PRAISE FOR *Delirium*:

"Lena's gradual awakening is set against a convincing backdrop of totalitarian horror. The abrupt ending leaves enough unanswered questions to set breathless readers up for volume two of this trilogy."
—*Kirkus Review* (starred review)

"Oliver writes beautifully, with well-measured mastery."—Juliana Baggott, writing in NPR's "Hooray for YA: Teen Novels for Readers of All Ages"

"Oliver's deeply emotional and incredibly well-honed prose commands the readers' attention and captures their hearts. With a pulse-pounding tempo and unforeseen twists and turns, Lauren Oliver has opened the door on a fantastic new series; the second book can't come soon enough."
—*New York Journal of Books*

"In a thick climate of fear, Oliver spins out a suspenseful story of awakening and resistance with true love at its core."—*The Horn Book*

PRAISE FOR *Pandemonium*:

"This is a romance in the purest of senses, where just the longing for the faintest taste of love is worth the greatest of risks. Like all successful second volumes, this expands the world and ups the stakes, setting us up for the big finale."—ALA *Booklist*

"Following directly on the heels of *Delirium*, *Pandemonium* is equally riveting. The underlying theme that love will win out regardless of prohibition is a powerful idea that will speak to teens."—*School Library Journal*

"If you crave the heart-stopping action of the arena from *The Hunger Games* combined with a destined-to-be-doomed love story then this sequel is perfect for you!"—Seventeen.com

PRAISE FOR *Requiem*:

"Is there a theme more perfect for YA readers than choosing what you want from life rather than being told?"—ALA *Booklist*

"The love triangle between Lena, Alex, and Julian is dramatic, bringing so much pain for all three of them that it almost makes the case for the Cure; the focus shift to Lena's relationship with her mother, her friend, and her cousin reminds readers that romantic love is not the only type that is abolished in the Cure's quest for order."—*BCCB*

requiem

LAUREN OLIVER

HARPER
An Imprint of HarperCollins*Publishers*

Requiem
Copyright © 2013 by Laura Schechter
HarperCollins Children's Books, a division of HarperCollins Publishers,
195 Broadway, New York, NY 10007.
www.epicreads.com

Library of Congress Cataloging-in-Publication Data
Oliver, Lauren.
  Requiem / Lauren Oliver. — 1st ed.
    p. cm.
  Sequel to: Pandemonium.
  Summary: "While Lena navigates the increasingly dangerous Wilds, her best
friend, Hana, lives a safe, loveless life in Portland."—Provided by publisher.
  ISBN 978-0-06-201454-2 (pbk.)
  [1. Government, Resistance to—Fiction. 2. Love—Fiction. 3. Best friends—
Fiction. 4. Friendship—Fiction. 5. Marriage—Fiction. 6. Maine—Fiction.
7. Science fiction.] I. Title.
PZ7.O475Req 2013   2012030236
[Fic]—dc23   CIP
                                                                            AC

Typography by Erin Fitzsimmons
15 16 17 LP/RRDH   10 9 8 7 6 5 4 3
❖
First paperback edition, 2014

For Michael, who took down the walls

Lena

I've started dreaming of Portland again.

Since Alex reappeared, resurrected but also changed, twisted, like a monster from one of the ghost stories we used to tell as kids, the past has been finding its way in. It bubbles up through the cracks when I'm not paying attention, and pulls at me with greedy fingers.

This is what they warned me about for all those years: the heavy weight in my chest, the nightmare-fragments that follow me even in waking life.

I warned you, Aunt Carol says in my head.

We told you, Rachel says.

You should have stayed. That's Hana, reaching out across an expanse of time, through the murky-thick layers of memory, stretching a weightless hand to me as I am sinking.

About two dozen of us came north from New York City: Raven, Tack, Julian, and me, and also Dani, Gordo, and Pike, plus fifteen or so others who are largely content to stay quiet and follow directions.

And Alex. But not my Alex: a stranger who never smiles, doesn't laugh, and barely speaks.

The others, those who were using the warehouse outside White Plains as a homestead, scattered south or west. By now, the warehouse has no doubt been stripped and abandoned. It isn't safe, not after Julian's rescue. Julian Fineman is a symbol, and an important one. The zombies will hunt for him. They will want to string the symbol up, and make it bleed meaning, so that others will learn their lesson.

We have to be extra careful.

Hunter, Bram, Lu, and some of the other members of the old Rochester homestead are waiting for us just south of Pough-keepsie. It takes us nearly three days to cover the distance; we are forced to circumnavigate a half-dozen Valid cities.

Then, abruptly, we arrive: The woods simply run out at the edge of an enormous expanse of concrete, webbed with thick fissures, and still marked very faintly with the ghostly white outlines of parking spaces. Cars, rusted, picked clean of various parts—rubber tires, bits of metal—still sit in the lot. They look small and faintly ridiculous, like ancient toys left out by a child.

The parking lot flows like gray water in all directions, running up at last against a vast structure of steel and glass: an old shopping mall. A sign in looping cursive script, streaked white with bird shit, reads EMPIRE STATE PLAZA MALL.

The reunion is joyful. Tack, Raven, and I break into a run. Bram and Hunter are running too, and we intercept them in the middle of the parking lot. I jump on Hunter, laughing, and he throws his arms around me and lifts me off my feet. Everyone is shouting and talking at once.

Hunter sets me down, finally, but I keep one arm locked around him, as though he might disappear. I reach out and wrap my other arm around Bram, who is shaking hands with Tack, and somehow we all end up piled together, jumping and shouting, our bodies interlaced, in the middle of the brilliant sunshine.

"Well, well, well." We break apart, turn around, and see Lu sauntering toward us. Her eyebrows are raised. She has let her hair grow long, and brushed it forward, so it pools over her shoulders. "Look what the cat dragged in."

It's the first time I've felt truly happy in days.

The short months we have spent apart have changed both Hunter and Bram. Bram is, against all odds, heavier. Hunter has new wrinkles at the corners of his eyes, although his smile is as boyish as ever.

"How's Sarah?" I say. "Is she here?"

"Sarah stayed in Maryland," Hunter says. "The homestead is thirty strong, and she won't have to migrate. The resistance is trying to get word to her sister."

"What about Grandpa and the others?" I am breathless, and there is a tight feeling in my chest, as though I am still being squeezed.

Bram and Hunter exchange a small glance.

"Grandpa didn't make it," Hunter says shortly. "We buried him outside Baltimore."

Raven looks away, spits on the pavement.

Bram adds quickly, "The others are fine." He reaches out and places a finger on my procedural scar, the one he helped me fake to initiate me into the resistance. "Looking good," he says, and winks.

We decide to camp for the night. There's clean water a short distance from the old mall, and a wreckage of houses and business offices that have yielded some usable supplies: a few cans of food still buried in the rubble; rusted tools; even a rifle, which Hunter found cradled in a pair of upturned deer hooves, under a mound of collapsed plaster. And one member of our group, Henley, a short, quiet woman with a long coil of gray hair, is running a fever. This will give her time to rest.

By the end of the day, an argument breaks out about where to go next.

"We could split up," Raven says. She is squatting by the pit she has cleared for the fire, stoking the first, glowing splinters of flame with the charred end of a stick.

"The larger our group, the safer we are," Tack argues. He has pulled off his fleece and is wearing only a T-shirt, so the ropy muscles of his arms are visible. The days have been warming slowly, and the woods have been coming to life. We can feel the spring arriving, like an animal stirring lightly in its sleep, exhaling hot breath.

But it's cold now, when the sun is low and the Wilds are swallowed by long purple shadows, when we are no longer moving.

"Lena," Raven barks out. I've been staring at the beginnings of the fire, watching flame curl around the mass of pine needles, twigs, and brittle leaves. "Go check on the tents, okay? It'll be dark soon."

Raven has built the fire in a shallow gully that must once have been a stream, where it will be somewhat sheltered from the wind. She has avoided setting up camp too close to the mall and its haunted spaces; it looms above the tree line, all twisted black metal and empty eyes, like an alien spaceship run aground.

Up the embankment a dozen yards, Julian is helping set up the tents. He has his back to me. He, too, is wearing only a T-shirt. Just three days in the Wilds have already changed him. His hair is tangled, and a leaf is caught just behind his left ear. He looks skinnier, although he has not had time to lose weight. This is just the effect of being here, in the open, with salvaged, too-big clothing, surrounded by savage wilderness, a perpetual reminder of the fragility of our survival.

He is securing a rope to a tree, yanking it taut. Our tents are old and have been torn and patched repeatedly. They don't stand on their own. They must be propped up and strung

5

between trees and coaxed to life, like sails in the wind.

Gordo is hovering next to Julian, watching approvingly.

"Do you need any help?" I pause a few feet away.

Julian and Gordo turn around.

"Lena!" Julian's face lights up, then immediately falls again as he realizes I don't intend to come closer. I brought him here, with me, to this strange new place, and now I have nothing to give him.

"We're okay," Gordo says. His hair is bright red, and even though he's no older than Tack, he has a beard that grows to the middle of his chest. "Just finishing up."

Julian straightens and wipes his palms on the back of his jeans. He hesitates, then comes down the embankment toward me, tucking a strand of hair behind his ear. "It's cold," he says when he's a few feet away. "You should go down to the fire."

"I'm all right," I say, but I put my hands into the arms of my wind breaker. The cold is inside me. Sitting next to the fire won't help. "The tents look good."

"Thanks. I think I'm getting the hang of it." His smile doesn't quite reach his eyes.

Three days: three days of strained conversation and silence. I know he is wondering what has changed, and whether it can be changed back. I know I'm hurting him. There are questions he is forcing himself not to ask, and things he is struggling not to say.

He is giving me time. He is patient, and gentle.

"You look pretty in this light," he says.

"You must be going blind." I intend it as a joke, but my voice sounds harsh in the thin air.

Julian shakes his head, frowning, and looks away. The leaf, a vivid yellow, is still tangled in his hair, behind his ear. In that moment, I'm desperate to reach out, remove it, and run my fingers through his hair and laugh with him about it. *This is the Wilds*, I'll say. *Did you ever imagine?* And he'll lace his fingers through mine and squeeze. He'll say, *What would I do without you?*

But I can't bring myself to move. "You have a leaf in your hair."

"A what?" Julian looks startled, as though I've recalled him from a dream.

"A leaf. In your hair."

Julian runs a hand impatiently through his hair. "Lena, I—"

Bang.

The sound of a rifle shot makes us both jump. Birds start out of the trees behind Julian, temporarily darkening the sky all at once, before dispersing into individual shapes. Someone says, "Damn."

Dani and Alex emerge from the trees beyond the tents. Both of them have rifles slung across their shoulders.

Gordo straightens up.

"Deer?" he asks. The light is nearly all gone. Alex's hair looks almost black.

"Too big for a deer," Dani says. She is a large woman, broad across the shoulders with a wide, flat forehead and almond-eyes. She reminds me of Miyako, who died before we went south last winter. We burned her on a frigid day, just before the first snow.

"Bear?" Gordo asks.

"Might have been," Dani replies shortly. Dani is harder-edged than Miyako was: She has let the Wilds whittle her down, carve her to steel.

"Did you hit it?" I ask, too eager, though I already know the answer. But I am willing Alex to look at me, to speak to me.

"Might have just clipped it," Dani says. "Hard to tell. Not enough to stop it, though."

Alex says nothing, doesn't register my presence, even. He keeps walking, threading his way through the tents, past Julian and me, close enough that I imagine I can smell him— the old smell of grass and sun-dried wood, a Portland smell that makes me want to cry out, and bury my face in his chest, and inhale.

Then he is heading down the embankment as Raven's voice floats up to us: "Dinner's on. Eat up or miss out."

"Come on." Julian grazes my elbow with his fingertips. Gentle, patient.

My feet turn me, and move me down the embankment, toward the fire, which is now burning hot and strong; toward the boy who becomes shadow standing next to it, blotted out by the smoke. That is what Alex is now: a shadow-boy, an illusion.

For three days he has not spoken to me or looked at me at all.

Hana

Want to know my deep, dark secret? In Sunday school, I used to cheat on the quizzes.

I could never get into *The Book of Shhh*, not even as a kid. The only section of the book that interested me at all was "Legends and Grievances," which is full of folk-tales about the world before the cure. My favorite, the Story of Solomon, goes like this:

Once upon a time, during the days of sickness, two women and an infant went before the king. Each woman claimed that the infant was hers. Both refused to give the child to the other woman and pleaded their cases passionately, each claiming that she would die of grief if the baby were not returned solely to her possession.

The king, whose name was Solomon, listened to both their speeches, and at last announced that he had a fair solution.

"We will cut the baby in two," he said, "and that way each of you will have a portion."

The women agreed that this was just, and so the executioner was brought forward, and with his ax, he sliced the baby cleanly in two.

And the baby never cried, or so much as made a sound, and the mothers looked on, and afterward, for a thousand years, there was a spot of blood on the palace floor that could never be cleaned or diluted by any substance on earth. . . .

I must have been only eight or nine when I read that passage for the first time, but it really struck me. For days I couldn't get the image of that poor baby out of my head. I kept picturing it split open on the tile floor, like a butterfly pinned behind glass.

That's what's so great about the story. It's real. What I mean is, even if it didn't *actually* happen—and there's debate about the Legends and Grievances section, and whether it's historically accurate—it shows the world truthfully. I remember feeling just like that baby: torn apart by feeling, split in two, caught between loyalties and desires.

That's how the diseased world is.

That's how it was for me, before I was cured.

In exactly twenty-one days, I'll be married.

My mother looks as though she might cry, and I almost hope

that she will. I've seen her cry twice in my life: once when she broke her ankle and once last year, when she came outside and found that protesters had climbed the gate, and torn up our lawn, and pried her beautiful car into pieces.

In the end she says only, "You look lovely, Hana." And then: "It's a little too big in the waist, though."

Mrs. Killegan—*Call me Anne,* she simpered, the first time we came for a fitting—circles me quietly, pinning and adjusting. She is tall, with faded blond hair and a pinched look, as though over the years she has accidentally ingested various pins and sewing needles. "You're sure you want to go with the cap sleeves?"

"I'm sure," I say, just as my mom says, "You think they look too young?"

Mrs. Killegan—Anne—gestures expressively with one long, bony hand. "The whole city will be watching," she says.

"The whole country," my mother corrects her.

"I like the sleeves," I say, and I almost add, *It's my wedding.* But that isn't true anymore—not since the Incidents in January, and Mayor Hargrove's death. My wedding belongs to the people now. That's what everybody has been telling me for weeks. Yesterday we got a phone call from the National News Service, asking whether they could syndicate footage, or send in their own television crew to film the ceremony.

Now, more than ever, the country needs its symbols.

We are standing in front of a three-sided mirror. My mother's frown is reflected from three different angles. "Mrs. Killegan's

11

right," she says, touching my elbow. "Let's see how it looks at three-quarters, okay?"

I know better than to argue. Three reflections nod simultaneously; three identical girls with identical ropes of braided blond hair in three identical white, floor-skimming dresses. Already, I hardly recognize myself. I've been transfigured by the dress, by the bright lights in the dressing room. For all my life I have been Hana Tate.

But the girl in the mirror is not Hana Tate. She is Hana Hargrove, soon-to-be wife of the soon-to-be mayor, and a symbol of all that is right about the cured world.

A path and a road for everyone.

"Let me see what I have in the back," Mrs. Killegan says. "We'll slip you into a different style, just so you'll have a comparison." She slides across the worn gray carpet and disappears into the storeroom. Through the open door, I see dozens of dresses sheathed in plastic, dangling limply from garment racks.

My mother sighs. We've been here for two hours already, and I'm starting to feel like a scarecrow: stuffed and poked and stitched. My mother sits on a faded footstool next to the mirrors, holding her purse primly in her lap so it won't touch the carpet.

Mrs. Killegan's has always been the nicest wedding shop in Portland, but it, too, has clearly felt the lingering effects of the Incidents, and the security crackdowns the government implemented in their aftermath. Money is tighter for practically everybody, and it shows. One of the overhead bulbs is out, and the shop has a musty smell, as though it has not been cleaned recently. On one wall, a pattern of moisture has begun bubbling the wallpaper, and earlier I noticed a large brown stain on one of the striped settees. Mrs. Killegan caught me looking and casually tossed a shawl down to conceal it.

"You really do look lovely, Hana," my mother says.

"Thank you," I say. I know I look lovely. It might sound egotistical, but it's the truth.

This, too, has changed since my cure. When I was uncured, even though people always told me I was pretty, I never *felt* it. But after the cure, a wall came down inside me. Now I see that yes, I am quite simply and inarguably beautiful.

I also no longer care.

"Here we are." Mrs. Killegan reemerges from the back, holding several plastic-swathed gowns over her arm. I swallow a sigh, but not quickly enough. Mrs. Killegan places a hand on my arm. "Don't worry, dear," she says. "We'll find the perfect dress. That's what this is all about, isn't it?"

I arrange my face into a smile, and the pretty girl in the mirror arranges her face with me. "Of course," I say.

Perfect dress. Perfect match. A perfect lifetime of happiness.

Perfection is a promise, and a reassurance that we are not wrong.

Mrs. Killegan's shop is in the Old Port, and as we emerge onto the street I inhale the familiar scents of dried seaweed and old

13

wood. The day is bright, but the wind is cold off the bay. Only a few boats are bobbing in the water, mostly fishing vessels or commercial rigs. From a distance, the scat-splattered wood moorings look like reeds growing out of the water.

The street is empty except for two regulators and Tony, our bodyguard. My parents decided to employ security services just after the Incidents, when Fred Hargrove's father, the mayor, was killed, and it was decided that I should leave college and get married as soon as possible.

Now Tony comes everywhere with us. On his days off, he sends his brother, Rick, as a substitute. It took me a month to be able to distinguish between them. They both have thick, short necks and shiny bald heads. Neither of them speaks much, and when they do, they never have anything interesting to say.

That was one of my biggest fears about the cure: that the procedure would switch me off somehow, and inhibit my ability to think. But it's the opposite. I think *more* clearly now. In some ways, I even feel things more clearly. I used to feel with a kind of feverishness; I was filled with panic and anxiety and competing desires. There were nights I could hardly sleep, days when I felt like my insides were trying to crawl out of my throat.

I was infected. Now the infection has gone.

Tony is leaning against the car. I wonder if he has been standing in that position for all three hours we've been in Mrs. Killegan's. He straightens up as we approach, and opens the door for my mother.

14

"Thank you, Tony," she says. "Was there any trouble?"

"No, ma'am."

"Good." She gets into the backseat, and I slide in after her. We've had this car for only two months—a replacement for the one that was vandalized—and just a few days after it arrived, my mom came out of the grocery store to find that someone had keyed the word *PIG* into the paint. Secretly, I think that my mom's real motivation for hiring Tony was to protect the new car.

After Tony shuts the door, the world outside the tinted windows gets tinged a dark blue. He turns the radio to the NNS, the National News Service. The commentators' voices are familiar and reassuring.

I lean my head back and watch the world begin to move. I have lived in Portland all my life and have memories of almost every street and every corner. But these, too, seem distant now, safely submerged in the past. A lifetime ago I used to sit on those picnic benches with Lena, luring seagulls with bread crumbs. We talked about flying. We talked about escape. It was kid stuff, like believing in unicorns and magic.

I never thought she would actually do it.

My stomach cramps. I realize I haven't eaten since breakfast. I must be hungry.

"Busy week," my mother says.

"Yeah."

"And don't forget, the *Post* wants to interview you this afternoon."

"I haven't forgotten."

"Now we just need to find you a dress for Fred's inauguration, and we'll be all set. Or did you decide to go with the yellow one we saw in Lava last week?"

"I'm not sure yet," I say.

"What do you mean, you're not sure? The inauguration's in *five days*, Hana. Everyone will be looking at you."

"The yellow one, then."

"Of course, I have no idea what *I'll* wear. . . ."

We've passed into the West End, our old neighborhood. Historically, the West End has been home to many of the higher-ups in the church and the medical field: priests of the Church of the New Order, government officials, doctors and researchers at the labs. That's no doubt why it was targeted so heavily during the riots following the Incidents.

The riots were quelled quickly; there's still much debate about whether the riots represented an actual movement or whether they were a result of misdirected anger and the passions we're trying so hard to eradicate. Still, many people felt that the West End was too close to downtown, too close to some of the more troubled neighborhoods, where sympathizers and resisters are concealed. Many families, like ours, have moved off-peninsula now.

"Don't forget, Hana, we're supposed to speak with the caterers on Monday."

"I know, I know."

We take Danforth to Vaughan, our old street. I lean forward

slightly, trying to catch a glimpse of our old house, but the Andersons' evergreen conceals it almost entirely from view, and all I get is a flash of the green-gabled roof.

Our house, like the Andersons' beside it and the Richards' opposite, is empty and will probably remain so. Still, we see not a single FOR SALE sign. No one can afford to buy. Fred says that the economic freeze will remain in place for at least a few years, until things begin to stabilize. For now, the government needs to reassert control. People need to be reminded of their place.

I wonder if the mice are already finding their way into my old room, leaving droppings on the polished wood floors, and whether spiders have started webbing up the corners. Soon the house will look like 37 Brooks, barren, almost *chewed-*looking, collapsing slowly from termite rot.

Another change: I can think about 37 Brooks now, and Lena, and Alex, without the old strangled feeling.

"And I'll bet you never reviewed the guest list I left in your room?"

"I haven't had time," I say absently, keeping my eyes on the landscape skating by our window.

We maneuver onto Congress, and the neighborhood changes quickly. Soon we pass one of Portland's two gas stations, around which a group of regulators stands guard, guns pointing toward the sky; then dollar stores and a Laundromat with a faded orange awning; a dingy-looking deli.

Suddenly my mom leans forward, putting one hand on the

back of Tony's seat. "Turn this up," she says sharply.

He adjusts a dial on the dashboard. The radio voice gets louder.

"Following the recent outbreak in Waterbury, Connecticut—"

"God," my mother says. "Not *another* one."

"—all citizens, particularly those in the southeast quadrants, have been strongly encouraged to evacuate to temporary housing in neighboring Bethlehem. Bill Ardury, chief of Special Forces, offered reassurances to worried citizens. 'The situation is under control,' he said during his seven-minute address. 'State and municipal military personnel are working together to contain the disease and to ensure that the area is cordoned off, cleansed, and sanitized as soon as possible. There is absolutely no reason to fear further contamination—"

"That's enough," my mother says abruptly, sitting back. "I can't listen anymore."

Tony begins fiddling with the radio. Most stations are just static. Last month, the big story was the government's discovery of wavelengths that had been co-opted by Invalids for their use. We were able to intercept and decode several critical messages, which led to a triumphant raid in Chicago, and the arrest of a half dozen key Invalids. One of them was responsible for planning the explosion in Washington, DC, last fall, a blast that killed twenty-seven people, including a mother and a child.

I was glad when the Invalids were executed. Some people complained that lethal injection was too humane for convicted terrorists, but I thought it sent a powerful message: We are not the evil ones. We are reasonable and compassionate. We stand for fairness, structure, and organization.

It's the other side, the uncureds, who bring the chaos.

"It's really disgusting," my mother says. "If we'd started bombing when the trouble first—Tony, look out!"

Tony slams on the brakes. The tires screech. I go shooting forward, narrowly avoiding cracking my forehead on the headrest in front of me before my seat belt jerks me backward. There is a heavy thump. The air smells like burned rubber.

"Shit," my mother is saying. "Shit. What in *God's* name—?"

"I'm sorry, ma'am, I didn't see her. She came out from between the Dumpsters. . . ."

A young girl is standing in front of the car, her hands resting flat on the hood. Her hair is tented around her thin, narrow face, and her eyes are huge and terrified. She looks vaguely familiar.

Tony rolls down his window. The smell of the Dumpsters—there are several of them, lined up next to one another—floats into the car, sweet and rotten. My mother coughs, and cups a palm over her nose.

"You okay?" Tony calls out, craning his head out the window.

The girl doesn't respond. She is panting, practically hyperventilating. Her eyes skate from Tony to my mother in the backseat, and then to me. A shock runs through me.

Jenny. Lena's cousin. I haven't seen her since last summer, and she's much thinner. She looks older, too. But it's unmistakably her. I recognize the flare of her nostrils, her proud, pointed chin, and the eyes.

She recognizes me, too. I can tell. Before I can say anything, she wrenches her hands off the car hood and darts across the street. She's wearing an old, ink-stained backpack that I recognize as one of Lena's hand-me-downs. Across one of its pockets two names are colored in black bubble letters: Lena's, and mine. We penned them onto her bag in seventh grade, when we were bored in class. That's the day we first came up with our little code word, our pump-you-up cheer, which later we called out to each other at cross-country meets. *Halena*. A combination of both our names.

"For heaven's sake. You'd think the girl was old enough to know not to dart in front of traffic. She nearly gave me a heart attack."

"I know her," I say automatically. I can't shake the image of Jenny's huge, dark eyes, her pale skeleton-face.

"What do you mean, you *know* her?" My mother turns to me.

I close my eyes and try to think of peaceful things. The bay. Seagulls wheeling against a blue sky. Rivers of spotless white fabric. But instead I see Jenny's eyes, the sharp angles of her cheek and chin. "Her name is Jenny," I say. "She's Lena's cousin—"

"Watch your mouth," my mom cuts me off sharply. I realize, too late, that I shouldn't have said anything. Lena's name is worse than a curse word in our family.

For years, Mom was proud of my friendship with Lena. She

saw it as a testament to her liberalism. *We don't judge the girl because of her family,* she would tell guests when they brought it up. *The disease isn't genetic; that's an old idea.*

She took it as almost a personal insult when Lena contracted the disease and managed to escape before she could be treated, as though Lena had deliberately done it to make her look stupid.

All those years we let her into our house, she would say out of nowhere, in the days following Lena's escape. *Even though we knew what the risks were. Everyone warned us. . . . Well, I guess we should have listened.*

"She looked thin," I say.

"Home, Tony." My mom leans her head against the headrest and closes her eyes, and I know the conversation is over.

Lena

I wake in the middle of the night from a nightmare. In it, Grace was trapped beneath the floorboards in our old bedroom in Aunt Carol's house. There was shouting from downstairs—a fire. The room was full of smoke. I was trying to get to Grace, to rescue her, but her hand kept slipping from my grasp. My eyes were burning, and the smoke was choking me, and I knew if I didn't run, I would die. But she was crying and screaming for me to save her, save her. . . .

I sit up. I repeat Raven's mantra in my head—*the past is dead, it doesn't exist*—but it doesn't help. I can't shake the feeling of Grace's tiny hand, wet with sweat, slipping from my grip.

The tent is overcrowded. Dani is pressed up on one side of me, and there are three women curled up against her.

Julian has his own tent for now. It is a small bit of courtesy. They are giving him time to adjust, as they did when I first escaped to the Wilds. It takes time to get used to the feeling of closeness, and bodies constantly bumping yours. There is no privacy in the Wilds, and there can be no modesty, either.

I could have joined Julian in his tent. I know that he expected me to, after what we shared underground: the kidnapping, the kiss. I brought him here, after all. I rescued him and pulled him into this new life, a life of freedom and feeling. There is nothing to stop me from sleeping next to him. The cureds—the zombies—would say that we are already infected. We wallow in our filth, the way that pigs wallow in muck.

Who knows? Maybe they're right. Maybe we are driven crazy by our feelings. Maybe love *is* a disease, and we would be better off without it.

But we have chosen a different road. And in the end that is the point of escaping the cure: We are free to choose.

We are even free to choose the wrong thing.

I won't be able to go back to sleep right away. I need air. I ease out from under the tangle of sleeping bags and blankets and fumble in the dark for the tent flap. I wriggle out of the tent on my stomach, trying not to make too much noise. Behind me, Dani kicks in her sleep and mutters something unintelligible.

The night is cool. The sky is clear and cloudless. The moon looks closer than usual, and it paints everything with a silvery glow, like a fine layering of snow. I stand for a moment, relishing the feeling of stillness and quiet: the peaks of the tents touched with moonlight; the low-hanging branches, just barely budding with new leaves; the occasional hooting of an owl in the distance.

In one of the tents, Julian is sleeping.

And in another: Alex.

I move away from the tents. I head down toward the gully, past the remains of the campfire, which by now is nothing more than charred bits of blackened wood and a few smoking embers. The air still smells, faintly, like scorched metal and beans.

I'm not sure where I'm going, and it's stupid to wander from camp—Raven has warned me a million times against it. At night, the Wilds belong to the animals, and it's easy to get turned around, lost among the growth, the slalom of trees. But I have an itch in my blood, and the night is so clear, I have no trouble navigating.

I hop down into the dried-out riverbed, which is covered in a layer of rocks and leaves and, occasionally, a relic from the old life: a dented metal soda can, a plastic bag, a child's shoe. I walk south for a few hundred feet, where I'm prevented from going farther by an enormous, felled oak. Its trunk is so wide that, horizontal, it nearly reaches my chest. A vast network of roots arch up toward the sky like a dark pinwheel spray of water from a fountain.

There's a rustling behind me. I whip around. A shadow shifts, turns solid, and for a second my heart stops—I'm not protected; I have no weapons, nothing to fend off a hungry animal. Then the shadow emerges into the open and takes the shape of a boy.

In the moonlight, it's impossible to tell that his hair is the exact color of leaves in the autumn: golden brown, and shot through with red.

"Oh," Alex says. "It's you." These are the first words he has spoken to me in more than three days.

There are a thousand things I want to say to him.

Please understand. Please forgive me.

I prayed every day for you to be alive, until the hope became painful.

Don't hate me.

I still love you.

But all that comes out is: "I couldn't sleep."

Alex must remember that I was always troubled by nightmares. We talked about it a lot during our summer together in Portland. Last summer—less than a year ago. It's impossible to imagine the vast distance I've covered since that time, the landscape that has formed between us.

"I couldn't sleep either," Alex says simply.

Just this, the simple statement, and the fact that he is speaking to me at all, loosens something inside me. I want to hold him, to kiss him the way I used to.

"I thought you were dead," I say. "It almost killed me."

"Did it?" His voice is neutral. "You made a pretty fast recovery."

"No. You don't understand." My throat is tight; I feel as though I'm being strangled. "I couldn't keep hoping, and then waking up every day and finding out it wasn't true, and you were still gone. I—I wasn't strong enough."

He is quiet for a second. It's too dark to see his expression: He is standing in shadow again, but I can sense that he is staring at me.

Finally he says, "When they took me to the Crypts, I thought they were going to kill me. They didn't even bother. They just left me to die. They threw me in a cell and locked the door."

"Alex." The strangled feeling has moved from my throat to my chest, and without realizing it, I have begun to cry. I move toward him. I want to run my hands through his hair and kiss his forehead and each of his eyelids and take away the memory of what he has seen. But he steps backward, out of reach.

"I didn't die. I don't know how. I should have. I'd lost plenty of blood. They were just as surprised as I was. After that it became a kind of game—to see how much I could stand. To see how much they could do to me before I'd—"

He breaks off abruptly. I can't hear any more; don't want to know, don't want it to be true, can't stand to think of what they did to him there. I take another step forward and reach for his chest and shoulders in the dark. This time, he doesn't push me away. But he doesn't embrace me either. He stands there, cold, still, like a statue.

"Alex." I repeat his name like a prayer, like a magic spell that will make everything okay again. I run my hands up his chest and to his chin. "I'm so sorry. I'm so, so sorry."

Suddenly he jerks backward, simultaneously finding my wrists and pulling them down to my sides. "There were days I would rather they have killed me." He doesn't drop my wrists; he squeezes them tightly, pinning my arms, keeping me immobilized. His voice is low, urgent, and so full of anger it pains me even more than his grip. "There were days I asked for it—prayed for it when I went to sleep. The belief that I would see you again, that I could find you—the hope for it—was the only thing that kept me going." He releases me and takes another step backward. "So no. I don't understand."

"Alex, *please*."

He balls his fists. "Stop saying my name. You don't know me anymore."

"I do know you." I'm still crying, swallowing back spasms in my throat, struggling to breathe. This is a nightmare and I will wake up. This is a monster-story, and he has come back to me a terror-creation, patched together, broken and hateful, and I will wake up and he will be here, and whole, and mine again. I find his hands, lace my fingers through his even as he tries to pull away. "It's me, Alex. Lena. Your Lena. Remember? Remember 37 Brooks, and the blanket we used to keep in the backyard—"

"Don't," he says. His voice breaks on the word.

"And I always beat you in Scrabble," I say. I have to

27

keep talking, and keep him here, and make him remember. "Because you always let me win. And remember how we had a picnic one time, and the only thing we could find from the store was canned spaghetti and some green beans? And you said to mix them—"

"Don't."

"And we did, and it wasn't bad. We ate the whole stupid can, we were so hungry. And when it started to get dark you pointed to the sky, and told me there was a star for every thing you loved about me." I'm gasping, feeling as though I am about to drown; I'm reaching for him blindly, grabbing at his collar.

"Stop." He grabs my shoulders. His face is an inch from mine but unrecognizable: a gross, contorted mask. "No more. It's done, okay? That's all done now."

"Alex, please—"

"Stop!" His voice rings out sharply, hard as a slap. He releases me and I stumble backward. "Alex is dead, do you hear me? All of that—what we felt, what it meant—that's done now, okay? Buried. Blown away."

"Alex!"

He has started to turn away; now he whirls around. The moon lights him stark white and furious, a camera image, two-dimensional, gripped by the flash. "I don't love you, Lena. Do you hear me? I *never* loved you."

The air goes. Everything goes. "I don't believe you." I'm crying so hard, I can hardly speak.

He takes one step toward me. And now I don't recognize him at all. He has transformed entirely, turned into a stranger. "It was a lie. Okay? It was all a lie. Craziness, like they always said. Just forget about it. Forget it ever happened."

"Please." I don't know how I stay on my feet, why I don't shatter into dust right there, why my heart keeps beating when I want it so badly to stop. "Please don't do this, Alex."

"Stop saying my name."

Then we both hear it: the crack and rustle of leaves behind us, the sound of something large moving through the woods. Alex's expression changes. The anger drops away and is replaced by something else: a frozen tenseness, like a deer just before it startles.

"Don't move, Lena," he says quietly, but his words are laced with urgency.

Even before I turn around, I can feel the looming shape behind me, the snuffle of animal breath, the *hunger*—craving, impersonal.

A bear.

It has picked its way into the gully and is now no more than four feet away from us. It is a black bear, its matted fur streaked silver in the moonlight, and *big*: five or six feet long, and, even on all four legs, almost as high as my shoulder. It looks from Alex to me, and back to Alex. Its eyes are just like pieces of carved onyx, dull, lifeless.

Two things strike me at once: The bear is skinny, starving. The winter has been hard.

Also: It is not afraid of us.

A jolt of fear shocks through me, shorting out the pain, shorting out all other thoughts besides one: *I should have brought a gun.*

The bear takes another step forward, swinging its massive head back and forth, evaluating us. I can see its breath steaming in the cold air, its peaked shoulder blades high and sharp.

"All right," Alex says, in that same low voice. He's standing behind me, and I can feel the tension in his body—ramrod straight, petrified. "Let's take it easy. Real slow. We're going to back away, all right? Nice and slowly."

He takes a single step backward and just that, that little movement, makes the bear tense up in a crouch, baring its teeth, which glisten bone white in the moonlight. Alex freezes again. The bear begins to growl. It is so close that I can feel the heat from its massive body, smell the sourness of its starving breath.

I should have brought a gun. No way to turn and run; that makes us prey, and the bear is looking for prey. *Stupid.* That is the rule of the Wilds: You must be bigger and stronger and tougher. You must hurt or be hurt.

The bear swings forward another step, still growling. Every muscle in my body is an alarm, screaming at me to run, but I stay rooted in place, forcing myself not to move, not to twitch.

The bear hesitates. I won't run. So maybe *not* prey, then.

It pulls back an inch—an advantage, a tiny concession.

I take it.

"Hey!" I bark, as loud as I can, and bring my arms above my head, trying to make myself look as large as possible. "Hey! Get out of here! Go on. *Go.*"

The bear withdraws another inch, confused, startled.

"I said *go.*" I reach out and strike against the nearest tree with my foot, sending a spray of bark in the bear's direction. As the bear still hesitates, uncertain—but not growling now, on the defensive, confused—I drop down into a crouch and scoop up the first rock I can get my fist around, and then I'm up and chucking it, hard. It connects just below the bear's left shoulder with a heavy thud. The bear shuffles backward, whimpering. Then it turns and bounds off into the woods, a fast black blur.

"Holy shit," Alex bursts out behind me. He exhales, long and loud, bends over, straightens up again. "Holy *shit.*"

The adrenaline, the release of tension, has made him forget; for a second, the new mask is dropped, and a glimpse of the old Alex is revealed.

I feel a brief surge of nausea. I keep thinking of the bear's wounded, desperate eyes, and the heavy thud of the rock against its shoulder. But I had no choice.

It is the rule of the Wilds.

"That was crazy. *You're* crazy." Alex shakes his head. "The old Lena would have bolted."

You must be bigger, and stronger, and tougher.

A coldness radiates through me, a solid wall that is growing, piece by piece, in my chest. He doesn't love me.

He never loved me.

It was all a lie.

"The old Lena is dead," I say, and then push past him, back down through the gully toward the camp. Each step is more difficult than the last; the heaviness fills me and turns my limbs to stone.

You must hurt, or be hurt.

Alex doesn't follow me, and I don't expect him to. I don't care where he goes, whether he stays in the woods all night, whether he never returns to camp.

As he said, all of that—the caring—is done now.

It's not until I've almost reached the tents that I begin crying again. The tears come all at once, and I have to stop walking and double up into a crouch. I want to bleed all the feelings out of me. For a second I think about how easy it would be to pass back to the other side, to walk straight into the laboratories and offer myself up to the surgeons.

You were right; I was wrong. Get it out.

"Lena?"

I look up. Julian has emerged from his tent. I must have woken him. His hair is sticking up at crazy angles, like the broken spokes of a wheel, and his feet are bare.

I straighten up, swiping my nose on the sleeve of my sweat-shirt. "I'm okay," I say, still hiccuping back tears. "I'm fine."

For a minute he stands there, looking at me, and I can tell that he knows why I'm crying, and he understands, and it's going to be all right. He opens his arms to me.

32

"Come here," he says quietly.

I can't move to him fast enough. I practically fall into him. He catches me and pulls me in tightly to his chest, and I let myself go again, let sobs run through me. He stands there with me and murmurs into my hair and kisses the top of my head and lets me cry over losing another boy, a boy I loved better.

"I'm sorry," I say over and over into his chest. "I'm sorry." His shirt smells like smoke from the fire, like mulch and spring growth.

"It's okay," he whispers back.

When I've calmed down a little, Julian takes my hand. I follow him into the dark cave of his tent, which smells like his shirt but even more so. I lie down on top of his sleeping bag and he lies down beside me, making a perfect seashell arc for my body. I curl up in this space—safe, warm—and let the last tears I will ever cry for Alex flow hot over my cheeks, and down into the ground, and away.

Hana

"H ana." My mother is looking at me expectantly. "Fred asked you to pass the green beans."

"Sorry," I say, forcing a smile. Last night, I hardly slept. I even had little snatches of dream—bare wisps of image that skittered away before I could focus on them.

I reach for the glazed ceramic dish—like everything in the Hargrove house, it is beautiful—even though Fred is more than capable of reaching it himself. This is part of the ritual. Soon I will be his wife, and we will sit like this every night, performing a well-choreographed dance.

Fred smiles at me. "Tired?" he says. In the past few months, we have spent many hours together; our Sunday dinner is just one of the many ways we have begun practicing merging our lives.

I've spent a long time scrutinizing his features, trying to figure out whether he is attractive, and in the end I have come up with this: He is very pleasant to look at. He is not as attractive as I am, but he is smarter, and I like his dark hair, and the way it falls over his right eyebrow when he has not had time to smooth it back.

"She *looks* tired," Mrs. Hargrove says. Fred's mother often talks about me as though I'm not in the room. I don't take it personally; she does it with everybody. Fred's father was mayor for more than three terms. Now that Mr. Hargrove is dead, Fred has been groomed to take his place. Since the Incidents in January, Fred campaigned tirelessly for the appointment, and it paid off. Only a week ago, a special interim committee appointed him the new mayor. He will be inaugurated publicly early next week.

Mrs. Hargrove is used to being the most important woman in the room.

"I'm fine," I say. Lena always said that I could lie my way out of hell.

The truth is, I'm not fine. I'm worried that I can't stop worrying about Jenny and how thin she looked.

I'm worried that I've been thinking of Lena again.

"Of course, the wedding preparations are very stressful," my mother says.

My father grunts. "You're not the one writing the checks."

This makes everybody laugh. The room is suddenly illuminated by a brief flash of light from outside: A journalist, parked in the bushes directly outside the window, is snapping our picture, which will then be sold to local newspapers and TV stations.

Mrs. Hargrove has arranged for paparazzi to be here tonight. She tipped the photographers off to the location of a dinner that Fred arranged for us on New Year's Eve, too. Photo opportunities are arranged and carefully plotted, so the public can watch our emerging story and see the happiness we've achieved by being paired so perfectly together.

And I *am* happy with Fred. We get along very well. We like the same things; we have a lot to talk about.

That's why I'm worried: Everything will go up in smoke if the procedure has not worked correctly.

"I heard on the radio that they've evacuated parts of Waterbury," Fred says. "Parts of San Francisco, too. Riots broke out over the weekend."

"Please, Fred," Mrs. Hargrove says. "Do we really have to talk about this at dinner?"

"It won't help to ignore it," Fred says, turning to her. "That's what Dad did. And look what happened."

"Fred." Mrs. Hargrove's voice is strained, but she manages to keep smiling. *Click.* Just for a second, the dining room walls are lit up by the camera's flash. "It really isn't the time—"

"We can't pretend anymore." Fred looks around the table, as though appealing to each of us. I drop my eyes. "The

36

resistance exists. It may even be growing. An epidemic—that's what this is."

"They've cordoned off most of Waterbury," my mother says. "I'm sure they'll do the same in San Francisco."

Fred shakes his head. "This isn't just about the infected. That's the problem. There's a whole system of sympathizers—a network of support. I won't do what Dad did," he says with sudden fierceness. Mrs. Hargrove has gone very still. "For years there were rumors that the Invalids existed, that their numbers were growing, even. You know it. Dad knew it. But he refused to believe."

I keep my head bent over my plate. A piece of lamb is sitting, untouched, next to green beans and fresh mint jelly. Only the best for the Hargroves. I pray that the journalists outside don't take a picture now; I'm sure my face is red. Everyone at the table knows that my former best friend tried to run off with an Invalid, and they know—or suspect—that I covered for her.

Fred's voice gets quieter. "By the time he accepted it—by the time he was willing to act—it was too late." He reaches out to touch his mother's hand, but she picks up her fork and begins eating again, stabbing green beans with such force, the tines of her fork make a sharp, clanging noise against the plate.

Fred clears his throat. "Well, I refuse to look the other way," he says. "It's time we all face this head-on."

"I just don't see why we have to talk about it at dinner," Mrs. Hargrove says. "When we're having a perfectly nice time—"

"May I be excused?" I ask too sharply. Everyone at the table turns to me in surprise. *Click*. I can only imagine what that picture will look like: my mother's mouth frozen in a perfect O, Mrs. Hargrove frowning, my father lifting a bloody piece of lamb to his lips.

"What do you mean, *excused*?" my mother says.

"See?" Mrs. Hargrove sighs and shakes her head at Fred. "You've made Hana unhappy."

"No, no. It's not that. It's just . . . You were right. I'm not feeling well," I say. I ball my napkin on the table and then, seeing my mother's look, fold it and drape it next to my plate. "I have a headache."

"I hope you're not coming down with something," Mrs. Hargrove says. "You can't be sick for the inauguration."

"She won't be sick," my mother says quickly.

"I won't be sick," I parrot. I don't know exactly what's wrong with me, but little points of pain are exploding in my head. "I just need to lie down, I think."

"I'll call Tony." My mom pushes away from the table.

"No, please." More than anything, I want to be left alone. In the past month, since my mother and Mrs. Hargrove determined that the wedding needed to be fast-tracked, to correspond with Fred's ascension to mayor, it seems the only time I can be alone is when I go to the bathroom. "I don't mind walking."

"Walking!" This provokes a miniature eruption. All of a sudden, everyone is speaking at once. My father is saying, *Out of the question*, and my mother says, *Imagine how* that *would look.* Fred leans toward me—*It isn't safe right now, Hana*—and Mrs. Hargrove says, *You must have a fever.*

In the end, my parents decide that Tony will drive me home and return for them later. This is a decent compromise. At least it means I'll have the house to myself for a bit. I stand up and bring my plate to the kitchen, despite Mrs. Hargrove's insistence that the housekeeper be allowed to do it. I scrape food into the trash, and flash back to the smell of the Dumpsters yesterday, the way that Jenny materialized from between them.

"I hope the conversation didn't upset you."

I turn around. Fred has followed me into the kitchen. He leaves a respectful distance between us.

"It didn't," I say. I'm too tired to reassure him further. I just want to go home.

"You don't have a fever, do you?" Fred looks at me steadily. "You look pale."

"I'm just tired," I say.

"Good." Fred puts his hands in his pockets, dark, creased in front, like my father's. "I was worried I'd gotten a defective one."

I shake my head, sure that I've misheard him. "What?"

"I'm kidding." Fred smiles. He has a dimple in his left cheek, and very nice teeth; I appreciate that about him. "I'll see you soon." He leans forward and kisses my cheek. I draw back involuntarily. I'm still not used to being touched by him. "Go get your beauty sleep."

"I will," I say, but he's already pushing out of the kitchen and returning to the dining room, where soon, dessert and coffee will be served. In three weeks, he will be my husband, and this will be my kitchen, and the housekeeper will be mine too. Mrs. Hargrove will have to listen to *me*, and I will choose what we eat every day, and there will be nothing left to want.

Unless Fred is right. Unless I am a defective one.

Lena

The argument continues: where to go, whether to split up.

Some members of the group want to loop south again, and then east to Waterbury, where there are rumors of a successful resistance movement and a large camp of Invalids flourishing in safety. Some want to head all the way out to Cape Cod, which is practically unpopulated and will therefore be a safer place to camp out. A few of us—Gordo, in particular—want to continue north and try to make a break across the U.S. border and into Canada.

In school we were always taught that other countries—places without the cure—had been ravaged by the disease and turned into wastelands. But this, like most other things we were taught, was no doubt a lie. Gordo has heard stories from trappers and drifters about Canada, and he makes it sound like Eden in *The Book of Shhh*.

"I say Cape Cod," Pike says. He has white-blond hair, ruthlessly trimmed down to the scalp. "If the bombing begins again—"

"If the bombing begins again, we won't be safe anywhere," Tack interrupts him. Pike and Tack are constantly butting heads.

"We're safer the farther we are from a city," Pike argues. If the resistance turns into a full-on rebellion, we can expect swift and immediate reprisals from the government. "We'll have more time."

"To what? Swim across the ocean?" Tack shakes his head. He is squatting next to Raven, who is repairing one of our traps. It's amazing how happy she looks here, sitting in the dirt, after a long day of hiking and trapping—happier than she did when we lived together in Brooklyn, posing as cureds, in our nice apartment with shiny edges and polished hard surfaces. There, she was like one of the women we studied in history class, who laced themselves up in corsets until they could barely breathe or speak: white-faced, stifled. "Look, we can't outrun this. We might as well join forces, build our numbers as best we can."

Tack catches my eye across the campfire. I smile at him. I don't know how much Tack and Raven have deciphered about what has happened between Alex and me, and what our history is—they've said nothing to me about it—but they have been nicer to me than usual.

"I'm with Tack," Hunter says. He tosses a bullet into the air, catches it on the back of his hand, then flips it into his palm.

"We could split up," Raven suggests for the hundredth time. It's obvious she doesn't like Pike, or Dani, either. In this new group, the lines of dominance haven't been so clearly drawn, and what Tack and Raven say doesn't automatically pass for gospel.

"We're not splitting up," Tack says firmly. But immediately he takes the trap from her and says, "Let me help you."

This is how Tack and Raven work: It's their private language of push and return, argument and concession. With the cure, relationships are all the same, and rules and expectations are defined. Without the cure, relationships must be reinvented every day, languages constantly decoded and deciphered.

Freedom is exhausting.

"What do you think, Lena?" Raven asks, and Pike, Dani, and the others swivel around to look at me. Now that I've proven myself to the resistance, my opinion carries weight. From the shadows, I can sense Alex looking at me too.

"Cape Cod," I say, feeding more kindling into the fire. "The farther we are from the cities, the better, and any advantage is better than none. It's not like we'll be alone. There will be other homesteaders there, other groups to join with." My voice rings out loudly in the clearing. I wonder if Alex has noticed this change: I have gotten louder and more confident.

There's a moment of quiet. Raven looks at me thoughtfully. Then, abruptly, she turns and shoots a glance over her shoulder. "What about you, Alex?"

"Waterbury," he answers immediately. My stomach knots up. I know it's stupid—I know the stakes are higher than the two of us—but I can't help but feel a flash of anger. Of course he disagrees with me. Of course.

"It's no advantage to be cut off from communication and information," he says. "There's a war on. We can try to deny it, we can try to bury our heads in the sand, but that's the truth. And the war will find us either way eventually. I say we meet it head-on."

"He's right," Julian pipes up.

I turn to him, startled. He hardly ever speaks in the evenings around the campfire. I don't think he feels comfortable yet. He is still the newbie, the outsider—and even worse, a convert from the other side. Julian Fineman, son of the late Thomas Fineman, founder and head of *Deliria*-Free America, and enemy to everything we stand for. It doesn't matter that Julian turned his back on his family and cause—and nearly gave up his life—to be here with us. I can tell that some people don't trust him.

Julian speaks with the measured cadence of a practiced public speaker. "There's no point in using avoidance tactics. This won't blow over. If the resistance grows, the government and the military will do anything they can to stop it. We'll have a better chance of fighting back if we put ourselves in the middle of things. Otherwise we'll just be rabbits in a hole, waiting to be flushed out."

Even though Julian agrees with Alex, he is careful to keep his eyes trained on Raven. Julian and Alex never speak to or even look at each other, and the others are careful not to comment on it.

"I say Waterbury," Lu puts in, which surprises me. Last year, she didn't want anything to do with the resistance. She wanted to disappear into the Wilds, make a homestead as far as possible from the Valid cities.

"All right, then." Raven stands up, brushing off the back of her jeans. "Waterbury it is. Any other objections?"

We're all silent for a minute, looking at one another, our faces consumed by shadow. No one speaks. I'm not happy with the decision, and Julian must sense it. He puts a hand on my knee and squeezes.

"Then it's decided. Tomorrow we can—"

Raven is cut off by the sound of shouting, a sudden flurry of voices. We all rise—an instinctive response.

"What the hell?" Tack has shouldered his rifle and is scanning the mass of trees that surround us, a tangled wall of branches and vines. The woods have fallen silent again.

"Shh." Raven holds up a hand.

Then: "I need help out here, guys!" And then, "Shit." There is a collective release, a relaxation of tension. We recognize Sparrow's voice. He wandered away earlier to do his business in the woods.

"We got you, Sparrow!" Pike calls out. Figures race into the trees, turning to shadow as soon as they leave the small circumference of brightness cast by the fire. Julian and I stay where we are, and I notice that Alex does too. There is a confusion of voices and instructions—"Her legs, her legs, grab her legs"—and then Sparrow, Tack, Pike, and Dani are emerging once again into the clearing, each pair saddled with a body. At first I think they are each hauling an animal, bundled in tarps, but then I see a pale white arm, dangling toward the ground, starkly illuminated by the fire, and my stomach turns.

People.

"Water, get water!"

"Grab the kit, Raven, she's bleeding."

For a moment, I'm paralyzed. As Tack and Pike place the bodies down on the ground, near the fire, two faces are revealed: one old, dark, weather-beaten; a woman who has been in the Wilds for most of her life, if not all of it. Saliva is bubbling at the corners of her mouth, and her breathing is hoarse and full of fluid.

The other face is unexpectedly lovely. She must be my age or even a little younger. Her skin is the color of the inside of an almond, and her long, dark-brown hair is fanned out behind her in the dirt. For a moment I am jettisoned back to my own escape to the Wilds. Raven and Tack must have found me exactly this way—more dead than not, beaten and bruised.

Tack swivels around and catches me staring.

"A little help, Lena," he says sharply. His voice snaps me

46

out of my trance. I go and kneel beside him, next to the older woman. Raven, Pike, and Dani are taking care of the girl. Julian hovers behind me.

"What can I do?" he asks.

"We need clean water," Tack says without looking up. He has his knife out and is cutting away her shirt. In places it seems almost melded with her skin—and then I see, horrified, that her lower half is badly burned, her legs covered with open sores and infection. I have to close my eyes for a second and will myself not to be sick. Julian brushes my shoulder once with his hand, then goes off in search of the water.

"Shit," Tack mutters, as he uncovers yet another wound; this one a long, ragged cut along her shin, deep and welling with infection. "Shit." The woman lets out a gurgled moan and then falls silent. "Don't tap out on me now," he says. He whips off his wind breaker. Sweat glistens on his forehead. We are close to the fire, which the others are stoking higher.

"I need a kit." Tack grabs a hand towel and begins ripping it into strips, expertly and quickly. These will be tourniquets. "Someone get me a *damn* kit."

The heat is a wall next to us. The dark smoke blots out the sky. It weaves its way into my thoughts, too, distorting my impressions, which begin to take on the quality of dream: the voices, the movement, the heat and the smell of bodies, all fractured and senseless. I can't tell whether I am kneeling there for minutes or hours. At some point Julian returns, carrying a bucket of steaming water. Then he leaves and returns again. I am helping to clean the woman's wounds, and after a time I stop seeing her body as skin and flesh, but as something twisted and warped and weird, like the dark pieces of petrified wood we turn up in the forest.

Tack tells me what to do and I do it. More water, cold this time. Clean cloth. I stand, move, take the objects that are given to me and return with them. More minutes pass; more hours.

At some point I look up and it is not Tack next to me, but Alex. He is sewing up a cut on the woman's shoulder, using a regular sewing needle and long, dark thread. He is pale with concentration, but he moves fluidly and quickly. He has obviously had practice. It occurs to me that there is so much I never knew about him—his past, his role in the resistance, what his life was like in the Wilds, before he came to Portland, and I feel a flash of grief so intense it almost makes me cry out: not for what I lost, but for the chances I missed.

Our elbows touch. He draws away.

The smoke is coating my throat now, making it difficult to swallow. The air smells like ash. I continue cleaning the woman's wooden legs and body, the way I used to help my aunt polish the mahogany table once a month, carefully and slowly.

Then Alex is gone, and Tack is next to me again. He puts his hands on my shoulders and draws me gently backward.

"It's okay," he's saying. "Leave it. It's all right. She doesn't need you anymore."

For a second I think, *We did it, she's safe now*. But then, as Tack pilots me toward the tents, I see her face lit up in the glow of the fire—white, waxen, eyes open and staring blindly at the sky—and I know that she's dead, and everything we did was for nothing.

Raven is still kneeling by the younger girl's side, but her ministrations are less frantic now, and I can hear that the girl is breathing regularly.

Julian is already in the tent. I'm so tired, I feel as though I'm sleepwalking. He moves over and makes a space for me, and I practically collapse into him, into that little question mark formed by his body. My hair reeks of smoke.

"Are you okay?" Julian whispers, finding my hand in the dark.

"Fine," I whisper back.

"Is *she* okay?"

"Dead," I say shortly.

Julian sucks in a breath, and I feel his body stiffen behind me. "I'm sorry, Lena."

"You can't save them all," I say. "That's not how it works." That is what Tack would say, and I know it's true, even if, deep down, I still don't quite believe it.

Julian squeezes me, and kisses the back of my head, and then I let myself tunnel down into sleep, and away from the smell of burning.

Hana

For a second night, the fog of my sleep is disturbed by an image: two eyes, floating up through darkened murk. Then the eyes are disks of light, headlights bearing down on me—I'm frozen in the middle of the road, surrounded by the heavy smells of garbage and car exhaust . . . gripped, motionless, in the roaring heat from an engine. . . .

I wake up just before midnight, sweating.

This can't be happening. Not to me.

I stand up and fumble toward the bathroom, bumping my shin against one of the unpacked boxes in my room. Even though we moved in late January, more than two months ago, I haven't bothered to unpack anything other than the basics.

In less than three weeks I'll be married, and I'll have to move again. Besides, my old belongings—the stuffed animals and books and funny porcelain figurines I used to collect as a kid—don't mean very much to me anymore.

In the bathroom, I splash cold water on my face, trying to shock out the memory of those headlight-eyes, the tightness in my chest, the terror of being flattened. I tell myself it doesn't mean anything, that the cure works a little bit differently for everyone.

Outside the window, the moon is round and improbably bright. I press my nose up to the glass. Across the street is a house nearly identical to ours, and next to it is another mirror-image house. On and on they go, dozens of replicas: the same gabled roofs, newly constructed and meant to look old.

I feel a need to move. I used to get the itch all the time, when my body was crying out for a run. I haven't run more than once or twice since I was cured—the few times I tried, it just wasn't the same—and even now, the idea has no appeal. But I want to do *something*.

I change into a pair of old sweatpants and a dark sweatshirt. I put on an old baseball cap, too, which belonged to my father—partly to keep my hair back, and partly so that if anyone does happen to be out, I won't be recognized. Technically, it isn't illegal for me to be out past curfew, but I have no desire to field questions from my parents. It's not something that Hana Tate, soon-to-be Hana Hargrove, would do. I don't want them to know I've been having trouble sleeping.

I can't give them a reason to be suspicious.

I lace up my sneakers and tiptoe to the bedroom door. Last summer, I used to sneak out all the time. There was the forbidden rave in the warehouse behind Otremba's Paints and the party in Deering Highlands that was raided; there were nights on the beach at Sunset Park and illegal meet-ups with uncured boys, including the time at Back Cove when I let Steven Hilt put a hand on the inside of my bare thigh and time seemed to stop.

Steven Hilt: dark eyelashes, neat straight teeth, the smell of pine needles; the drop in my stomach whenever he looked at me.

The memories seem like snapshots from someone else's life.

I ease downstairs in near-total silence. I find the latch on the front door and turn it by minuscule increments, so that the bolt withdraws soundlessly.

The wind is chilly and rustles the holly shrubs that encircle our yard, just inside the iron gate. The shrubs, too, are a feature of WoodCove Farms: *For security and protection,* the real estate brochures said, *and a real measure of privacy.*

I pause, listening for sounds of passing patrols. Nothing. But they can't be too far off. WoodCove advertises a twenty-four-hour, seven-day-a-week volunteer guard corps. Still, the community is large, and full of dozens of offshoots and cul-de-sacs. With any luck, I'll be able to avoid them.

Down the front walk, down the flagstone path, to the iron gate. A blur of black bats skirts past the moon, sending shadows skating across the lawn. I shiver. Already, the itch is draining out of me. I think about returning to bed, burrowing under the soft blankets and the pillows scented faintly of detergent; waking up refreshed to a nice big breakfast of scrambled eggs.

Something bangs in the garage. I spin around. The garage door is partially open.

My first thought is of a photographer. One of them has jumped the gate and camped out in the yard. But I quickly dismiss the idea. Mrs. Hargrove has carefully orchestrated all our press opportunities, and so far, I haven't been an object of attention unless I'm with Fred.

My second thought is *gas thief.* Recently, because of government-mandated restrictions, especially in the poorer parts of the city, there has been a rash of break-ins throughout Portland. It was especially bad during the winter: Furnaces were drained of oil, and cars of gas; houses were raided and vandalized. In February, there were two hundred burglaries alone, the largest number of crimes since the cure was made mandatory forty years ago.

I consider heading inside and waking my dad. But that would mean questions, and explanations.

Instead I cross the yard toward the garage, keeping my eye on the half-open door, checking for signs of movement. The grass is coated with dew, which soaks rapidly into my sneakers. I have a prickly, all-over body feeling. Someone is watching me.

A twig snaps behind me. I whirl around. A ripple of wind again disturbs the holly. I take a deep breath and turn back to the garage. My heart drums high in my throat, an uncomfortable and unfamiliar feeling. I have not been afraid—really afraid— since the morning of my cure, when I couldn't even unknot the hospital gown because my hands were shaking so badly.

"Hello?" I whisper.

Another rustle. Something—or someone—is definitely in the garage. I stand a few feet outside the door, struck rigid with fear. Stupid. This is stupid. I'll go into the house and wake Dad. I'll say I heard a noise, and I'll deal with questions later.

Then, faintly: a mewling sound. A cat's eyes blink momentarily at me in the open door.

I exhale. A stray cat—nothing more. Portland is lousy with them. Dogs, too. People buy them, and then can't afford or don't care to keep them, and dump them in the streets. For years they've been breeding. I've heard there are whole packs of wild dogs that roam around the Highlands.

I move forward slowly. The cat watches me. I put my hand on the garage door, ease it open a few more inches.

"Come on," I coo. "Come on out of there."

The cat bolts back into the garage. It darts past my old bike, knocking against the kickstand. The bike starts to totter, and I spring forward and grab it before it can crash to the ground. The handlebars are dusty; even though it's practically pitch-dark, I can feel the grime.

I keep one hand on the bike, steadying it, and feel for the

switch on the wall. I flick on the overhead lights. Immediately, the normalcy of the garage reasserts itself: the car, the trash cans, the lawn mower in the corner; cans of paint and extra tanks of gas stacked neatly in the corner, in a pyramid formation. The cat is crouched among them. At least the cat looks relatively clean—it's not frothing at the mouth or covered with scabs. Nothing to be afraid of. One more step toward her, and she bolts again; this time shooting around the car and circling past me, out into the yard.

As I lean the bike up against the garage wall, I notice the faded purple scrunchie still looped around one handle. Lena and I used to have identical bicycles, but she teased me that hers was faster. We were always switching bikes by accident, after dumping them down on the grass or the beach. She would hop up on the seat, barely able to reach the pedals, and I'd climb on her bike all scrunched up like a toddler, and we would ride home together, laughing hysterically. One day she bought two scrunchies from her uncle's convenience store— purple for me, blue for her—and insisted we keep them fixed around the handles, so we could differentiate them.

The scrunchie is now creased with dirt. I haven't ridden my bike since last summer. This hobby, like Lena, has faded into the past. Why were Lena and I best friends? What did we talk about? We had nothing in common. We didn't like the same foods or the same music. We didn't even believe in the same things.

And then she left, and it broke my heart so completely I

could hardly breathe. If I hadn't been cured, I'm not sure what I would have done.

I can admit, now, that I must have loved Lena. Not in an Unnatural way, but my feelings for her must have been a kind of sickness. How can someone have the power to shatter you to dust—and also to make you feel so whole?

The urge to walk has drained away completely. All I want to do is fall into bed.

I turn off the lights and close the door to the garage, making sure I hear the latch slide shut.

As I turn back to the house, I see a piece of paper lying on the grass, already spotted with moisture. It wasn't there a minute ago. Someone has obviously pushed it through the gate while I was in the yard.

Someone *was* watching me—could be watching me even now.

I cross the yard slowly. I see myself reach the paper. I see myself bend to pick it up.

It is a grainy black-and-white photo that has obviously been reproduced from the original: It shows a man and a woman kissing. The woman in the picture is bent backward, her fingers laced in the man's hair. He is smiling even as he kisses her.

At the bottom of the flyer are printed the words: THERE ARE MORE OF US THAN YOU THINK.

Instinctively, I crumple the flyer in my fist. Fred was right: The resistance is here, nesting among us. They must have access to copiers, to paper, to messengers.

A door bangs in the distance, and I jump. Suddenly the night seems alive. I practically sprint to the front porch and completely forget to be quiet as I slip inside the door, triple-locking it behind me. For a moment I stand in the hall, the flyer still balled in my hand, breathing in the familiar smells of furniture polish and Clorox.

In the kitchen, I throw the paper in the trash. Then, thinking better of it, I stuff it into the garbage disposal instead. I'm no longer worried about waking my parents. I just want to get rid of the picture, get rid of the words—a threat, no doubt about it. *There are more of us than you think.*

I wash my hands with hot water and fumble clumsily back to my bedroom. I don't even bother to undress, just kick off my shoes, take off the baseball hat, and climb under the covers. Even though the heat is humming, I still don't feel warm.

Long, dark fingers are enclosing me. Velvet-gloved hands, soft and perfumed, are wrapping around my throat, and Lena is whispering from somewhere far away—*What did you do?*—and then, mercifully, the fingers release, the hands drop from around my throat, and I am falling, falling, into a deep and dreamless sleep.

Lena

When I open my eyes, the tent is full of hazy green light as the sun is transformed into color by the thin tent walls. The ground beneath me is slightly damp, as it always is in the mornings; the ground exhales dew, shakes off the nighttime freeze. I can hear voices and the clang of metal pots. Julian is gone.

I can't remember how long it has been since I've slept so deeply. I don't even remember dreaming. I wonder whether this is what it is like to be cured, to wake up refreshed and renewed, undisturbed by the long, shadowy fingers that reach for you in sleep.

Outside, the air is unexpectedly warm. The woods are full

of birdsong. Clouds skate giddily across a pale blue sky. The Wilds are boldly asserting the arrival of spring, like the first proud, puff-chested robins to appear in March.

I go down to the small stream where we've been drawing our water. Dani has just emerged from bathing and is standing totally naked, toweling off her hair with a T-shirt. Nudity used to shock me, but now I hardly notice it; she could be a dark, water-slicked otter shaking itself in the sun. Still, I head downstream from where she is, stripping off my shirt to splash my face and underarms and dunk my head underwater, gasping a little as I come up. The water is still ice-cold, and I can't bring myself to submerge.

Back at the camp, I see that the body of the old woman has already been removed. Hopefully they've found somewhere to bury her. I think of Blue, and how we had to leave her out in the snow while the ice clotted her dark lashes and sealed her eyes shut, and of Miyako, who was burned. Ghosts, shadow-figures in my dreams. I wonder whether I will ever be rid of them.

"Morning, sunshine," says Raven, without looking up from the jacket she is patching. She is holding several needles in her mouth, fanned out between her lips, and she has to speak through them. "Sleep well?" She doesn't wait for me to answer. "There's some grub on the fire, so eat up before Dani gets hold of seconds."

The girl we rescued last night is awake and sitting near Raven, at a short distance from the fire, with a red blanket draped around her shoulders. She is even lovelier than I thought. Her eyes are vivid green, and her skin is luminous and soft-looking.

"Hi," I say as I move between her and the fire. She gives me a shy smile but doesn't speak, and I feel a rush of sympathy for her. I remember how terrified I was when I escaped into the Wilds and found myself among Raven and Tack and the others. I wonder where she has come from, and what terrible things she has seen.

At the edge of the fire, a dented pot is half-buried in the ash. Inside is a small bit of oatmeal-and-black-bean stew, left over from our dinner last night. It's charred crunchy and practically tasteless. I spoon some into a tin cup and force myself to eat quickly.

As I'm finishing, Alex stomps his way out of the woods, carrying a plastic jug of water. I glance up instinctively to see whether he will acknowledge me, but as usual he keeps his eyes locked on air over my head.

He passes beyond me and stops by the new girl.

"Here," he says. His voice is gentle, the voice of the old Alex, the Alex of my memories. "I brought you some water. Don't worry. It's clean."

"Thanks, Alex," she responds. The name sounds wrong in her mouth and makes me feel off-kilter, the way I used to feel as a kid at the Strawberry Festival at Eastern Prom, standing in the hall of fun-house mirrors: like everything has been distorted.

Tack, Pike, and some of the others come pushing out of the

woods just after Alex, elbowing their way through the weave of branches. Julian is one of the last to emerge, and I stand up and find myself running toward him, barreling into his arms.

"Whoa." He laughs, stumbling backward a little and squeezing me, obviously surprised and pleased. I am never this affectionate with him during the day, in front of the others. "What was that for?"

"I missed you," I say, feeling breathless for no reason. I put my forehead on his collarbone, place one hand on his chest. Its rhythm reassures me: He is real, and he is now.

"We did a full sweep," Tack is saying. "Three-mile circumference. Everything looks good. The Scavengers must have gone in a different direction."

Julian tenses. I turn around and face Tack.

"Scavengers?" I ask.

Tack shoots me a look and doesn't answer. He has stopped in front of the new girl. Alex is still sitting beside her. Their arms are separated by only a few inches, and I start to fixate on the negative space between their shoulders and elbows, like one-half of an hourglass.

"You don't remember what day they came?" he asks the girl, and I can tell he's struggling not to seem impatient. On the surface, Tack is all bite—bite and rough edges, just like Raven. That's why they go so well together.

The girl chews her lip. Alex reaches out and touches her hand, gentle and reassuring, and I am suddenly filled, head to toe, with the feeling that I am going to be sick.

"Go on, Coral," he says. Coral. Of course she would be named Coral. Beautiful and delicate and special.

"I—I don't remember." Her voice is almost as low as a boy's.

"Try," Tack says. Raven shoots him a look. Her expression is clear. *Don't push it.*

The girl draws the blanket a little tighter around her shoulders. She clears her throat. "They came a few days ago—three, four. I don't know exactly. We found an old barn, totally intact. . . . We'd been crashing there. There was just a small group of us. There was David and Tigg and—and Nan." Her voice breaks a bit, and she sucks in a breath. "And a few others—eight of us total. We've stuck together since I first came to the Wilds. My grandfather was a priest of one of the old religions." She looks up at us defiantly, as though she is daring us to criticize her. "He refused to convert to the New Order and was killed." She shrugs. "Ever since then, my family was tracked. And when my aunt turned out to be a sympathizer . . . well, we were blacklisted. Couldn't get a job, couldn't get paired to save our lives. There wasn't a landlord in Boston who would rent to us—not that we had any money to pay."

Bitterness has crept into her voice. I can tell that it is only the recent trauma that has made her seem fragile. Under normal circumstances, she is a leader—like Raven. Like Hana.

I feel another stab of jealousy, watching Alex watching her.

"The Scavengers," Tack prompts her.

"Let it go, Tack," Raven breaks in. "She's not ready to talk about it."

"No, no. I can. It's just . . . I hardly remember . . ." Again she shakes her head, this time looking puzzled. "Nan had trouble with her joints. She didn't like to be alone in the dark when she had to use the bathroom. She was worried she might fall." She squeezes her knees closer to her chest. "We took turns walking with her. It was my turn that night. That's the only reason I'm not . . . That's the only reason . . ." She trails off.

"The others are dead, then?" Tack's voice is hollow.

She nods. Dani mutters, "Shit," and toes some dirt into the air, aiming at nothing.

"Burned," the girl says. "While they were sleeping. We saw it happen. The Scavengers surrounded the place and just—*phoomf*. It went up like a match. Nan lost her head. Went hurtling straight back toward the barn. I went after her . . . after that, I don't remember much. I thought she was on fire . . . and then I remember I woke up in a ditch, and it was raining . . . and then you found us. . . ."

"Shit, shit, shit." Each time Dani says the word, she toes up another spray of dirt.

"You're not helping," Raven snaps.

Tack rubs his forehead and sighs. "They've cleared out of the area," he says. "That's a break for us. We'll just have to hope we don't cross paths."

"How many were there?" Pike asks Coral. She shakes her head. "Five? Seven? A dozen? Come on. You have to give us something to—"

"I want to know why," Alex interjects. Even though he speaks softly, everyone instantly gets quiet and listens. I used to love that about him: the way he can take command of a situation without raising his voice, the ease and confidence he has always radiated.

Now I am supposed to feel nothing, so I focus on the fact that Julian is behind me, only inches away; I focus on the fact that Alex's and Coral's knees are touching, and he doesn't draw away or seem to mind at all.

"*Why* the attack? Why burn the barn down? It doesn't make sense." Alex shakes his head. "We all know the Scavengers are out to loot and rob, not ravage. This wasn't theft—it was massacre."

"The Scavengers are working with the DFA," Julian says. He glosses fluidly over the words, although they must be difficult for him. The DFA was his father's organization, his family's lifework, and up until Julian and I were thrown together only a few short weeks ago, it was Julian's lifework as well.

"Exactly." Alex stands up. Even though he and Julian are once again speaking off each other, call-and-response, he refuses to look in our direction. He keeps his eyes on Raven and Tack. "It's not about survival for them anymore, is it? It's about payday. The stakes are higher and the goals are different."

No one contradicts him. Everyone knows he is right. The Scavengers never cared about the cure. They came into the Wilds because they didn't belong in—or were pushed out of—normal society. They came with no allegiance or affiliation, no sense of honor or ideals. And although they were always ruthless, their attacks used to serve a purpose—they pillaged and robbed, took supplies and weapons, and didn't mind killing in the process.

But murder with no meaning and no gain . . .

That is very different. That is contract killing.

"They're picking us off." Raven speaks slowly, as though the idea is just occurring to her. She turns to Julian. "They're going to hunt us down like—like animals. Is that it?"

Now everyone looks at him—some curiously, some with resentment.

"I don't know." He stutters very lightly over the words. Then: "They can't afford to let us live."

"Now can I say *shit*?" Dani asks sarcastically.

"But if the DFA and the regulators are using the Scavengers to kill us, it's proof that the resistance has power," I protest. "They see us as a threat. That's a good thing."

For years, the Invalids living in the Wilds were actually *protected* by the government, whose official position was that the disease, *amor deliria nervosa*, had been wiped out during the blitz, and all the infected people eradicated. Love was no more. To recognize that Invalid communities existed would have been an admission of failure.

But now the propaganda can't hold. The resistance has become too large and too visible. They can't ignore us any longer, or pretend that we don't exist—so now they must try to wipe us out.

"Yeah, we'll see how good it feels when the Scavengers fry us in our sleep," Dani fires back.

"Please." Raven gets to her feet. A ribbon of white runs through her black hair; I've never noticed it before, and I wonder whether it has always been there or only recently appeared. "We'll just have to be more careful. We'll scout locations for our camps more closely, and keep someone on guard at night. All right? If they're hunting us, we'll just have to be faster and smarter. And we'll have to work *together*. There are more of us every day, right?" She looks pointedly at Pike and Dani, then turns her gaze back to Coral. "Do you think you're strong enough to walk?"

Coral nods. "I think so."

"All right, then." Tack is obviously getting antsy. It must be at least ten o'clock. "Let's make final rounds. Check the traps; work on getting packed up. We'll shove off as soon as we can."

Tack and Raven no longer have undisputed control of the group, but they can still get people to *move*, and in this case, no one argues. We've been camping near Poughkeepsie for almost three days, and now that we have decided on a destination, we're all eager to get there.

The group breaks up as people begin to scatter into the trees. We've been traveling together for a little less than a week, but each of us has already assumed a different role. Tack and Pike are the hunters; Raven, Dani, Alex, and I take turns manning the traps; Lu hauls and boils water. Julian packs and unloads and repacks. Others repair clothing and patch tents. In the Wilds, existence depends on order.

On that, the cureds and the uncureds agree.

I fall into step behind Raven, who is stalking up a short incline, toward a series of bombed-out foundations, where a block of houses must once have stood. There is evidence of raccoons here.

"She's coming with us?" I burst out.

"Who?" Raven seems surprised to see me next to her.

"The girl." I try to keep my voice neutral. "Coral."

Raven raises an eyebrow at me. "She doesn't have much of a choice, does she? It's either that or she stays and starves."

"But . . ." I can't explain why I feel, stubbornly, that she shouldn't be trusted. "We don't know anything about her."

Raven stops walking. She turns to me. "We don't know anything about *anyone*," she says. "Don't you get that yet? You don't know shit about me, I don't know shit about you. *You* don't even know shit about you."

I think of Alex—the strange, stony figure of a boy I thought I once knew. Maybe he hasn't changed that much. Maybe I *never* really knew him at all.

Raven sighs and rubs her face with both hands. "Look, I meant what I said back there. We're all in this together, and we have to act like it."

"I get it," I say. I look back toward the camp. From a distance, the red blanket draped across Coral's shoulders looks jarring, like a spot of blood on a polished wood floor.

"I don't think you do," Raven says. She steps in front of me, forcing me to meet her gaze. Her eyes are hard, nearly black. "This—what's happening now—is the only thing that matters. It's not a game. It's not a joke. This is war. It's bigger than you or me. It's bigger than all of us combined. We don't matter anymore." Her voice softens. "Remember what I always told you? The past is dead."

I know, then, that she's talking about Alex. My throat begins to tighten, but I refuse to let Raven see me cry. I won't cry over Alex ever again.

Raven starts walking again. "Go on," she calls back over her shoulder. "You should help Julian pack up the tents."

I look over my shoulder. Julian already has half the tents dismantled. As I watch, he collapses yet another one, and it shrinks into nothing, like a mushroom sprouting in reverse.

"He's got it under control," I say. "He doesn't need me." I move to follow her.

"Trust me"—Raven whirls around, her black hair fanning behind her—"he needs you."

For a second we just stand there, looking at each other. Something flashes in Raven's eyes, an expression I can't quite decipher. A warning, maybe.

Then she quirks her lips into a smile. "I'm still in charge, you know," she says. "You have to listen to me."

So I turn around and go back down the hill, toward the camp, toward Julian, who needs me.

Hana

In the morning I wake up momentarily disoriented: The room is drowning in sunlight. I must have forgotten to close the blinds.

I sit up, pushing the covers to the foot of my bed. Seagulls are calling outside, and as I stand, I see that the sun has touched the grass a vivid green.

In my desk I find one of the few things I bothered to unpack: *AfterCure*, the thick manual I was given after my procedure, which, according to the introduction, "contains the answers to the most common—and uncommon!—questions about the procedure and its aftereffects."

I flip quickly to the chapter on dreaming, scanning several

pages that detail, in boring technical terms, the unintended side effect of the cure: dreamless sleep. Then I spot a sentence that makes me want to hug the book to my chest: "As we have repeatedly emphasized, people are different, and although the procedure minimizes variances in temperament and personality, it must of necessity work differently for everybody. About five percent of cureds still report having dreams."

Five percent. Not a huge amount, but still, not a freakishly small percentage either.

I feel better than I have in days. I close the book, making a sudden resolution.

I will ride my bike to Lena's house today.

I haven't been anywhere near her house on Cumberland in months. This will be my way of paying tribute to our old friendship and of putting to rest the bad feeling that has bugged me since I saw Jenny. Lena may have succumbed to the disease, but it was, after all, partly my fault.

That must be why I still think of her. The cure doesn't suppress *every* feeling, and the guilt is still pushing through.

I will bike by the old house and see that everyone is okay, and I will feel better. Guilt requires absolution, and I have not absolved myself for my part in her crime. Maybe, I think, I'll even bring over some coffee. Her aunt Carol used to love the stuff.

Then I'll return to my life.

I splash water on my face, pull on a pair of jeans and my favorite fleece, soft from years of going in the dryer, and twist my hair up in a messy bun. Lena used to make a face whenever I wore it this way. *Unfair,* she'd say. *If I tried to do that, I'd look like a bird crapped a nest on my head.*

"Hana? Is everything okay?" my mother calls to me from the hallway, her voice muffled, concerned. I open the door.

"Fine," I say. "Why?"

She squints at me. "Were you—were you singing?"

I must have been humming unconsciously. I feel a hot shock of embarrassment.

"I was trying to think of the words to some song Fred played me," I say quickly. "I can't remember more than a few words."

My mother's face relaxes. "I'm sure you can find it on LAMM," she says. She reaches out and cups my chin, scans my face critically for a minute. "Did you sleep well?"

"Perfectly," I say. I detach myself from her grip and head toward the stairs.

Downstairs, Dad is pacing the kitchen, dressed for work except for a tie. I can tell just by looking at his hair that he has been watching the news for a while. Since last fall, when the government issued its first statement acknowledging the existence of the Invalids, he insists on keeping the news running almost constantly, even when we leave the house. As he watches, he twirls his hair between his fingers.

On the news, a woman with an orange-lipstick mouth is saying, *"Outraged citizens stormed the police station on State Street this morning, demanding to know how the Invalids were able to move freely through the city streets to deliver their threats...."*

Mr. Roth, our neighbor, is sitting at the kitchen table, spinning a mug of coffee between his palms. He is becoming a regular fixture in our house.

"Good morning, Hana," he says without taking his eyes off the screen.

"Hi, Mr. Roth."

Despite the fact that the Roths live across from us, and Mrs. Roth is always talking about the new clothes she has bought her older daughter, Victoria, I know that they are struggling. Neither of their children made a particularly good match, mostly because of a small scandal that attached itself to Victoria, who was rumored to have been forced into an early procedure after being caught in the streets after curfew. Mr. Roth's career has stalled, and the signs of financial difficulty are there: They no longer use their car, although it still sits, gleaming, beyond the iron gate in the driveway. And the lights go off early; obviously, they are trying to conserve electricity. I suspect that Mr. Roth has been stopping by so much because he no longer has a working television.

"Hi, Dad," I say as I scoot past the kitchen table.

He grunts at me in response, grabbing and twisting another bit of hair. The newscaster says, *"The flyers were distributed in a dozen different areas, and were even slipped into playgrounds and elementary schools."*

The footage cuts to a crowd of protesters standing on the steps of city hall. Their signs read TAKE BACK OUR STREETS and *DELIRIA*-FREE AMERICA. The DFA has received an outpouring of support since its leader, Thomas Fineman, was assassinated last week. Already he is being treated as a martyr, and memorials to him have sprung up across the country.

"Why isn't anyone doing anything to protect us?" a man is saying into a microphone. He has to shout over the noise of the other protesters. *"The police are supposed to keep us safe from these lunatics. Instead they're swarming the streets."*

I remember how frantic I was to get rid of the flyer last night, as though doing so would mean that it had never existed. But of course the Invalids didn't target us specifically.

"It's outrageous!" my dad explodes. I've seen him raise his voice only two or three times in my life, and he's only ever totally lost it once: when they announced the names of the people who had been killed during the terrorist attacks, and Frank Hargrove—Fred's father—was among those listed as dead. We were all watching TV in the den, and suddenly my father turned and threw his glass against the wall. It was so shocking, my mother and I could only stare at him. I'll never forget what he said that night: Amor deliria nervosa *isn't a disease of love. It's a disease of selfishness.* "What's the *point* of the National Security Administration if—"

Mr. Roth cuts in. "Come on, Rich, have a seat. You're getting upset."

"Of course I'm upset. These *cockroaches* . . ."

In the pantry, boxes of cereal and bags of coffee are lined neatly in multiples. I tuck a bag of coffee under my arm and rearrange the others so the gap isn't noticeable. Then I grab a piece of bread and smear some peanut butter on it, even though the news has almost completely killed my hunger.

I pass back through the kitchen and am halfway down the hall before my dad turns and calls, "Where are you going?"

I angle my body away from him, so the bag of coffee isn't visible. "I thought I'd go on a bike ride," I say brightly.

"A bike ride?" my dad repeats.

"The wedding dress has been getting a little tight." I gesture expressively with the folded piece of bread. "Stress eating, I guess." At least my ability to lie hasn't changed since my cure.

My dad frowns. "Just stay away from downtown, okay? There was an incident last night. . . ."

"Vandalism," Mr. Roth says. "And nothing more."

Now the television is showing footage of the terrorist incidents in January: the sudden collapse of the eastern side of the Crypts, captured by a grainy handheld camera; fire licking up from city hall; people pouring out of stalled buses and running, panicked and confused, through the streets; a woman crouched in the bay, dress billowing behind her on the swells, screaming that judgment has arrived; a mass of floating dust blowing through the city, turning everything chalk-white.

"This is just the beginning," my father responds sharply. "They obviously meant the message to be a warning."

"They won't be able to pull anything off. They're not organized."

"That was what everyone said last year, too, and we ended up with a hole in the Crypts, a dead mayor, and a city full of psychopaths. Do you know how many prisoners escaped that day? Three hundred."

"We've tightened security since then," Mr. Roth insists.

"Security didn't stop the Invalids from treating Portland like a giant post office last night. Who knows what could happen?" He sighs and rubs his eyes. Then he turns to me. "I don't want my only daughter blown to bits."

"I won't go downtown, Dad," I say. "I'll stay off-peninsula, okay?"

He nods and turns back to the television.

Outside, I stand on the porch and eat my bread with one hand, keeping the bag of coffee tucked under my arm. I realize, too late, that I'm thirsty. But I don't want to go back inside.

I kneel down, transfer the coffee into my old backpack—still smelling, faintly, like the strawberry gum I used to chew—and shove the baseball hat over my ponytail again. I put on sunglasses, too. I'm not particularly afraid of being spotted by photographers, but I don't want to risk running into anyone I know.

I retrieve my bike from the garage and wheel it into the street. Everyone says that riding a bike is a skill that stays with you forever, but for a moment after I climb on the seat I wobble wildly, like a toddler just learning to ride. After a few teetering seconds, I manage to find my balance. I angle the bike downhill and begin coasting down Brighton Court, toward the gatehouse and the border of WoodCove Farms.

There's something reassuring about the *tic-tic-tic* of my

wheels against the pavement, and the feel of the wind on my face, raw and fresh. I don't get the same feeling I used to have from running, but it does bring contentment, like settling into clean sheets at the end of a long day.

The day is perfect, bright, and surprisingly cold. On a day like today, it seems impossible to imagine that half the country is blighted by the rise of insurgents; that Invalids are running like sewage through Portland, spreading a message of passion and violence. It seems impossible to imagine that anything is wrong in the whole world. A bed of pansies nods at me, as though in agreement, as I zip by them, picking up speed, letting the slope carry me forward. I whiz through the iron gates and past the gatehouse without stopping, raising a hand in a gesture of quick salute, although I doubt Saul recognizes me.

Outside WoodCove Farms, the neighborhood quickly changes. Government-owned plots run up against seedy lots, and I pass three mobile home parks in a row, which are crowded with outdoor charcoal grills and fire pits and shrouded over by a film of smoke and ash, since the people who live here use electricity only sparingly.

Brighton Avenue carries me on-peninsula, and technically across the border and into downtown Portland. But city hall, and the cluster of municipal buildings and laboratories where people have gathered to protest, is still several miles away. The buildings this far from the Old Port are no more than a few stories high, and interspersed with corner delis, cheap Laundromats, run-down churches, and long-disused gas stations.

I try to remember the last time I went to Lena's house, instead of she to mine, but all I get is a mash-up of years and images, the smell of tinned ravioli and powdered milk. Lena was embarrassed by her cramped home, and by her family. She knew what people said. But I always liked going to her house. I'm not sure why. I think at the time it was the mess that appealed to me—the beds crammed closely together in the upstairs room, the appliances that never worked correctly, fuses that were always powering down, a washing machine that sat rusting, used only as a place for storing winter clothes.

Even though it has been eight months, I navigate the way to Lena's old house easily, even remembering to shortcut through the parking lot that backs up onto Cumberland.

By this point, I'm sweating, and I stop my bike a few doors down from the Tiddles' house, wrestling off my hat and running a hand through my hair so I at least look semi-presentable. A door bangs down the street, and a woman emerges onto her porch, which is cluttered with broken furniture and even, mysteriously, a rust-spotted toilet seat. She is carrying a broom, and she begins sweeping back and forth, back and forth, over the same six inches of porch, her eyes locked on me.

The neighborhood is worse, much worse, than it used to be. Half the buildings are boarded up. I feel like a diver on a new submarine, coasting past the wreck of a tanked ship. Curtains stir in the windows, and I have a sense of unseen eyes following my progress down the street—and anger, too, simmering inside all the sad, sagging homes.

I start to feel incredibly stupid for coming. What will I say? What *can* I say?

But now that I'm so close, I can't turn around until I've seen it: number 237, Lena's old house. As soon as I wheel my bike up to the gate, I can tell that the house has been abandoned for some time. Several shingles are missing from the roof, and the windows have been boarded up with fungus-colored wood. Someone has painted a large red *X* over the front door, a symbol that the house was harboring disease.

"What do you want?"

I spin around. The woman on the porch has stopped sweeping; she holds the broom in one hand and shields her eyes with the other.

"I was looking for the Tiddles," I say. My voice rings out too loudly on the open street. The woman keeps staring at me. I force myself to move closer to her, wheeling my bike across the street and up to her front gate, even though something inside me is revolting, telling me to go. I do not belong here.

"Tiddles moved off last fall," she says, and begins sweeping again. "They weren't welcome around here no more. Not after—" She breaks off suddenly. "Well. Anyways. Don't know what happened to them, and don't care, either. They can rot away in the Highlands as far as I'm concerned. Spoiling the neighborhood, making it hard for everybody else—"

"Is that where they went?" I seize on the small bit of information. "To Deering Highlands?"

Instantly, I can tell I've put her on her guard. "What business is it to you?" she says. "You Youth Guard or something? This is a good neighborhood, a clean neighborhood." She jabs at the porch with her broom, as though trying to tamp down invisible insects. "Read the Book every day and passed all my reviews just like anybody else. But still people come poking and prying, digging up trouble—"

"I'm not from the DFA," I say to reassure her. "And I'm not trying to cause trouble."

"Then what are you trying to do?" She squints at me closely, and I see a flicker of recognition pass across her face. "Hey. Have you been around here before or something?"

"No," I say quickly, and jam the hat back onto my head. I'll get no more help here, I can tell.

"I'm sure I know you from somewhere," the woman says as I climb onto my bike. I know it will click for her any second: That's the girl who got paired with Fred Hargrove.

"You don't," I say, and I push off into the street.

I should let it go. I know I should let it go. But more than ever, I have an urge to see Lena's family again. I need to know what has happened since she left.

I haven't been to Deering Highlands since last summer, when Alex, Lena, and I used to hang out in 37 Brooks, one of the neighborhood's many abandoned houses. 37 Brooks is where Lena and Alex were caught by the regulators, and the reason they attempted a last-minute, poorly planned escape.

Deering Highlands, too, is even more run-down than I remember it. The neighborhood was practically abandoned years ago, after a string of busts in the area gave it the reputation of being tainted. When I was little, the older kids used to tell stories of the ghosts of uncureds who'd died of *amor deliria nervosa* and still wandered the streets. We used to dare each other to go into the Highlands and put a hand on the derelict buildings. You had to keep your hand there for a full ten seconds, just enough time for the disease to seep through your fingertips.

Lena and I did it together once. She chickened out after four seconds, but I waited the whole ten, counting slowly, and loud, so the girls who were watching could hear. I was the hero of second grade for a full two weeks.

Last summer, there was a raid on an illegal party in the Highlands. I was there. I let Steven Hilt lean in and whisper to me, his mouth bumping against my ear.

It was one of four illegal parties I'd attended since graduation. I remember how thrilled I was sneaking through the streets, long past curfew, my heart clawing up to my throat, and how Angelica Marston and I would meet the next day to laugh about how we'd gotten away with it. We spoke in whispers about kissing and threatened to run away to the Wilds, as though we were little girls talking about Wonderland.

That's the point. It was kid stuff. A big game of make-believe.

It was never supposed to happen to me, to Angie, or to anyone else. It definitely wasn't supposed to happen to Lena.

After the raid, the neighborhood was officially repossessed by the city of Portland, and a number of the houses were razed. The plan was to set up new low-income condos for some of the municipal workers, but construction stalled after the terrorist incidents, and as I cross over into the Highlands, all I see is rubble: holes in the ground, and trees felled and left with their roots exposed to the sky, dirty, churned earth, and rusting metal signs declaring it a hard-hat area.

It's so quiet that even the sound of my wheels as they turn seems overloud. A thought comes to me suddenly, unbidden—*Quiet through the grave go I; or else beneath the graves I lie*—the old rhyme we used to whisper as kids when we passed a graveyard.

A graveyard: That's exactly what the Highlands is like now.

I climb off my bike and lean it against an old street sign, which points the way to Maple Avenue, another street of large, carved bowls of dark earth and uprooted trees.

I walk down Maple for a bit, feeling increasingly stupid. There is no one here. That is obvious. And Deering Highlands is a large neighborhood, a tangle of small streets and cul-de-sacs. Even if Lena's family is squatting somewhere around here, I won't necessarily find them.

But my feet keep stepping one in front of the other, as though controlled by something other than my brain. The wind sweeps quietly over the bare lots, and the air smells like rot. I pass an old foundation, exposed to the air, and it reminds me, weirdly, of the X-rays my dentist used to show me: toothy gray structures, like a jaw split open and tacked to the ground.

Then I smell it: wood smoke, faint but definite, threaded underneath the other smells.

Someone is having a fire.

I turn left at the next intersection and start down Wynnewood Road. This is the Highlands I remember from last summer. Here the houses were never razed. They still loom, gloomy and vacant, behind thick stands of ancient pine trees.

My throat begins to tighten and release, tighten and release. I can't be far from 37 Brooks now. I have a sudden terror of coming across it.

I make a decision: If I come to Brooks Street, it will be a sign that I should turn around. I'll go home; I'll forget about this ridiculous mission.

"Mama, Mama . . . help me get home . . ."

The singsong voice stops me. I stand still for a minute, holding my breath, trying to locate the source of the sound.

"I'm out in the woods, I'm out on my own . . ."

The words are from an old nursery rhyme about the monsters that were rumored to live in the Wilds. Vampires. Werewolves. Invalids.

Except that the Invalids, it turns out, are real.

I step out of the road and into the grass, weaving through the trees that line the street. I move slowly, careful to touch my toes lightly to the ground before shifting my weight forward—the voice is so quiet, so faint.

The road turns a corner, and I see a girl squatting in the middle of the street, in a large patch of sunshine, her stringy dark hair hanging like a curtain in front of her face. She is all bones. Her kneecaps are like two spiky sails.

She is holding a filthy doll in one hand and a stick in the other. Its end is whittled to a point. The doll has hair made of matted yellow yarn, and eyes of black buttons, although only one of them is still attached to its face. Its mouth is no more than a stitch of red yarn, also unraveling.

"I met a vampire, a rotten old wreck . . ."

I close my eyes as the rest of the lines from the rhyme come back to me.

Mama, Mama, put me to bed
I won't make it home, I'm already half-dead
I met an Invalid, and fell for his art
He showed me his smile, and went straight for my heart.

When I open my eyes again, she looks up, briefly, as she stabs the air with her makeshift stake, as though warding off a vampire. For a moment, everything in me stills. It's Grace, Lena's younger cousin. Lena's favorite cousin.

It's Grace, who never, ever said a word to anyone, not once in the six years I watched her grow from an infant.

"Mommy, put me to bed . . ."

Even though it's cool in the shade of the trees, a bead of sweat has gathered between my breasts. I can feel it tracing its way down to my stomach.

"I met an Invalid, and fell for his art . . ."

Now she takes the stick and begins working it against the doll's neck, as though making a procedural scar. "Safety, Health, and Happiness spells *Shh*," she singsongs.

Her voice is pitched higher now, a lullaby coo. "Shh. Be a good girl. This won't hurt at all, I promise."

I can't watch anymore. She's jabbing at the doll's flexible neck, making its head shudder in response as though it is nodding yes. I step out of the trees.

"Gracie," I call to her. Unconsciously, I've extended one arm, as though I'm approaching a wild animal.

She freezes. I take another careful step toward her. She is gripping the stick in her fist so tightly, her knuckles are white.

"Grace." I clear my throat. "It's me, Hana. I'm a friend—I was a friend of your cousin, Lena."

Without warning, she's up on her feet and running, leaving the doll and the stick behind. Automatically, I break into a sprint and tear after her down the street.

"Wait!" I call out. "Please—I'm not going to hurt you."

Grace is *fast*. She has put fifty feet of distance between us already. She disappears around a corner, and by the time I reach it, she's gone.

I stop running. My heart drums hard in my throat, and there's a foul taste in my mouth. I take off my hat and swipe at the sweat on my forehead, feeling like a complete idiot.

"Stupid," I say out loud. Because it makes me feel better, I repeat, a little louder, "Stupid."

There's a titter of laughter from somewhere behind me. I spin around: no one. The hair pricks up on my neck; all of a sudden I have the feeling I'm being watched, and it occurs to me that if Lena's family is here, there must be others, too. I notice that cheap plastic shower curtains are hung in the windows of the house across the street; next to it is a yard layered with plastic debris—toys and tubs and plastic building blocks, but neatly arranged, as though someone has recently been playing there.

Feeling suddenly self-conscious, I retreat into the protection of the trees, keeping my eyes on the street, scanning for signs of movement.

"We have a right to be here, you know."

The whispering voice comes from directly behind me. I whirl around, so startled that for a moment I can't speak. A girl has just emerged from the trees. She stares at me with wide brown eyes.

"Willow?" I choke out.

Her eyelids flicker. If she recognizes me, she doesn't acknowledge it. But it's definitely her—Willow Marks, my old classmate, who got pulled out of school just before we graduated, after rumors circulated that she had been found with a boy, an uncured, in Deering Oaks Park after curfew.

"We have a right," she repeats, in that same urgent whisper.

She twists her long, thin hands together. "A road and a path for everybody . . . That is the promise of the cure. . . ."

"Willow." I take a step backward and almost trip over myself. "Willow, it's me. Hana Tate. We had math together last year. Mr. Fillmore's class. Remember?"

Her eyelids flutter. Her hair is long and hopelessly tangled. I remember how she used to dye streaks of it different colors. My parents always said she would get into trouble. They told me to stay away from her.

"Fillmore, Fillmore," she repeats. When she turns her head, I see that she has the three-pronged procedural mark, and I remember that she was pulled abruptly out of school just a few months short of graduation: Everyone said that her parents forced her into an early procedure. She frowns and shakes her head. "I don't know . . . I'm not sure . . ." She brings her fingernails to her mouth, and I see that her cuticles are gnawed to shreds.

My stomach surges. I need to get out of here. I never should have come.

"Good to see you, Willow," I say. I start to inch slowly around her, trying not to move too quickly even though I'm desperate to break into a run.

All of a sudden, Willow reaches out and puts an arm around my neck, pulling me close, as though she wants to kiss me. I cry out and strain against her, but she is surprisingly strong.

With one hand, she begins feeling her way across my face, prodding my cheeks and chin, like a blind person. The feel of her nails on my skin makes me think of small, sharp-clawed rodents.

"Please." To my horror, I find that I am almost crying. My throat is spasming; fear makes it hard to breathe. "Please let me go."

Her fingers find my procedural scar. All at once, she seems to deflate. For a second, her eyes click into focus, and when she looks at me, I see the old Willow: smart and defiant and, now, in this moment, defeated.

"Hana Tate," she says sadly. "They got you, too."

Then she releases me, and I run.

Lena

Coral slows us down. She has no visible injuries, now that she has bathed and had various cuts and scrapes bandaged, but she is obviously weak. She falls behind as soon as we begin to move, and Alex hangs back with her. In the early part of the day, even though I try to ignore it, I can hear the ribbon of their conversation weaving up and through the other voices. Once, I hear Alex burst out laughing.

In the afternoon, we come across a large oak. Its trunk has been gouged and slashed with various lines. I let out a cry of recognition as soon as I see it: a triangle, followed by a number and a rudimentary arrow. It's Bram's knife pattern, the specific series of markings he used during relocation from the northern homestead last year to mark our progress and help us find our way back in the spring.

This mark I remember specifically; it indicates the way to a house we came across last year, intact and inhabited by a family of Invalids. Raven must recognize it too.

"Jackpot," she says, grinning. Then she raises her voice to the group. "This way to a roof!" There are whoops and exclamations. Just a week outside of civilization makes us crave the simplest things: roofs and walls and tubs full of steaming water. Soap.

It's less than a mile to the house, and when I see the gabled roof, covered in a fur of brown and tangled ivy, my heart leaps. The Wilds—so vast and changeable, so disorienting—also make us lust for the familiar.

I burst out to Julian, "We stopped here last autumn. During the journey south from Portland. I remember that broken window—see how they've patched it with wood? And the little stone chimney peeking up over the ivy."

I notice, though, that the house is more run-down than it was even six short months ago. Its stone facade is darker, coated with a slick surface of black mold that has webbed itself into the caulking. The small clearing around the house, where last year we pitched our tents, is overgrown with high brown grasses and thorned plants.

There is no smoke piping from the chimney. It must be cold inside the house with no fire going. Last autumn the kids ran out to intercept us when we were halfway to the front door. They were always outside, laughing and shouting, teasing one another. Now there is quiet and stillness, except the wind through the ivy, a slow sigh.

I begin to feel uneasy. The others must feel it too. We've covered the last mile quickly, moving together as one large group, buoyed by the promise of a real meal, an indoor space, a chance to feel like humans. But now everyone falls silent.

Raven reaches the door first. She hesitates with a fist raised; then she knocks. The sound is hollow and overloud in the stillness. Nothing happens.

"Maybe they're out gathering," I say. I'm trying to quell the panic that is building, the spiky sense of fear I used to get whenever I ran past the graveyard in Portland. *Better go fast,* Hana used to say, *or they'll reach out and grab your ankles.*

Raven doesn't answer. She puts her hand on the knob and turns. The door opens.

She turns to Tack. He unslings his rifle and passes in front of her into the house. Raven seems relieved that he has taken the lead. She removes a knife from the belt she wears on her hips and follows him inside. The rest of us flow in after them.

It smells terrible. A little light penetrates the darkness, spilling in from the open door and piercing the wooden slats that cover the broken window. We can just see the bare outlines of the furniture, much of it smashed or overturned. Someone lets out a cry.

"What happened?" I whisper. Julian finds my hand in the darkness and squeezes. Nobody answers. Tack and Raven move farther into the room, their shoes crunching on broken glass. Tack takes the butt of his rifle and slams it, hard, against the wooden slats in the window; they break apart easily, and more light flows into the room.

No wonder it smells so bad; there is food, rotted, spilling out of an overturned copper pot. When I take a step forward, insects scurry into the corners. I fight down a surge of nausea.

"God," Julian mutters.

"I'll check the upstairs," Tack says, at normal volume, which makes me jump. Someone clicks on a flashlight, and the beam sweeps over the littered floor. Then I remember that I, too, have a flashlight, and I fumble in my backpack for it.

I move with Julian into the kitchen, keeping the flashlight in front of me, rigid, as though it will protect us. There are more signs of struggle here—a few smashed glass jars, more insects and rotting food. I draw my sleeve up to my nose and breathe through it. I pass the beam of light over the pantry shelves. They are still fairly well-stocked: jars of pickled vegetables and meats are lined neatly next to bundles of dried jerky. The jars are labeled with neat, handwritten script that identifies their contents, and I feel a sudden vertigo, a wild swinging, as I remember a woman with fire-red hair, bending over a jar with her pen, smiling, saying, *There's hardly any paper left at all. Soon we'll have to guess at what's what.*

"Clear," Tack announces. We hear him thudding back downstairs, and Julian draws me through the short hallway and into the main room, where most of the group is still assembled.

"Scavengers again?" Gordo asks gruffly.

Tack passes a hand through his hair.

"They weren't looking for food or supplies," I say. "The pantry's still stocked."

"Maybe it wasn't Scavengers at all," Bram says. "Maybe the family just took off."

"What? And trashed the place before they split?" Tack toes a metal cup. "And left their food behind?"

"Maybe they were in a hurry," Bram insists. But I can tell even he doesn't believe it; the atmosphere in the house is rancid, wrong. This is a house where something very bad has happened, and all of us can feel it.

I move toward the open door and step out onto the porch, inhaling clean, outside smells, scents of space and growth. I wish we'd never come.

Half the group has already retreated outside. Dani is moving across the yard slowly, parting the grasses with a hand—looking for what, I don't know—as though she is wading through knee-high water. From the back of the house I hear shouted conversation; then Raven's voice, rising above the noise. "Get back, get back. Don't go down there. I *said*, don't go down there."

My stomach tightens. She found something.

She comes around the side of the house, breathless. Her eyes are shiny, bright with anger.

But all she says is, "I found them." She doesn't have to say that they're dead.

"Where?" I croak.

"Bottom of the hill," she says shortly, then she pushes past me, back into the house. I don't want to return inside, to the smell and the darkness and the fine layering of death that covers everything—that's what it is, that *wrong*-thing, that evil silence—but I do.

"What did you find?" Tack asks. He's still standing in the middle of the room. Everyone else surrounds him in a semicircle, frozen, quiet, and for a moment, when I reenter the room, I have the impression of statues, gripped in gray light.

"Evidence of a fire," Raven says, and then adds, a little more quietly, "Bone."

"I knew it." Coral's voice sounds high and slightly hysterical. "They were here. I *knew* it."

"They're gone now," Raven says soothingly. "They won't be back."

"It wasn't Scavengers."

All of us whip around. Alex is standing in the doorway. Something red—a ribbon, or strip of fabric—is balled loosely in his fist.

"I told you not to go down there," Raven says. She is glaring at him—but beneath the anger, I see fear as well.

He ignores her and passes into the room, shaking out the fabric as he does, holding it up for us to see: It's a long strip of red plastic tape. At intervals it is imprinted with an image of a skull and crossbones, and the words CAUTION: BIOHAZARD.

"The whole area's cordoned off," Alex says. He keeps his face neutral, but his voice has a strangled quality, as though he is speaking through a muffler.

Now *I* feel like the statue. I want to speak, but my mind has gone blank.

"What does it mean?" Pike says. He has been in the Wilds since he was a child. He knows hardly anything about life inside the bordered places—about the regulators and the health initiatives, the quarantines and the prisons, the fears of contamination.

Alex turns to him. "The infected aren't buried. They're either kept apart, in the prison yards, or they're burned." For just a second, Alex's eyes slide to mine. I am the only person here who knows that his father's body was buried in the tiny prison courtyard of the Crypts, unmarked, uncelebrated; I am the only person who knows that for years Alex visited the makeshift grave and wrote his father's name in marker on a stone, to keep him from being forgotten. *I'm sorry,* I try to think to him, but his eyes have already passed over me.

"Is it true, Raven?" Tack asks sharply.

She opens her mouth, then closes it again. For a second I think she'll deny it. But at last she says, in a tone of resignation, "It looks like regulators."

There's a collective inhale.

"Fuck," Hunter mutters.

Pike says, "I don't believe it."

"Regulators . . ." Julian repeats. "But that means . . ."

"The Wilds aren't safe anymore," I finish for him. The panic is building now, cresting in my chest. "The Wilds aren't *ours* anymore."

"Happy now?" Raven asks Alex, shooting him a dirty look.

"They had to know," he says shortly.

"All right." Tack holds up his hands. "Settle down. This doesn't change anything. We already knew the Scavengers were on the prowl. We'll just have to be on our guard. Remember, the regulators don't know the Wilds. They're not used to wilderness or open territory. This is *our* land."

I know Tack is doing his best to reassure us, but he's wrong about one thing: Something *has* changed. It's one thing to bomb us from the skies. But the regulators have broken through the barriers, real and imagined, that have been keeping our worlds apart. They've torn through the fabric of invisibility that has cloaked us for years.

Suddenly I remember one time coming home to find that a raccoon had somehow worked its way into Aunt Carol's house and chewed through all the cereal boxes, scattering crumbs in every room. We cornered it in the bathroom and Uncle William shot it, saying it probably carried disease. The raccoon had left crumbs in my sheets; it had been in my bed. I washed the sheets a full three times before I would sleep in them again, and even then I had dreams of tiny claws digging into my skin.

"Let's get some of this mess cleared out," Tack says. "We'll fit as many people inside as we can. The rest will camp outside."

"We're *staying* here?" Julian bursts out.

Tack stares at him hard. "Why not?"

"Because . . ." Julian looks helplessly at everyone else. No one will meet his gaze. "People were killed here. It's just . . . *wrong.*"

"What's *wrong* is heading back into the Wilds when we've got a roof, and a pantry stocked with food, and better traps here than the pieces of crap we've been using," Tack says sharply. "The regulators have been here once. They won't be back again. They did their job the first time around."

Julian looks to me for help. But I know Tack too well, and I know the Wilds, too. I just shake my head at Julian. *Don't argue.*

Raven says, "We'll get the smell out faster if we break open some more windows."

"There's firewood stacked and split out back," Alex says. "I can get a fire started."

"All right, then." Tack doesn't look at Julian again. "It's settled. We camp here for the night."

We pile the debris out back. I try not to look too much at the shattered bowls, the splintered chairs, or think about the fact that six months ago I sat in them, warm and fed.

We scrub the floors with vinegar we find in the cupboards, and Raven gathers some dried grass from the yard outside and burns it in the corners, until the sweet, choking smell of rot is finally driven out.

Raven sends me out with a few small traps, and Julian volunteers to come with me. He's probably looking for an excuse to get away from the house. I can tell that even after we've cleaned the rooms of almost all evidence of the struggle, he's still uncomfortable.

We walk in silence for a bit, across the overgrown yard, into the thick tangle of trees. The sky is stained pink and purple, and the shadows are thick, stark brushstrokes on the ground. But the air is still warm, and several trees are crowned with tiny green leaves.

I like seeing the Wilds this way: skinny, naked, not yet clothed in spring. But reaching, too, grasping and growing, full of want and a thirst for sun that gets slaked a little bit more every day. Soon the Wilds will explode, drunk and vibrant.

Julian helps me place the traps, tamping them down in the soft dirt to conceal them. I like this feeling: of warm earth; of Julian's fingertips.

When we've positioned all three traps and marked their locations by tying a length of twine around the trees that encircle them, Julian says, "I don't think I can go back there. Not yet."

"Okay." I stand up, wiping my hands on my jeans. I'm not ready to go back either. It's not just the house. It's Alex. It's the group, too, the fighting and factions, resentments and push-back. It's so different from what I found when I first came to the Wilds at the old homestead: There, everyone seemed like family.

Julian straightens up too. He runs a hand through his hair. Abruptly he says, "Remember when we first met?"

"When the Scavengers—?" I start to say, and he cuts me off.

"No, no." He shakes his head. "Before that. At the DFA meeting."

I nod. It's still strange to imagine that the boy I saw that day—the poster child for the anti-*deliria* cause, the embodiment of correctness—could be even remotely connected to the boy who walks beside me, hair tangled across his forehead

97

like twisted strands of caramel, face ruddy from cold.

This is what amazes me: that people are new every day. That they are never the same. You must always invent them, and they must invent themselves, too.

"You left your glove. And you came in and found me looking at photographs. . . ."

"I remember," I say. "Surveillance images, right? You told me you were looking for Invalid camps."

"That was a lie." Julian shakes his head. "I just—I liked seeing all that openness. That space, you know? But I never imagined—even when I dreamed about the Wilds and the unbordered places—I didn't think it could really be like this."

I reach out and take his hand, give it a squeeze. "I knew you were lying," I say.

Julian's eyes are pure blue today, a summer color. Sometimes they turn stormy, like the ocean at dawn; other times they are as pale as new sky. I am learning them all. He traces my jaw with one finger. "Lena . . ."

He's looking at me so intently, I begin to feel anxious. "What's wrong?" I say, trying to keep my voice light.

"Nothing." He reaches for my other hand too. "Nothing's wrong. I—I want to tell you something."

Don't, I want to say, but the word breaks apart in a fizz of laughter, the hysterical feeling I used to get just before tests. He has accidentally smudged a bit of dirt across his cheekbone, and I start to giggle.

"What?" He looks exasperated.

Now that I've started laughing, I can't stop. "Dirt," I say, and reach out to touch his cheek. "Covered in it."

"Lena." He says it with such force, I finally go quiet. "I'm trying to tell you something, okay?"

For a second we stand there in silence, staring at each other. The Wilds are perfectly still for once. It's as though even the trees are holding their breath. I can see myself reflected in Julian's eyes—a shadow self, all form, no substance. I wonder what I look like to him.

Julian sucks in a deep breath. Then, all in a rush, he says, "I love you."

Just as I blurt out, "Don't say it."

There's another beat of silence. Julian looks startled. "What?" he finally says.

I wish I could take the words back. I wish I could say *I love you, too.* But the words are caught in the cage of my chest. "Julian, you have to know how much I care about you." I try to touch him, and he jerks backward.

"Don't," he says. He looks away from me. The silence stretches long between us. It is growing darker by the minute. The air is textured with gray, like a charcoal drawing that has begun to smudge.

"It's because of him, isn't it?" he says at last, clicking his eyes back to mine. "Alex."

I don't think Julian has ever said his name.

"No," I say too forcefully. "It's not him. There's nothing between us anymore."

He shakes his head. I can tell he doesn't believe me.

"Please," I say. I reach for him again, and this time he lets me run my hand along his jaw. I crane onto my tiptoes and kiss him once. He doesn't pull away, but he doesn't kiss me back, either. "Just give me time."

Finally he gives in. I take his arms and wind them around my body. He kisses my nose, and then my forehead, then traces his way to my ear with his lips.

"I didn't know it would be like this," he says in a whisper. And then: "I'm scared."

I can feel his heart beating through the layers of our clothing. I don't know what, exactly, he is referring to—the Wilds, the escape, being with me, loving someone—but I squeeze him tightly, and rest my head on the flat slope of his chest.

"I know," I say. "I'm scared too."

Then, from a distance, Raven's voice echoes through the thin air. "Grub's on! Eat up or opt out!"

Her voice startles a flock of birds. They go screaming into the sky. The wind picks up, and the Wilds come alive again with rustling and scurrying and creaking: a constant nonsense-babble.

"Come on," I say, and take Julian back toward the dead house.

Hana

Explosions: a sudden shattering of the sky. First one, then another; then a dozen of them, rapid gunfire sounds, smoke and light and bursts of color against a pale-blue evening sky.

Everyone applauds as the final round of fireworks blooms above the terrace. My ears are ringing, and the smell of smoke makes my nostrils burn, but I clap too.

Fred is officially the mayor of Portland now.

"Hana!" Fred moves toward me, smiling, as cameras light up around him. During the fireworks, as everyone surged onto the terraces of the Harbor Golf and Country Club, we were separated. Now he seizes my hands.

"Congratulations," I say. More cameras go off—*click, click, click*—like another miniature volley of fireworks. Every time I blink, I see bursts of color behind my eyelids. "I'm so happy for you."

"Happy for *us*, you mean," he says. His hair—which he gelled and combed so carefully—has over the course of the night become increasingly unruly, and migrated forward, so a stray lock of hair falls over his right eye. I feel a rush of pleasure. This is my life and my place: here, next to Fred Hargrove.

"Your hair," I whisper. He brings a hand automatically to his head, patting his hair into place again.

"Thank you," he says. Just then a woman I recognize vaguely from the staff of the *Portland Daily* shoulders up to Fred.

"Mayor Hargrove," she says, and it gives me a thrill to hear him referred to that way. "I've been trying to get a word with you all night. Do you have a minute—?"

She doesn't wait to hear his response but draws him away from me. He turns his head over his shoulder and mouths, *Sorry*. I give him a small wave to show that I understand.

Now that the fireworks are done, people flow back into the ballroom, where the reception will continue. Everyone is laughing and chattering. This is a good night, a time of celebration and hope. In his speech, Fred promised to restore order and stability to our city and to root out the sympathizers and resisters who have nested among us—like termites, he said, slowly eroding the basic structure of our society and our values.

No more, he said, and everyone applauded.

This is what the future looks like: happy pairs, bright lights and pretty music, tasteful draped linens and pleasant conversation. Willow Marks and Grace, the rotting houses of Deering Highlands, and the guilt that compelled me out of the house and onto my bike yesterday—all of it seems like a bad dream.

I think of the way Willow looked at me, so sadly: *They got you, too.*

They didn't get *me*, I should have said. *They saved me.*

The last, wispy fingers of smoke have dispersed. The green hills of the golf course are swallowed in purple shadow.

For a second I stand on the balcony, enjoying the order of it all: the trimmed grass and carefully plotted landscape, the pattern of day into night into day again, a predictable future, a life without pain.

As the crowd on the terrace thins, I catch the eye of a boy standing at the opposite side of the deck. He smiles at me. He looks familiar, although for a moment I can't place him. But as he begins moving toward me, I feel a jolt of recognition.

Steve Hilt. I almost don't believe it.

"Hana Tate," he says. "I guess I can't call you Hargrove yet, can I?"

"Steven." Last summer I called him Steve. Now it seems inappropriate. He is changed; that must be why I didn't recognize him at first. As he inclines his head toward a waitress, depositing his empty wineglass on a tray, I see he has been cured.

But it is more than that: He is heavier, his stomach a round swell under his button-down shirt, his jawline blurring into his neck. His hair is combed straight across his forehead, the same way my dad wears it.

I try to remember the last time I saw him. It might have been the night of the raid in the Highlands. I had gone to the party mostly because I was hoping to see him. I remember standing in the half-dark basement while the floor thudded with the rhythm of the music, sweat and moisture coating the walls, the smell of alcohol and sunscreen and bodies packed into a tight space. And he had pressed his body against mine—he was so thin then, tall and skinny and tan—and I had let him slide his hands around my waist, under my shirt, and he had leaned down and pressed his lips against mine, opened my mouth with his tongue.

I believed I loved him. I believed he loved me.

And then: the first scream.

Gunfire.

Dogs.

"You look good," Steven says. Even his voice sounds different. Again, I can't help but think of my father, the easy, low-belly voice of a grown-up.

"So do you," I lie.

He tips his head, gives me a look that says both *Thanks* and *I know*. Unconsciously, I withdraw a few inches. I can't believe that I kissed him last summer. I can't believe that I risked everything—contagion, infection—on this boy.

104

But no. He was a different boy back then.

"So. When is the happy event? Next Saturday, isn't it?" He puts his hands in his pockets and rocks back on his heels.

"The Friday after." I clear my throat. "And you? You've been paired, then?" It never occurred to me last summer to ask.

"Sure have. Celia Briggs. Do you know her? She's at UP now. We won't be married until she's finished."

I do know Celia Briggs. She went to New Friends Academy, a St. Anne's rival school. She had a hook nose and a loud, rattling laugh, which made it always sound as though she was fighting a bad throat infection.

As though he can tell what I'm thinking, Steven says, "She's not the prettiest girl, but she's decent. And her dad's chief of the Regulatory Office, so we'll be all set up. That's how we scored an invite to this shindig." He laughs. "Not bad, I have to say."

Even though we are practically the only two people left on the deck, I suddenly feel claustrophobic.

"I'm sorry." I have to force myself to look at him. "I should get back to the party. It was great seeing you, though."

"Pleasure's mine," he says, and winks. "Enjoy yourself."

I can only nod. I step through the French doors and snag the hem of my dress on a splinter in the threshold. I don't stop; I give my dress a sharp tug and hear it tear. I push through knots of partygoers: the wealthiest and most important members of the Portland community, everyone scented and powdered and well-dressed. As I make my way through the room, I pick up on snatches of conversation, an ebb and flow of sound.

"You know Mayor Hargrove has ties to the DFA."

"Not publicly."

"Not yet."

Seeing Steven Hilt has destabilized me for reasons I can't understand. Someone presses a glass of champagne into my hand, and I drink it quickly, unthinkingly. The bubbles fizz in my throat, and I have to stifle a sneeze. It has been a long time since I've had anything to drink.

People whirl around the room, around the band, dancing two-step and waltz, arms rigid, steps graceful and defined: patterns forming and reforming, dizzying to watch. Two women, both tall, with the regal looks of birds of prey, stare at me as I push past them.

"Very pretty girl. Healthy-looking."

"I don't know. I heard her scores were rigged. I think Hargrove could have done better. . . ."

The women move off into the swirl of dancers, and I lose the thread of their voices. Different conversations overwhelm them.

"How many kids have they been assigned?"

"Don't know, but she looks like she can handle a litter of 'em."

Heat starts to climb into my chest and cheeks. Me: They're talking about me.

I look around for my parents or Mrs. Hargrove and don't spot them. I can't see Fred, either, and I have a moment of panic—I'm in a room full of strangers.

That's when it hits me that I have no friends anymore. I

suppose that I will make friends with Fred's friends now—people in our class and rank, people who share similar interests. People like these people.

I take a deep breath, trying to calm down. I shouldn't feel this way. I should feel brave, and confident, and careless.

"Apparently there were some problems with her last year before she was cured. She started manifesting symptoms. . . ."

"So many of them do, don't they? That's why it's so important that the new mayor aligns himself with the DFA. If they can shit a diaper, they can be cured. That's what I say."

"Please, Mark, give it a rest. . . ."

Finally I spot Fred across the room, surrounded by a small crowd and flanked by two photographers. I try to push my way toward him but am blocked by the crowd, which seems to be growing as the evening goes on. An elbow hits me in the side, and I stumble against a woman holding a large glass of red wine.

"Excuse me," I murmur, pushing past her. I hear a gasp and a few nervous titters, but I'm too focused on getting through the crowd to worry about what has attracted their attention.

Then my mother is barging toward me. She grabs my elbow, hard.

"What happened to your dress?" she hisses.

I look down and see a bright red stain spreading across my chest. I have the inappropriate urge to laugh; it looks as though I've been shot. Mercifully, I manage to suppress it.

"A woman spilled on me," I say, detaching myself from her. "I was just about to go to the bathroom." As soon as I say it, I feel relieved: I'll get a break in the bathroom.

"Well, hurry up." She shakes her head at me, as though it's my fault. "Fred is going to make a toast soon."

"I'll hurry," I tell her.

In the hall, it's much cooler, and my footsteps are suctioned away by the plush carpet. I head for the women's room, ducking my head to avoid making eye contact with the handful of guests who have trickled out into the hall. A man is talking loudly, ostentatiously, into a cell phone: Everyone here has that kind of money. The air smells like potpourri and, faintly, cigar smoke.

When I reach the bathroom, I pause with my hand on the door. I can hear voices murmuring inside, and a burst of laughter. Then a woman says, very clearly, "She'll make a good wife for him. It's a good thing, after what happened with Cassie."

"Who?"

"Cassie O'Donnell. His first pair. You don't remember?"

I pause with my hand on the door. Cassie O'Donnell. Fred's first wife. I've been told practically nothing about her. I hold my breath, hoping they'll continue speaking.

"Of course, of course. What was it? Two years ago now?"

"Three."

Another voice: "You know, my sister went to grade school

with her. She went by her middle name then. Melanea. Stupid name, don't you think? My sister says she was a perfect little bitch. But I guess she got hers in the end."

"The mills of God . . ."

Footsteps cross toward me. I take a step back, but not quickly enough. The door flies open. A woman is standing in the doorway. She is probably only a few years older than I am, and punch-bowl pregnant. Startled, she draws back to allow me room to enter.

"Were you coming in?" she asks pleasantly. She betrays no signs of discomfort or embarrassment, even though she must suspect that I've overheard her conversation. Her gaze ticks down to the stain on my dress.

Behind her, two women are lined up in front of the mirror, watching me with identical expressions of curiosity and amusement. "No," I blurt, and spin around and keep going down the hall. I can imagine the women turning to one another, smirking.

I round a corner and plunge blindly down another hallway, this one even quieter and cooler than the last one. I shouldn't have had the champagne; it has made me dizzy. I steady myself against the wall.

I haven't thought very much about Cassie O'Donnell, Fred's first pair. All I know is that they were married for more than seven years. Something terrible must have happened; people don't get divorced anymore. There's no need. It's practically illegal.

Maybe she couldn't have children. If she were biologically defective, it would be grounds for divorce.

Fred's words come back to me: *I was afraid I'd gotten a defective one.* It's cool in the hall, and I shiver.

A sign indicates the way to additional restrooms down a carpeted flight of stairs. Here it is totally quiet except for a low, electrical hum. I keep my hand on the thick banister to steady myself in my heels.

At the bottom of the stairs I pause. This floor isn't carpeted, and it's mostly swallowed in darkness. I've been to the Harbor Club only twice before, both times with Fred and his mother. My parents were never members, although my father is thinking of joining now. Fred says that half the country's business is conducted in golf clubs like this one; there's a reason, he says, that the Consortium made golf the national sport nearly thirty years ago.

A perfect golf game uses not a single wasted movement: Order, form, and efficiency are its trademarks. All this, I learned from Fred.

I pass several large banquet halls, all dark, that must be used for private functions, and finally recognize the vast clubhouse cafe where Fred and I once had lunch together. I find the women's bathroom at last: a pink room, like a gigantic perfumed pincushion.

I pull my hair into an updo and blot my face quickly with paper towels. There's nothing I can do about the stain, so I detach the sash from around my waist and tie it around my shoulders loosely, knotting it between my breasts. It's not the best I've ever looked, but at least I'm semi-presentable.

Now that I've oriented myself, I realize I can take a short-cut back to the ballroom by going left instead of right out of the bathroom and heading to the elevator banks. As I move down the hall, I hear the low murmur of voices and a burst of television static.

A half-open door leads into a kitchen prep area. Several waiters—ties loosened, shirts partially unbuttoned, aprons off and balled up on the counter—are gathered around a small TV. One of them has his feet up on the shiny metal counter.

"Turn it up," one of the kitchen girls says, and he grunts and leans forward, swinging his legs off the counter, to poke at the volume button. As he settles back in his chair, I catch sight of the image on the screen: a swaying mass of green, threaded with wisps of dark smoke. I feel a small, electric thrill, and without meaning to, I freeze.

The Wilds. Has to be.

A newscaster is saying, *"In an effort to exterminate the last breeding grounds of the disease, regulators and government troops are penetrating the Wilds. . . ."*

Cut to: governmental ground troops, dressed in camouflage, bumping along an interstate highway, waving and grinning at the cameras.

"As the Consortium gathers to debate the future of these uncharacterized areas, the president made an unscheduled speech to the press, in which he vowed to root out the remaining Invalids and

111

see them punished or treated."

Cut to: President Sobel, doing his infamous lean into the podium, as though he can barely keep himself from toppling it over into the audience of cameras.

"It will take time and troops. It will take fearlessness and patience. But we will win this war. . . ."

Cut back to: The puzzle-piece vision of green and gray, smoke and growth, and tiny, forked tongues of fire. And then another image: more growth, a narrow river winding between the pine trees and willows. And then another, this time in a place where the trees have been burned all the way down to the red soil.

"What you're seeing now are aerial images from all over the country, where our troops have been deployed to hunt down the last harborers of the disease. . . ."

For the first time, it strikes me that Lena is, in all probability, dead. It's stupid that I have not thought of it until now. I watch the smoke rising up from the trees and imagine little bits of Lena floating away with it: nails, hair, eyelashes, all gone to ash.

"Turn it off," I say without meaning to.

All four waiters turn around at once. Immediately, they push out of their chairs, readjust their ties, and begin tucking their shirts into their high-waisted black pants.

"Can we do anything for you, miss?" one of them, an older man, asks politely. Another reaches out and turns off the television. The resulting silence is unexpected.

"No, I . . ." I shake my head. "I was just trying to find my way back to the ballroom."

The older waiter blinks once, his face impassive. He steps out into the hall and points toward the elevators, which are less than ten feet away. "You'll just want to go up one floor, miss. The ballroom is at the end of the hall." He must think I'm an idiot, but he keeps smiling pleasantly. "Would you like me to escort you upstairs?"

"No," I say too forcefully. "No, I'll be fine." I practically take off running down the hallway. I can feel the waiter's eyes on me. I'm relieved that the elevator arrives quickly, and I exhale as the doors slide shut behind me. I lean my forehead briefly against the elevator wall, which feels cool against my skin, and inhale.

What's wrong with me?

When the elevator doors slide open, the sound of voices swells—a roar of applause—and I round the corner and step into the fierce glare of the ballroom just as a thousand voices echo, "To your future wife!"

I see Fred onstage, raising a glass of champagne, the color of liquid gold. I see a thousand bright and bloated faces turned toward me, like swollen moons. I see more champagne, more liquid, more swimming.

I bring my hand up. I wave. I smile.

More applause.

In the car on the way home from the party, Fred is quiet. He has insisted that he would like to be alone with me, and has sent his mother and my parents ahead of us with a different driver. I had assumed he had something to say to me, but so far, he hasn't spoken. His arms are crossed, and he has tucked his chin to his chest. He looks almost as though he is sleeping. But I recognize the gesture; he has inherited it from his father. It means that he is thinking.

"I think it was a success," I say, after the silence becomes intolerable.

"Mmm." He rubs his eyes.

"Are you tired?" I ask.

"I'm all right." He lifts his chin. Then, abruptly, he leans forward and knocks on the window that separates us from the driver. "Pull over for a second, Tom, will you?"

Tom pulls the car over immediately and cuts the engine. It's dark, and I can't see exactly where we are. On either side of the car are looming walls of dark trees. Once the headlights switch off, it's practically pitch-black. The only light comes from a streetlamp fifty feet ahead of us.

"What are we—?" I start to ask, but Fred turns to me and cuts me off.

"Remember the time I explained the rules of golf to you?" he says.

I'm so startled, both by the urgency in his voice and the randomness of the question, I can only nod.

"I told you," he says, "about the importance of the caddy. Always a step behind—an invisible ally, a secret weapon. Without a good caddy, even the best golfer can be sunk."

"Okay." The car feels small and too hot. Fred's breath smells sour, like alcohol. I fumble to open the window, but of course, I can't. The engine is off; the windows are locked.

Fred runs a hand agitatedly through his hair. "Look, what I'm saying is that you're my caddy. Do you understand that? I expect you—I need you—to be behind me one hundred percent."

"I am," I say, and then clear my throat and repeat it. "I am."

"Are you sure?" He leans forward another inch and places a hand on my leg. "You'll support me always, no matter what?"

"Yes." I feel a flicker of uncertainty—and beneath that, fear. I have never seen Fred so intense before. His hand is gripping my thigh so tightly, I'm worried he'll leave a mark. "That's what pairing is about."

Fred stares at me for a second longer. Then, all at once, he releases me.

"Good," he says. He taps casually against the driver's window once more, which Tom takes as a signal to start the car again and keep driving. Fred leans back, as though nothing has happened. "I'm glad we understand each other. Cassie never *understood* me. She didn't listen. That was a big part of the problem." The car starts moving again.

"Cassie?" My heart knocks against my rib cage.

"Cassandra. My first pair." Fred smiles tightly.

"I don't understand," I say.

For a moment he doesn't say anything. Then, abruptly: "Do you know what my father's problem was?" I can tell he doesn't expect an answer, but I shake my head anyway. "He believed in people. He believed that if people could only be shown the right way—the way to health and order, a way to be free of unhappiness—they would make the right choice. They would obey. He was naive." Fred turns to me again. His face has been swallowed up by darkness. "He didn't understand. People are stubborn and stupid. They're irrational. They're destructive. That's the point, isn't it? That's the whole reason for the cure. People will no longer destroy their own lives. They won't be capable of it. Do you understand?"

"Yes." I think of Lena and those pictures of the Wilds on fire. I wonder what she would be doing now had she stayed. She would be sleeping soundly in a decent bed; she would rise tomorrow to the sun coming up over the bay.

Fred turns back to the window, and his voice becomes steely. "We've been lax. We've allowed too much freedom already, and too much occasion for rebellion. It must stop. I won't allow it anymore; I won't watch my city, my country, be consumed from inside. It ends now."

Even though Fred and I are separated by a foot of space, I'm as frightened of him as I was when he was grabbing my thigh. I have never seen him like this, either—hard and foreign.

"What are you planning to do?" I ask.

"We need a system," he says. "We'll reward people who follow the rules. It's the same principle, really, as training a dog."

I flash to the woman at the party: *She looks like she can handle a litter of 'em.*

"And we'll punish the people who don't conform. Not bodily, of course. This is a civilized country. I plan on appointing Douglas Finch as the new minister of energy."

"Minister of energy?" I repeat. I've never heard the term.

We reach a stoplight—one of the few that still work downtown. Fred gestures vaguely at it.

"Power isn't free. Energy isn't free. It has to be earned. Electricity—light, heat—will be given to the people who have earned it."

For a moment I can't think of any response. Power-outages and blackouts have always been mandatory during certain hours of the night, and in the poorer neighborhoods, especially now, many families simply choose to do without dishwashers and laundry machines. They're just too expensive to maintain.

But everyone has always had the *right* to electricity.

"How?" I finally ask.

Fred takes my question literally. "It's simple, actually. The grid's already in place, and all this stuff is computerized nowadays. It's simply a matter of collecting the data and a few keystrokes. One click turns on the juice; one click turns it off. Finch will be in charge of all that. And we can reevaluate every six months or so. We want to be fair about it. Like I said, this is a civilized country."

"There will be riots," I say.

Fred shrugs. "I expect a certain amount of initial resistance," he says. "That's why it's so important that you be on my side. Look, once we get the right people behind us—the important people—everyone else will fall in line. They'll have to." Fred

117

reaches out and takes my hand. He squeezes it. "They'll learn that rioting and resistance will just make things worse. We need a zero-tolerance policy."

My mind is spinning. No power means no lights, no refrigeration, no working ovens. No furnaces.

"What will people do for heat?" I blurt out.

Fred laughs a little, indulgently, as though I'm a puppy and have just learned a new trick. "Summer's almost here," he says. "I don't think heat will be a problem."

"But what happens when it starts to get cold?" I persist. In Maine, the winters often last from September until May. Last year we had eighty inches of snow. I think of skinny Grace, with her doorknob elbows, her shoulder blades like peaked wings. "What will they do then?"

"I guess they'll find out that freedom doesn't keep you warm," he says, and I can hear the smile in his voice. He leans forward and knocks on the driver's window again. "How about some music? I'm in the mood for a little music. Something upbeat—don't you think, Hana?"

Lena

Night is coming quickly, and with it, the cold.

We're lost.

We're looking for an old highway that should lead us toward Waterbury. Pike is convinced we're too far north; Raven thinks we're too far south.

We're striking out mostly blind, using a compass and a series of old sketches that have been passed back and forth among other traders and Invalids, filled in a little at a time, showing a random scattering of landmarks: rivers; dismantled roads and old towns, bombed by the blitz; the borders of the established cities, so we know to avoid them; ravines and impassable places. Direction, like time, is a general thing, deprived of boundaries and borders. It is an endless process of interpretation and reinterpretation, doubling back and adjusting.

We come to a stop while Pike and Raven argue it out. My shoulders are aching. I unload my pack and sit on top of it, take a swig of water from the jug I have looped to the belt around my waist. Julian is hovering behind Raven, red-faced, his hair dark with sweat and his jacket tied around his waist. He's trying to see beyond her, to the map that Pike is holding. He is getting skinnier.

At the periphery of the group, Alex is sitting, like me, on his pack. Coral does the same, inching closer to him so their knees are touching. Over the course of a few short days, they have become practically inseparable.

Even though I want to, I can't bring myself to look away from him. I don't understand what he and Coral have to talk about. They talk while they hike, and while they set up camp. They talk at mealtimes, sequestered in the corner. Meanwhile, he hardly speaks with anyone else, and he has not exchanged a single word with me since our confrontation with the bear.

She must have asked him a question, because I see him shake his head.

And then, just for a second, both of them look up at me. I turn away quickly, heat rushing to my cheeks. They were talking about me. I know it. I wonder what she asked him.

Do you know that girl? She's staring at you.

Do you think Lena's pretty?

I squeeze my fists until my nails dig into the flesh of my

palms, inhale deeply, and will away the thought. Alex and what he thinks of me are irrelevant.

Pike is saying, "I'm telling you, we should have gone east at the old church. It's marked on the map."

"That isn't a church," Raven argues, snatching the map back from him. "It's the tree we passed earlier—the one split by lightning. And it means we should have continued north."

"I'm telling you, that's a *cross*—"

"Why don't we send out scouts?" Julian interrupts them. Startled into silence, they turn to him. Raven frowns, and Pike stares at Julian with open hostility. My stomach starts squirming, and I silently pray in his direction: *Don't get involved. Don't say anything stupid.*

But Julian continues calmly, "We move more slowly as a group, and it's a waste of our time and energy if we're headed in the wrong direction." For a second I see his old self float to the surface, the Julian of conferences and posters, the youth leader of the DFA, self-assured. "So I say two people head north—"

"Why north?" Pike breaks in angrily.

Julian barely misses a beat. "Or south, whichever. Hike for half a day, look for the highway. If it isn't there, hike in the other direction. At least we'll get more of a sense of the terrain. We can help orient the group."

"We?" Raven parrots.

Julian looks at her. "I want to volunteer," he says.

"It's not safe," I burst out, climbing to my feet. "There are

Scavengers patrolling—maybe regulators, too. We need to stick together. Otherwise we're easy prey."

"She's right," Raven says, turning back to Julian. "It isn't safe."

"I've dealt with Scavengers before," Julian argues.

"And almost died," I fire back.

He smiles. "I didn't, though."

"I'll go with him." Tack spits a thick wad of tobacco onto the ground and wipes his mouth with the back of his hand. I glare at him. He ignores me. He has made no secret of the fact that he thinks it was a mistake to have rescued Julian and a liability to have him with us. "You know how to shoot a gun?"

"No," I say. "He doesn't." Now everyone's looking at me, but I don't care. I don't know what Julian's trying to prove, but I don't like it.

"I can handle a gun," Julian lies quickly.

Tack nods. "All right, then." He extracts another bit of tobacco from a pouch he wears around his neck and balls it into his mouth. "Let me unload some of my pack. We'll leave in half an hour."

"Okay, everyone." Raven raises her arms in a gesture of resignation. "We might as well camp here."

The group, as one, begins to shed packs and shake supplies out on the ground, like a single animal molting its skin. I grab Julian's arm and draw him away from everybody else.

"What was that about?" I'm struggling to keep my voice down. I can see Alex watching us. He looks amused. I wish I had something to throw at him.

I take Julian and swivel him around, so he blocks Alex from my view.

"What do you mean?" He shoves his hands in his pockets.

"Don't play dumb," I say. "You shouldn't have volunteered to scout. This isn't a joke, Julian. We're in the middle of a war."

"I don't think it's a joke." His calmness is infuriating. "I know better than anyone else what the other side is capable of, remember?"

I look away, biting my lip. He has a point. If anyone knows about the tactics of the zombies, it's Julian Fineman.

"You still don't know the Wilds," I insist. "And Tack won't protect you. If you get attacked—if anything happens, and it's a question of you or the rest of us—he'll leave you. He won't endanger the group."

"Lena." Julian puts his hands on my shoulders and forces me to look at him. "Nothing's going to happen, okay?"

"You don't know that," I say. I know I'm overreacting, but I can't help it. For some reason, I feel like crying. I think of the quietness of Julian's voice as he said *I love you*, the steadiness of his rib cage rising and falling against my back as we sleep.

I love you, Julian. But the words don't come.

"The others don't trust me," Julian says. I open my mouth to protest, but he cuts me off. "Don't try and deny it. You know it's true."

I don't contradict him. "So what? You need to prove yourself?"

He sighs and rubs his eyes. "I chose to make my place here, Lena. I chose to make my place with you. Now I have to earn

123

it. It's not about proving myself. But like you said, there's a war on. I don't want to sit on the sidelines." He leans forward and kisses my forehead once. He still hesitates for just a fraction of a second before he kisses me, as though he has to shake out that old fear, the terror of touch and contamination. "Why are you so upset about this? Nothing will happen."

I'm scared, I want to say. *I have a bad feeling. I love you and don't want you to get hurt.* But again, it's as though the words are trapped, buried under past fears and past lives, like fossils compressed under layers of dirt.

"We'll be back in a few hours," Julian says, and cups my chin briefly. "You'll see."

But they aren't back by dinnertime, and they aren't back by the time we rake dirt over the fire, extinguishing it for the night. It's a liability now, and even though we'll be colder, and Julian and Tack will have trouble finding their way to us without it, Raven is insistent.

I volunteer to stay up and stand watch. I'm too anxious to sleep. Raven gives me an extra coat from our store of clothing. The nights are still edged with a hard chill.

A few hundred feet from the camp is a slight incline, and an old cement wall, still imprinted with ghostly loops of graffiti, that will shield me from the wind. I huddle up with my back against the stone, cupping the mug of water Raven boiled for me earlier to help warm my fingers. My gloves were lost, or stolen, somewhere between the New York homestead and here, and now I have to do without.

The moon rises and touches the camp—the slumbering forms, the domed tents and makeshift shelters—with a fine white sheen. In the distance, a water tower, still intact, hovers over the trees like a steel insect, perched on long, spindly legs. The sky is clear and cloudless, and thousands of stars float out of the darkness. An owl hoots, a hollow, mournful sound that echoes through the woods. From even this short distance, the camp looks peaceful, wrapped up in its white haze, surrounded by the splintered wrecks of old houses: roofs collapsed into the ground, a swing set, overturned, its plastic slide still protruding from the dirt.

After two hours, I'm yawning so much my jaw aches, and my whole body feels as though it has been filled with wet sand. I lean my head back against the wall, struggling to keep my eyes open. The stars above me blur together . . . they became one beam of light—sunshine—Hana is stepping out of the sunshine, leaves in her hair, saying, *"Wasn't it a funny joke? I was never planning to get cured, you know. . . ."* Her eyes are locked on mine, and as she steps forward, I see she's about to put her foot in a trap. I try to warn her, but—

Snap. I jolt awake, heart throbbing in my throat, and quickly, as quietly as possible, move into a crouch. The air is still again, but I know I didn't imagine or dream the sound: the sound of a twig snapping.

The sound of a footstep.

Let it be Julian, I think. *Let it be Tack.*

I scan the camp and see a shadow moving between the tents. I tense up and reach forward, ever so slowly, easing the rifle into my hands. My fingers are swollen with cold, and clumsy. The gun feels heavier than it did earlier.

The figure steps into a patch of moonlight, and I exhale. It's just Coral. Her skin shines a vivid white in the moonlight, and she is wearing an oversized sweatshirt that I recognize as belonging to Alex. My stomach clenches. I bring the rifle up to my shoulder, swing the muzzle toward her, think: *Bang*.

I bring the gun down quickly, ashamed.

My former people were not totally wrong. Love is a kind of possession. It's a poison. And if Alex no longer loves me, I can't bear to think that he might love somebody else.

Coral disappears into the woods, probably to pee. My legs are cramping, so I straighten up. I'm too tired to stand guard any longer. I'll go down and wake up Raven, who volunteered to replace me.

Snap. Another footstep, this one closer and on the east side of the camp. Coral went north. Instantly, I'm on alert again.

Then I see him: He inches slowly forward, gun raised, emerging from behind a thick copse of evergreens. I can tell right away he's not a Scavenger. His posture is too perfect, his gun too pristine, his clothing well-fitted.

My heart stops. A regulator. Must be. And that means the Wilds really have been breached. Despite all the evidence, a part of me has been hoping it wasn't true.

For a second everything gets silent, and then frighteningly

loud, as the blood rushes to my head, pounding in my ears, and the night seems to light up with frightening hoots and screams, alien and wild, animals prowling the dark. My palms are sweating as I bring the gun once more to my shoulder. My throat is dry. I track the regulator as he moves closer to the camp. I put my finger on the trigger. Panic is building in my chest. I don't know whether to shoot. I've never shot anything from this distance. I've never shot a person. I don't even know that I *could*.

Shit, shit, shit, shit. I wish Tack were here.

Shit.

What would Raven do?

He reaches the edge of the camp. He lowers his gun, and I move my finger off the trigger. Maybe he's just a scout. Maybe he's supposed to report back. That will give us time to move, to clear out, to prepare. Maybe we'll be okay.

Then Coral reemerges from the woods.

For a split second she stands there, frozen stiff and white as though framed in a photographer's flash. For a split second, he doesn't move either.

Then she gasps, and he swings his gun toward her, and without thinking or planning on it, my finger finds the trigger again and pulls. The regulator's knee goes and he cries out, sinking to the ground.

Then everything is chaos.

The kick of the rifle knocks me backward, and I stumble, trying to keep my balance. A jagged tooth of rock bites sharply into my back, and pain shoots from my ribs to my shoulder. There are more gunshots—one, two—and then shouting. I sprint down toward the camp. In less than a minute, it has unfolded, opened, turned into a swarm of people and voices.

The regulator is lying facedown in the dirt, arms and legs splayed. A pool of blood extends like a dark shadow around him. Dani is standing near him with her handgun out. She must have been the one to kill him.

Coral has her arms wrapped around her waist, looking shocked and slightly guilty, as though she somehow summoned the regulator to her. She is uninjured, which is a relief. I'm glad that my instincts were to save her. I think about centering her in my crosshairs earlier, and feel another pulse of shame. This is not the person I wanted to become: Hatred has carved a permanent place inside me, a hollow where things are so easily lost.

Hatred, too, the zombies warned me about.

Pike, Hunter, and Lu are all talking at the same time. The rest of our group huddles in a semicircle around them, pale and frightened-looking in the moonlight, their eyes hollows, like resurrected ghosts.

Only Alex isn't standing. He's squatting, quickly and methodically repacking his backpack.

"All right." Raven speaks quietly, but the urgency there commands our attention. "Let's look at the facts. We have a dead regulator on our hands."

Someone whimpers.

128

"What are we doing?" Gordo breaks in. His face is wild with panic. "We have to *go*."

"Go where?" Raven demands. "We don't know where they are, what direction they're coming from. We could be running straight into a trap."

"Shh." Dani hushes us sharply. For a second there is total stillness, except for the low moan of wind through the trees and an owl calling. Then we hear it: from the south, the distant echo of voices.

"I say we stay and fight," Pike says. "This is *our* territory."

"We don't fight unless we have to," Raven says, turning on him. "We don't know how many regulators there are, or what kind of weapons they have. They're better fed and stronger than we are."

"I'm sick of running," Pike fires back.

"We're not running," she says calmly. She turns back to the rest of the group. "We're going to divide. Spread out around the camp. Hide. Some of us can head down to the old riverbed. I'll be watching from the hill. Rocks, bushes, whatever looks like it will conceal you—use it. Climb a tree, for shit's sake. Just stay out of sight." She looks to each of us in turn. Pike stubbornly refuses to meet her gaze.

"Take your guns, knives—anything you have. But remember, we don't fight unless we have to. Don't do anything until my signal, okay? *Nobody moves*. Nobody breathes, coughs, sneezes, or farts. Is that clear?"

Pike spits on the ground. No one speaks.

"All right," Raven says. "Let's go."

The group breaks up, quickly and wordlessly. People blur past me and become shadows; the shadows fold themselves into the dark. I push my way to Raven, who has knelt down beside the dead regulator and is checking him for weapons, money, whatever might be of use.

"Raven." Her name catches in my throat. "Do you think—?"

"They'll be fine," she says without looking up. She knows I was going to ask about Julian and Tack. "Now get out of here."

I move through the camp at a jog, find my backpack heaped next to several others at the edge of the fire pit. I sling my pack over my right shoulder; next to the rifle, the strap digs painfully into my skin. I grab two of the other packs and swing them onto my left shoulder.

Raven jogs past me. "Time to go, Lena." She, too, dissipates into the darkness.

I stand up, then notice that someone unpacked the medical supplies last night. If anything happens—if we *have* to run, and can't come back—we'll need those.

I remove one of the backpacks and kneel down.

The regulators are getting closer. I can pick out individual voices now, individual words. I am suddenly aware that the camp has been totally cleared out. I'm the only one left.

I unzip the backpack. My hands are shaking. I wrestle a sweatshirt out of the backpack, begin stuffing it instead with Band-Aids and bacitracin.

A hand clamps down on my shoulder.

"What the *hell* are you doing?" It's Alex. He gets a hand under my arm and hauls me to my feet. I just manage to zip up the backpack. "Come on."

I try to wrench my arm away, but he keeps a firm grip on me, practically dragging me into the woods, away from the camp. I flash back to the raid night in Portland when Alex led me like this through a black maze of rooms; when we huddled together on the piss-smelling floor of a storage shed and he gently wrapped my wounded leg, his hands soft and strong and strange on my skin.

He kissed me that night.

I push the memory away.

We plunge down a steep embankment, sinking through a rotten layer of loam and damp leaves, toward a jutting lip of land that forms a natural cave, a hollowed-out spot in the hillside. Alex pilots me into a crouch and practically pushes me into the small, dark space.

"Watch it." Pike is there too: a few glistening teeth, a bit of solid darkness. He shifts slightly to accommodate us. Alex slides beside me, knees drawn to his chest.

The tents are no more than fifty feet away from us, up the hill. I say a silent prayer that the regulators will think we've run, and not waste their time searching.

The waiting is agony. The voices from the woods have dropped away. The regulators must be moving slowly now, stalking us, drawing closer. Maybe they're even in the camp, threading their way past the tents: deadly, silent shadows.

131

The space is too narrow, the darkness intolerable. The idea comes to me, suddenly, that we are wedged in a coffin.

Alex shifts next to me. The back of his hand brushes up against my arm. My throat goes dry. His breathing is quicker than usual. I go stiff, perfectly rigid, until he withdraws his hand. It must have been an accident.

Another agonizing stretch of silence. Pike mutters, "This is stupid."

"Shh." Alex hushes him sharply.

"Sitting here like rats in a trap . . ."

"I swear, Pike . . ."

"*Both* of you be quiet," I whisper fiercely. We lapse into silence again. After a few more seconds, someone shouts. Alex tenses up. Pike eases his rifle off his shoulder, jabbing me in the side with his elbow. I bite back a cry.

"They've cleared out." The voice floats down to us from the camp. So they've arrived. I guess now that they've found the tents empty, they don't think they need to be quiet anymore. I wonder what their plan was: surround us, mow us down while we slept.

I wonder how many there are.

"Damn. You were right about the shots we heard. It's Don."

"Dead?"

"Yup."

There's a faint rustling sound, as though someone is kicking through the tents. "Look at how they live out here. Packed together. Mucking around in the dirt. Animals."

"Careful. It's all contaminated."

So far, I've counted six voices.

"It smells, doesn't it? I can *smell* them. Shit."

"Breathe through your mouth."

"Bastards," Pike mutters.

"Shh," I say reflexively, even though anger has gripped me, too, alongside the fear. I hate them. I hate every single one of them, for thinking that they are better than us.

"Where do you think they're headed?"

"Wherever it is, they can't have gone far."

Seven distinct voices in all. Maybe eight. It's hard to tell. And we are about two dozen. Still, as Raven said, it's impossible to know what kind of weapons they're carrying, whether there are reinforcements waiting nearby.

"Let's wrap it up here, then. Chris?"

"Got it."

My thighs have started to cramp. I ease my weight backward to get some relief, pressing up against Alex. He doesn't pull away. Once again, his hand brushes my arm, and I'm not sure if it's accidental, or a gesture of reassurance. For a second—despite everything else—my insides go white and electric, and Pike and the regulators and the cold zoom away, and there is only Alex's shoulder against my shoulder, and his ribs expanding and contracting against mine, and the rough warmth of his fingers.

The air smells like gasoline.

The air smells like fire.

I jolt into awareness. Gasoline. Fire. Burning. They're burning our things. Now the air is popping and crackling.

133

The regulators' voices are muffled behind the noise. Ribbons of smoke stream down over the hillside, float into our view, writhing like airborne snakes.

"Bastards," Pike says again, his voice strangled. He starts to rocket out of the hollow and I reach for him, try to pull him backward.

"Don't. Raven said to wait for her signal."

"Raven's not in charge." He breaks away from me and slides onto his stomach, holding his rifle in front of him like a sniper.

"*Don't*, Pike."

Either he doesn't hear me or he ignores me. He begins inching up the hill on his stomach.

"Alex." Panic is filling me like a tide. The smoke, the anger, the roar of the fire as it spreads—all of it is making it impossible to think.

"Shit." Alex moves past me and starts to reach for Pike. By now, only his boots are still visible. "Pike, don't be a goddamn idiot—"

Bang. Bang.

Two shots. The noise seems to echo and amplify in the hollow space. I cover my ears.

Then: *bang, bang, bang, bang.* Gunshots from everywhere, and people screaming. A shower of dirt rains on me from above. My ears are ringing, and my head is full of smoke.

Focus.

Alex has already pushed out of the hollow and I follow him, trying to wrestle the gun off my shoulder. At the last second

I shrug off the backpacks. They'll only slow me down.

Explosions from all sides, and the roar of an inferno.

The woods are full of smoke and fire. Orange and red flames shoot between the black trees—stark, stiff-necked, like witnesses frozen in horror. Pike is kneeling, half-concealed behind a tree, shooting. His face is lit orange from the fire, and his mouth is open in a roar. I see Raven moving through the smoke. The air is alive with gunshots: so many of them that it reminds me of sitting at the Eastern Prom with Hana on Independence Day and watching the fireworks display, the rapid staccato and the flashes of dazzling color. The smell of smoke.

"Lena!"

I don't have time to see who calls my name. A bullet whizzes past me and lodges itself in the tree directly behind me, sending off a spray of bark. I unfreeze, dart forward, and position myself flat against the large trunk of a sugar maple. Several feet ahead of me, Alex has taken refuge behind a tree as well. Every few seconds he pokes his head around the trunk, fires off a few rounds, then ducks back into safety.

My eyes are watering. I crane my head cautiously around the trunk, trying to distinguish the figures grappling in the dark, backlit by the fire. From a distance, they look almost like dancers—pairs swaying, wrestling, dipping, and spinning.

I can't tell who is who. I blink, cough, palm my eyes. Pike has disappeared.

There: I see Dani's face briefly as she turns to the fire. A regulator has jumped her from behind, has an arm thrown around her neck. Dani's eyes are bulging, her face purple. I bring my gun up, then lower it again. Impossible to aim from here, not as they stagger back and forth. Dani is twisting and bucking like a bull trying to shake its rider.

There's another chorus of gunshots. The regulator withdraws his arm from Dani's neck, clutching his elbow, shouting in pain. He turns toward the light, and I can see blood bubbling between his fingers. I have no idea who fired or whether the bullet was aimed at Dani or the regulator, but the momentary release gives Dani the advantage she needs. She fumbles at her belt for her knife, heaving and gagging. She is obviously tired, but she moves with the dumb persistence of an animal being worked to death.

She swings her arm up toward the regulator's neck; metal flashes in her fist. After she stabs him, he jerks, a huge convulsion. His face registers surprise. He totters forward onto his knees, and then onto his face. Dani kneels next to him, wedges a boot under his body, and uses the purchase to bring her knife out of his neck.

Somewhere, beyond the wall of smoke, a woman screams. I track my rifle helplessly from one side of the burning camp to the other, but everything is confusion and blur. I have to get closer. I can help no one where I am.

I break into the open, staying as low as possible, and move toward the fire and the chaos of bodies, past Alex, who is tracking the action from behind a sycamore.

"Lena!" he shouts as I dart by him. I don't respond. I need

to focus. The air is hot and thick. The fire is leaping from tree branches now, a deadly canopy above us; flames braid themselves around the trunks, turning them a chalky white. The sky is obscured behind all the smoke. This is all that is left of our camp, of the supplies we gathered so carefully—the clothing we hunted for, scrubbed in the river, wore to tatters; and the tents we mended so painstakingly, until they were crisscrossed with stitches: this hungry, all-consuming heat.

Fifteen feet from me, a man the size of a boulder has brought Coral to the ground. I start toward her when someone tackles me from behind. As I'm falling, I jab hard behind me with the butt of my rifle. The man spits out a curse and pulls back several inches, giving me time and space to roll onto my back. I use my gun like a baseball bat, swinging it toward his jaw. It connects with a sickening crack, and he slumps sideways.

Tack was right about one thing: The regulators aren't trained for combat like this. Almost all their fighting has been done from the air, from the cockpit of a bomber, from a distance.

I scramble to my feet and sprint toward Coral, who is still on the ground. I don't know what happened to the regulator's gun. But he has his hands coiled around her neck.

I raise the butt of my rifle high above my head. Coral's eyes flick to mine. As I'm bringing the rifle down on the regulator's head, he whips around toward me. I manage to graze the side of his shoulder, but I'm carried off balance by the force of my swing. I stumble, and he sweeps an arm at my shins and sends me sprawling flat. I bite down on my lip and taste blood.

I want to turn onto my back, but suddenly there's a weight on top of me, knocking me flat, crushing the air from my lungs. The gun is ripped from my hand.

I can't breathe. My face is pressed to the dirt. Something—a knee? an elbow?—is digging into my neck. Bursts of light explode behind my eyelids.

Then there's a *thwack*, and a grunt, and the weight is released. I twist around, sucking in air, kicking away from the regulator. He is still straddling me, but he is now slumped sideways, eyes closed, a small bit of blood trickling from his forehead, where he was hit. Alex is standing above me, gripping his rifle.

He leans down and grabs my elbow, hauls me to my feet. Then he picks up my rifle and passes it to me. Behind him, the fire is still spreading. The swaying dancers have dispersed. Now I can't see anything but a huge wall of flame and several forms huddled on the ground. My stomach lurches. I can't tell who has fallen, whether they are our people.

Next to us, Gordo lifts Coral and slings her over his back. She moans, eyelids fluttering, but doesn't wake up.

"Come on," Alex shouts. The noise of the fire is tremendous: a cacophony of cracking and popping, like a slurping, sucking monster.

Alex leads us away from the fire, using the butt of his rifle to swipe a clear path through the woods. I recognize that we're heading in the direction of a small stream we located yesterday. Gordo pants loudly behind me, and I'm still dizzy, and not very steady on my feet. I keep my eyes locked on the back

138

of Alex's jacket, and I think of nothing but moving, one foot in front of the other, getting as far from the fire as possible.

"Coo-ee!"

As we draw close to the stream, Raven's call echoes to us through the woods. To our right, a flashlight cuts through the darkness. We shoulder through a thick tangle of dead growth and emerge onto a gentle slope of stony land, through which a shallow stream is pushing resolutely. The break in the canopy above us allows moonlight to penetrate. It streaks the surface of the stream with silver, makes the pale pebbles lining the banks glow slightly.

Our group is crouching, huddled together, a hundred feet away on the other side of the stream. Relief breaks in my chest. We're intact; we survived. And Raven will know what to do about Julian and Tack. She will know how to find them.

"Coo-ee!" Raven calls again, angling a flashlight in our direction.

"We see you," Gordo grunts. He pushes ahead of me, his breathing now a hoarse rasp, and sloshes across the stream to the other side.

Before we can cross, Alex whirls around and takes two steps back to me. I'm startled to see that his face is twisted in anger.

"What the hell was that about?" he demands. When I can only stare at him, he goes on, "You could have died, Lena. If it wasn't for me, you *would* be dead."

"Is this your way of asking for a thank-you?" I'm shaky, and tired, and disoriented. "You could just learn to say please, you know."

"I'm not kidding." Alex shakes his head. "You should have stayed where you were. You didn't need to go charging in there like some kind of hero."

I feel a flicker of anger. I hold on to it and coax it into life. "Excuse me," I say. "If I hadn't charged in there, your new— your new *girlfriend* would be dead right now." I've rarely had occasion to use the word in my life, and it takes me a second to remember it.

"She's not your responsibility," Alex says evenly.

Instead of making me feel better, his response makes me feel worse. Despite everything that has happened tonight, it's this stupid, basic fact that makes me feel like I am going to cry: He didn't deny that she was his girlfriend.

I swallow back the sick taste in my mouth. "Well, I'm not your responsibility either, remember? You can't tell me what to do." I've found the thread of anger again. Now I'm following it, pulling myself forward on it, hand over hand. "Why do you even care, anyway? You hate me."

Alex stares at me. "You really don't get it, do you?" His voice is hard.

I cross my arms and squeeze tight, trying to squeeze back the pain, to push it deep under the anger. "Don't get *what*?"

"Forget it." Alex shoves a hand through his hair. "Forget I said anything at all."

"Lena!"

I turn. Tack and Julian have just emerged from the woods on the other side of the stream, and Julian runs toward me, splashing through the water without seeming to register it. He charges straight past Alex and sweeps me up in his arms, lifting me off the ground. I let out a single, muffled sob into his shirt.

"You're okay," he whispers. He's squeezing me so tightly, I can hardly breathe. But I don't mind. I don't want him to let go, ever.

"I was so worried about you," I say. Now that my anger at Alex has drained away, the need to cry is resurging, pushing at my throat.

I'm not sure Julian understands me. My voice is muffled by his shirt. But he gives me another hard squeeze before setting me down. He brushes the hair back from my face.

"When you and Tack didn't come back . . . I thought maybe something had happened. . . ."

"We decided to camp for the night." Julian looks guilty, as though his absence was somehow the cause of the attack. "Tack's flashlight went bust and we couldn't see a damn thing when the sun went down. We were worried about getting lost. We were probably only half a mile from here." He shakes his head. "When we heard the shots, we came as fast as we could." He touches his forehead to mine and adds, a little softer, "I was so scared."

"I'm fine," I say. I keep my arms wrapped around his waist. He is so steady, so solid. "There were regulators—seven or eight of them, maybe more. But we chased them off."

Julian finds my hand and laces his fingers in mine.

"I should have stayed with you," he says, his voice breaking a little.

I bring his hand to my lips. This simple thing—the fact that I can kiss him like this, freely—suddenly seems like a miracle. They have tried to squeeze us out, to stamp us into the past. But we are still here.

And there are more of us every day.

"Come on," I say. "Let's make sure the others are okay."

Alex must have crossed the stream and rejoined the group already. At the edge of the water, Julian doubles down and sweeps an arm behind my knees, so I stumble backward and into his arms. He picks me up, and I put my arms around his neck and rest my head against his chest: His heart is a steady rhythm, reassuring. He wades across the stream and deposits me on the other side.

"Nice of you to join us," Raven is saying to Tack, as Julian and I push our way into the circle. But I can hear the relief in her voice. Despite the fact that Raven and Tack are often fighting, it's impossible to imagine one without the other. They are like two plants that have grown around each other—they strangle and squeeze and support at the same time.

"What are we supposed to do?" Lu asks. She is an indistinct shape in the darkness. Most of the faces in the circle are ovals of dark, individual features fragmented by the small patches of moonlight. A nose is visible here; a mouth there; the barrel of a gun.

"We go to Waterbury, like we planned," Raven says firmly.

"With what?" Dani says. "We have nothing. No food. No blankets. Nothing."

"It could have been worse," Raven says. "We got out, didn't we? And we can't be too far."

"We aren't." Tack speaks up. "Julian and I found the highway. It's a half day from here. We're too far north, just like Pike said."

"I guess we can forgive you, then," Raven says, "for almost getting us killed."

Pike, for the first time in his life, has nothing to say.

Raven sighs dramatically. "Okay. I admit it. I was wrong. Is that what you want to hear?"

Again: no response.

"Pike?" Dani ventures, into the silence.

"Shit," Tack mutters. Then he says again, "Shit."

Another pause. I shiver. Julian puts his arm around me, and I lean into him.

Raven says quietly, "We can light a small fire. If he's lost, it will help him find his way to us."

This is her gift to us. She knows—just like we all know in that instant, deep down—that Pike is dead.

God forgive me, for I have sinned. Cleanse me of these passions, for the diseased will wallow in the dirt with the dogs, and only the pure will ascend into heaven.

People aren't supposed to change. That's the beauty of pairing—people can be plotted together, their interests made to intersect, their differences minimized.

That's what the cure promises.

But it's a lie.

Fred isn't Fred—at least, he's not the Fred I thought he was. And I'm not the Hana I was supposed to be; I'm not the Hana everyone *told* me I would be after my cure.

The realization brings with it a physical disappointment—and a feeling, too, of relief.

The morning after Fred's inauguration, I get up and take a shower, feeling alert and very refreshed. I'm overly conscious of the brightness of the lights, the beeping of the coffee machine from downstairs, and the *thump-thump-thump* of the clothes in the dryer. Power, power, power all around us: We pulse with it.

Mr. Roth has once again come over to watch the news. If he behaves, maybe the minister of energy will give him his juice back, and then I won't have to see him every morning. I could speak to Fred about it.

The idea makes me want to laugh.

"Morning, Hana," he says, keeping his eyes locked on the TV.

"Good morning, Mr. Roth," I say cheerfully, and pass into the pantry. I scan the well-stocked shelves, run my fingers over the boxes of cereal and rice, the identical jars of peanut butter, a half-dozen jams.

I'll have to be careful, of course, to steal only a little at a time.

I make my way directly to Wynnewood Road, where I saw Grace playing with the doll. I again abandon my bike early and go most of the way on foot, careful to stick closely to the trees. I listen for voices. The last thing I want is to be taken by surprise by Willow Marks again.

My backpack digs painfully into my shoulders, and underneath the straps, my skin is slippery with sweat. It's heavy. I can hear liquid sloshing around when I move, and I just pray that the lid of the old glass milk jug—which I've filled with as much gasoline from the garage as I could get away with stealing—is screwed on tightly.

Once again, the air is scented faintly with wood smoke. I wonder how many of the houses are occupied, and which other families have been forced to live way out here, scraping out a living. I don't know how they make it through the winters. No wonder Jenny, Willow, and Grace look so pale and drawn—it's a miracle that they're still alive.

I think of what Fred said: *They must learn that freedom will not keep them warm.*

So disobedience will kill them slowly.

If I can find the Tiddles' house, I can leave them the food I've stolen, and the bottle of gasoline. It's a small thing, but it's *something*.

As soon as I turn onto Wynnewood—only two streets away from Brooks—I once again see Grace in the street, this time squatting on the sidewalk directly in front of a weathered gray house, chucking stones in the grass as though she is trying to skip them over water.

I take a deep breath and step out of the trees. Grace tenses up instantly.

"Please don't run," I say softly, because she looks like she's about to bolt. I take a tentative step toward her and she scrambles to her feet, so I stop walking. Keeping my eyes on Grace's, I unsling the backpack from my shoulder. "You might not remember me," I say. "I was a friend of Lena's." I choke a little on her name and have to clear my throat. "I'm not going to hurt you, okay?"

The backpack clinks against the sidewalk when I set it down, and her eyes flit to it briefly. I take this as an encouraging sign and move into a crouch, still keeping my eyes on her, willing her not to run. Slowly, I unzip the backpack.

Now her eyes are darting between the bag and me. She relaxes her shoulders a little.

"I brought you a couple of things," I say, slowly reaching into the bag and withdrawing what I've stolen: a bag of oatmeal; Cream of Wheat and two boxes of macaroni and cheese; cans of soup; vegetables and tuna fish; a package of cookies. I lay them all out on the sidewalk, one by one. Grace takes a quick step forward and then stops herself.

Last, I remove the old milk jug full of gasoline. "This is for you too," I say. "For your family." I see movement in an upstairs window and feel a quick jolt of alarm. But it's only a dirty towel, strung up like a curtain, fluttering in the wind.

Suddenly she darts forward and snatches the bottle from my hands.

"Be careful," I say. "It's gasoline. It's very dangerous. I thought you could use it for burning things," I finish lamely.

Grace doesn't say anything. She's trying to stuff her arms with all the food I've brought. When I crouch down and try to help her, she grabs the pack of cookies and presses it protectively to her chest.

"Easy," I say. "I'm just trying to help."

She sniffs, but allows me to help her stack and gather up the cans of vegetables and soup. We're just a few inches apart, so close I can smell her breath, sour and hungry. There is dirt under her fingernails, streaks of grass on her knees. I've never been this close to Grace before, and I find myself searching her face for a resemblance to Lena. Grace's nose is sharper, like Jenny's, but she has Lena's big brown eyes and dark hair.

I feel a quick pulse of something: a squeeze deep in my stomach, an echo from another time, feelings that should have been quieted forever by now.

No one can know, or even suspect.

"I have more to give you," I tell Grace quickly as she stands up, holding a teetering pile of packages and bags in her arms, along with the plastic bottle. "I'll come back. I can only bring a little bit at a time."

She just stands there, staring at me with Lena's eyes.

"If you're not here, I'll leave the food for you somewhere safe. Somewhere it won't get—damaged." I stop myself at the last second from saying *stolen*. "Do you know a good hiding place?"

She turns abruptly and darts around the side of the gray house, through a patch of overgrown grass and high weeds. I'm not sure whether she intends for me to follow her, but I do. The paint is peeling; one of the shutters hangs crookedly from a window on the second floor, tapping lightly in the wind.

At the back of the house, Grace waits for me by a large wooden door set in the ground, which must lead to a cellar. She sets down the pile of food carefully in the grass, then grabs the rusted metal handle of the trapdoor and heaves. Underneath the door is a gaping mouth of darkness, and a set of wooden stairs descending into a small, packed-dirt space. The room is empty except for several crooked wooden shelves, which contain a flashlight, two bottles of water, and some batteries.

"This is perfect," I say. For just a second, a smile flits across Grace's face.

I help her carry the food down into the cellar and stock it on the shelves. I place the bottle of gasoline against one wall. She keeps the package of cookies hugged to her chest, though, and refuses to let it go. The room smells bad, like Grace's breath: sour and earthy. I'm glad when we emerge back into the sunshine. The morning has left a heavy feeling in my chest that refuses to dissolve.

"I'll be back," I say to Grace.

I've nearly rounded the corner when she speaks.

"I remember you," she says, her voice hardly louder than a whisper. I spin around, surprised. But she is already darting away into the trees, and disappears before I have a chance to reply.

Lena

The dawn is double: a twin smoky glow at the horizon and behind us, above the trees, where the fire continues to smolder. The clouds and the drifts of black smoke are almost indistinguishable.

In the dark, and the confusion, we didn't realize we were missing two members of our group: Pike and Henley. Dani wants to go back and look for their bodies, but the fire makes it impossible. We can't even go back to forage for cans that will not have burned, and supplies that have made it through the flames.

Instead, as soon as the sky is light, we push forward.

We walk in silence, in a straight line, our eyes trained on

the ground. We must get to the camp at Waterbury as soon as possible—no detours, no resting, no explorations of the ruins of old towns, picked clean of useful supplies long ago. The air is charged with anxiety.

We can count ourselves lucky for one thing: that Raven's map was with Julian and Tack and has not been destroyed with the rest of our supplies.

Tack and Julian walk together at the front of the line, occasionally stopping to consult notations they've made on the map. Despite everything that has happened, it gives me a rush of pride to watch Tack consulting Julian, and a different kind of pleasure too—vindication, because I know Alex will also have noticed.

Alex, of course, takes up the rear with Coral.

It's a warm day—so warm that I have removed my jacket and rolled my long-sleeved shirt to the elbows—and the sun is splashed liberally over the ground. It's almost impossible to believe that only hours ago we were attacked, except that Pike's and Henley's voices are missing from the murmured conversation.

Julian is ahead of me. Alex is behind me. So I push forward—exhausted, my mouth still full of the taste of smoke, my lungs burning.

Waterbury, Lu has told us, is the beginning of a new order. An enormous camp has amassed outside the city's wall, and many of the city's Valid residents have fled. Portions of Waterbury have been totally evacuated; other parts of the city are barricaded against the Invalids on the other side.

Lu has heard that the Invalid camp is almost like a city itself: Everyone pitches in, everyone helps repair shelters and hunt for food and gather water. It has so far been safe from retaliation, partly because no one has remained who *can* retaliate. The municipal offices were destroyed, and the mayor and his deputies were chased out.

There, we'll build shelters out of branches and salvaged brick, and finally find a place for ourselves.

In Waterbury, everything will be okay.

The trees begin to thin, and we pass old, graffiti-covered benches and half-shell underpasses, speckled with mold; a roof, intact, sitting on a field of grass, as though the rest of the house has been simply suctioned underground; stretches of road that, leading nowhere, are now part of a nonsense-grammar. This is the language of the world *before*—a world of chaos and confusion and happiness and despair—before the blitz turned streets to grids, cities to prisons, and hearts to dust.

We know we're getting close.

In the evening, when the sun begins to set, the anxiety comes sweeping back. None of us wants to spend another night alone, exposed, in the Wilds, even if we have managed to put the regulators off our trail for now.

From ahead, there is a shout. Julian has circled away from Tack and fallen into step beside me, although we have been mostly walking in silence.

"What is it?" I ask him. I'm so tired I am numb. I can't see past the people ahead of me. The group is fanning out over what looks as though it was once an old parking lot. Most of the pavement is gone. Two streetlamps, empty of lightbulbs, are staked into the ground. Next to one of them, Tack and Raven have both stopped.

Julian cranes onto his tiptoes. "I think . . . I think we're there." Even before he finishes speaking, I am pushing through the group, angling for a look.

At the edge of the old parking lot, the ground drops away suddenly and cuts sharply downward. A series of switchback trails leads down the hillside to a barren, treeless portion of land.

The camp is not like I've envisioned it at all. I've been imagining real houses, or at least solid structures, nestled between trees. This is simply a vast, teeming field, a patchwork of blankets and trash, and hundreds and hundreds of people, pushing almost directly up against the city's wall, stained red in the dying light. Fires burn sporadically across the great, dark expense, winking like lights from a distant city. The sky, electric at the horizon, is otherwise stretched dark and tight, like a metal lid that has been screwed shut over waste.

For a moment I flash back to the twisted underground people Julian and I met when we were trying to escape the Scavengers, and their grimy, smoky, underground world.

I've never seen so many Invalids. I have never seen so many people, period.

Even from here, we can smell them.

My chest feels like it has caved in.

"What is this place?" Julian mutters. I want to say something to comfort him—I want to tell him it will be okay—but I feel weighted down, dull with disappointment.

"This is it?" Dani is the one to voice what we must all be feeling. "This is the big dream? The new order?"

"We have friends here, at least," Hunter says quietly. But even he can't keep up the act. He shoves a hand through his hair so it sticks up in all directions. His face is white; all day, he has been hacking as he walked, his breath coming wet and ragged. "And we had no choice, anyway."

"We could have gone to Canada, like Gordo said."

"We wouldn't have made it there without our supplies," Hunter says.

"We would still *have* our supplies if we had headed north in the first place," Dani fires back.

"Well, we didn't. We're here. And I don't know about you guys, but I'm thirsty as hell." Alex pushes his way through the line. He has to sidestep down the hill to the first switchback trail, sliding a little on the steep slope, sending a spray of gravel skidding down toward the camp.

He pauses when he reaches the path and looks back up at us. "Well? Are you coming?" His eyes slide over the whole group. When he looks at me, a small shock pulses through me, and I quickly drop my eyes. For a split second, he had looked almost like my Alex again.

Raven and Tack move forward together. Alex is right

about one thing—we don't have a choice now. We won't make it another few days in the Wilds, not without any traps, or supplies, and vessels to boil our water. The rest of the group must know this, because they follow Raven and Tack, sidestepping down toward the dirt path one after another. Dani mutters something under her breath, but follows at last.

"Come on." I reach for Julian's hand.

He draws back. His eyes are fixed on the vast, smoky plain below us, and the dingy patchwork of blankets and makeshift tents. For a moment, I think he's going to refuse. Then he jerks forward, as though pushing his way through an invisible barrier, and precedes me down the hill.

At the last second, I notice that Lu is still standing on the ridge. She looks tiny, dwarfed by the enormous evergreens behind her. Her hair is nearly down to her waist now. She is staring not at the camp, but at the wall beyond it: the stained-red stone that marks the beginning of the other world. The zombie world.

"You coming, Lu?" I say.

"What?" She looks startled, as though I've woken her up. Then, immediately: "I'm coming." She casts one more look at the wall before following us. Her face is troubled.

The city of Waterbury looks, at least from this distance, dead: no smoke floats up from the factory chimneys; no lights shine from the darkened, glass-enclosed towers. It is the empty husk of a city, almost like the ruins we pass in the Wilds. Except this time, the ruin is on the other side of the walls.

And I wonder what about it, exactly, makes Lu afraid.

Once we reach the ground, the smell is thick, almost unbearable: the stink of thousands of unwashed bodies and unwashed, hungry mouths; urine; old fires and tobacco. Julian coughs, mutters, "God." I bring my sleeve to my mouth, trying to inhale through it.

The periphery of the camp is ringed with large metal drums and old, rust-spotted trash cans, in which fires have been lit. People crowd around the fires, cooking or warming their hands. They look at us with suspicion as we pass. Immediately, I can tell that we are not welcome.

Even Raven looks uncertain. It's not clear where we should go, or who we should speak to, or whether the camp is organized at all. As the sun is finally swallowed by the horizon, the crowd becomes a mass of shadows: faces lit up, grotesque and contorted by the flickering light. Shelters have been constructed hastily from bits of corrugated tin and scraps of metal; other people have created makeshift tents with dirty bedsheets. Still others are lying, huddled, on the ground, pressing against one another for warmth.

"Well?" Dani says. Her voice is loud, a challenge. "What now?"

Raven is about to respond when suddenly a body rockets into her, nearly pushing her over. Tack reaches out to steady her, barks, "Hey!"

The boy who catapulted into Raven—skinny, with the jutting jaw of a bulldog—doesn't even glance at her. Already, he is plowing back toward a dingy red tent, where a small crowd has assembled. A man—older, bare-chested but wearing a long, flapping winter coat—is standing with his fists balled, his face screwed up with fury.

"You filthy pig!" he spits. "I'm going to fucking kill you."

"Are you crazy?" Bulldog's voice is surprisingly shrill. "What the *hell* are you—"

"You stole my goddamn can. Admit it. You stole my can." Bits of spit are collected at the corners of the old man's mouth. His eyes are wide, wild. He turns a full circle, appealing to the crowd. Then he raises his voice. "I had a whole can of tuna, unopened. Sitting right with my things. He *stole* it."

"I never touched it. You're out of your mind." Bulldog starts to turn away. The man in the ragged coat lets out a roar of fury.

"Liar!"

He leaps. For a second, it seems he is suspended in midair, his coat flapping behind him like the great leathery wings of a bat. Then he lands on the boy's back, pinning him to the ground. All at once the crowd is a surge, shouting, pressing forward, cheering them on. The boy rolls on top of the man, straddling him, pounding him. Then the older man kicks him off and wrestles the boy's face into the dirt. He is shouting, but his words are unintelligible. The boy thrashes and manages to buck the old man off, sending him into the side of a metal drum. The man screams. The fire has obviously been burning for a long time. The metal must be hot.

Someone shoves me from behind, and I nearly go sprawling to the ground. Julian just manages to get his hand around my arm, keeping me on my feet. The crowd is seething now: The voices and bodies have become one, like dark water teeming with a many-headed, many-armed monster.

This is not freedom. This is not the new world we imagined. It can't be. This is a nightmare.

I push through the crowd after Julian, who never lets go of my hand. It's like moving through a violent tide, a surge of different currents. I'm terrified that we've lost the others, but then I see Tack, Raven, Coral, and Alex, standing a little ways off, scanning the crowd for the rest of our group. Dani, Bram, Hunter, and Lu fight their way to us.

We huddle close together and wait for the others. I scan the crowd for Gordo, for his chest-length beard, but all I see is blur and haze, faces merging in and out behind clouds of oily smoke. Coral begins to cough.

The others don't come. Eventually we are forced to admit that we've been separated from them. Raven says, halfheartedly, that they will no doubt track us down. We need to find somewhere we can safely camp, and someone who might be willing to share food and water.

We ask four different people before we find one who will help us. A girl—probably no more than twelve or thirteen, and dressed in clothes so filthy they have all turned a uniform, dingy gray—directs us to speak to Pippa, and gestures to a portion of the camp illuminated more brightly than the rest.

As we make our way toward the place she indicated, I can feel the young girl watching us. I turn around once to look at her. She has a blanket pulled over her head, and her face is fluid with shadows, but her eyes are enormous, luminous. I think of Grace and feel a sharp pain in my chest.

It seems the camp is actually subdivided into little areas, each claimed by a different person or group of people. As we push toward the series of small campfires that apparently mark the beginning of Pippa's domain, we hear dozens of fights breaking out over borders and boundaries, property and possessions.

Suddenly Raven lets out a shout of recognition. "Twiggy!" she cries, and breaks into a run. I see her barrel into a woman's arms—the first time I have ever seen Raven voluntarily embrace anyone besides Tack—and when she pulls away, they both begin talking and laughing at once.

"Tack," Raven is saying, "you remember Twiggy! You were with us—what?—three summers ago?"

"Four," the woman corrects her, laughing. She is probably thirty, and her nickname must be ironic. She's built like a man: heavy, with broad shoulders and no hips. Her hair is cropped close to her scalp. She has a man's laugh, too, deep and full-throated. I like her immediately. "I've got a new name now, you know," she says, and winks. "Around here, people call me Pippa."

The bit of land Pippa has claimed for herself is larger and better organized than anything we have yet seen in the camp. There is real shelter: Pippa has constructed, or claimed, a large wooden shed with a roof, enclosed on three sides. Inside the hut are several crudely made benches, a half-dozen battery-operated lanterns, piles of blankets, and two refrigerators—one large, kitchen-sized, and one miniature—both chained shut and padlocked. Pippa tells us that this is where she keeps the food and medical supplies she has managed to gather. She has, additionally, recruited several people to man the camp-fires constantly, boil the water, and keep out anybody with an inclination to steal.

"You wouldn't believe the shit I've seen around here," she says. "Last week someone was killed over a goddamn cigarette. It's crazy." She shakes her head. "No wonder the zombies didn't bother bombing us. Waste of ammunition. We'll kill each other off just fine at this rate." She gestures for us to sit on the ground. "Might as well park here for a bit. I'll get some food on. There isn't a lot. I was expecting a new delivery. We've been getting help from the resistance. But something must have happened."

"Patrols," Alex says. "There were regulators just south of here. We ran into a group of them."

Pippa doesn't seem surprised. She must have already known that the Wilds have been breached. "No wonder you all look like shit," she says mildly. "Go on. Kitchen's about to open. Take a load off."

Julian is very quiet. I can feel the tension in his body. He keeps looking around as though he expects someone to leap out at him from the shadows. Now that we are on this side of the campfires, encircled by warmth and light, the rest of the camp looks like a shadowy blur: a writhing, roiling darkness, swelling with animal sounds.

I can only imagine what he must think of this place, what he must think of *us*. This is the vision of the world that he has always been warned against: a world of the disease is a world of chaos and filth, selfishness and disorder.

I feel unjustifiably angry with him. His presence, his anxiety, is a reminder that there is a difference between his people and mine.

Tack and Raven have claimed one of the benches. Dani, Lu, Hunter, and Bram squeeze onto the other one. Julian and I take a seat on the ground. Alex remains standing. Coral sits directly in front of him, and I try not to pay attention to the fact that she is leaning back, resting against his shins, and the back of her head is touching his knee.

Pippa removes a key from around her neck and unlocks the large refrigerator. Inside it are rows and rows of canned food, as well as bags of rice. The bottom shelves are packed with bandages, antibacterial ointment, and bottles of ibuprofen. As Pippa moves, she tells us about the camp, and the riots in Waterbury that led to its creation.

"Started in the streets," she explains as she dumps rice into a large, dented pot. "Kids, mostly. Uncureds. Some of them were riled up by the sympathizers, and we got some members of the R in as moles, too, to keep everybody fired up."

She moves precisely, without wasting any energy. People

materialize out of the dark to help her. Soon she has placed various pots on one of the fires at the periphery. Smoke—delicious, threaded with food smells—drifts back to us.

Immediately there is a shift, a difference in the darkness that surrounds us: A circle of people has gathered, a wall of dark, hungry eyes. Two of Pippa's men stand guard over the pots, knives drawn.

I shiver. Julian doesn't put his arm around me.

We eat rice and beans straight out of a communal pot, using our hands. Pippa never stops moving. She walks with her neck jutting forward, as though she constantly expects to encounter a barrier and intends to head-butt her way through it. She doesn't stop talking, either.

"The R sent me here," she says. Raven has asked her how she came to be in Waterbury. "After all the riots in the city, we thought we had a good chance to organize a protest, plan a large-scale opposition. There are two thousand people in the camp right now, give or take. That's a lot of manpower."

"How's it going?" Raven asks.

Pippa squats by the campfire and spits. "How does it look like it's going? I've been here a month and I've found maybe a hundred people who care about the cause, who are willing to fight. The rest are too scared, too tired, or too beat down. Or they just don't care."

"So what are you going to do?" Raven asks.

Pippa spreads her hands. "What can I do? I can't force them

to get involved, and I can't tell people what to do. This isn't Zombieland, right?"

I must be making a face, because she looks at me sharply.

"What?" she says.

I look at Raven for guidance, but her face is impassive. I look back to Pippa. "There must be some way . . ." I venture.

"You think so?" Her voice gets a hard edge. "How? I have no money; I can't bribe them. We don't have enough force to threaten them. I can't convince them if they won't listen. Welcome to the free world. We give people the power to choose. They can even choose the wrong thing. Beautiful, isn't it?" She stands abruptly and moves away from the fire. When she speaks again, her voice is composed. "I don't know what will happen. I'm waiting for word from higher up. It might be better to move on, leave this place to rot. At least we're safe for the moment."

"What about fears of attack?" Tack says. "You don't think that the city will retaliate?"

Pippa shakes her head. "The city was mostly evacuated after the riots." Her mouth quirks into a small smile. "Fear of contagion—the *deliria* spreading through the streets, turning us all into animals." Then the smile fades. "I'm telling you something. The things I've seen here . . . They might be right."

She takes the stack of blankets and passes them to Raven. "Here. Make yourself useful. You'll have to share. The blankets are even harder to keep around than the pots. Bed down wherever you can find the space. Don't wander too far, though.

There are some crazies around here. I've seen it all—botched procedures, loons, criminals, the lot. Sweet dreams, kiddies."

It's only when Pippa mentions sleep that I realize how exhausted I am. It has been more than thirty-six hours since I've slept, and until now I have been fueled primarily by fear of what will happen to us. Now my body is leaden. Julian has to help me to my feet. I follow him like a sleepwalker, blindly, hardly conscious of my surroundings. We move away from the three-sided hut.

Julian stops by a campfire that has been allowed to burn out. We are at the very base of the hill, and here the slope is even steeper than the one we came down, and no path has been beaten in its side.

I don't care about the hardness of the ground, the bite of the frost, the continued shouts and hoots from all around us, a darkness alive and menacing. As Julian settles behind me and wraps the blankets around us both, I'm already somewhere else: I am at the old homestead, in the sickroom, and Grace is there, speaking to me, saying my name over and over. But her voice is drowned out by the fluttering of black wings, and when I look up I see that the roof has been blown apart by the regulators' bombs, and instead of a ceiling there is only the dark night sky, and thousands and thousands of bats, blotting out the moon.

Hana

I wake up as the dawn is barely washing over the horizon. An owl hoots somewhere outside my window, and my room is full of drifting dark shapes.

In fifteen days, I will be married.

I join Fred to cut the ribbon at the new border wall, a fifteen-foot-tall, concrete and steel-reinforced structure. The new border wall will replace all the electrified fences that have always encircled Portland.

The first phase of construction, completed just two days after Fred officially became mayor, extends from the Old Port past Tukey's Bridge and all the way to the Crypts. The second phase will not be completed for another year, and will place a wall all the way down to the Fore River; two years after that, the final wall will go up, connecting the two, and the modernization and strengthening of the border will be complete, just in time for Fred's reelection.

At the ceremony, Fred steps forward with a pair of oversized scissors, smiling at the journalists and photographers clustered in front of the wall. It's a brilliantly sunny morning—a day of promise and possibility. He raises the scissors dramatically toward the thick red ribbon strung across the concrete. At the last second he stops, turns, and gestures me forward.

"I want my future wife to usher in this landmark day!" he calls out, and there is a roar of approval as I come forward, blushing, feigning surprise.

This has all been rehearsed, of course. He plays his role. And I am very careful to play mine, too.

The scissors, manufactured for show, are dull, and I have trouble getting the blades through the ribbon. After a few seconds, my palms begin to sweat. I can feel Fred's impatience behind his smile, can feel the weighted stare of his associates and committee members, all of them watching me from a small, cordoned-off area next to the pack of journalists.

Snip. At last I work the scissors through the ribbon, and the ribbon flutters to the ground, and everyone cheers in front of the high, smooth concrete wall. The barbed wire at its top glistens in the sun, like metal teeth.

Afterward, we adjourn to the basement of a local church for a small reception. People snack on brownies and cheese squares off paper napkins, and sit in folding chairs, balancing plastic cups of soda on their laps.

This, too—the informality, the neighborhood feel, the church basement with its clean white walls and the faint smell of turpentine—was carefully planned.

Fred receives congratulations and answers questions about policy and planned changes. My mother is glowing, happier than I have ever seen her, and when she catches my eye across the room, she winks. It occurs to me that this is what she has wanted for me—for us—all my life.

I drift through the crowd, smiling, making polite conversation when I am needed. Underneath the laughter and chatter, I am pursued by a snake-hiss of sound, a name that follows me everywhere.

Prettier than Cassie . . .

Not as slender as Cassie . . .

Cassie, Cassie, Cassie . . .

Fred is in a great mood as we drive home. He loosens his tie and unbuttons his collar, rolls up his sleeves to the elbow, and opens the windows so the breeze sweeps into the car, blowing his hair across his face.

Already he looks more like his father. His face is red—it was hot in the church—and for a second I can't help but imagine what it will be like after we are married, and how soon he will want to get started on having babies. I close my eyes and visualize the bay, let the image of Fred on top of me break apart on its waves.

"They were eating it up," Fred says excitedly. "I threw out a couple hints—here and there—about Finch and the Department of Energy, and you could just tell everyone was going ape shit."

All of a sudden, I can no longer keep the question down: "What happened to Cassandra?"

His smile falters. "Were you even listening?"

"I was. They were eating it up. Going ape shit." He winces a little when I say the word *shit*, even though I'm only parroting his words back to him. "But you reminded me—I've been meaning to ask. You never told me what happened to her."

Now the smile is completely gone. He turns toward the window. The afternoon sunshine stripes his face in alternating patterns of light and shadow. "What makes you think something *happened*?"

I keep my voice light. "I just meant—I wanted to know why you got divorced."

He swivels quickly to look at me, eyes narrow, as though hoping to catch the lie on my face. I keep my face neutral. He relaxes a little.

"Irreconcilable differences." The smile returns. "They must have made a mistake when they evaluated her. She wasn't right for me at all."

We stare at each other, both of us smiling, doing our duty, keeping our respective secrets.

"You know one of the things I like best about you?" he asks, reaching for my arm.

"What?"

He jerks me suddenly close to him. Surprised, I cry out. He pinches the soft skin on the inside of my elbow, sending a sharp zip of pain down my arm. Tears prick my eyes, and I inhale deeply, willing them back.

"That you don't ask too many questions," he says, and pushes me away from him roughly. "Cassie asked too many questions."

Then he leans back, and we drive the rest of the way in silence.

Late afternoon used to be my favorite time of day—mine, and Lena's. Is it still?

I don't know. My feelings, my old preferences, are just out of reach—not eradicated completely, as they should have been, but like shadows, burning away whenever I try to focus on them.

I don't ask questions.

I just go.

The ride to Deering Highlands already feels easier. Thankfully, I don't encounter anyone. I deposit the supplies of food and gasoline in the underground cellar that Grace showed me.

Afterward, I make for Preble Street, where Lena's uncle used to have his little corner grocery store. As I suspected, it is now closed and shuttered. Metal grates have been drawn over its windows; beyond the latticed steel, I see graffiti scrawls across the glass, now indecipherable, faded by rain and weather. The awning, a royal blue, is torn up and half-dismantled. One thin, spindly metal support, like the jointed leg of a spider, has come free of the fabric and swings pendulum-like in the wind. A small placard fixed to one of the metal grates says COMING SOON! BEE'S SALON AND BARBER.

The city no doubt forced him to close his doors, or the customers stopped coming, worried that they would be guilty by association. Lena's mother, Lena's uncle William, and now Lena . . .

Too much bad blood. Too much disease.

No wonder they're hiding in the Deering Highlands. No wonder Willow is hiding there as well. I wonder whether it was by choice—or whether they were coerced, threatened, or even bribed to leave a better neighborhood.

I don't know what possesses me to go around back, to the narrow alley and the small blue door that used to lead to the storeroom. Lena and I used to hang out here together when she was stocking shelves after school.

The sun slants hard over the sloped roofs of the buildings around me, skipping right over the alley, which is dark and cool. Flies buzz around a Dumpster, droning and then colliding with the metal. I climb off my bike and lean it against one of the beige concrete walls. The sounds from the street—people shouting to one another, the occasional rumble of a bus—already seem distant.

I step toward the blue door, which is streaked with pigeon shit. Just for a moment, time seems to fold in two, and I imagine that Lena will fling open the door for me, as she always did. I'll grab a seat on one of the crates of baby formula or canned green beans, and we'll split a bag of chips and a soda stolen from stock, and we'll talk about . . .

What?

What did we talk about then?

School, I guess. The other girls in our class, and track meets, and the concert series in the park and who was invited to whose birthday party, and things we wanted to do together.

Never boys. Lena wouldn't. She was far too careful.

Until, one day, she wasn't.

That day I remember perfectly. I was still in shock because of the raids the night before: the blood and the violence, the chorus of shouting and screaming. Earlier that morning, I had thrown up my breakfast.

I remember Lena's expression when he knocked on the door: eyes wild, terrified, body stiff; and how Alex had looked at her when she finally let him into the storeroom. I remember exactly what he was wearing, too, and the mess of his hair, the sneakers with their blue-tinged laces. His right shoe was untied. He didn't notice.

He didn't notice anything but Lena.

I remember the hot flash that stabbed through me. Jealousy.

I reach out for the door handle, suck in a deep breath, and pull. It's locked, of course. I don't know what I was expecting, and why I feel so disappointed. It *would* be locked. Beyond it, the dust will be settling on the shelves.

This is the past: It drifts, it gathers. If you are not careful, it will bury you. This is half the reason for the cure: It clean-sweeps; it makes the past, and all its pain, distant, like the barest impression on sparkling glass.

But the cure works differently for everybody; and it does not work perfectly for all.

I'm resolved to help Lena's family. Their store was taken away and their apartment reclaimed, and for that I am partly responsible. I was the one who encouraged her to go to her first illegal party; I was the one who always egged her on, asking her about the Wilds, talking about leaving Portland.

And I was also the one who helped Lena escape. I got the note to Alex informing him she had been caught and that her procedural date had been changed. If it weren't for me, Lena would have been cured. She might be sitting in one of her courses at the University of Portland, or walking the streets of the Old Port with her pair. The Stop-N-Save would still be open, and the house on Cumberland would be occupied.

But the guilt goes even deeper than that. It, too, is dust: Layers and layers of it have accumulated.

Because if it weren't for me, Lena and Alex would never have been caught at all.

I told on them.

I was jealous.

God forgive me, for I have sinned.

Lena

I wake up to motion and noise. Julian is gone.

The sun is high, the sky cloudless, and the day still. I kick off the blankets and sit up, blinking hard. My mouth tastes like dust.

Raven is kneeling nearby, feeding twigs, one at a time, to one of the campfires. She glances up at me. "Welcome to the land of the living. Sleep well?"

"What time is it?" I ask.

"After noon." She straightens up. "We're about to head down to the river."

"I'll come with you." Water: That's what I need. I need to wash and drink. My whole body feels like it's coated in grime.

"Come on, then," she says.

Pippa is sitting at the edge of her camp, talking with an unfamiliar woman.

"From the resistance," Raven explains when she sees me looking, and my heart does a funny stutter in my chest. My mother is with the resistance. It's possible the stranger knows her. "She's a week late. She was coming from New Haven with supplies but got waylaid by patrols."

I swallow. I'm afraid to ask the stranger for news. I'm terrified I'll once again be disappointed.

"Do you think Pippa's going to leave Waterbury?" I ask.

Raven shrugs. "We'll see."

"Where will we go?" I ask her.

She shoots me a small smile, reaches out and touches my elbow. "Hey. Don't worry so much, okay? That's my job."

I feel a rush of affection for her. Things between us have not been the same since I found out that she and Tack used me—and Julian—for the movement. But I would be lost without her. We all would be.

Tack, Hunter, Bram, and Julian are standing together, holding makeshift buckets and containers of various sizes. They have obviously been waiting for Raven. I don't know where Coral and Alex are. I don't see Lu, either.

"Hey, sleeping beauty," Hunter says. He has obviously slept well. He looks a hundred times better than he did yesterday, and he isn't coughing anymore.

"Let's get this party started," Raven says.

We leave the relative safety of Pippa's camp and push into the jostle of people, through the maze of patched-together shelters and makeshift tents. I try not to breathe too deeply. It stinks of unwashed bodies and—even worse—of bathroom smells. The air is thick with flies and gnats. I can't wait to wade into the water, to wash away the smells and the dirt. In the distance, I can just make out the dark thread of the river, winding along the south side of the camp. Not too much farther now.

The press of tents and shelters eventually peters out. Ribbons of old pavement, now cracked and fragmented, crisscross the landscape. Vast squares of concrete mark the foundation of old houses.

As we approach the river, we see a crowd has gathered along its banks. People are shouting, pushing and shoving their way to the water.

"*Now* what's the problem?" Tack mutters.

Julian hitches the buckets higher on his shoulder and frowns, although he stays silent.

"There's no problem," Raven says. "Everyone's just excited about a shower." But her voice is strained.

We force our way into the thick tangle of bodies. The smell is overwhelming. I gag, but there's no space to move, no way to bring a hand over my mouth. Not for the first time, I'm grateful to be only five foot two; at least it allows me to squeeze through the smallest openings between people, and I fight to the front of the crowd first, breaking out onto the steep, stony banks of the river, while the mass of people continues to swell behind me, fighting toward the river.

Something is wrong. The water is extremely low—no more than a trickle, a foot or so wide and hardly that deep, and churned mostly to mud. As the river winds back toward the city, it is filled with a moving jigsaw puzzle of people, swelling into the riverbank, desperate to fill their containers. From a distance, they look like insects.

"What the hell?" Raven finally pushes her way onto the bank and stands next to me, stunned.

"The water's running out," I say. Facing this sluggish stream of mud, I begin to panic. Suddenly I am thirstier than I have ever been in my life.

"Impossible," Raven says. "Pippa said the river was flowing fine just yesterday."

"Better take what we can," Tack says. He, Hunter, and Bram have finally fought their way through the crowd. Julian follows a moment afterward. His face is red with sweat. His hair is plastered to his forehead. For a moment, my heart aches for him. I should never have asked him to join me here; I should never have asked him to cross.

More and more people are flowing down toward the river and fighting for what little water remains. There is no choice; we must fight alongside them. As I'm moving into the water, someone pushes me out of the way, and I end up falling backward, landing hard on the rocks. Pain shoots up my spine, and it takes me three tries to stand up. Too many people are streaming by me, shoving me. Eventually, Julian has to fight his way back through the crowd and help me to my feet.

In the end, we manage to get only a fraction of the water we wanted, and we lose some of it on the way back to Pippa's camp, when a man stumbles into Hunter, upsetting one of his buckets. The water we have collected is filled with fine silt and will be reduced even further once we manage to boil away the mud. I would cry if I thought I could waste the water.

Pippa and the woman from Resistance are standing in the middle of a small circle of people. Alex and Coral have returned. I can't help but imagine where they have been together. Stupid, when there are so many other things to worry about; but still the mind will circle back to this one thing.

Amor deliria nervosa: *It affects your mind so that you cannot think clearly, or make rational decisions about your own well-being. Symptom number twelve.*

"The river—" Raven starts to say as we get closer, but Pippa cuts her off.

"We heard," she says. Her face is grim. In the daylight, I see Pippa is older than I originally thought. I assumed she was in her early thirties, but her face is deeply lined, and her hair is gray at the temples. Or maybe that is only the effect of being here, in the Wilds, and waging this war. "It isn't flowing."

"What do you mean?" Hunter says. "A river doesn't stop flowing overnight."

"It does if it's dammed," Alex says.

For a second there's silence.

177

"What do you mean, *dammed*?" Julian speaks first. He, too, is trying not to panic. I can hear it in his voice.

Alex stares at him. "Dammed," he repeats. "As in, stopped. Blocked up. Obstructed or confined by a—"

"But who dammed it?" Julian cuts in. He refuses to look at Alex, but it's Alex who responds.

"It's obvious, isn't it?" He shifts slightly, angling his body toward Julian. There's a hot, electric tension in the air. "The people on the other side." He pauses. "Your people."

Julian still isn't used to losing his temper. He opens his mouth and then shuts it. He says, very calmly, "What did you say?"

"Julian." I place a hand on his arm.

Pippa jumps in. "Waterbury was mostly evacuated before I arrived," she says. "We thought it was because of the resistance. We took it as a sign of progress." She lets out a harsh bark of laughter. "Obviously, they had other plans. They've cut off the water source in the city."

"So we'll leave," Dani says. "There are other rivers. The Wilds is full of them. We'll go somewhere else." Her suggestion meets with silence. She stares from Pippa to Raven.

Pippa runs a hand over the short fuzz of her hair.

"Yeah, sure." The woman from the resistance speaks up. She has a funny accent, all lilts and melody, like drawn butter. "The people we can gather, the ones who can be mobilized—we can leave. We can scatter, break up, go back into the Wilds. But there are probably patrols waiting for us. No doubt they're gathering even now. Easier for them if we're in smaller groups—less of a chance we'll be able to fight. Plus, it looks better for the press. Large-scale slaughter is harder to cover up."

"How do you know so much about it?"

I turn around. Lu has just joined the group. She is slightly breathless, and her face is shiny, as though she has been running. I wonder where she has been all this time. As usual, her hair is loose, plastered to her neck and forehead.

"This is Summer," Pippa says evenly. "She's with Resistance. She's the reason you'll be eating tonight." The subtext is clear: *Watch what you say.*

"But we *have* to leave." Hunter's voice is practically a bark. I get the urge to reach out and squeeze his hand. Hunter never loses his temper. "What other choice do we have?"

Summer doesn't flinch. "We could fight back," she says. "We've all been looking for a chance to rally together, make something of this mess." She gestures to the array of shelters, like pieces of enormous metal shrapnel, glittering vastly toward the horizon. "That was the point of coming to the Wilds, wasn't it? For all of us? We were tired of being told what to choose."

"But how will we fight?" I feel shyer in front of this woman, with her soft, musical voice and her fierce eyes, than I have in front of anyone for a while. But I press on. "We're weak as it is. Pippa said we're disorganized. Without water—"

"I'm not suggesting we go head-to-head," she interrupts me. "We don't even know what we're dealing with—how many people are left in the city, whether there are patrols gathering in the Wilds. What I'm suggesting is that we take the river back."

"But if the river's dammed—"

Again, she cuts me off. "Dams can be exploded," she says simply.

We are silent for another second. Raven and Tack exchange a glance. Largely from habit, we wait for one of them to speak.

"What's your plan?" Tack says, and just like that, I know it's real: This is happening. This will happen.

I close my eyes. An image flashes—emerging from the van with Julian after our escape from New York City; believing, in that moment, that we had escaped the worst, that life would begin again for us.

Instead life has only grown harder.

I wonder whether it will ever end.

I feel Julian's hand on my shoulder: a squeeze, a reassurance. I open my eyes.

Pippa squats and draws a large teardrop shape in the ground with a thumb. "Let's say this is Waterbury. We're here." She marks an X at the southeast side of the larger end. "And we know that when the fighting started, the cureds retreated to the west side of the city. My guess is that the block is some-where here." She hazards an X on the east side, where the teardrop begins to narrow.

"Why?" Raven says. Her face is alive again, alert. For a moment, when I look at her, I get a small chill. She lives for this—the fight, the battle for survival. She actually *enjoys* it.

Pippa shrugs. "It's my best guess. That part of the city was mostly park anyway—they've probably just flooded it completely, rerouted the water flow. They'll have shored up defenses there, of course, but if they had enough firepower to rout us, they'd have attacked already. We're talking whatever forces they've gathered in a week or two."

She looks up at us, to make sure we're following. Then she draws a sweeping arrow around the base of the teardrop, pointing upward. "They'll probably expect us to go north, toward the water flow. Or they think we'll scatter." She draws lines radiating in various directions from the base of the teardrop; now it looks like a deranged, bearded smiley face. "I think instead we should make a direct attack, send a small force into the city, bust open the dam." She draws a line, sweepingly, through the teardrop, cutting it in half.

"I'm in," Raven says. Tack spits. He doesn't have to say he's in too.

Summer folds her arms, looking down at Pippa's diagram. "We'll need three separate groups," she says slowly. "Two diversionary, to create problems here and here"— she bends down and marks X's at two distinct places along the periphery—"and one smaller force to get in, do the job, and get out."

"I'm in," Lu pipes up. "As long as I can be part of the main force. I don't want any of this side-business shit."

This surprises me. At the old homestead, Lu never expressed

interest in joining the resistance. She never even got a fake procedural mark. She just wanted to stay as far as possible from the fighting; she wanted to pretend that the other side, the cured side, didn't exist. Something must have changed in the months we've been apart.

"Lu can come with us." Raven grins. "She's a walking good-luck charm. That's how she got her name. Isn't it, Lucky?"

Lu doesn't say anything.

"I want to be part of the main force too," Julian speaks up suddenly.

"Julian," I whisper. He ignores me.

"I'll go wherever you need me," Alex says. Julian glances at him, and for a second I feel the resentment between them, a blunt, hard-edged force.

"So will I," Coral says.

"Count us in." Hunter speaks for him and Bram.

"I want to be the one who lights the match," Dani says.

Other people are chiming in now, volunteering for different tasks. Raven looks at me. "What about you, Lena?"

I can feel Alex's eyes on me. My mouth is so dry; the sun is so blinding. I look away, toward the hundreds and hundreds of people who have been driven out of their homes, out of their lives, to this place of dust and dirtiness, all because they wanted the power to feel, to think, to choose for themselves. They couldn't have known that even this was a lie—that we never really choose, not entirely. We are always being pushed and squeezed down one road or another. We have no choice but to step forward, and then step forward again, and then step forward again; suddenly we find ourselves on a road we haven't chosen at all.

But maybe happiness isn't in the choosing. Maybe it's in the fiction, in the pretending: that wherever we have ended up is where we intended to be all along.

Coral shifts, and moves her hand to Alex's arm.

"I'm with Julian," I say at last. This, after all, is what I have chosen.

Hana

efore going home, I spend some time zigzagging through the streets near the Old Port, trying to clear my head of Lena, and the guilt; trying to clear it of Fred's voice: *Cassie asked too many questions.*

I bump onto the curb and pedal as fast as I can, as though I can push out my thoughts through my feet. In just two short weeks, I won't have even this freedom; I'll be too known, too visible, too followed. Sweat trickles down my scalp. An old woman emerges from a store and I barely have time to swerve, jump the curb, and skate back into the street, before I hit her.

"Idiot!" she shouts.

"Sorry!" I call over my shoulder, but the word gets lost in the wind.

Then, out of nowhere—a barking dog, a huge blur of black fur, leaps for me. I jerk my handlebars to the right and lose my balance. I tumble off the bike, hitting the ground hard on my elbow, and skid several feet as pain rips up my right side. My bike thuds next to me, screeching across the concrete, and someone is yelling, and the dog is still barking. One of my feet is entangled in the spokes of my front wheel. The dog circles me, panting.

"Are you okay?" A man speed-walks across the street. "Bad dog," he says, smacking the dog's head roughly. The dog slinks several feet away, whimpering.

I sit up, extracting my foot carefully from my bike. My right arm and shin are cut up, but miraculously, I don't think I've broken anything. "I'm all right." I pull myself carefully to my feet, rolling my ankles and wrists slowly, checking for pain. Nothing.

"You should watch where you're going," the man says. He looks annoyed. "You could have been killed." Then he stalks off down the street, whistling for his dog to follow. The dog trots after him, head down.

I pick up my bike and wheel it onto the sidewalk. The chain has come off the stay, and one handlebar is slightly crooked, but other than that, it looks okay. As I bend down to adjust the chain, I notice that I've landed directly in front of the Center for Organization, Research, and Education. I must have been circling it for the past hour.

The CORE keeps Portland's public records: the incorporation documents for its businesses, but also the names, birth dates, and addresses of its citizens; copies of their birth, marriage, medical, and dental records; violations against them and report cards and annual review scores, as well as evaluation results and suggested matches.

An open society is a healthy society; transparency is necessary to trust. That's what *The Book of Shhh* teaches. My mom used to phrase it differently: Only people who have something to hide make a fuss about privacy.

Without consciously making the decision, I lock my bike to a streetlamp and jog up the stairs. I push through the revolving doors and step into a large, plain lobby, decorated with gray linoleum floor tiles and buzzing overhead lights.

A woman sits behind a fake-wood desk, in front of an ancient-looking computer. Behind her a heavy chain is hung across an open doorway; from it, a large sign is dangling: PERSONNEL AND AUTHORIZED CORE EMPLOYEES ONLY.

The woman barely glances at me as I approach the desk. A small plastic name tag identifies her as TANYA BOURNE, SECURITY ASSISTANT.

"Can I help you?" she asks in a monotone. I can tell that she doesn't recognize me.

"I hope so," I say cheerfully, placing my hands on the desk and forcing her to meet my gaze. Lena used to call it my *Buy a bridge* look. "See, my wedding's coming up, and I completely flaked on Cassie, and now I have barely any time to track her down. . . ."

The woman sighs and resettles in her chair.

"And of course Cassie *has* to be there. I mean, even if we haven't spoken . . . well, she invited me to *her* wedding, and it just wouldn't be nice, would it?" I let out a giggle.

"Miss?" she prompts tiredly.

I giggle again. "Oh, sorry. Babbling—it's a bad habit. I guess I'm just nervous, you know, because of the wedding and everything." I pause and suck in a deep breath. "So can you help me?"

She blinks. Her eyes are a dirty-bathwater color. "What?"

"Can you help me find Cassie?" I ask, squeezing my hands into fists, hoping she won't notice. *Please say yes.* "Cassandra O'Donnell."

I watch Tanya carefully, but she doesn't appear to recognize the name. She heaves an exaggerated sigh, pushes up from her chair, and moves over to a tiered stack of papers. She moves back to me and practically slaps it on the desk. It's as thick as a medical intake form—at least twenty pages long. "Personal Information Requests may be sent to CORE, attention Census Department, and will be processed within ninety days—"

"Ninety days!" I cut her off. "My wedding's in *two* weeks."

She draws her mouth into a line. Her whole face is the color of bad water. Maybe being here day after day, under the dull, buzzing lights, has begun to pickle her. She says determinedly, "Expedited Personal Information Request Forms must be accompanied by a personal statement—"

"Look." I spread my fingers flat on the counter and press my frustration down through my palms. "The truth is, Cassandra is a little witch, okay? I don't even *like* her."

Tanya perks up a little.

The lies come fluidly. "She always said I'd flunk my evaluations, you know? And when she got an eight, she went on about it for days. Well, you know what? I scored higher than she did, and my pair is better, and my wedding will be better too." I lean a little closer, drop my voice to a whisper. "I want her to be there. I want her to see it."

Tanya studies me closely for a minute. Then, slowly, her mouth hitches into a smile. "I knew a woman like that," she says. "You'd think God's garden grew under her feet." She turns her attention to her computer screen. "What'd you say her name was again?"

"Cassandra. Cassandra O'Donnell."

Tanya's nails click exaggeratedly against the keyboard. Then she shakes her head and frowns. "Sorry. No one listed by that name."

My stomach does a weird turn. "Are you sure? I mean, you've spelled it correctly and everything?"

She swivels the computer screen around to face me. "Got over four hundred O'Donnells. Not one Cassandra."

"What about Cassie?" I'm fighting a bad feeling—a feeling I have no name for. Impossible. Even if she were dead, she would show up in the system. The CORE keeps records of everyone, living or dead, for the past sixty years.

She readjusts the screen and *click-click-click*s again, then shakes her head. "Uh-uh. Sorry. Maybe you got the wrong spelling?"

"Maybe." I try to smile, but my mouth won't obey. It doesn't make any sense. How does a person disappear? A thought occurs to me: Maybe she was invalidated. It's the only thing that makes any sense. Maybe her cure didn't work, maybe she caught the *deliria*, maybe she escaped to the Wilds.

That would fit. That would be a reason for Fred to divorce her.

". . . work out in the end."

I blink. Tanya has been speaking. She stares at me patiently, obviously expecting a reply. "I'm sorry—what did you say?"

"I said that I wouldn't worry too much about it. These things have a way of working out. Everyone gets what's right for them in the end." She laughs loudly. "The gears of God don't turn unless all the pieces fit right. Know what I mean? And you got your right fit, and she'll get hers."

"Thanks," I say. I can hear her laughing again as I cross back toward the revolving doors; the sound follows me out onto the street, rings faintly in my head even when I am several blocks away.

Lena

The sky doesn't set so much as break apart. The horizon is brick-colored. The rest of the sky is streaked with shock-red tendrils.

The river has slowed to a bare trickle. Fights break out over water. Pippa warns us not to leave her circle, and posts guards around its periphery. Summer has already split. Either Pippa doesn't know where she has gone, or won't share her plans with us.

In the end, Pippa decides that smaller is better: The fewer people we involve, the less chance of a screwup. The best fighters—Tack, Raven, Dani, and Hunter—will be responsible for the main action: getting to the dam, wherever it is, and taking it down. Lu insists on going with them and so does Julian, and even though neither one is a trained fighter, Raven relents.

I could kill her.

"We'll need guards, too," she says. "Lookouts. Don't worry. I'll bring him back safely."

Alex, Pippa, Coral, and one of Pippa's crew, nicknamed Beast—I can only assume because of his tangle of wild black hair and the dark beard that obscures his mouth—will form one diversionary force. Somehow I get roped into heading up the second one. Bram will be my support.

"I wanted to stay with Julian," I tell Tack. I don't feel comfortable complaining directly to Pippa.

"Yeah? Well, I wanted bacon and eggs this morning," he says, without glancing up. He's rolling a cigarette.

"After all I did for you," I say, "you still treat me like a child."

"Only when you act like one," he says sharply, and I remember a fight I had with Alex once, a lifetime ago, after I had first discovered that my mom had been imprisoned in the Crypts my whole life. I haven't thought about that moment, and Alex's sudden outburst, in forever. That was just before he told me he loved me for the first time. That was just before I said it back.

I feel suddenly disoriented and have to squeeze my nails into my palms until I feel a brief shock of pain. I don't understand how everything changes, how the layers of your life get buried. Impossible. At some point, at some time, we must all explode.

"Look, Lena." Now Tack raises his head. "We're asking you to do this because we trust you. You're a leader. We need you."

I'm so startled by the sincerity of his tone, I can't think of a response. In my old life, I was never a leader. Hana was the leader. I got to follow along. "When does it end?" I say finally.

"I don't know," Tack says. It's the first time I've ever heard him admit to not knowing something. He tries to roll up his cigarette, but his hands are shaking. He has to stop, and try again. "Maybe it doesn't." Finally he gives up and throws the cigarette down in disgust. For a moment we stand there in silence.

"Bram and I need a third," I say at last. "That way if something happens, if one of us goes down, the other one still has backup."

Tack looks up at me again. I'm reminded that he, too, is young—twenty-four, Raven once told me. In that second, he looks it. He looks like a grateful kid, like I've just offered to help with his homework.

Then the moment passes, and his face goes hard again. He removes his pack of tobacco, and some rolling papers, and begins again. "You can have Coral," he says.

The part of the mission that frightens me the most is the journey through the camp. Pippa gives us one of the battery-operated lanterns, which Bram carries. In its jerky glow, the crowd around us is broken into pieces and fragments: the flash of a grin here; a woman, bare-breasted, nursing a baby, staring at us resentfully. A tide of people barely break apart to let us through, then reform and refold behind us. I have a sense of their sucking need: Already, the moans have started, the whispers of *water, water.* From everywhere, too, comes the sound of shouting; stifled cries in the darkness; fists into flesh.

We reach the riverbank, now eerily quiet. There are no more people teeming in its depths, fighting over water. There is no more water to fight over—only a tiny trickle, no wider than a finger, black with silt.

It's a mile to the wall, and then another four northwest along its perimeter, to one of the better-fortified areas. A problem there will bring the most attention and pull the largest number of security forces away from the point Raven, Tack, and the others need to breach.

Earlier, Pippa opened the second, smaller fridge, revealing shelves packed with weapons she had been sent by the resistance. Tack, Raven, Lu, Hunter, and Julian were each provided with guns. We've had to make do with a half-empty bottle of gasoline, stuffed with an ancient rag: a *beggar's purse*, Pippa called it. By silent consensus I have been elected the one to carry it. As we walk, it seems to grow heavier in my backpack, bumping uncomfortably against my spine. I can't help but imagine sudden explosions, being blown accidentally to bits.

We reach the place where the camp runs up against the city's southern border wall, a wave of people and tents lapping up against the stone. This part of the wall, and the city beyond it, has been abandoned. Enormous, dark floodlights crane their necks over the camp. Only a single bulb remains intact: It sends a bright white light forward, painting the out-line of things clearly, leaving the detail and the depth out, like a lighthouse beaming out over dark water.

We follow the border wall north and finally leave the camp behind. The ground underneath us feels dry. The carpet of pine needles cracks and snaps each time we take a step. Other than that, once the noise of the camp recedes, it is silent.

Anxiety gnaws at my stomach. I'm not too worried about our role—if all goes well, we won't even have to breach the wall—but Julian is in way over his head. He has no idea what he's doing, no idea what he's getting into.

"This is crazy," Coral says suddenly. Her voice is high, shrill. She must have been fighting down panic all this time. "It'll never work. It's suicide."

"You didn't have to come," I say sharply. "No one asked you to volunteer."

It's as though she doesn't hear me. "We should have packed up, gotten out of here," she says.

"And left everyone else to fend for themselves?" I fire back.

Coral says nothing. She's obviously just as unhappy as I am that we've been forced to work together—probably even unhappier, since I'm the one in charge.

We weave between the trees, following the erratic motions of Bram's lantern, which bobs in front of us like an overgrown firefly. Every so often, we cross ribbons of concrete, radi-ating outward from the city's walls. Once, these old roads would have led to other towns. Now they run aground into earth, flowing like gray rivers around the bases of new trees. Signs—choked with brown ivy—point the way to towns and restaurants long dismantled.

I check the small plastic watch that Beast lent me: eleven thirty p.m. It has been an hour and a half since we set out. We have another half hour before we are supposed to light the rag and send the purse over the wall. This will be timed with a simultaneous explosion on the eastern side, just south of where Raven, Tack, Julian, and the others will be crossing. Hopefully, the two explosions will divert attention away from the breach.

This far from the camp, the border becomes better maintained. The high concrete wall is undamaged and clean. The floodlights become functional and more numerous: enormous, wide-open, dazzling eyes at intervals of twenty or thirty feet.

Beyond the floodlights, I can make out the black silhouettes of looming apartment complexes, glass-fronted buildings, church spires. I know we must be getting close to the downtown center, an area that, unlike some of the outlying residential portions of the city, was not completely evacuated.

Adrenaline starts working its way through me, making me feel very alert. I'm suddenly aware that the night isn't silent at all. I can hear animals scurrying all around us, the pitter-patter of small bodies rustling through the leaves.

Then: voices, faintly, intermingling with the wood sounds.

"Bram," I whisper at him. "Turn off the lantern."

He does. We all stop moving. The crickets are singing,

beating the air into bits, ticking off seconds. I can hear the shallow, desperate pattern of Coral's breathing. She's scared.

Voices again, and a bit of drifting laughter. We are hugging the woods, concealed in a thick wedge of dark between two floodlights. As my eyes adjust, I see a tiny glowing light—an orange firefly—hovering above the wall. It flares, fades, then flares again. A cigarette. Guard.

Another burst of laughter breaks the silence, this time louder, and a man's voice says, "No frigging way." *Guards*, plural.

So. There are watch points along the way. This is both good and bad news. More guards means more people to sound the alarm, more forces to divert from the main breach. But it will also make it more dangerous to get close to the wall.

I gesture for Bram to keep moving. Now that the lantern is off, we have to go slowly. I check the watch again. Twenty minutes.

Then I see it: a metal structure rising above the wall like an overgrown birdcage. An alarm tower. Manhattan, which had a wall similar to this one, had similar alarms. Inside the wire cage is a lever that will trip security alarms all across the city, summon regulators and police to the border.

The alarm tower is situated, mercifully, in one of the dark spaces between floodlights. Still, it's a good bet that there are guards working that portion of the border, even if we can't see them. The top of the wall is bulk and shadow, and any number of regulators could be sheltered there.

I whisper for Bram and Coral to stop. We are still a good

hundred feet from the wall, and concealed in the shadow of looming evergreens and oaks.

"We'll detonate as close to the alarm tower as possible," I say, keeping my voice low. "If the explosion doesn't trip the alarm, the guards will. Bram, I need you to take out one of the floodlights farther on. Not too far, though. If there are guards in the tower, I want them pulled away from their position. I'm going to need to get closer before I can toss this thing." I ease off my backpack.

"What am I going to do?" Coral asks.

"Stay here," I say. "Watch. Cover me if something goes wrong."

"That's bullshit," she says halfheartedly.

I check my watch again. Fifteen minutes. Almost go-time. I wrestle the bottle out of my backpack. It feels larger than it did earlier, and harder to carry. I can't immediately find the matchbook Tack gave me, and I have a momentary panic that it somehow got lost in the dark—but then I remember I put it in my pocket for safekeeping.

Light the rag, throw the bottle, Pippa told me. *Nothing to it.*

I take a deep breath, exhale silently. I don't want Coral to know that I'm nervous. "Okay, Bram."

"Now?" His voice is soft but calm.

"Go now. But wait for my whistle."

He unfolds from his crouch, then moves away from us soundlessly; he is soon absorbed by the greater dark. Coral and I wait in silence. At one point our elbows collide, and she

197

jerks back. I scoot a little away from her, scanning the wall, trying to make out whether the shadows I see are people, or just tricks of the night.

I check my watch, then check it again. Suddenly the minutes seem to be tumbling forward. 11:50. 11:53. 11:55.

Now.

My throat is parched. I can hardly swallow, and I have to lick my lips twice before I manage a whistle.

For several long, agonizing moments, nothing happens. There's no longer any point in pretending that I'm not afraid. My heart is jackhammering in my chest, and my lungs feel like they've been flattened.

Then I see him. Just for a second, as he darts toward the wall, he crosses into the path of the floodlight and he is lit up, frozen, a photographic still; then the darkness swallows him again, and a second later there's a tremendous shattering, and the floodlight goes dark.

Instantly, I'm up on my feet and running for the wall. I'm aware of shouting, but I can't make out any words, don't focus on anything but the wall and the alarm tower behind it. Now that the floodlight is out, the tower's silhouettes have come into starker relief, backlit by the moon and a few scattered lights from the city. Fifteen feet from the wall, I press myself against the trunk of a young oak. I put the beggar's purse between my thighs and struggle to get a match lit. The first one sputters out.

"Come on, come on," I mutter. My hands are shaking. Matches two and three don't stay lit.

A staccato of gunfire breaks the stillness. The shots sound random—they're firing blind, and I say a quick prayer that Bram is back in the trees already, concealed and safe, watching to make sure the rest of the plan goes off.

Match four catches. I move the bottle from between my thighs, touch the match tip to the rag, watch it flare up, white and hot.

Then I move out from the shelter of the trees, breathe deep, and throw.

The bottle spins toward the wall, a dizzying circle of flame. I brace myself for the explosion, but it never comes. The rag, still flaming, detaches from the mouth of the bottle and floats to the ground. I am temporarily mesmerized, watching its path—like a fiery bird, listing and damaged, collapsing into the undergrowth massed at the base of the wall. The bottle shatters harmlessly against the concrete.

"What the fuck? *Now* what's the problem?"

"Fire, looks like."

"Probably your damn cigarette."

"Stop bitching and get me a hose."

Still no alarm. The guards are probably used to vandalism from the Invalids, and neither a damaged floodlight nor a dinky fire is enough to cause them concern. It's possible it won't matter—Alex, Pippa, and Beast's diversion is more important, closer to where the action is—but I can't shake the fear that maybe their plan hasn't worked either. That will leave a city full of guards, prepped, primed, attentive.

That will be sending Raven, Tack, Julian, and the rest of them into slaughter.

Without consciously deciding to move, I'm on my feet again, sprinting toward an oak close to the wall that looks like it will support my weight. All I know is I have to get over the wall and trigger the alarm myself. I wedge my foot against a knot in the tree trunk and haul myself upward. I'm weaker than I was last fall, when I used to climb to the nests quickly, daily, without a problem. I thud back down to the ground.

"What are you doing?"

I spin around. Coral has emerged from the trees.

"What are *you* doing?" I turn back to the tree and try again, picking a different grip this time. No time, no time, no time.

"You said to cover for you," she says.

"Keep your voice down," I whisper sharply. I'm surprised that she actually cared enough to follow me. "I have to get over the wall."

"And do what?"

I try a third time—managing to skim the branches above my head with my fingertips—before my legs give out and I'm forced to jump back to the ground. My fourth attempt is worse than the first three. I'm losing control, I'm not thinking straight.

"*Lena*. What are you planning to do?" Coral repeats.

I spin around to look at her. "Give me a boost," I whisper.

"A what?"

"Come on." The panic is creeping into my voice. If Raven and the others haven't already crossed, they'll be trying to any second. They're *counting* on me.

Coral must hear the change in my tone, because she doesn't ask any more questions. She laces her fingers together and squats so I can wedge my foot in the cradle formed by her hands. Then she lifts me, grunting, and I shoot upward and manage to pull myself into the branches, which fan out from the trunk like the spokes of an umbrella laid bare. One branch extends almost all the way to the wall. I lean down onto my stomach, pressing myself flat against the bark, scooting forward like an inchworm.

The branch begins to sink under my weight. Another foot or so, and it begins to sway. I can't go any farther. As the branch sinks, the distance between my position and the top of the wall increases; any farther, and I'll have no chance of making it over.

I take a deep breath and move into a crouch, keeping my hands tightly wrapped around the branch, which is swaying lightly underneath me. There's no time to worry or debate. I spring up and toward the wall and the branch moves with me, like a springboard, as my weight is released.

For a second I'm airborne, weightless. Then the wall's concrete edge drives hard into my stomach, knocking the wind out of me. I just manage to hook both my arms over the wall and pull myself over, dropping onto the elevated pathway that the guards walk during their patrol. I pause in the shadows to get control of my breathing.

But I can't rest for very long. I hear a sudden eruption of sound: guards calling to one another, and heavy footsteps jogging in my direction. They'll be on me in no time, and I'll have lost my chance.

I stand and sprint toward the alarm tower.

"Hey! Hey, *stop!*"

Shapes materialize from the dark: one, two, three guards, all men, moonlight on metal. Guns.

The first shot dings off one of the steel supports of the alarm tower. I throw myself into the small, open-air tower as more shots rattle the air. My vision is tunneling and everything sounds distant. Disjointed images flash in my head, like stills from different movies: Shots. Firecrackers. Screaming. Children on the beach.

And then all I can see is the small lever, illuminated from above by a single bulb encased in metal wiring: EMERGENCY ALARM.

Time seems to wind down. My arm looks like someone else's, floating toward the lever, agonizingly slow. The lever is in my hand: the metal is surprisingly cold. Slowly, slowly, slowly, the hand grips; the arm pushes.

Another shot, the ring of metal all around me: a fine, high vibration.

Then, all at once, the night is pierced with a shrill, wailing cry, and time shudders back to normal speed. The sound is so tremendous, I can feel it in my teeth. An enormous bulb at the top of the alarm tower lights up and begins turning, sending a sweep of red across the city.

There are arms reaching for me through the metal scaffolding: spider arms, huge and hairy. One of the guards grabs my wrist. I reach out and wrap a hand around the back of his neck, pull him suddenly forward, and he collides forehead-first with one of the steel supports. His grip on me releases as he staggers backward, cursing.

"Bitch!"

I burst free from the tower. Two steps, over the wall, and I'll be fine, I'll be free. Bram and Coral will be waiting in the trees . . . we'll lose the guards in the darkness and the shadows. . . .

I can make it. . . .

That's when Coral comes over the wall. I'm so startled, I stop running. This isn't protocol. Before I have time to ask her what she's doing, an arm is wrapped around my waist, hauling me backward. I smell leather and feel hot breath on my neck. Instincts take over; I shove my elbow back into the guard's stomach, but he doesn't release me.

"Hold still," he snarls.

Everything is short bursts: Someone is screaming, and a hand is around my throat. Coral is in front of me, pale and lovely, hair streaming behind her, arm raised—a vision.

She's holding a rock.

Her arm pinwheels, a graceful, pale arc, and I think, *She's going to kill me*.

Then the guard grunts, and the arm around my waist goes slack, and the hand releases as he crumples to the ground.

But now they are appearing from everywhere. The alarm is still screaming, and at intervals the scene is lit up in red: two guards on our left; two guards on our right. Three guards, shoulder to shoulder, pressed against the wall, blocking our path to the other side.

Sweep: The light cuts over us again, illuminating a metal

stairway behind us, stretching down into the narrow chasm of city streets.

"This way," I pant. I reach out and tug Coral down the stairs. This move was unexpected, and it takes the guards a moment to react. By the time they reach the stairway, Coral and I have hit the street. Any second more guards will arrive, summoned by the alarm. But if we can find a dark corner . . . Somewhere to hide and wait it out . . .

Only a few streetlamps are still lit. The streets are dark. A smattering of gunfire rings out, but it's clear the guards are firing at random.

We make a right, then a left, then another right. Footsteps drum toward us. More patrols. I hesitate, wondering whether we should go back the way we came. Coral puts a hand on my arm and draws me toward a thick triangle of shadow: a recessed doorway, scented with cat urine and cigarette smoke and half-concealed behind a pillared entry. We crouch in the shadows. A minute later, a blur of bodies goes by, a buzz of walkie-talkie voices and heavy breathing.

"Alarm's still going. Position twenty-four is saying there's been a breach."

"We're waiting for backup to start the sweep."

As soon as they pass, I turn to Coral.

"What the hell were you doing?" I say. "Why did you follow me?"

"You said I was supposed to back you up," she says. "I got freaked when I heard the alarm. I thought you must be in trouble."

"What about Bram?" I say.

Coral shakes her head. "I don't know."

"You shouldn't have risked it," I say sharply. Then I add, "Thank you."

I start to climb to my feet, but Coral draws me back.

"Wait," she whispers, and brings her fingers to her lips. Then I hear it: more footsteps, moving in the opposite direction. Two figures come into view, moving fast.

One of them, a man, is saying, "I don't know how you lived with that filth for so long. . . . I'm telling you, I couldn't have done it."

"It wasn't easy." The second one is a woman. I think her voice sounds familiar.

As soon as they pass out of view, Coral nudges me. We need to move away from the area, which will soon be crawling with patrols; they'll probably turn on the streetlamps, too, so their search will be easier.

We need to head south. Then we'll be able to cross back into the camp.

We move quickly, in silence, sticking close to the buildings, where we can easily duck into alleys and doorways. I'm filled with the same suffocating fear I felt when Julian and I escaped through the tunnels and had to make our way through the underground.

Abruptly, all the streetlamps come on at once. It's as though the shadows were an ocean, and the tide has gone out, leaving a barren, ridged landscape of empty streets. Instinctively, Coral and I duck into a darkened doorway.

"Shit," she mutters.

"I was afraid this would happen," I whisper. "We'll have to stick to the alleys. We'll stick to the darkest places we can find."

Coral nods.

We move like rats: We scamper from shadow to shadow, hiding in the small spaces: in the alleys and the cracks, the darkened doorways and behind the Dumpsters. Twice more, we hear patrols approaching us and have to duck into the shadows, until the buzz of static walkie-talkies, and the rhythm of footsteps, is gone.

The city changes. Soon, the buildings thin out. At last the sound of the alarm, still wailing, is no more than a distant cry, and we sink gratefully back into an area where the streetlamps are dark. The moon above us is high and bloated. The apartments on either side of us have the empty, forlorn look of children separated from their parents. I wonder how far we are from the river, whether Raven and the others managed to explode the dam, whether we would have heard it. I think of Julian and feel a twist of anxiety and also regret. I've been hard on him. He's doing his best.

"Lena." Coral stops and points. We're moving past a park; at its center is a sunken amphitheater. For a second, confusedly, I have the impression of dark oil, shimmering between its stone seats; the moon is shining down onto a slick black surface.

Then I realize: *water.*

Half the theater is flooded. A coating of scattered leaves is swirling across its surface, disturbing the watery reflections of the moon, stars, and trees. It's strangely beautiful. I take an unconscious step forward, onto the grass, which squelches under my feet. Mud bubbles up beneath my shoes.

Pippa was right. The dam must have forced the water over the riverbanks and flooded some of the downtown areas. That must mean we're in one of the neighborhoods that was evacuated after the protests.

"Let's get to the wall," I say. "We shouldn't have any trouble crossing."

We continue skirting the periphery of the park. The silence around us is deep, complete, and reassuring. I'm starting to feel good. We've made it. We did what we were supposed to do—with any luck, the rest of our plan went off too.

At one corner of the park is a small stone rotunda, surrounded by a fringe of dark trees. If it weren't for the single, old-fashioned lantern burning on the corner, I would have missed the girl sitting on one of its stone benches. Her head is dropped between her knees, but I recognize her long, streaked hair and her mud-caked purple sneakers. Lu.

Coral sees her at the same time I do. "Isn't that . . . ?" she starts to ask, but I'm already breaking into a run.

"Lu!" I cry out.

She looks up, startled. She must not recognize me immediately; for a second her face is vivid white, frightened. I drop into a squat in front of her, put my hands on her shoulders.

"Are you all right?" I say breathlessly. "Where are the others? Did something happen?"

"I . . ." She trails off and shakes her head.

"Are you hurt?" I straighten up, keeping my hands on her shoulders. I don't see any blood, but she's trembling slightly under my hands. She opens her mouth and then closes it again. Her eyes are wide and vacant. "Lu. Talk to me." I lift my hands from her shoulders to her face, giving her a gentle shake, trying to snap her out of it. As I do, my fingertips skim the skin behind her left ear.

My heart stops. Lu lets out a small cry and tries to jerk away from me. But I keep my hands wrapped tightly around the back of her neck. Now she is bucking and twisting, trying to fight her way from my grasp.

"Get away from me," she practically spits.

I don't say anything. I can't speak. All my energy is in my hands now, and my fingers. She is strong, but she has been taken by surprise, and I manage to haul her to her feet and pin her back against a stone column. I drive my elbow into her neck, forcing her to turn, coughing, to the left.

Dimly I'm aware of Coral's voice. "What the hell are you *doing*, Lena?"

I wrench Lu's hair away from her face, so that her neck is exposed, white and pretty.

I can see the frantic flutter of her pulse—just beneath the neat, three-pronged scar on her neck.

The mark of the procedure. A real one.

Lu is cured.

The past few weeks cycle back to me: Lu's quietness, and her changes in temperament. The fact that she grew her hair long and brushed it carefully forward every day.

"When?" I croak out. I still have my forearm pressed against her throat. Something black and old is rising up inside of me. *Traitor.*

"Let me go," she gasps. Her left eye rolls back to look at me.

"When?" I repeat, and give her throat a nudge. She cries out.

"Okay, okay," she says, and I ease the pressure, just a little. But I keep her pinned against the stone. "December," she croaks. "Baltimore."

My head is spinning. Of course. It was Lu I heard earlier. The regulator's words come back to me with new, terrible meaning: *I don't know how you lived with that filth for so long.* And hers: *It wasn't easy.*

"Why?" I choke out the words. When she doesn't answer me immediately, I lean into her again. "Why?"

She starts speaking in a hoarse rush. "They were right, Lena. I know that now. Think of all those people out there in the camps, in the Wilds . . . like animals. That's not happiness."

"It's freedom," I say.

"Is it?" Her eye is huge; her iris has been swallowed by black. "Are *you* free, Lena? Is this the life you wanted?"

I can't respond. The anger is a thick, dark mud, a rising tide in my chest and throat.

Lu's voice drops to a silken whisper, like the noise of a snake through the grass. "It's not too late for you, Lena. It doesn't matter what you've done on the other side. We'll wipe that out; we'll start clean. That's the whole point. We can take all that away . . . the past, the pain, all your struggling. You can start again."

For a second, we both stand there staring at each other. Lu is breathing hard.

"All of it?" I say.

Lu tries to nod, and grimaces as she once again encounters my elbow. "The anxiety, the unhappiness. We can make it go away."

I ease the pressure off her neck. She sucks in a deep, grateful breath. I lean in very close to her and repeat something that Hana once said to me a lifetime ago.

"You know you can't be happy unless you're unhappy sometimes, right?"

Lu's face hardens. I've given her just enough space to maneuver, and when she goes to swing at me, I catch her left wrist and twist it behind her back, forcing her to double over. I wrestle her to the ground, press her flat, force a knee between her shoulder blades.

"Lena!" Coral shouts. I ignore her. A single word drums through me: *Traitor. Traitor. Traitor.*

"What happened to the others?" I say. My words are high and strangled, clutched in the web of anger.

"It's too late, Lena." Lu's face is half-mashed against the ground, but still she manages to twist her mouth into a horrible smile, a leering half grin.

It's a good thing I don't have a knife on me. I would drive it straight into her neck. I think of Raven smiling, laughing. *Lu can come with us. She's a walking good-luck charm.* I think of Tack dividing his bread, giving her the largest share when she complained about being hungry. My heart feels like it's crumbling to chalk, and I want to scream and cry at the same time. *We trusted you.*

"Lena," Coral repeats. "I think—"

"Be quiet," I say hoarsely, keeping my focus locked on Lu. "Tell me what happened to them or I'll kill you."

She struggles under my weight, and continues beaming that horrible twisted grin at me. "Too late," she repeats. "They'll be here before nightfall tomorrow."

"What are you talking about?"

Her laughter is a rattle in her throat. "You didn't think it would last, did you? You didn't think we'd let you keep playing in your little camp, in your filth—" I twist her arms another inch toward her shoulder blades. She cries out, and then continues speaking in a rush. "Ten thousand soldiers, Lena. Ten thousand soldiers against a thousand hungry, thirsty, diseased, disorganized uncureds. You'll be mowed down. Obliterated. *Poof.*"

I think I'm going to be sick. My head is thick, fluid-feeling. Distantly, I'm aware that Coral is speaking to me again. It takes a moment for the words to work their way through the murk, through the watery echoes in my head.

"Lena. I think someone's coming."

She has barely spoken the words when a regulator—probably the one we saw with Lu earlier—rounds the corner, saying, "Sorry that took so long. Shed was locked—"

He breaks off when he sees Coral and me, and Lu on

the ground. Coral shouts and lunges for him but clumsily, off balance. He pushes her backward, and I hear a small crack as her head collides with one of the stone columns of the portico. The regulator lunges forward, swinging his flashlight at her face. She manages to duck, barely, and the flashlight crashes hard against the stone pillar and sputters into darkness.

The regulator has thrown too much weight into the swing, and his balance is upset. This gives Coral just enough time to break past him, away from the pillar. She's swaying on her feet, and obviously unsteady. She staggers around to face him, but clutching one hand to the back of her head. The regulator regains his footing and his hand goes to his belt. Gun.

I rocket to my feet. I have no choice but to release Lu from underneath me. I dive at the regulator and grab him around the waist. My weight and momentum carry us both off our feet, and we hit the ground together, rolling once, arms and legs tangled together. The taste of his uniform and sweat is in my mouth, and I can feel the weight of his gun digging against my thigh.

Behind me, I hear a shout, and a body thudding to the ground. I pray that it's Lu and not Coral.

Then the regulator breaks free of my grip and scrambles to his feet, pushing me off him roughly. He is panting, red-faced. Bigger than I am, and stronger—but slower, too, in bad shape. He fumbles with his belt, but I'm on my feet before he can get the gun from its holster. I grab his wrist, and he lets out a roar of frustration.

Bang.

The gun goes off. The explosion is so unexpected, it sends a jolt through my whole body; I feel it ringing all the way up into my teeth. I jump backward. The regulator screams out in pain and crumples; a dark black stain is spreading down his right leg and he rolls over onto his back, clutching his thigh. His face is contorted, wet with sweat. The gun is still in its holster—a misfire.

I step forward and take the gun off him. He doesn't resist. He just keeps moaning and shuddering, repeating, "Oh shit, oh shit."

"What the hell did you do?"

I whip around. Lu is standing, panting, staring at me. Behind her, I see Coral lying on the ground, on her side, her head resting on one arm and her legs curled up toward her chest. My heart stops. *Please don't let her be dead.* Then I see her eyelids flutter, and one of her hands twitch. She moans. Not dead, then.

Lu takes a step toward me. I raise the gun, level it at her. She freezes.

"Hey, now." Her voice is warm, easy, friendly. "Don't do anything stupid, okay? Just hold on."

"I know what I'm doing," I say. I'm amazed to see how steady my hand is. I'm amazed that this—wrist, finger, fist, gun—belongs to me.

She manages to smile. "Remember the old homestead?" she says in that same smooth lullaby-voice. "Remember when Blue and I found all those blueberry bushes?"

"Don't you dare talk to me about what I remember," I practically spit. "And don't talk about Blue, either." I cock the gun. I see her flinch. Her smile falters. It would be so easy. Flex and release. Bang.

"Lena," she says, but I don't let her finish. I take a step closer to her, closing the distance between us, then wrap one arm around her neck and draw her into an embrace, shoving the muzzle of the revolver into the soft flesh of her chin. Her eyes begin rolling, like a horse's when it's frightened; I can feel her bucking against me, shaking, trying to wrestle away from me.

"Don't move," I say in a voice that doesn't sound like my own. She goes limp—all except for her eyes, which keep rolling, terrified, from my face to the sky.

Flex and release. A simple motion; a twitch.

I can smell her breath, too: hot and sour.

I push her away from me. She falls back, gasping, as though I've been choking her.

"Go," I say. "Take him"—I gesture to the regulator, who is still moaning, and clutching his thigh—"and go."

She licks her lips nervously, her eyes darting to the man on the ground.

"Before I change my mind," I add.

She doesn't hesitate after that; she squats and slings the regulator's arm around her shoulders, helping him to his feet. The stain on his pants is black, spreading from mid-thigh down to his kneecap. I find myself hoping, cruelly, that he'll bleed out before they can find help.

"Let's go," Lu whispers to him, her eyes still locked on me. I watch as she and the regulator hobble off down the street. Each one of his steps is punctuated by a cry of pain. As soon as the darkness has swallowed them, I exhale. I turn around and see that Coral is sitting up, rubbing her head.

"I'm all right," she says when I go to help her up. She climbs to her feet unsteadily. She blinks several times, as though trying to clear her vision.

"You sure you can walk?" I ask, and she nods. "Come on," I say. "We've got to find our way out of here."

Lu and the regulator will give us away at their first opportunity. If we don't hurry, any minute we'll be surrounded. I feel a deep spasm of hatred, thinking of the fact that Tack shared his dinner with Lu only a few days ago, thinking of the fact that Lu accepted it from him.

Thankfully, we make it to the border wall without encountering any patrols, and locate a rusty metal stairwell that leads up to the guards' walkway, which is also empty; we must be at the southernmost end of the city right now, very close to the camp, and security is concentrated in more populated portions of Waterbury.

Coral mounts the stairs shakily and I go behind her, to make sure she won't fall, but she refuses my help and jerks away from me when I place a hand on her back. In just a few hours, my respect for her has increased tenfold. As we reach the walkway, the alarm in the distance finally stops, and the sudden quiet is somehow scarier: a silent scream.

Getting down the other side of the wall is trickier. The drop from the top is a good fifteen feet, onto a steep, loose slope of gravel and rock. I go first, swinging out, hand over hand, on one of the disabled floodlights; when I let go and drop to the ground, I slide forward several feet, thudding onto my knees, and feel the gravel bite through my denim. Coral follows after me, her face pale with concentration, landing with a small cry of pain.

I don't know what I was expecting—I had feared, I think, that the tanks would have already arrived, that we would find the camp already consumed by fire and chaos—but it stretches before us as it ever did, a vast and pitted field of peaked tents and shelters. Beyond it, across the valley, are the high cliffs, capped with a shaggy black mass of trees.

"How long do you think we have?" Coral says. I know without asking that she means before the troops come.

"Not long enough," I say.

We move in silence toward the outskirts of the camp— walking the periphery will still be quicker than trying to navigate the maze of people and tents. The river is still dry. The plan obviously failed. Raven and the others did not manage to disable the dam—not that it matters much, at this point.

All these people . . . thirsty, exhausted, weak. They'll be easier to corral.

And, of course, far easier to kill.

By the time we make it back to Pippa's camp, my throat is so dry I can hardly swallow. For a second, when Julian rushes toward me, I don't recognize his face: It is a collection of random shapes and shadows.

Behind him, Alex turns away from the fire. He meets my eyes and starts toward me, mouth open, hands extended. Everything freezes, and I know I've been forgiven and I reach out my hands—reach out my arms to him . . .

"Lena!" Then Julian is sweeping me into his arms, and I snap back into myself, press my cheek against his chest. Alex must have been reaching for Coral; I hear him murmuring to her, and as I pull away from Julian, I see that Alex is leading Coral back toward one of the campfires. I was so sure, for just that one second, that he was reaching for me.

"What happened?" Julian asks, cupping my face and bending down a little bit so that we're nearly eye to eye. "Bram told us—"

"Where's Raven?" I say, cutting him off.

"I'm right here." She flows out of the dark, and suddenly I am surrounded: Bram, Hunter, Tack, and Pippa, all speaking at once, firing questions at me.

Julian keeps one hand on my back. Hunter offers me a drink from a plastic jug, which is mostly empty. I take it gratefully.

"Is Coral okay?"

"You're bleeding, Lena."

"God. What *happened*?"

"There's no time." The water has helped, but still the words shred my throat. "We have to leave. We have to get everyone we can, and we have to—"

"Slow down, slow down." Pippa holds up both hands. Half her face is lit by the fire; the other is plunged in darkness. I think of Lu and feel nauseous: a half person, a two-faced traitor.

"Start from the beginning," Raven says.

"We had to fight," I say. "We had to go inside."

"We thought you might have been taken," Tack says. I can tell he's hopped up, anxious; everybody is. The whole group is charged with bad electricity. "After the ambush—"

"Ambush?" I repeat sharply. "What do you mean, ambush?"

"We never made it to the dam," Raven says. "Alex and Beast managed to get their blast off okay. We were a half-dozen feet from the wall when a group of regulators started swarming us. It was like they were *waiting*. We would have been screwed if Julian hadn't spotted the movement and given the alarm early."

Alex has joined the group. Coral gets clumsily to her feet, her mouth a fine, dark line. I think she looks more beautiful than I've ever seen her. My heart squeezes once, tight, in my chest. I can see why Alex likes her.

Maybe even why he loves her.

"We beat it back here," Pippa pipes up. "Then Bram showed up. We've been debating whether to go looking—"

"Where's Dani?" I notice, for the first time, that she isn't with the group.

"Dead," Raven says shortly, avoiding my eyes. "And Lu was taken. We couldn't get to them in time. I'm sorry, Lena," she finishes in a softer voice, and looks at me again.

I feel another surge of nausea. I wrap my arms around my stomach, as though I can press it deep and down. "Lu wasn't taken," I say. My voice comes out as a bark. "And they *were* waiting for you. The regulators. It was a trap."

There's a second of silence. Raven and Tack exchange a glance. Alex is the one who speaks.

"What are you talking about?"

It's the first time he has spoken to me directly since that night on the banks, after the regulators burned our camp.

"Lu isn't what we thought she was," I say. "She isn't *who* we thought she was. She's been cured."

More silence: a sharp, shocked minute of it.

Finally Raven bursts out, "How do you know?"

"I saw the mark," I say. Suddenly I'm exhausted. "And she told me."

"Impossible," Hunter says. "I was with her. . . . We went to Maryland together. . . ."

"It's not impossible," Raven says slowly. "She told me she'd broken off from the group for a while, spent some time floating between homesteads."

"She was only gone for a few weeks." Hunter looks at Bram for confirmation. Bram nods.

"That's time enough." Julian speaks softly. Alex glares at him. But Julian's right: It is time enough.

Raven's voice is strained. "Go on, Lena."

"They're bringing in troops," I say. Once the words leave my mouth I feel like I've been socked in the stomach.

There's another moment of silence. "How many?" Pippa demands.

"Ten thousand." I can barely speak the words.

There is a sharp intake of breath, gasps from all around the circle. Pippa stays laser-focused on me. "When?"

"Less than twenty-four hours," I say.

"*If* she was telling the truth," Bram says.

Pippa runs a hand through her hair, making it stick up in spikes. "I don't believe it," she says, but adds almost immediately, "I was worried something like this might happen."

"I'll fucking kill her," Hunter says softly.

"What do we do now?" Raven addresses the comment to Pippa.

Pippa is silent for a second, staring at the fire. Then she rouses herself. "We do nothing," she says firmly, sweeping her eyes deliberately around the group: from Tack and Raven to Hunter and Bram; to Beast and Alex and Coral, and to Julian. Finally her eyes click to mine, and I involuntarily draw back. It's as though a door has closed inside her. For once, she isn't pacing. "Raven, you and Tack will lead the group to a safe house just outside of Hartford. Summer told me how to get there. Some contacts from the resistance will be there in the next few days. You'll have to wait it out."

"What about you?" Beast asks.

Pippa pushes her way out of the circle, stepping into the three-sided structure at the center of camp and moving toward the old refrigerator. "I'll do what I can here," she says.

Everyone speaks at once. Beast says, "I'm staying with you."

Tack bursts out, "That's suicide, Pippa."

And Raven says, "You're no match for ten thousand troops. You'll be mowed down—"

Pippa raises a hand. "I'm not planning to fight," she says. "I'll do what I can to spread the word about what's coming. I'll try to clear the camp."

"There's no *time*." Coral speaks up. Her voice is shrill. "The troops are already on their way. . . . There's no time to move everyone, no time to get the word out—"

"I said I would do what I can." Now Pippa's voice turns sharp. She removes the key from around her neck and opens the lock around the fridge, removing food and medical equipment from the darkened shelves.

"We won't leave without you," Beast says stubbornly. "We'll stay. We'll help you clear the camp."

"You'll do what I say," Pippa says, without turning around to face him. She squats and begins pulling blankets from under the bench. "You'll go to the safe house and you'll wait for the resistance."

"No," he says. "I won't." Their eyes meet: Some wordless dialogue flows between them, and at last, Pippa nods.

"All right," she says. "But the rest of you need to clear out."

"Pippa—" Raven starts to protest.

Pippa straightens up. "No arguing," she says. Now I know where Raven learned her hardness, her way of leading people. "Coral is right about one thing," Pippa continues quietly. "There's hardly any time. I expect you out of here in twenty minutes." She sweeps her eyes around the circle again. "Raven, take the supplies you think you'll need. It's a day's walk to the safe house, more if you have to circumvent the troops. Tack, come with me. I'll make you a map."

The group breaks up. Maybe it's the exhaustion, or the fear, but everything seems to happen as it does in a dream: Tack and Pippa are crouching over something, gesticulating; Raven is rolling up food in blankets, tying up the bundles with old cord; Hunter is urging me to have more water and then, suddenly, Pippa is pressing us to *go, go*.

The moon beats down on the switchback paths cut in the hill, tawny-colored and dry, as though steeped in old blood. I shoot a last glance back down at the camp, at the sea of writhing shadows—people, all those people, who don't know that even now the guns and the bombs and the troops are drawing closer.

Raven must sense it too: the new terror in the air, the proximity of death, the way an animal must feel when it is caught in a trap. She turns and shouts down to Pippa.

"Please, Pippa." Her voice rolls off the bare slope. Pippa is standing at the bottom of the dirt path, watching us. Beast is standing behind her. She's holding a lantern, which illuminates her face from below, carves it into stone, into planes of shadow and light.

222

"Go," Pippa says. "Don't worry. I'll meet you at the safe house."

Raven stares at her for a few more seconds, and then begins to turn around again.

Then Pippa calls, "But if I'm not there in three days, don't wait."

Her voice never loses its calm. And I know, now, what the look was that I saw earlier in her eyes. It was beyond calm. It was resignation.

It was the look of someone who knows she will die.

We leave Pippa behind, standing in the dark, teeming bowels of the camp, while the sun begins to stain the sky electric, and from all sides the guns draw closer.

Hana

On Saturday morning I make my visit to Deering Highlands. It is becoming almost routine. I'm happy that I manage to avoid seeing Grace—the streets are still, silent, wrapped in an early-morning mist—and happy, too, that the shelves of the underground room are looking fuller already.

Back at home, I shower in too-hot water, until my skin is pink. I scrub carefully, under my fingernails even, as though the smell of the Highlands, and all the people living there, might have clung to me. But I can't be too careful. If Cassie was invalidated because she caught the disease, or because Fred suspected her of it, I can only imagine what he will do to me and to my family if he discovers that the cure did not work perfectly.

I need to know—for good, for sure—what happened to Cassandra.

Fred is spending the day golfing with several dozen campaign donors and supporters, including my father. My mother is meeting Mrs. Hargrove at the club for lunch. I wave good-bye to my parents cheerfully and then kill time for a half hour, too antsy to watch TV or do anything but pace.

When a sufficient amount of time has elapsed, I gather up the final guest list and seating chart for the wedding, shuffling them roughly into a folder. There's no point in being secretive about where I'm going, so I call Rick, Tony's brother, and wait on the front porch for him to pull up the car.

"To the Hargroves', please," I say brightly as I slide into the backseat.

I try not to fidget too much. I don't want Rick to know that I'm nervous. I don't want any questions. But he doesn't pay any attention to me at all. He keeps his eyes on the road. His bald head, nestled in his shirt collar, reminds me of a swollen pink egg.

At the Hargroves' house, all three cars are missing from the circular driveway. So far, so good.

"Wait here," I say to Rick. "I won't be long."

A girl I recognize as a member of the household staff opens the door. She can't be more than a few years older than I am and has a permanent look of dull suspicion, like a dog kicked too many times in the head.

"Oh!" she says when she sees me, and hesitates, clearly uncertain about whether to let me in.

I start talking immediately. "I ran over here as fast as I could. Can you believe after all that, my mom forgot to bring the plans to lunch? Mrs. Hargrove needs approval over the seating chart, of course."

"Oh!" the girl says again. She frowns. "But Mrs. Hargrove isn't here. She's at the club."

I let out a groan, making a big show of surprise. "When my mom said they were having lunch, I just assumed . . ."

"They're at the club," she repeats nervously. She's clinging to that piece of information like a lifeline.

"So stupid of me," I say. "And of course I don't have time to run to the club now. Maybe I could just drop them for Mrs. Hargrove . . . ?"

"I can give them to her, if you like," she offers.

"No, no. You don't have to," I say quickly. I lick my lips. "If I can just pop inside for a minute, I'll leave her a quick note. Tables six and eight may have to be swapped, and I'm not sure what to do with Mr. and Mrs. Kimble. . . ."

The girl retreats to let me in. "Of course," she says, opening the door a little wider to admit me.

I pass in front of her. Although I've been to the Hargroves' many times, the house feels different without its owners present. Most rooms are dark, and it's so quiet I can hear the creaking of footsteps above, the rustle of fabric several rooms away. Goose bumps pop up on my arms. It's cool in the hall, but it's also the feel of the place—like the whole house is holding its breath, waiting for a disaster.

Now that I'm here, I'm not sure where to begin. Fred must have kept records of his wedding to Cassie, and probably of his divorce, too. I've never been inside his study, but he pointed it out to me during my first visit, and there's a good chance that any documents he keeps will be there. But first I have to get rid of the girl.

"Thanks so much," I say as she ushers me into the living room. I beam her my brightest smile. "I'll just plop down here and write a note. You'll tell Mrs. Hargrove the plans are on the coffee table, right?" I intend for her to take this as a hint to leave me, but she just nods and stands there, watching me dumbly.

I'm improvising now, grasping at excuses. "Can you do me a favor? Since I'm already here, can you run upstairs and try to find the color swatches we lent to Mrs. Hargrove ages ago? The florist needs them back. And Mrs. Hargrove said she left them for me in her bedroom—probably on the desk or something."

"Color swatches . . . ?"

"A big book of them," I say. And then, because she still hasn't moved: "I'll just wait here while you get them."

At last she leaves me alone. I wait until I hear her footsteps retreat upstairs before venturing back out to the hallway.

The door to Fred's study is closed but, thankfully, unlocked. I slip inside and close the door quietly. My mouth is dry and my heart is speed-racing in my throat. I have to remind myself that I haven't done anything wrong. At least not yet. Techni-cally, this is my house too, or it will be very soon.

I feel for the light on the wall. It's a risk—anyone could see the light spilling under the door—but then fumbling around in the dark, overturning furniture, will bring them running as well.

The room is dominated by a large desk and a stiff-backed leather chair. I recognize one of Fred's golf trophies and the sterling-silver paperweight sitting on the otherwise empty bookcases. In one corner is a large metal filing cabinet; next to it, on the wall, is a large painting of a man, presumably a hunter, standing in the middle of various animal carcasses, and I look away quickly.

I head for the filing cabinet, which is also unlocked. I rifle through stacks of financial information—bank statements and tax returns, receipts and deposit slips—dating back nearly a decade. One drawer holds all the employee informa-tion, including photographed copies of the staff's ID cards. The girl who showed me in is named Eleanor Latterly, and she's my age exactly.

And then, stuffed in the back of the lowest drawer, I find it: an unmarked folder, slender, containing Cassie's birth and marriage certificates. There's no record of a divorce, only a letter, folded in two, typed on thick stationery.

I scan the first line quickly. *This letter is in regard to the physical and mental state of Cassandra Melanea Hargrove, b. O'Donnell, who was admitted to my care—*

I hear footsteps crossing quickly toward the study. I shove the folder back in place, push the cabinet closed with a foot, and stuff the letter into my back pocket, thanking God I thought to wear jeans. I grab a pen off the desk. When Eleanor swings the door open, I triumphantly flourish a pen before she has a chance to speak.

"Found it!" I say cheerfully. "Can you believe I didn't think to bring a pen? My brain is cheese today."

She doesn't trust me. I can tell. But she can't exactly accuse me outright. "There was no book of swatches," she says slowly. "No book anywhere, that I could see."

"Weird." A bead of sweat trickles between my breasts. I watch her eyes tick around the whole room, as though looking for anything disturbed or displaced. "I guess we've all got our messages crossed today. Excuse me." I have to shove past her, moving her bodily out of the way. I barely remember to scrawl a quick note to Mrs. Hargrove—*For your approval!* I write, even though I don't really care what she thinks. Eleanor hovers behind me the whole time, like she thinks I'm going to steal something.

Too late.

The whole operation has taken only ten minutes. Rick still has the engine on. I slide into the backseat. "Home," I tell him. As he maneuvers the car out of the driveway, I think I can see Eleanor watching me from the front window.

It would be safer to wait until I was home to read the note, but I can't stop myself from unfolding it. I take a closer look at the letterhead: *Sean Perlin, MD, Chief Surgical Supervisor, Portland Laboratories.*

The letter is brief.

To Whom It May Concern:

This letter is in regard to the physical and mental state of Cassandra Melanea Hargrove, b. O'Donnell, who was admitted to my care and supervision for a period of nine days.

In my professional opinion, Mrs. Hargrove suffers acute delusions provoked by an entrenched mental instability; she is fixated on the Bluebeard myth and relates the story to her fears of persecution; she is profoundly neurotic and unlikely, in my opinion, to improve.

Her condition seems of the degenerative kind and may have been provoked by certain chemical imbalances resultant from the procedure, although this is impossible to say definitively.

I read the letter several times. So I was right—there *was* something wrong with her. She went screwy. Maybe the procedure unhinged her, like it did for Willow Marks. Strange that no one noticed before she married Fred, but I guess sometimes these things are gradual.

Still, the knot in my stomach refuses to unravel. Beneath the doctor's polished prose is a separate message: a message of fear.

I remember the story of Bluebeard: the story of a man, a handsome prince, who keeps a locked door in his beautiful castle. He tells his new bride that she may enter any room but that one. But one day her curiosity overwhelms her, and she discovers a room of murdered women, strung from their heels. When he finds out she disobeyed his order, he adds her to that horrible, bloody collection.

The fairy tale terrified me when I was a kid, especially the image of the women heaped together, arms pale and eyes sightless, gutted.

I fold the letter carefully and return it to my back pocket. I'm being stupid. Cassie was defective, like I thought she was, and Fred had every reason to divorce her. Just because she no longer shows up in the system doesn't mean anything terrible happened to her. Maybe it was just an administrative error.

But the whole ride home, I can't help but picture Fred's strange smile, and the way he said, *Cassie asked too many questions.*

And I can't help the thought that rises, unbidden, unwanted: *What if Cassie was right to be afraid?*

Lena

For the first half of the day we see no evidence of troops, and it occurs to me that Lu might have been lying. I feel a welling of hope: Maybe the camp won't be attacked after all, and Pippa will be fine. Of course there's still the problem of the dammed river, but Pippa will figure it out. She's like Raven: born to survive.

But in the afternoon, we hear shouting in the distance. Tack holds up a hand and gestures for silence. We all freeze, and then, when Tack motions, disperse into the woods. Julian has adjusted to the Wilds well, and to our need for camouflage. One second he is standing next to me; the next he has melted behind a small group of trees. The others vanish just as quickly.

I duck behind an old concrete wall, which appears to have been dropped randomly from above. I wonder what kind of structure it used to belong to; and suddenly, I have a memory of the story Julian told me when we were imprisoned together, of a girl named Dorothy whose house spirals up into the air on the powerful surges of a tornado, and who ends up in a magical land.

As the sound of shouting gets louder and the noise of clanking weaponry and heavy boot steps swells to a pounding rhythm, I find myself fantasizing that we, too, will be whisked away—all of us, all the Invalids, the people pushed and elbowed out of normal society—will vanish on a puff of air, and wake up and find ourselves somewhere different.

But this is not a fairy tale. This is April in the Wilds, and black mud seeping up around my damp sneakers; and clouds of hovering gnats; and held breath and waiting.

The troops are several hundred feet away from us, down a gently sloping embankment and across a trickling stream. From our elevated position, we can easily see the long line of soldiers as it comes into view, a blur of uniforms weaving in and out of trees. The shifting diamond pattern of leaves merges perfectly with the shifting, blurry mass of men and women, suited up in camouflage, hauling machine guns and tear gas. It seems there is no end to them.

Finally the flow of soldiers trickles away, and by silent understanding we all regroup and begin walking again. The silence is electric and uneasy. I try not to think about those people at the camp, cupped in a bowl of land, trapped. An old expression comes back to me—*like shooting fish in a barrel*—and I feel a wild and inappropriate desire to laugh. That's what they are, all those Invalids: wild-eyed, pale-bellied fishes, rolling up toward the sun, as good as dead.

We make it to the safe house in slightly more than twelve hours. The sun has made a complete revolution and is now sinking down over the trees, breaking up into watery streaks of yellow and orange. It reminds me of the poached eggs my mother used to make me when I was sick as a small child, how the yolk would seep across the plate, a vivid and startling gold, and I feel a sharp stab of homesickness. I'm not even sure whether I'm missing my mother, or simply the old routine of my life: a life of school and playdates and rules that kept me safe; boundaries and borders; bath time and curfews. A simple life.

The safe house is marked by a small wooden over-structure, no larger than an outhouse latrine, fitted with a clumsily constructed door. The whole thing must have been assembled from scraps after the blitz. When Tack heaves open the door on its rusted hinges—these, too, twisted and bent—we can just make out a few steps tunneling down into a dark hole.

"Wait." Raven kneels, fumbling in one of the packs she took from Pippa, and produces a flashlight. "I'll go first."

The air is thick with must and something else—a sour-sweet smell I can't identify. We follow Raven down the steeply pitched stairs. She aims the flashlight around a room that is surprisingly spacious and clean: shelves, a few rickety tables, a kerosene stove. Beyond the stove is another darkened doorway, leading to additional rooms. I feel a flicker of warmth in my chest. It reminds me of the homestead near Rochester.

"There should be lanterns around here somewhere." Raven advances several paces into the room. The light zigzags across the clean-swept concrete floor, and I see a small pair of blinking eyes, a flash of gray fur. Mice.

Raven finds a pile of dusty battery-operated lanterns in the corner. It takes three lanterns to beat away all the shadows in the room. Normally Raven would insist on conserving energy, but I think she feels—as we all feel—that tonight we need as much light as we can. Otherwise, images of the camp will come pressing back, carried on silken shadow fingers: all those people, trapped, helpless. We must focus instead on this bright, small, underground room, and its illuminated corners and wooden shelves.

"Do you smell that?" Tack says to Bram. He picks up one of the lanterns and carries it into the next room. "Bingo!" he shouts.

Raven is already rifling through the pack, removing supplies. Coral has found large metal jugs full of water stored on one of the lower shelves, and has crouched down, swigging gratefully. But the rest of us follow Tack into the second room.

Hunter says, "What is it?"

Tack is standing, holding the lantern up to reveal a wall crisscrossed with a diamond-lattice of wooden shelves. "Old wine cellar," he says. "I thought I smelled the booze." Two bottles of wine, and one bottle of whiskey, remain. Immediately, Tack uncaps the whiskey and takes a swig, before offering it to Julian, who accepts after only a split-second hesitation. I start to protest—I'm sure he's never had a drink before, would practically swear to it—but before I can speak he has taken a long sip and, miraculously, managed to swallow without gagging.

Tack breaks into one of his rare smiles and claps Julian on the shoulder. "You're all right, Julian," he says.

Julian wipes his mouth with the back of his hand. "That wasn't bad," he says, gasping a little, and Tack and Hunter laugh. Alex takes the bottle from Julian wordlessly and swigs.

All the exhaustion of the past few days hits me at once. Beyond Tack, across the room from the lattice-shelves, are several narrow cots, and I practically stagger to the one closest to me.

"I think . . ." I start to say as I lie down, curling my knees to my chest. There are no blankets and no pillow on the cot, but still I feel as though I'm sinking into something heavenly: a cloud, a feather. No. I am the feather. I am drifting away. *I'm going to sleep for a bit*, I mean to finish, but I don't get the words out before, already, I am.

I wake up gasping in total darkness. For a moment I panic, thinking I'm back in the underground cell with Julian. I sit up, heart slamming against my ribs, and only when I hear Coral murmur on the cot next to mine do I remember where I am.

The room smells bad, and there's a bucket next to Coral's bed. She must have thrown up earlier.

A wedge of light cuts through the open doorway, and I hear muffled laughter from the next room.

Someone placed a blanket over me while I was sleeping. I push it to the bottom of the cot and stand up. I have no idea what time it is.

Hunter and Bram are sitting together in the next room, bent close together, laughing. They have the slightly sweaty, glassy-eyed look of people who have been drinking. The whiskey bottle is sitting between them, nearly empty, along with a plate bearing the remains of what must have been dinner: beans, rice, nuts.

They go quiet as soon as I walk into the room, and I know that whatever they were laughing about, it was private.

"What time is it?" I say, moving over to the jugs of water. I crouch down and lift a jug straight to my mouth without bothering to pour it into a cup. My knees, arms, and back are sore, my body still heavy with exhaustion.

"Probably midnight," Hunter says. So I haven't been sleeping for more than a few hours.

"Where's everybody else?" I ask.

Hunter and Bram exchange a small look. Bram tries to suppress a smile.

"Raven and Tack went midnight trapping," he says, raising an eyebrow. This is an old joke, a code we invented at the old homestead. Raven and Tack managed to keep their romantic

237

relationship a secret for close to a year. But one time, Bram couldn't sleep and decided to take a walk, and he caught them sneaking around together. When he confronted them, Tack blurted out, "Trapping!" even though it was close to two a.m. and all the traps had been cleared and set earlier in the day.

"Where's Julian?" I say. "Where's Alex?"

There's another fractional pause. Now Hunter is struggling not to laugh. He's definitely drunk—I can tell by the rash-like patches of red in his cheeks.

"Outside," Bram says, and then he can't help himself, and lets out a loud snort of laughter. Instantly, Hunter starts laughing too.

"Outside? Together?" I stand up, confused, getting irritated. When neither responds, I persist. "What are they *doing*?"

Bram struggles to control himself. "Julian wanted to learn how to fight—"

Hunter finishes for him. "Alex volunteered to teach him." They dissolve into laughter again.

My whole body goes hot, then cold. "What the *hell*?" I burst out, and the anger in my voice makes them, at last, go quiet. "Why didn't you wake me up?" I direct the question mostly to Hunter. I don't expect Bram to understand. But Hunter is my friend, and he's too sensitive not to have noticed the tension between Alex and Julian.

For a second, Hunter looks guilty. "Come on, Lena. It's no big deal. . . ."

I'm too furious to respond. I grab a flashlight from the shelves and head for the stairs.

"Lena, don't be mad. . . ."

I drown out the rest of Hunter's words by pounding my feet extra hard. Stupid, stupid, stupid.

Outside, the sky is cloudless and glittering with bright points of light. I grip the flashlight tightly in one hand, trying to funnel all my anger through my fingers. I don't know what kind of game Alex is playing, but I'm sick of it.

The woods are still—no sign of Tack or Raven, no sign of anyone. As I stand in the dark, listening, it strikes me that the air is very warm; we must be halfway into April now. Soon summer will be here. For a moment, a flood of memories rides up, surging on the air and the smell of honeysuckle: Hana and I squeezing lemon juice on our hair to lighten it, stealing sodas from the cooler in Uncle William's store and taking them down to Back Cove; clam-pot dinners on the old wooden porch when it was too hot to eat inside; following Gracie's tricycle down the street, wobbling on my bike, trying not to pass her.

The memories bring, as they always do, a deep ache inside me. But I'm used to it by now, and I wait for the feeling to pass, and it does.

I turn on the flashlight and sweep it across the woods. In its pale-yellow beam, the web of trees and bushes looks bleached, surreal. I switch the flashlight off again. If Julian and Alex went off together somewhere, I have very little hope of finding them.

I'm just about to head back inside when I hear a shout. Fear shoots straight through me. Julian's voice.

I plunge into the tangle of growth to my right, pushing toward the sound, swiping with my flashlight to help clear the interlaced path of creepers and pine branches.

After a minute, I burst into a large clearing. For a second I feel disoriented, thinking I've stumbled onto the edge of a large silver lake. Then I see that it's a parking lot. A heap of rubble at one end marks what must have once been a building.

Alex and Julian are standing a few feet away from me, breathing hard, glaring at each other. Julian is holding his hand to his nose, and blood is coming through his fingers.

"Julian!" I start toward him. Julian keeps his eyes locked on Alex.

"I'm okay, Lena," he says. His voice sounds muffled and strange. When I place a hand on his chest, he gently removes it. He smells faintly of alcohol.

I whirl around to face Alex. "What the *hell* did you do?"

His eyes flick to mine for just a second. "It was an accident," he says neutrally. "I swung too high."

"Bullshit," I spit out. I turn back to Julian. "Come on," I say in a low voice. "Let's go inside. We'll clean you up."

He takes his hand away from his nose, then brings his shirt to his face, wiping the remaining blood off his lip. Now his shirt is coated with dark streaks, glistening almost black in the night. "No way," he says, still without looking at me. "We were just getting started. Weren't we, Alex?"

"Julian—" I start to plead. Alex cuts me off.

"Lena's right," he says, his tone deliberately light. "It's late.

We can barely see anything out here. We can pick up again tomorrow."

Julian's voice is also light—but beneath it I can hear a hard edge of anger, a bitterness I don't recognize. "No time like the present."

The silence stretches between them, electric and dangerous.

"Please, Julian." I reach for his wrist and he shakes me off. I turn once again to Alex, willing him to look at me, to break eye contact with Julian. The tension between them is cresting, peaking, like something black and murderous rising underneath the surface of the air. *"Alex."*

Alex looks at me finally, and for a second I see a look of surprise cross his face—as though he hadn't realized I was there, or as though he is only just seeing me. It's followed quickly by an expression of regret, and just like that the tension ebbs away and I can breathe.

"Not tonight," Alex says shortly. Then he turns around and goes to push back into the woods.

In an instant, before I can react or cry out, Julian charges and tackles him from behind. He brings Alex tumbling to the concrete, and all of a sudden they are spitting and grunting, rolling over each other, wrestling each other into the ground. Then I do scream—both their names, and *stop*, and *please*.

Julian is on top of Alex. He draws his fist up; I hear the heavy thud as he swings it down against Alex's cheek. Alex spits at him, gets a hand on Julian's jaw, forcing his head back, pushing Julian up and off. Distantly, I think I hear shouting, but I can't focus on it, can't do anything but scream until my throat is sore. There are lights, too, flashing in my peripheral vision, as though I'm the one getting hit, as though my vision is exploding with bursts of color.

Alex manages to gain the advantage and presses Julian back against the ground. He swings twice, hard, and I hear a horrible crack. Blood is flowing freely across Julian's face now.

"Alex, please!" I'm crying now. I want to pull him off Julian, but fear has frozen me in place, rooted me to the ground.

But either Alex doesn't hear me or he chooses to ignore me. I've never seen him look like this: his face lit up with anger, transfigured in the moonlight to something raw and harsh and terrifying. I can't even scream anymore, can't do anything but cry convulsively, feel nausea build in my throat. Everything is surreal, slow-motion.

Then Tack and Raven burst through the trees on a blaze of sudden light—sweating, out of breath, carrying lanterns— and Raven is shouting and gripping me by the shoulders, and Tack pulls Alex off Julian—"What the *fuck* are you doing?"—and everything begins moving at normal speed again. Julian coughs once and lies back against the ground. I break away from Raven and run toward him, dropping to my knees. I know immediately that his nose is broken. His face is dark with blood, and his eyes are two slits as he struggles to sit up.

"Hey." I put a hand on his chest, swallowing back the spasms in my throat. "Hey, take it easy."

Julian relaxes again. I feel his heart beating up into my palm.

"What *happened*?" Tack is shouting.

Alex is standing a little ways away from where Julian is lying. All his anger is gone; instead he looks shocked, his hands limp at his sides. He's staring at Julian, looking puzzled, as though he doesn't know how Julian got there.

I stand up and move toward him, feeling the anger crawl into my fingers. I wish I could wrap them around his neck, choke him.

"What the hell is the matter with you?" My voice is low. I have to push the words out past the hard lump of anger in my throat.

"I—I'm sorry," Alex whispers. He shakes his head. "I didn't mean . . . I don't know what happened. I'm sorry, Lena."

If he keeps looking at me like that—pleading, willing me to understand—I know I'll start to forgive him.

"Lena." He takes a step toward me, and I take a step back. For a moment we stand there; I can feel the pressure of his eyes on me, and the pressure, too, of his guilt. But I won't look at him. I can't.

"I'm sorry," he repeats again, too low for Raven and Tack to hear. "I'm sorry for everything."

Then he turns and pushes back into the woods, and he's gone.

Hana

Out of the shifting liquid of my sleep, the dream rises and takes shape:

Lena's face.

Lena's face, floating out of the shadow. No. Not shadow. She is pushing up from the ash, from a deep drift of cinders and char. Her mouth is open. Her eyes are closed.

She is screaming.

Hana. She is screaming for me. The ash is tumbling like sand into her open mouth, and I know she will soon be buried again, forced into silence, back into the dark. And I know, too, that I have no chance of reaching her—no hope of saving her at all.

Hana, she screams, while I stand motionless.

Forgive me, I say.

Hana, help.

Forgive me, Lena.

"Hana!"

My mother is standing in the doorway. I sit up, bewildered and terrified, Lena's voice echoing in my mind. I dreamed. I am not supposed to dream.

"What's wrong?" She's silhouetted in the doorway; behind her, I can just make out the small night-light outside my bathroom. "Are you sick?"

"I'm fine." I pass a hand across my forehead. It comes away wet. I'm sweating.

"Are you sure?" She moves as though to come into the room, but at the last second remains in the doorway. "You cried out."

"I'm sure," I say. And then, because she seems to be expecting more: "Nerves, I guess, about the wedding."

"There's nothing at all to be nervous about," she says, sounding annoyed. "Everything's under control. It will all work beautifully."

I know she is talking about more than the ceremony itself. She means the marriage in general: It has been tabulated and coordinated—made to work beautifully, engineered for efficiency and perfection.

My mother sighs. "Try and get some sleep," she says. "We're going to a church at the labs with the Hargroves at nine thirty.

245

The final dress fitting's at eleven. *And* there's the interview for *House and Home*."

"Good night, Mom," I say, and she withdraws without closing the door. Privacy means less to us than it once did: another unanticipated benefit, or side effect, of the cure. Fewer secrets.

At least, fewer secrets in *most* cases.

I go to the bathroom and splash water on my face. Although the fan is on, I still feel overheated. For a second, when I look into the mirror, I can almost see Lena's face staring at me from behind my eyes—a memory, a vision of a buried past.

Blink.

She's gone.

Lena

Alex is not back when Raven, Tack, Julian, and I return to the safe house. Julian has revived and has insisted he is fine to walk, but Tack keeps an arm around his shoulders anyway. Julian is unsteady on his feet and still bleeding freely. As soon as we reach the safe house, Bram and Hunter babble excitedly about what happened until I give them the dirtiest look I can. Coral comes to the doorway, blinking sleepily, one arm around her stomach.

Alex is not back by the time we've cleaned Julian off—"Broken," he says with a wince, in a thick voice, when Raven skates a finger over the bridge of his nose—and he is not back by the time we all, finally, lie down in our cots with our thin blankets, and even Julian manages to sleep, breathing noisily through his mouth.

By the time we wake up, Alex has already come and gone. His belongings are missing, as well as a jug of water and one of the knives.

He has left nothing except for a note, which I find neatly folded under one of my sneakers.

The Story of Solomon is the only way I know how to explain.

And then, in smaller letters:

Forgive me.

Hana

Thirteen days until the wedding. The presents have already begun to trickle in: soup bowls and salad tongs, crystal vases, mountains of white linen, monogrammed towels, and things I've had no name for before now: ramekins; zesters; pestles. This is the language of married, adult life, and it is completely foreign to me.

Twelve days.

I sit and write thank-you cards in front of the television. My father leaves at least one TV on practically all the time now. I wonder if this is partly because he wants to prove that we can afford to waste electricity.

For what seems like the tenth time today, Fred steps onto

the screen. His face is tinged orange with foundation. The sound is muted, but I know what he is saying. The news has been broadcasting and rebroadcasting the announcement about the Department of Energy and Power, and Fred's plans for Black Night.

On the night of our wedding, one-third of the families in Portland—anyone suspected of sympathizing or resisting—will be plunged into darkness.

The lights burn bright for those who obey; the others will live in shadow all the days of their lives (*The Book of Shhh*, Psalm 17). Fred used that quote in his speech.

Thank you for the lace-edged linen napkins. They are exactly what I would have chosen for myself.

Thank you for the crystal sugar bowl. It will look perfect on the dining room table.

The doorbell rings. I hear my mother head to the door, and the murmur of muffled voices. A moment later, she comes into the room, red-faced, agitated.

"Fred," she says as he steps into the room behind her.

"Thank you, Evelyn," he says in a clipped voice, and she takes it as a cue to leave us. She closes the door behind her.

"Hi." I climb to my feet, wishing I were wearing something other than an old T-shirt and ratty shorts. Fred is dressed in dark jeans and a white button-down, sleeves rolled to the elbows. I feel his eyes sweep over me, absorbing my messy hair, the rip in the hem of my shorts, the fact that I am wearing no makeup. "I wasn't expecting you."

He doesn't say anything. There are two Freds looking at me now, screen-Fred and the real thing. Screen-Fred is smiling, leaning forward, easy and relaxed. The real Fred stands stiffly, glaring at me.

"Is—is something wrong?" I say after the silence has extended several seconds. I cross the room to the TV and turn it off, partly so I don't have to watch Fred watching me, and partly because I can't stand the double vision.

When I turn around again, I suck in a quick breath. Fred has moved closer, silently, and he is now standing a mere six inches away, face white and furious. I have never seen him look this way before.

"What—?" I start to say, but he cuts me off.

"What the hell is this?" He reaches into his jacket and pulls out a folded manila envelope, throws it down on the glass coffee table. The motion sends several photographs fanning out of the envelope and onto the table.

There I am, frozen, preserved in a camera lens: *Click*. Walking, head down, next to a dilapidated house—the Tiddles' house in Deering Highlands—empty backpack looped over one shoulder. *Click*. From behind: pushing through a blur of green growth, reaching up to swat away a low-hanging branch. *Click*. Turning, surprised, scanning the woods behind me, looking for a source of the sound, the soft rustle of movement, the click.

"Do you want to explain to me," Fred says coldly, "what you were doing in Deering Highlands on Saturday?"

251

A flash of anger goes through me, and also fear. *He knows.* "You're having me followed?"

"Don't flatter yourself, Hana," he says in the same flat tone. "Hugo Bradley's a friend of mine. He works for the *Daily*. He was on assignment, and he saw you going into the Highlands. Naturally, he was curious." His eyes have darkened. They're the color of wet concrete. "What were you doing?"

"Nothing," I say quickly. "I was exploring."

"Exploring." Fred practically spits the word. "Do you understand, Hana, that the Highlands is a condemned neighborhood? Do you have any idea what kind of people live there? Criminals. Infected people. Sympathizers and rebels. They nest in those buildings like cockroaches."

"I wasn't doing anything," I insist. I wish he wouldn't stand so close. I'm suddenly paranoid he'll be able to *smell* the fear, the lies, the way dogs can.

"You were *there*," Fred says. "That's bad enough." Although we're separated by only a few inches, he moves forward. I unconsciously step backward, bumping into the television console behind me. "I've just gone on record saying we won't tolerate any more civil disobedience. Do you know how bad it would look if people found out my pair was sneaking around in Deering Highlands?" Once again, he inches forward. Now I have nowhere to go, and force myself to stay very still. He narrows his eyes. "But maybe that was the whole point. You're trying to embarrass me. Mess with my plans. Make me seem like an idiot."

The edge of the TV console is digging into the back of my thighs. "I hate to break it to you, Fred," I say, "but not everything I do is about you. In fact, most things I do are about *me*."

"Cute," he says.

For a second we stand there, staring at each other. The stupidest thought comes to me: When Fred and I were getting paired, where was this, this hard, cold center, listed among his Characteristics and Qualities?

Fred draws away a few inches, and I allow myself to exhale.

"Things will be very bad for you if you go back there," he says.

I force myself to meet his gaze. "Is that a warning or a threat?"

"It's a promise." His mouth quirks into a small smile. "If you're not with me, you're against me. And tolerance is not one of my virtues. Cassie would tell you that, but I'm afraid she doesn't get much of an audience these days." He barks a laugh.

"What—what do you mean?" I wish I could keep the tremor from my voice.

He narrows his eyes. I hold my breath. For a second I think he'll admit it—what he did to her, where she is.

But he simply says, "I won't have you ruin what I've worked so hard to achieve. You will listen to me."

"I'm your pair," I say. "Not your dog."

It happens lightning-quick. He closes the distance between us, and his hand is around my throat, and the breath is crushed out of me. Panic, heavy and black, sits in my chest. Can't breathe.

Fred's eyes, stony and impenetrable, swim in my vision. "You're right," he says. He is totally calm now as he tightens his fingers around my throat. My vision shrinks to a single point: those eyes. For a second, everything goes dark—*blink*—and then he is there again, staring at me, speaking in that lullaby-voice. "You aren't my dog. But you will still learn to sit when I tell you. You will still learn to obey."

"Hello? Anyone here?"

The voice echoes from the foyer. Instantly Fred releases me. I suck in a breath, then start to cough. My eyes are stinging. My lungs stutter in my chest, trying to suck in air.

"Hello?"

The door swings open and Debbie Sayer, my mother's hairdresser, bursts into the room. "Oh!" she says, and stops. Her face reddens when she sees Fred and me. "Mayor Hargrove," she says. "I didn't mean to interrupt. . . ."

"You didn't interrupt," Fred says. "I was on my way out."

"We had an appointment," Debbie adds uncertainly. She looks at me. I swipe a hand across my eyes; it comes away damp. "We were going to talk styles for the wedding. . . . I didn't get the time wrong, did I?"

The wedding: It seems absurd now, a bad joke. This is my promised path: with this monster, who can smile in one moment and squeeze my throat in the next. I feel tears pushing at my eyes again and press my palms against my eyelids, willing them back.

"No." My throat is raw. "You're right."

"Are you okay?" Debbie asks me.

"Hana suffers from allergies," Fred answers smoothly, before I've had a chance to respond. "I've told her a hundred times to get a prescription. . . ." He reaches out and takes my hand, squeezes my fingers—too hard, but not so much that Debbie will notice. "She's very stubborn."

He withdraws his hand. I bring my aching fingers behind my back, flexing them, still fighting the urge to cry. "I'll see you tomorrow," Fred says, directing a smile toward me. "You haven't forgotten about the cocktail party, have you?"

"I haven't forgotten," I say, refusing to look at him.

"Good." He crosses the room. In the hall, I hear him begin to whistle.

Debbie begins chattering the moment he is out of earshot. "You're so lucky. Henry—that's my pair, you know—looks as though he's had his face squashed by a rock." She laughs. "He's a good match for me, though. We're big supporters of your husband—or soon-to-be, I guess we should say. Big supporters."

She places a blow dryer, two brushes, and a translucent bag of pins side by side on top of the thank-you cards and the photographs, which she has not noticed. "You know, Henry met your husband just recently at a fund-raiser. *Where* is my hair spray?"

I close my eyes. Maybe this is all a dream—Debbie, the wedding, Fred. Maybe I'll wake up, and it will be last summer, or two summers ago, or five: before any of this was real.

"I knew he would make a great mayor. Didn't mind Hargrove Senior, and I'm sure he did his best, but if you want my opinion, he was just a little soft. He actually wanted the Crypts *torn apart*. . . ." She shakes her head. "I say, bury them there and let them rot."

I snap suddenly to attention. "What?"

She descends on me with her hairbrush, tugging and pulling. "Don't get me wrong—I *liked* Hargrove Senior. But I think he had the wrong idea about certain kinds of people."

"No, no." I swallow. "What did you say after that?"

She tilts my chin forcefully up toward the light and examines me. "Well, I think they should be left to rot in the Crypts—criminals, I mean, and sick people." She begins looping hair, experimenting with the way it falls.

Stupid. I've been so stupid.

"And then you think of the way he *died*." Fred's father died January 12, the day of the Incidents, after the bombs went off in the Crypts. The whole eastern facade was blown clean away; prisoners suddenly found themselves in cells with no walls, and yards with no fences. There was a mass insurrection; Fred's father arrived with the police, and died trying to restore order.

My ideas come hard and fast, like a thick snow, building a white wall I can't get above or around.

Bluebeard kept a locked room, a secret space where he stashed his wives. . . . Locked doors, heavy bolts, women rotting in stone prisons . . .

Possible. It's possible. It fits. It would explain the note, and why she wasn't in CORE's system. She might have been invalidated. Some prisoners are. Their identities, their histories, their whole lives are erased. *Poof.* A single keystroke, a metal door sliding shut, and it's as though they never existed.

Debbie prattles on. "Good riddance, I say, and they should be grateful we don't just shoot 'em on the spot. Did you hear about what happened in Waterbury?" She laughs, a sound too loud for the quiet room. Small bursts of pain fire off in my head.

On Saturday morning, in just a single hour, an enormous camp of resisters outside Waterbury was eradicated. Only a handful of our soldiers were injured.

Debbie grows serious again. "You know what? I think the lighting's better upstairs, in your mom's room. Don't you think?"

I find myself agreeing, and before I know it I am also moving. I float up the stairs in front of her. I lead the way to my mother's bedroom as though I am drifting, or dreaming, or dead.

Lena

A dull feeling settles over us after Alex's departure. He was causing problems, but he was still one of us, one of the group, and I think everyone—except for Julian—feels the loss.

I walk around in a near daze. Despite everything, I took comfort in his presence, in seeing him, in knowing he was safe. Now that he has gone off on his own, who knows what will happen to him? He is no longer mine to lose, but the grief is there, a gnawing sense of disbelief.

Coral is pale, and silent, and wide-eyed. She doesn't cry. She doesn't eat much, either.

Tack and Hunter talked about going after him, but Raven

quickly made them see the foolishness of the idea. He no doubt had many hours' head start, and a single person, moving rapidly on foot, is even harder to track than a group. They'd be wasting time, resources, and energy.

There's nothing we can do, she said, careful to avoid looking at me, *but let him go.*

So we do. Suddenly there is no amount of lanterns that can chase away the shadows that often fall between us, the shades of other people and other lives lost to the Wilds, to this struggle, to the world split in two. I can't help but think of the camp, and of Pippa, and the line of soldiers we saw threading through the woods.

Pippa said we could expect the contacts from Resistance within three days, but the third day winds slowly into evening with no sign of anyone.

Each day, we get a little more stir-crazy. It's not anxiety, exactly. We have enough food and, now that Tack and Hunter have found a stream nearby, enough water. Spring is here: The animals are out, and we have begun trapping successfully.

But we are completely cut off—from news of what has happened in Waterbury and what is happening in the rest of the country. It's far too easy to imagine, as another morning washes like a gentle wave over the old, towering oaks, that we are the only people left in the world.

I can no longer bear to be inside, underground. Each day, after whatever lunch we can scrounge up, I pick a direction and start walking, trying not to think about Alex and about his message to me, and usually finding that I can think of nothing else.

Today, I go east. It's one of my favorite times of day: that perfect in-between moment when the light has a liquid feel, like a slow pour of syrup. Still, I can't shake loose the knot of unhappiness in my chest. I can't shake loose the idea that the rest of our lives might simply look like this: this running, and hiding, and losing the things we love, and burrowing underground, and scavenging for food and water.

There will be no turn in the tide. We will never march back into the cities, triumphant, crying out our victory in the streets. We will simply eke out a living here until there is no living to be eked.

The Story of Solomon. Strange that Alex picked that story, of all the stories in *The Book of Shhh*, when it was the one that so consumed me after I found out he was alive. Could he have known, somehow? Could he have known that I felt just like that poor, severed baby in the story?

Was he trying to tell me that he felt the same way?

No. He told me that our past together, and what we shared, was dead. He told me he never loved me.

I keep pushing through the woods, barely paying attention to where I'm going. The questions in my head are like a strong tide, dragging me back over and over to the same places.

The Story of Solomon. A king's judgment. A baby cleaved in two and a stain of blood seeping into the floor . . .

At a certain point, I realize I have no idea how long I've

been walking, or how far I've ended up from the safe house. I haven't been paying attention to the landscape as I go, either—a rookie's error. Grandpa, one of the oldest Invalids at the homestead near Rochester, used to tell stories of sprites that supposedly lived in the Wilds, switching the location of trees and rocks and rivers, just to confuse people. None of us actually believed in that stuff, but the message was true enough: The Wilds is a mess, a shifting maze, and will turn you around in circles.

I begin retracing my steps, looking for places my heel has left imprints in the mud, scanning for signs of trampled underbrush. I force all thoughts of Alex out of my head. It's too easy to get lost in the wilderness; if you are not careful, you will be swallowed up in it forever.

I see a flash of sunlight between the trees: the stream. I drew water just yesterday, and should be able to navigate back from here. But first, a quick wash. By this point, I'm sweating.

I push through the last bit of undergrowth, onto a wide bank of sun-bleached grass and flat stone.

I stop.

Someone else is already here: a woman, crouching, forty feet down from me on the opposite bank, her hands submerged in the water. Her head is down, and all I can see is a tangle of gray hair, streaked with white. For a second I think she might be a regulator, or a soldier, but even from a distance I can tell her clothes are not standard-issue. The backpack next to her is patched and old; her tank top is stained with yellow rings of sweat.

A man hidden from view calls out something unintelligible, and she responds, without looking up, "Just another minute."

My body goes tight and still. I know that voice.

She draws a bit of fabric out of the water, a piece of clothing she has been washing, and straightens up. As she does, my breath stops. She holds the cloth taut between two hands and winds it rapidly around itself, then unwinds it just as quickly, sending a pinwheel of water arching across the bank.

And I am suddenly five years old again, standing in our laundry room in Portland, listening to the throaty gurgle of soapy water draining slowly from the sink, watching her do the same thing with our shirts, our underwear; watching the stippling of water across the tile walls; watching her turn and clip, clip, our clothing to the lines crisscrossing our ceiling, and then turn again, smiling at me, humming to herself. . . .

Lavender soap. Bleach. T-shirts dripping onto the floor. It is now. I am there.

She is here.

She spots me and freezes. For a second she doesn't say anything, and I have time to notice how different she is from my memory of her. She is so much harder now, her face so sharp with angles and lines. But underneath it I detect another face, like an image hovering just underneath the surface of water: the laughing mouth and round, high cheeks, the sparkling eyes.

Finally she says, "Lena."

I inhale. I open my mouth.

I say, "Mom."

For an interminable minute we just stand there, staring at each other, as the past and present continue to converge and then separate: my mother now, my mother then.

She starts to say something. Just then two men come crashing out of the woods, mid-conversation. As soon as they spot me, they raise their rifles.

"Wait," my mother says sharply, raising a hand. "She's with us."

I'm not breathing. I exhale as the men lower their guns. My mother continues to stare at me—silent, amazed, and something else. Afraid?

"Who are you?" one of the men says. He has brilliant red hair, streaked with white. He looks like an enormous marmalade cat. "Who are you with?"

"My name is Lena." Miraculously, my voice doesn't tremble. My mother flinches. She always used to call me Magdalena, and hated the abbreviation. I wonder whether it still bothers her after all this time. "I came from Waterbury with some others."

I wait for my mother to give some indication that we know each other—that I'm her *daughter*—but she doesn't. She exchanges a look with her two companions. "Are you with Pippa?" the red-haired man says.

I shake my head. "Pippa stayed," I say. "She directed us to

come here, to the safe house. She told us the resistance would be coming."

The other man, who is brown and wiry, laughs shortly and shoulders his rifle. "You're looking at it," he says. "I'm Cap. This is Max"—he jerks his thumb toward the marmalade-cat man—"and this is Bee." He inclines his head toward my mother.

Bee. My mother's name is Annabel. This woman's name is Bee. My mother is always moving. My mother had soft hands that smelled like soap, and a smile like the first bit of sunlight creeping over a trimmed lawn.

I do not know who this woman is.

"Are you heading back to the safe house?" Cap asks.

"Yes," I manage to say.

"We'll follow you," he says with a half bow that, given our surroundings, seems more than a little ironic. I can feel my mother watching me again, but as soon as I look at her, she averts her eyes.

We walk in near silence back to the safe house, although Max and Cap exchange a few scattered words of conversation, mostly coded talk I don't understand. My mother—Annabel, Bee—is quiet. As we near the safe house, I find myself unconsciously slowing, desperate to extend the walk, willing my mother to say something, to acknowledge me.

But all too soon we have reached the splintered over-structure, and the stairway leading underground. I hang back, allowing Max and Cap to pass down the stairs first. I'm hoping my mother will take the hint too and delay for a moment, but she just follows Cap underground.

"Thanks," she says softly as she passes me.

Thanks.

I can't even be angry. I'm too shocked, too dazed by her sudden appearance: this mirage-woman with the face of my mother. My body feels hollow, my hands and feet huge, balloonlike, as though they belong to someone else. I watch the hands feel their way down the wall, watch the feet go *clomp-clomp-clomp* down the stairs.

For a second I stand at the base of the stairwell, disoriented. In my absence, everyone has returned. Tack and Hunter talk over each other, firing off questions; Julian rises from a chair as soon as he sees me; Raven bustles around the room, organizing, ordering people around.

And in the middle of it, my mother—removing her pack, taking a chair, moving with unconscious grace. Everyone else breaks apart into flutter and flurry, like moths circling a flame, undifferentiated blurs against the light. Even the room looks different now that she's inside it.

This must be a dream. It has to be. A dream of my mother who is not really my mother, but someone else.

"Hey, Lena." Julian cups my chin in his hands and leans down to give me a kiss. His eyes are still swollen and ringed with purple. I kiss him back automatically. "You okay?" He pulls away from me, and I purposely avoid his eyes.

"I'm okay," I tell him. "I'll explain later." There's a bubble of air caught in my chest, making it hard to breathe or speak.

He doesn't know. Nobody knows, except for Raven and maybe Tack. They've worked with Bee before.

Now my mother won't look at me at all. She accepts a cup of water from Raven and begins to drink. And just that—that small motion—makes anger uncoil inside me.

"I shot a deer today," Julian is saying. "Tack spotted it halfway across the clearing. I didn't think I had a chance—"

"Good for you," I cut him off. "You pulled a trigger."

Julian looks hurt. I've been horrible to him for days now. This is the problem: Take away the cure, and the primers, and the codes, and you are left with no rules to follow. Love comes only in flashes.

"It's food, Lena," he says quietly. "Didn't you always tell me that this wasn't a game? I'm playing for real—for keeps." He pauses. "To stay." He emphasizes the last part, and I know that he is thinking of Alex, and then I can't help but think of him too.

I need to keep moving, find my balance, get away from the stifling room.

"Lena." Raven is at my side. "Help me get some food on, will you?"

This is Raven's rule: Stay busy. Go through the motions. Stand up.

Open a can. Pull water.

Do something.

I follow her automatically to the sink.

"Any news from Waterbury?" Tack asks.

For a moment there is silence. My mother is the one to speak.

"Gone," she says simply.

Raven accidentally slices too hard through a strip of dried meat, and pulls her finger away, gasping, sucking it in her mouth.

"What do you mean, *gone*?" Tack's voice is sharp.

"Wiped out." This time Cap speaks up. "Mowed down."

"Oh my God." Hunter thuds heavily into a chair. Julian is standing perfectly rigid, taut, hands clenched; Tack's face has turned stony. My mother—the woman who was my mother—sits with her hands folded on her lap, motionless, expressionless. Only Raven continues moving, wrapping a kitchen towel around her cut finger, sawing through the dried meat, back and forth, back and forth.

"So what now?" Julian asks, voice tight.

My mother looks up. Something old and deep flexes inside me. Her eyes are still the vivid blue I remember, still unchanged, like a sky to tumble into. Like Julian's eyes.

"We have to move," she says. "Give support where it can do good. The resistance is still gathering strength, gathering *people*—"

"What about Pippa?" Hunter bursts out. "Pippa said to wait for her. She said—"

"*Hunter,*" Tack says. "You heard what Cap said." He lowers his voice. "Wiped out."

There's another moment of heavy silence. I see a muscle twitch in my mother's jaw—a new tic—and she turns away, so I can see the faded green number tattooed along her neck, just beneath the vicious spate of angry scars, the products of all her failed procedures. I think about the years she spent in her tiny, windowless cell in the Crypts, chipping away at the walls with the metal pendant my father had given her, carving the word *Love* endlessly over the stone. And somehow, now, after less than a year of freedom, she has entered the resistance. More than that. She is at its center.

I don't know this woman at all; I don't know how she became who she is, or when her jaw began to twitch and her hair began to gray, and she began to pull a veil over her eyes, and avoid the gaze of her daughter.

"So where do we go?" Raven asks.

Max and Cap exchange a look. "There's something stirring up north," Max says. "In Portland."

"Portland?" I parrot the word without meaning to speak. My mother glances up at me, and I think she looks afraid. Then she drops her eyes.

"That's where you come from, right?" Raven asks me.

I lean back against the sink, close my eyes for a second, and have a vision of my mother on the beach, running ahead of me, laughing, kicking up dark sand, a loose green tunic dress snapping around her ankles. I open my eyes again quickly and manage to nod.

"I can't go back there."

The words come out with more force than I intended, and everyone turns to look at me.

"If we go anywhere, we all go together," Raven says.

"There's a big underground in Portland," Max says. "The network is growing—has been since the Incidents. That was only the beginning. What's going to happen next . . ." He shakes his head, eyes bright. "It's going to be big."

"I can't," I repeat. "And I won't." Memories are coming fast: Hana running next to me by Back Cove, our sneakers squelching in the mud; fireworks over the bay on the Fourth of July, sending tentacles of light over the water; Alex and me lying, laughing, on the blanket at 37 Brooks; Grace shivering next to me in the bedroom at Aunt Carol's, wrapping her thin arms around my waist, her smell of grape bubblegum. Layers and layers of memories, a life I have tried to bury and kill—a past that was dead, like Raven always said—suddenly surging, threatening to pull me under.

And with the memories comes the guilt, another feeling I have tried so hard to bury. I left them: Hana and Grace, and Alex, too. I left them and I ran, and I didn't look back.

"It's not your decision," Tack says.

Raven says, "Don't be a baby, Lena."

Normally, I back down when Raven and Tack gang up on me. But not today. I push the guilt down under a heavy fist of anger. Everyone is staring at me, but I can feel my mother's eyes like a burn—her blank curiosity, as though I'm a specimen in a museum, some ancient, foreign tool whose purpose she's trying to decipher.

"I won't." I slam down the can opener, too hard, on the counter.

"What's the matter with you?" Raven says in a low voice. But it has gone so quiet in the room, I'm sure that everyone hears.

My throat is so tight I can hardly swallow. I realize, all of a sudden, that I am on the verge of tears. "Ask her," I manage to say, jerking my chin toward the woman who calls herself Bee.

There's another moment of silence. All the eyes turn on my mother now. At least she looks guilty—she knows she's a fraud, this woman who wants to lead a revolution for love and doesn't even acknowledge her own daughter.

Just then Bram comes sailing down the stairs, whistling. He's holding a large knife, which is wet with blood—he must have been cutting up the deer. His T-shirt is streaked with it too. He stops when he sees us standing there in silence.

"What's up?" he says. "What'd I miss?" Then, as he takes in my mom, Cap, and Max: "Who are you?"

The sight of all that blood makes my stomach heave. We're killers, all of us: We kill our lives, our past selves, the things that mattered. We bury them under slogans and excuses. Before I can begin crying, I wrench away from the sink and push past Bram so roughly, he lets out a yelp of surprise. I pound up the stairs and throw myself outside, into the open air and the warm afternoon and the throaty sound of the woods opening up to spring.

But even outside I feel claustrophobic. There's no place to go. There's no way to escape the crushing sense of loss, the endless exhaustion of time sawing away at the people and things that I've loved.

Hana, Grace, Alex, my mother, the sea-spray salt-air Portland mornings and the distant cries of the wheeling seagulls—all of them broken, splintered, lodged somewhere deep, impossible to shake loose.

Maybe, after all, they were right about the cure. I am no happier than I was when I believed that love was a disease. In many ways, I am less happy.

I get only a few minutes away from the safe house before I stop fighting the pressure behind my eyes. My first cries are convulsions, and bring up the taste of bile. I let go completely. I sink onto the tangle of undergrowth and soft moss, put my head between my legs, and sob until I can't breathe, until I'm spitting up on the leaves between my legs. I cry for everything I abandoned and because I, too, have been left behind—by Alex, by my mom, by time that has cut through our worlds and separated us.

I hear footsteps behind me and know, without turning around, that it will be Raven. "Go away," I say. My voice sounds thick. I drag the back of my hand across my cheeks and nose.

But it's my mother who responds. "You're angry at me," she says.

I stop crying at once. My whole body goes cold and still. She squats down beside me, and even though I'm careful not to look up, not to look at her at all, I can *feel* her, can smell the sweat from her skin and hear the ragged pattern of her breathing.

"You're angry at me," she repeats, and her voice hitches

a little. "You think I don't care."

Her voice is the same. For years I used to imagine that voice lilting over those forbidden words: *I love you. Remember. They cannot take it.* Her last words to me before she went away.

She shuffles forward and squats next to me. She hesitates, then reaches out and places her palm against my cheek, and turns my head toward hers so I'm forced to look at her. I can feel the calluses on her fingers.

In her eyes, I see myself reflected in miniature, and I tunnel back to a time before she left, before I believed she was gone forever, when her eyes welcomed me into every day and shepherded me, every night, into sleep.

"You turned out even more beautiful than I'd imagined," she whispers. She, too, is crying.

The hard casement inside me breaks.

"Why?" is the only word that comes. Without intending to or even thinking about it, I allow her to draw me against her chest, let her wrap her arms around me. I cry into the space between her collarbones, inhaling the still-familiar smell of her skin.

There are so many things I need to ask her: *What happened to you in the Crypts? How could you let them take you away? Where did you go?* But all I can say is: "Why didn't you come for me? After all those years—all that time—why didn't you come?" Then I can't speak at all; my sobs become shudders.

"Shh." She presses her lips to my forehead, strokes my hair, just like she used to when I was a child. I am a baby once again in her arms—helpless and needy. "I'm here now."

She rubs my back while I cry. Slowly, I feel the darkness drain out of me, as though pulled away by the motion of her hand. Finally I can breathe again. My eyes are burning, and my throat feels raw and sore. I draw away from her, wiping my eyes with the heel of my hand, not even caring that my nose is running. I'm suddenly exhausted—too tired to be hurt, too tired to be angry. I want to sleep, and sleep.

"I never stopped thinking about you," my mother says. "I thought of you every day—you and Rachel."

"Rachel was cured," I say. The exhaustion is a heaviness; it blankets out every feeling. "She got paired and she left. And you let me think you were dead. I'd still think you were dead if—" *If it weren't for Alex,* I think, but don't say. Of course my mother doesn't know the story of Alex. She knows none of my stories.

My mother looks away. For a second I think she will begin to cry again. But she doesn't. "When I was in that place away, thinking of you—my two beautiful girls—was the only thing that kept me going. It was the only thing that kept me sane." Her voice holds an edge, an undercurrent of anger, and I think of visiting the Crypts with Alex: the stifling darkness and echoing, inhuman cries; the smell of Ward Six, the cells like cages.

I persist, stubbornly: "It was hard for me, too. I had no one. And you could have come for me after you escaped. You could have told me . . ." My voice breaks, and I swallow. "After you found me at Salvage—we were touching, you could have shown me your face, you could have said something. . . ."

"Lena." My mom reaches out to touch my face again, but this time she sees me stiffen, and she drops her hand with a sigh. "Did you ever read the Book of Lamentations? Did you read about Mary Magdalene and Joseph? Did you ever wonder why I named you what I did?"

"I read it." I read the Book of Lamentations at least a dozen times at least; it is the chapter of *The Book of Shhh* I know the best. I looked for clues, for secret signs from my mother, for whispers from the dead.

The Book of Lamentations is a story of love. More than that: It's a story of sacrifice.

"I just wanted you to be safe," my mother says. "Do you understand that? Safe, and happy. Anything I could do . . . even if it meant I couldn't be with you . . ."

Her voice gets thick and I have to look away from her, to stop the grief from welling up once again. My mother aged in a small square room with only a bit of eked-out hope, words scratched on the walls day by day, to keep her going.

"If I hadn't believed, if I hadn't been able to trust that . . . There were many times I thought about . . ." She trails off.

There's no need for her to finish her sentence. I understand what she means: There were times she wanted to die.

I remember I used to imagine her sometimes standing on the edge of a cliff, coat billowing behind her. I would *see* her. For one second, she would always remain suspended in the air, hovering, like a vision of an angel. But always, even in my head, the cliff disappeared, and I would see her falling. I wonder if, in some way, she was reaching out to me through the echoes of space on those nights—whether I could sense her.

For a while we let silence stretch between us. I dry the moisture from my face with my sleeve. Then I stand up. She stands with me. I'm amazed, as I was when I realized that she had been the one to rescue me from Salvage, that we are roughly the same height.

"So what now?" I say. "Are you taking off again?"

"I'll go where the resistance needs me," she says.

I look away from her. "So you *are* leaving," I say, feeling a dull weight settle in my stomach. Of course. That's what people do in a disordered world, a world of freedom and choice: They leave when they want. They disappear, they come back, they leave again. And you are left to pick up the pieces on your own.

A free world is also a world of fracture, just like *The Book of Shhh* warned us. There is more truth in Zombieland than I wanted to believe.

The wind blows my mother's hair across her forehead. She twists it back behind her ear, a gesture I remember from years ago. "I need to make sure that what happened to me—what I was made to give up—doesn't happen again to anyone." She finds my eyes, forcing me to look at her. "But I don't want to leave," she adds quietly. "I—I'd like to know you now, Magdalena."

I cross my arms and shrug, trying to find some of the hardness I have built during my time in the Wilds. "I don't even know where to begin," I say.

She spreads her hands, a gesture of submission. "Me neither. But we can, I think. *I* can, if you'll let me." She cracks a small smile. "You're part of the resistance too, you know. This is what we do: We fight for what matters to us. Right?"

I meet her eyes. They are the clear blue of the sky stretched high above the trees, a ceiling of color. I remember: Portland beaches, kite flying, macaroni salads, summertime picnics, my mother's hands, a lullaby-voice singing me to sleep.

"Right," I say.

We walk back, together, to the safe house.

Hana

The Crypts looks different from the way I remember it. I've been here only once before, on a school trip in third grade. Weirdly, I don't remember anything about the actual visit, only that Jen Finnegan threw up in the bus afterward, and the air stank like tuna fish, even after the bus driver opened all the windows.

The Crypts is situated at the northern border and backs up onto the Wilds and the Presumpscot River. That's why so many prisoners were able to escape during the Incidents. The exploding shrapnel took out huge chunks of the border wall; the inmates who made it out of their cells just ran straight into the Wilds.

After the Incidents, the Crypts was rebuilt, and a new, modern wing was attached. The Crypts was always monstrously ugly, but now it is worse than ever: The steel-and-cement addition runs up awkwardly against the old building, made of blackened stone, with its hundreds of tiny barred windows. It's a sunny day, and beyond the high roof, the sky is a vivid blue. The whole scene feels off to me: This is a place that should never see sunlight.

For a minute, I stand outside the gates, wondering whether I should turn around. I came by municipal bus, which took me all the way from downtown, emptying as we got closer and closer to this, its final destination. At last, I shared the bus with only the driver and a large, heavily made-up woman wearing nurse's scrubs. As the bus rolled away, kicking up sprays of mud and exhaust, for a wild second I thought of running after it.

But I have to know. I must.

So I follow the nurse as she shuffles toward the guard hut just outside the gates and flashes her ID card. The guard's eyes flick to me, and I wordlessly pass him a piece of paper.

He scans the photocopy. "Eleanor?"

I nod. I don't trust myself to speak. In the photocopy, it's impossible to make out many of her features, or distinguish the dishwater color of her hair. But if he looks too closely, he'll see the details don't line up: the height, the eye color.

Fortunately, he doesn't. "What happened to the original?"

"Went through the dryer," I reply promptly. "I had to apply to SVS for a replacement."

He turns his gaze back to the photocopy. I hope he can't hear my heart, which is beating loud and hard.

Getting the photocopy was no problem. A quick phone call to Mrs. Hargrove this morning, a proposed cup of tea, a twenty-minute chat, an expressed desire to use the bathroom—and then a two-minute detour to Fred's study instead. I couldn't risk being identified as Fred's future wife. If Cassie *is* here, it's possible that some of the wardens know Fred, too. And if Fred finds out I've been poking around the Crypts . . .

He has already told me I must not ask questions.

"Business?"

"Just . . . visiting."

The guard grunts. He hands back my paper and waves me on as the gates begin to shudder open. "Check in at the visitors' desk," he grunts. The nurse gives me a curious look before scuttling ahead of me across the yard. I can't imagine there are many visitors here.

That's the whole point. Lock them up and let them rot.

I cross the yard and pass through a heavy, bolted steel door, and find myself in a claustrophobic entrance hall, dominated by a metal detector and several massive guards. By the time I get through the door, the nurse has already unloaded her purse onto the conveyor belt and is standing with her arms and legs spread as a guard moves over her body with a wand, checking her for weapons. She hardly seems to notice; she's busy chatting with the woman manning the check-in desk to the right, which is situated behind bulletproof glass.

"Same as always," she's saying. "The baby kept me up all night. I'm telling you, if 2426 gives me more problems today, I'll put his ass on lockdown."

"Amen," says the woman behind the desk. Then she turns her eyes to me. "ID?"

We repeat the procedure all over again: I slide the paper through the gap in the window, explain that the original was ruined.

"How can I help you?" she asks.

I've been crafting my story carefully for the past twenty-four hours, but still I find the words come haltingly. "I—I'm here to visit my aunt."

"You know what ward she's in?"

I shake my head. "No, see . . . I didn't even know she was here. I mean, I just found out. For most of my life, I thought she was dead." The woman shows no reaction to this statement. "Name?"

"Cassandra. Cassandra O'Donnell." I squeeze my fists and focus on the pain running through my palms as she keys the name into her computer. I'm not sure whether I'm hoping her name will come up or not.

The woman shakes her head. She has watery blue eyes and a mass of frizzy blond hair, which in this light appears to be the same dull gray as the walls. "Nothing here. You got an intake month?"

How many years ago did Cassie disappear? I remember overhearing at Fred's inauguration that he has been without a pair for three years.

I hazard a guess. "January or February. Three years ago."

She sighs and hauls herself out of her chair. "Only went computerized last year." She passes out of view, then returns with a large, leather-bound book, which she sets down on her side of the counter with a bang. She flips forward a few pages, then opens a window in the glass and slides the book out to me.

"January and February," she says shortly. "It's all organized by date—if she came through here, she'll be there."

The book is oversized, its pages crisscrossed with spidery writing, intake dates, prisoner names, and corresponding prisoner numbers. The period from January through February runs several pages, and I'm uncomfortably aware of the woman watching me impatiently as I move my finger slowly down the column of names.

There's a tight feeling in my stomach. She's not here. Of course, I might have the dates wrong—or I might have been wrong altogether. Maybe she never came to the Crypts at all.

I think of Fred laughing, saying, *She doesn't get much of an audience these days.*

"Any luck?" the woman asks, without real interest.

"Just a second." A bead of sweat rolls down my spine. I flip to April and continue my search.

Then I see a name that stops me: *Melanea O.*

Melanea. That was Cassandra's middle name; I remember overhearing that at Fred's inauguration, and seeing it on the letter I stole from Fred's study.

"Here," I say. It makes sense that Fred would not have entered her under her real name. The point, after all, was to make her disappear.

I push the book back through the plate-glass window. The woman's eyes slide from *Melanea O* to the inmate number assigned to her: 2225. She keys this into the computer, repeating the number under her breath.

"Ward B," she says. "New wing." She types a few more commands into her keyboard, and a printer behind her shudders to life, regurgitating a small white sticker with VISITOR—WARD B printed neatly across it. She slides it through the window to me, along with another, thinner, leather-bound book. "Sign your name and date in the visitors' log, and mark the name of the person you're visiting. Place the sticker on your chest; it must be visible at all times. And you'll have to wait for an escort. Go on through security and I'll page someone down here to get you."

She runs through this last speech quickly, tonelessly. I fish a pen from my bag and write Eleanor Latterly in the allotted position, praying she doesn't ask to see my ID card. The visitor's log is very slender. Only three visitors have come here in the past week.

My hands have begun to shake. I have trouble wrestling off my jacket after the security guards instruct me that it must go on the conveyor belt. My bag and shoes are also placed in trays for inspection, and I have to stand with my arms and legs spread, as the nurse did, as one of the men pats me down roughly, waving a wand between my legs and over my breasts.

"Clear," he says, stepping aside to let me pass. Just past security is a small waiting area, outfitted with several cheap plastic chairs and a plastic table. Beyond that, I see various hallways branching, and signs pointing the way to different wards and portions of the complex. A TV is playing in the corner, muted: a political broadcast. I avert my eyes quickly, just in case Fred comes on the screen.

A nurse with tufts of black hair and a shiny, greasy face comes slapping down the hallway toward me, wearing blue hospital clogs and floral scrubs. Her name card reads JAN.

"You for Ward B?" she pants at me, when she comes close. I nod. Her perfume is vanilla, sickly sweet and too strong, but it still can't completely conceal the other smells of the place: bleach, body odor.

"This way." She pads in front of me to a heavy set of double doors, using a hip to bump them open.

Beyond the doors, the atmosphere changes. The hallway we've entered is sparkling white. This must be the new wing. The floors, walls, and even the ceiling are made of the same spotless paneling. Even the air smells different— cleaner and newer. It's very quiet, but as we move down the hall, I hear the occasional sounds of muffled voices, the beeping of mechanical equipment, the *slap-slap-slap* of another nurse's clogs down another hallway.

"Been here before?" Jan wheezes. I shake my head, and she shoots me a sidelong glance. "Thought not. We don't get many visitors around here. What's the point, I say."

"I just found out that my aunt—"

She cuts me off. "Gonna have to leave your bag outside the ward." Pant, pant, pant. "Even a nail file will do it in a pinch. And we'll have to give you some slippers. Can't have you wearin' those laces in the ward. Last year one of our guys strung himself up to a pipe, quick as a flash, when he got hold of some laces. Dead as a doornail by the time we found him. Who're you here for?"

She says all this so quickly, I can barely follow the thread of her conversation. An image flashes: someone swinging from the ceiling, laces knotted around the throat. In my mind, the person swings, revolving toward me. Weirdly, it's Fred's face I picture, huge and bulging and red.

"I'm here to see Melanea." I watch the nurse's face, see the name means nothing to her. "Number 2225," I add.

Apparently, people go solely by their numbers in the Crypts, because the nurse lets out a noise of recognition. "She won't give you no trouble," she says conspiratorially, as though she's sharing a great secret. "She's quiet as a church mouse. Well, not always. I remember the first few months, she was shouting and shouting. 'I don't belong here! I'm not crazy!'" The nurse laughs. "'Course, that's what they all say. And then you start listening, and they'll run your ear off talking little green men and spiders."

"She's—she's crazy then?" I say.

"Wouldn't be here if she wasn't, would she?" Jan says. She obviously doesn't expect an answer. We've arrived at another set of double doors, this one marked with a sign that reads

284

"Go on and grab yourself a pair of slippers," she resumes cheerfully, pointing.

Outside the doors are a bench and a small wooden bookcase, on which several plastic-sheathed hospital slippers have been placed. The furniture is obviously old, and looks strange in the middle of all the gleaming whiteness. "Leave your shoes and your bag right here. Don't worry; no one will take 'em. The criminals are in the old wards." She laughs again.

I sit on the bench and fumble with my shoelaces, wishing I'd thought to wear boots or flats instead. My fingers feel clumsy.

"So she screamed?" I prompt. "When she first came, I mean."

The nurse rolls her eyes. "Thought her husband was tryin' to do her in. Shouted conspiracy to anyone who'd listen."

My whole body goes cold. I swallow. "'Do her in'? What do you mean?"

"Don't worry." Jan waves a hand. "She went quiet pretty soon. Most of 'em do. Takes her medicine regular-like, doesn't give nobody no trouble." She pats my shoulder. "Ready?"

I can only nod, although *ready* is the last thing I feel. My body is filled with a need to turn, to run. But instead I stand up and follow Jan through the double doors into another hallway, as spotlessly white as the one we have just passed through, lined on both sides with white, windowless doors. Each step seems to be harder than the last. I can feel the chilly bite of the floor through the slippers, which are tissue-thin, and every time I put a heel down, a shiver runs all the way up my spine.

Too soon, we reach a door marked *2225.* Jan raps twice on

the door, hard, but doesn't seem to expect a response. She removes her key card from around her neck, holds it up to the scanner to the left of the door—"We got all new systems after the Incidents; neat, huh?"—and, when the lock slides open with a click, pushes the door open firmly.

"Got a visitor," she calls cheerfully as she passes into the room. This last step is the hardest. For a second I think I won't be able to do it. I have to practically throw myself forward, over the threshold, into the cell. As I do, the air leaves my chest.

She is sitting in the corner, in a plastic chair with rounded corners, staring out of a small window fitted with heavy iron bars. She doesn't turn when we enter, although I can make out her profile, which is just touched with the light filtering in from outside: the small, ski-jump nose, the exquisite little mouth, the long fringe of lashes, her seashell-pink ear and the neat procedural scar just beneath it. Her hair is long and blond, and hangs loose, nearly to her waist. I estimate that she's about thirty.

She is beautiful.

She looks like me.

My stomach lurches.

"Morning," Jan says loudly, as if Cassandra won't hear us otherwise, even though the room is tiny. It's too small to contain all of us comfortably, and even though the space is bare except for a cot, a chair, a sink, and a toilet, it feels overcrowded. "Brought somebody to see you. Nice surprise, isn't it?"

Cassandra doesn't speak. She doesn't even acknowledge us.

Jan rolls her eyes expressively, mouths *I'm sorry* to me. Out loud, she says, "Come on, now. Don't be rude. Turn around and say hello like a good girl."

Cassie does turn then, although her eyes pass over me completely and go directly to Jan. "May I have a tray, please? I missed breakfast this morning."

Jan puts her hands on her hips and says, in an exaggerated tone of reproach—as though she is speaking to a child— "Now that was silly of you, wasn't it?"

"I wasn't hungry," Cassie says simply.

Jan sighs. "You're lucky I'm feeling nice today," she says with a wink. "You okay here for a minute?" This question is directed to me.

"I—"

"Don't worry," Jan says. "She's harmless." She raises her voice and assumes the forced-cheerful tone. "Be right back. You be a good girl. Don't make no trouble for your guest." She turns once again to me. "Any problems, just hit the emergency button next to the door."

Before I can respond, she bustles into the hallway again, closing the door behind her. I hear the lock slide into place. Fear stabs, sharp and clear, through the muffling effects of the cure.

For a moment there is silence as I try to remember what I came here to say. The fact that I have found her—the mysterious woman—is overwhelming, and I suddenly can't think of what to ask her.

Her eyes click to mine. They are hazel, and very clear. Smart.

Not crazy.

"Who are you?" Now that Jan has left the room, her voice takes on an accusatory edge. "What are you doing here?"

"My name is Hana Tate," I say. I suck in a deep breath. "I'm marrying Fred Hargrove next Saturday."

Silence stretches between us. I feel her eyes sweeping over me and force myself to stand still. "His taste hasn't changed," she says neutrally. Then she turns back to the window.

"Please." My voice cracks a little. I wish I had some water. "I'd like to know what happened."

Her hands are still in her lap. She must have perfected this art over the years: sitting motionless. "I'm crazy," she says tonelessly. "Didn't they tell you?"

"I don't believe it," I say, and it's true, I don't. Now that I'm speaking to her, I know for a fact that she is sane. "I want the truth."

"Why?" She turns back to me. "Why do you care?"

So it won't happen to me; so I can stop it. That's the true and selfish reason. But I can't say that. She has no reason to help me. We are not made to care for strangers any longer.

Before I can think of anything to say, she laughs: a dry sound, as though her throat has been long in disuse. "You want to know what I did, don't you? You want to be sure you don't make the same mistake."

"No," I say, although of course she's right. "That's not what I—"

"Don't worry," she says. "I understand." A smile passes briefly across her face. She looks down at her hands. "I was paired with Fred when I was eighteen," she says. "I didn't go to university. He was older. They'd had trouble finding a match for him. He was picky—he was allowed to be picky, because of who his father was. Everyone said I was lucky." She shrugs. "We were married for five years."

That makes her younger than I thought. "What went wrong?" I ask.

"He got tired of me." She states this firmly. Her eyes flick to mine momentarily. "And I was a liability. I knew too much."

"What do you mean?" I want to sit down on the cot; my head feels strangely light, and my legs feel impossibly far away. But I'm afraid to move. I'm afraid even to breathe. At any second, she can order me out. She owes me nothing.

She doesn't answer me directly. "Do you know what he liked to do when he was a little kid? He used to lure the neighborhood cats into his yard—feed them milk, give them tuna fish, earn their trust. And then he would poison them. He liked to watch them die."

The room feels smaller than ever: stifling and airless.

She turns her gaze to me again. Her calm, steady stare disconcerts me. I will myself not to look away.

"He poisoned me, too," she says. "I was sick for months and months. He told me, finally. Ricin in my coffee. Just enough to keep me sick, in bed, dependent. He told me so I would know what he was capable of." She pauses. "He killed his own father, you know."

For the first time I wonder if maybe, after all, she is crazy. Maybe the nurse was right—maybe she does belong here. The idea is a deliverance. "Fred's father died during the Incidents," I say. "He was killed by Invalids."

She looks at me pityingly. "I know that." As though she is reading my mind, she adds, "I have eyes and ears. The nurses talk. And of course I was in the old wing, when the bombs exploded." She looks down at her hands. "Three hundred prisoners escaped. Another dozen were killed. I wasn't lucky enough to be in either group."

"But what has that got to do with Fred?" I ask. A whine has crept into my voice.

"Everything," she says. Her tone turns sharp. "Fred wanted the Incidents to happen. He wanted the bombs to go off. He worked with the Invalids—he helped plan it."

It can't be true; I can't believe her. I won't. "That doesn't make any sense."

"It makes perfect sense. Fred must have planned it for years. He worked with the DFA; they had the same idea. Fred wanted his father proven wrong about the Invalids—and he wanted his father dead. That way, Fred would be right, and Fred would be mayor."

A shock runs up my spine when she mentions the DFA. In March, at an enormous rally of *Deliria*-Free America in

New York City, Invalids attacked, killing thirty citizens and injuring countless more. Everyone compared it to the Incidents, and for weeks, security everywhere was tightened: IDs scanned, vehicles searched, homes raided, and patrols on the streets doubled.

But there were other whispers too—some people said that Thomas Fineman, the DFA's president, had known in advance what would happen, and had even allowed it. Then, two weeks later, Thomas Fineman was assasinated.

I don't know what to believe. My chest is aching with a feeling I can't remember how to name.

"I liked Mr. Hargrove," Cassandra says. "He felt sorry for me. He knew what his son was. He used to visit every so often, after Fred had me locked up. Fred got people to testify that I was a lunatic. Friends. Doctors. They committed me to life in this place." She gestures toward the small white room, her burial place. "But Mr. Hargrove knew I wasn't crazy. He told me stories about the world outside. He found my mother and father a place to live in Deering Highlands. Fred wanted them silenced too. He must have thought I'd told them . . . he must have thought they knew what I knew." She shakes her head. "But I hadn't. They didn't."

So Cassie's parents were forced into the Highlands, like Lena's family.

"I'm sorry," I say. It's the only thing I can think of, even though I know how flimsy it sounds.

Cassie doesn't seem to hear me. "That day—when the

bombs went off—Mr. Hargrove was visiting. He brought me chocolate." She turns to the window. I wonder what she is thinking; she is perfectly still again, her profile just traced with dull sunlight. "I heard he died trying to restore order. Then I felt sorry for *him*. Funny, isn't it? But I guess Fred got us both in the end."

"Here I am! Better late than never!"

Jan's voice makes me jump. I spin around; she is pushing through the door, carrying a plastic tray with a plastic cup of water and a small plastic bowl of lumpy oatmeal. I step out of the way as she plunks the tray down on the cot. I notice that the silverware is plastic, too. Of course, there would be no metal. No knives, either.

I think of the man swinging by his shoelaces, close my eyes, and think of the bay instead. The image breaks away on the waves. I open my eyes again.

"So what do you think?" Jan says brightly. "You want to tuck in now?"

"Actually, I think I'll wait," Cass says softly. Her gaze is still directed out the window. "I'm not hungry anymore."

Jan looks at me and rolls her eyes as though to say, *Crazies.*

Lena

We waste no time in leaving the safe house, now that it's been decided: We go to Portland as a group, to join with the resistance there and add our strength to the agitators. Something large is in the works, but Cap and Max refuse to say a word about it, and my mother claims they all know only the sketchiest details, anyway. Now that the wall has come down between us, I'm no longer so resistant to returning to Portland. In fact, a small part of me even looks forward to it.

My mother and I talk around the campfire while we eat; we talk late into the night until Julian pokes his head out of the tent, sleepy and disoriented, and tells me I should really get some sleep; or until Raven yells at us to shut the hell up.

We talk in the morning. We talk as we walk.

We talk about what my life in the Wilds, and hers, have been like. She tells me that she was involved in the resistance even when she was in the Crypts—there was a mole, a resister, a cured who still had sympathies for the cause and worked as a guard in Ward Six, where my mother was imprisoned. He was blamed for my mother's escape and became a prisoner himself.

I remember him: I saw him curled, fetus-like, in the corner of a tiny stone cell. I haven't told my mother this, though. I haven't told her that Alex and I gained admittance to the Crypts, because it would mean talking about him. And I can't bring myself to speak about him—not with her, not with anyone.

"Poor Thomas." My mother shakes her head. "He fought hard to get placed in Ward Six. He sought me out deliberately." She looks at me sideways. "He knew Rachel, you know—long ago. I think he always resented that he had to give her up. He stayed angry, even after his cure."

I squeeze my eyes shut against the sun. Long-buried images begin flashing: Rachel locked in her room, refusing to come out and eat; Thomas's pale, freckled face floating at the window, gesturing for me to let him in; crouching in the corner on the day they dragged Rachel to the labs, watching her kick and scream and bare her teeth, like an animal. I must have been eight—it was only a year after my mom died, or after I was told she had died.

"Thomas Dale," I blurt out. The name has stuck with me all these years.

My mom passes her hand absentmindedly through a field of waving grasses. In the sun, her age, and the lines on her face, are starkly obvious. "I barely remembered him. And of course, he had changed a great deal by the time I saw him again. It had been three, four years. I remember I caught him hanging around the house once when I came home early from work. He was terrified. He thought I would tell." She barks a laugh. "That was just before I was . . . taken."

"And he helped you," I say. I try to force his face into clarity in my mind, to make the details resurface, but all I see is the filthy figure curled on the floor in a grimy cell.

My mom nods. "He couldn't quite forget what he had lost. It stayed with him. It does, you know, for some people. I always thought it did for your father."

"So Dad *was* cured?" I don't know why I feel so disappointed. I didn't even remember him; he died of cancer when I was one.

"He was." A muscle twitches in my mom's jaw. "But there were times I felt . . . There were times it seemed as though he could still feel it, just for a second. Maybe I only imagined it. It doesn't matter. I loved him anyway. He was very good to me." She brings her hand unconsciously to her neck, as though feeling for the necklace she wore—my grandfather's military pendant, given to her by my dad. She used it to tunnel her way from the Crypts.

"Your necklace," I say. "You still aren't used to being without it."

She turns to me, squinting. She manages a small smile. "There are some losses we never get over."

I tell my mother about my life too, especially what has happened since crossing from Portland, and how I came to be involved with Raven, Tack, and the resistance. Occasionally we bring up memories from the time before, too—the lost time before she went away, before my sister was cured, before I was placed in Aunt Carol's house. But not too much.

As my mother said, there are some losses we never get over.

Certain subjects remain completely off-limits. She doesn't ask what compelled me to cross in the first place, and I don't volunteer to tell her. I keep Alex's note in a little leather pouch around my neck—a gift from my mom, procured from a trader earlier in the year—but it is a memento from a past life, like carrying the picture of someone who is dead.

My mother knows, of course, that I have found my way into loving. Occasionally, I catch her watching me with Julian. The look on her face—pride, grief, envy, and love commingled— reminds me that she is not just my mother, but a woman who has fought her whole life for something she has never truly experienced.

My dad was cured. And you can't love, not fully, unless you are loved in return.

It makes me ache for her, a feeling I hate and am somehow ashamed of.

Julian and I have found our rhythm again. It's as though we have skated over the past few weeks, skated over Alex's long shadow, and landed neatly on the other side. We can't get enough of each other. I'm amazed by every part of him again: his hands, his low, gentle way of speaking, all his different laughs.

At night, in the dark, we reach for each other. We lose ourselves in the nighttime rhythm, in the hoots and cries and moans from the animals outside. And despite the dangers of the Wilds, and the constant threat of regulators and Scavengers, I feel free for the first time in what feels like forever.

One morning I emerge from the tents and find that Raven has overslept, and it is instead Julian and my mom who have been stoking the fire. Their backs are turned toward me, and they are laughing about something. Faint wisps of smoke twist up into the fine spring air. For a moment I stand perfectly still, terrified, feeling as though I am on the brink of something—if I move at all, take a step forward or back, the image will break apart in the wind, and they'll scatter into dust.

Then Julian turns and sees me. "Morning, beauty," he says. His face is still bruised and swollen in places, but his eyes are exactly the color of early-morning sky. When he smiles, I think he is the most beautiful thing I have ever seen.

My mom grabs a bucket and stands. "I was going for a shower," she says.

"Me too," I say.

As I wade into the still-freezing stream, the wind raises goose bumps on my body. A cloud of swallows flies across the sky; the water carries a slight taste of grit; my mother hums downstream. This is not any kind of happiness that I imagined. It is not what I chose.

But it's enough. It is more than enough.

On the border of Rhode Island, we encounter another group of about two dozen homesteaders, who are on their way to Portland as well. All but two of them are on the side of the resistance, and the two who don't care to fight don't dare to be left alone. We are nearing the coast, and the detritus of old life is everywhere. We come across a massive cement honeycomb structure, which Tack identifies as an old parking garage.

Something about the structure makes me anxious. It's like a towering stone insect, outfitted with a hundred eyes. The whole group falls silent as we pass under its shadow. The hair on my neck is standing up, and even though it's stupid, I can't shake the feeling that we are being watched.

Tack, who is leading the group, holds up his hand. We all come to an abrupt stop. He cocks his head, obviously listening for something. I hold my breath. It's quiet, except for the usual rustle of animals in the woods, and the gentle sighing of the wind.

Then a fine spray of gravel lands on us from above, as though someone has accidentally toed it out of one of the upper levels of the parking garage.

Instantly, everything is blur and motion.

"Get down, get down!" Max yells as all of us are reaching

for weapons, unshouldering rifles, and dropping into the underbrush.

"Coo-ee!"

The voice, the shout, freezes us. I crane my head toward the sky, shielding my eyes from the sun. For a second, I'm sure I'm dreaming.

Pippa has emerged from the dark caverns of the honeycomb structure and stands on a sun-drenched ledge, waving a red handkerchief down at us, grinning.

"Pippa!" Raven cries out, her voice strangled. Only then do I believe it.

"Hey, yourself," Pippa shouts down. And slowly, from behind her, more and more people edge into view: masses of skinny, ragged people, packed into all the different levels of the garage.

When Pippa finally makes it to the ground, she is immediately engulfed by Tack, Raven, and Max. Beast is alive too; he lopes out into the sunshine directly behind Pippa, and it seems almost too much to believe. For fifteen minutes, we do nothing but shout and laugh and talk over one another, and not a single word gets said that anyone understands.

Finally, Max makes himself heard over the chaos of competing voices and laughter. "What happened?" He's laughing, breathless. "We heard no one escaped. We heard it was a massacre."

Instantly, Pippa grows serious. "It *was* a massacre," she says. "We lost hundreds. The tanks came and encircled the camp.

They used tear gas, machine guns, shells. It was a bloodbath. The screaming—" She breaks off. "It was awful."

"How did you get out?" Raven asks. We have all gotten quiet. Now it seems horrible that only a second earlier we were laughing, rejoicing in Pippa's safety.

"We had hardly any time," Pippa says. "We tried to warn everyone. But you know how it was—chaos. Hardly anyone would listen."

Behind her, Invalids are stepping tentatively out into the sunlight, emerging from the parking garage—wide-eyed, silent, nervous, like people who have weathered a hurricane and are amazed to see the world still exists. I can only imagine what they witnessed at Waterbury.

"How did you get around the tanks?" Bee asks. It's still hard for me to think of her as my mother when she acts like this, like a hardened member of the resistance. For now, I am content to allow her to exist doubly: She is my mother sometimes, and sometimes, a leader and a fighter.

"We didn't run," Pippa says. "There was no chance. The whole area was swarming with troops. We hid." A spasm of pain crosses her face. She opens her mouth, as though to say more, and then closes it again.

"Where did you hide?" Max presses.

Pippa and Beast exchange an indecipherable look. For a moment, I think Pippa will refuse to answer. Something happened at the camp, something she won't tell us.

Then she coughs and turns her eyes back to Max. "In the riverbed, at first, before the shooting started," she says. "It didn't take long for the bodies to start falling. We were protected under them, once they did."

"Oh my God." Hunter balls his fist into his right eye. He looks like he's about to be sick. Julian turns away from Pippa.

"We had no choice," Pippa says sharply. "Besides, they were already dead. At least their bodies didn't go to waste."

"We're glad you made it, Pippa," Raven says gently, and places a hand on Pippa's shoulder. Pippa turns to her gratefully, her face suddenly eager, open, like a puppy's.

"I was planning to get word to you at the safe house, but I figured you had already left," she says. "I didn't want to risk it when there were troops in the area. Too conspicuous. So I went north. We stumbled on the hive by accident." She jerks her chin to the vast parking structure. It really does look like a gigantic hive, now that there are figures, half-shadowed, peering down at us from its different levels, flitting through patches of light and then retreating once again into the darkness. "Figured it was a good place to hide out for a bit and wait for things to settle down."

"How many you got?" Tack asks. Dozens and dozens of people have descended and are standing, herded together, a little ways behind Pippa, like a pack of dogs that has been beaten and starved into submission. Their silence is disconcerting.

"More than three hundred," Pippa says. "Closer to four."

A huge number: still, only a fraction of the number of people who were camped outside Waterbury. For a moment I am filled with a blind, white-hot rage. We wanted the freedom to love, and instead we have been turned into fighters, savages. Julian moves close to me and puts his arm around my shoulder, allowing me to lean into him, as though he can sense what I am thinking.

"We've seen no sign of the troops," Raven says. "My guess is they came up from New York. If they had tanks, they must have used one of the service roads along the Hudson. Hopefully they've gone south again."

"Mission accomplished," Pippa says bitterly.

"They haven't accomplished anything." My mother speaks up again, but her voice is softer now. "The fight isn't over— it's only beginning."

"We're headed to Portland," Max says. "We have friends there—lots of them. There'll be payback," he adds with sudden fierceness. "An eye for an eye."

"And the whole world goes blind," Coral puts in quietly.

Everyone turns to look at her. She has barely spoken since Alex left, and I have been careful to avoid her. I feel her pain like a physical presence, a dark, sucking energy that consumes and surrounds her, and it makes me both pity and resent her. It's a reminder that he was no longer mine to lose.

"What did you say?" Max says with barely concealed aggression.

Coral looks away. "Nothing," she says. "It's just something I once heard."

"We have no choice," my mother insists. "If we don't fight, we'll be destroyed. It's not about payback." She shoots a look at Max, and he grunts and crosses his arms. "It's about survival."

Pippa runs a hand over her head. "My people are weak," she says finally. "We've been living on scraps—rats, mostly, and what we could forage in the woods."

"There will be food up north," Max says. "Supplies. Like I said, the resistance has friends in Portland."

"I'm not sure they'll make it," Pippa says, lowering her voice.

"Well, you can't stay here, either," Tack points out.

Pippa bites her lip and exchanges a look with Beast. He nods.

"He's right, Pip," Beast says.

Behind Pippa, a woman speaks up suddenly. She is so thin, she looks as though she has been whittled from ancient wood.

"We'll go." Her voice is surprisingly deep and forceful. Set in her sunken, shipwreck face, her eyes burn like two smoldering coals. "We'll fight."

Pippa exhales slowly. Then she nods.

"All right, then," she says. "Portland it is."

As we draw closer to Portland, as the light and land grow more familiar—lush with growth and smells I know from childhood, from my longest, oldest memories—I begin to make my plans.

Nine days after we left the safe house, our numbers now hugely swollen, we catch a glimpse of one of the Portland border fences. Only now it is no longer a fence. It's a huge cement wall, a faceless slab of stone, stained an unearthly pink in the dawn light.

I'm so startled, I stop short. "What the hell?"

Max is walking behind me, and has to dodge at the last

second. "New construction," he says. "Tightened border control. Tightened control everywhere. Portland's making an example." He shakes his head and mutters something.

This image—the sight of a wall, newly erected—has made my heart start pounding. I left Portland less than a year ago, but already, it has changed. I'm seized by a fear that everything will be different on the inside of the wall too. Maybe I won't recognize any of the streets. Maybe I won't be able to find my way to Aunt Carol's house.

Maybe I won't be able to find Grace.

I can't help but worry about Hana, too. I wonder where she will be once we begin pouring into Portland: the cast-out children, the prodigal sons, like the angels described in *The Book of Shhh* who were thrown out of heaven for harboring the disease, expelled by an angry god.

But I remind myself that my Hana—the Hana I knew and loved—is gone now.

"I don't like it," I say.

Max swivels around to look at me, one corner of his mouth quirked into a smile. "Don't worry," he says. "It won't be standing too much longer." He winks.

So. More explosions. It makes sense; we need to move a large number of people into Portland somehow.

A high, thin whistle disrupts the morning stillness. Beast. He and Pippa have been scouting ahead of the group this morning, tracing the periphery of the city, looking for other Invalids, signs of a camp or homestead. We turn toward the sound. We've been walking since midnight, but now we find renewed energy and move more quickly than we have all night.

The trees spit us out at the edge of a large clearing. The growth has been rigorously trimmed back, and a long, well-tended alley of green extends a quarter of a mile into the distance. In it are trailer homes propped on cinder blocks and chunks of concrete, as well as rusted truck beds, tents, and blankets strung up from tree branches to form makeshift canopies. People are already moving around the camp, and the air smells like smoking wood.

Beast and Pippa are standing a little ways away, conversing with a tall, sandy-haired man outside one of the trailers.

Raven and my mother begin shepherding the group into the clearing. I stay where I am, rooted to the spot. Julian, realizing I am not with the group, doubles back to me.

"What's the matter?" he asks. His eyes are red. He has been doing more than almost anyone—scouting, foraging, standing watch while the rest of us are sleeping.

"I—I know where we are," I say. "I've been here before."

I don't say *with Alex*. I don't have to. Julian's eyes flicker.

"Come on," he says. His voice is strained, but he reaches out and takes my hand. His palms have grown calloused, but his touch is still gentle.

I scan instinctively across the line of trailers, trying to pick out the one Alex had claimed for himself. But that was last summer, in the dark, and I was terrified. I don't remember any of its features but the roll-away, plastic-tarp roof, which won't be distinguishable from where I'm standing.

I feel a brief flicker of hope. Maybe Alex is here. Maybe he came back to familiar grounds.

The sandy-haired man is speaking to Pippa. "You got here just in time," he says. He is much older than he appeared from a distance—in his forties at least—although his neck is unblemished. He has obviously not spent any significant amount of time in Zombieland. "Game time is tomorrow at noon."

"*Tomorrow?*" Pippa repeats. She and Tack exchange a look. Julian squeezes my hand. I feel a pulse of anxiety. "Why so soon? If we had more time to plan—"

"And more time to eat," Raven cuts in. "Half our number is practically starving. They won't put up a very good fight."

The sandy-haired man spreads his hands. "It wasn't my decision. We've been coordinating with our friends on the other side. Tomorrow is our best chance for getting in. A large portion of security will be busy tomorrow—there's a public event down by the labs. They'll be pulled away from the perimeter to guard it."

Pippa rubs her eyes and sighs. My mother puts in, "Who's going in first?"

"We're still working out the details," he says. "We didn't know whether Resistance got the word out. We didn't know whether we could expect any help." When he speaks to my mom, his whole manner changes—he becomes more formal, and more respectful, too. I see his eyes skate down to the tattoo on her neck, the one that marks her as a former prisoner of

306

the Crypts. He obviously knows what it means, even if he has not spent time in Portland.

"You have help now," my mother says.

The sandy-haired man looks out over our group. More and more people are pushing out of the woods, flowing into the clearing, huddling together in the weak morning light. He starts slightly, as though he has only just become aware of our number. "How many of you are there?" he asks.

Raven smiles, showing all her teeth. "Enough," she says.

Hana

The Hargroves' house is blazing with light. As our car turns into the drive, I have the impression of a massive white boat run aground. In every single window, a lamp is burning; the trees in the yard have been strung with miniature white lights, and the roof is crowned with them as well.

Of course, the lights are not about celebration. They are a statement of power. We will have, control, possess, even waste—and others will wither away in the dark, sweat in the summer, freeze as soon as the weather changes.

"Don't you think it's lovely, Hana?" my mother says as black-suited attendants materialize from the darkness and open up the car door. They stand back and wait for us, hands folded—respectful, deferential, silent. Fred's work, probably. I think about his fingers tightening around my throat. *You will still learn to sit when I tell you. . . .*

And the flatness of Cassandra's voice, the dull resignation in her eyes. *He poisoned cats when he was little. He liked to watch them die.*

"Lovely," I echo.

She turns to me in the act of swinging her legs out of the car, and frowns slightly. "You're very quiet tonight."

"Tired," I say.

The past week and a half has slipped away so quickly, I can't remember individual days: Everything blurs together, turns the muddled gray of a confused dream.

Tomorrow, I marry Fred Hargrove.

All day I have felt as though I am sleepwalking, seeing my body move and smile and speak, get dressed and lotioned and perfumed, float down the stairs to the waiting car and now drift up the flagstone path to Fred's front door.

See Hana walk. See Hana stepping into the foyer, blinking in the brightness: a chandelier sending rainbow-shards of light across the walls; lamps crowding the hall table and bookshelves; candles burning in hard sterling candlesticks. See Hana turning into the packed living room, a hundred bright and bloated faces turning to look at her.

"There she is!"

"Here comes the bride . . ."

"And Mrs. Tate."

See Hana say hello, wave and nod, shake hands, and smile.

"Hana! Perfect timing. I was just singing your praises." Fred is striding across the room toward me, smiling, his loafers sinking soundlessly into the thick carpet.

See Hana give her almost-husband an arm.

Fred leans in to whisper, "You look very pretty." And then: "I hope you took our conversation to heart." As he says it, he pinches my arm, hard, on the fleshy inside just above my elbow. He gives his other arm to my mother, and we move into the room while the crowd parts for us, a rustle of silk and linen. Fred steers me through the room, pausing to chat with the most important members of city government and his largest benefactors. I listen and laugh at the right moments, but all the time I still feel as though I am dreaming.

"Brilliant idea, Mayor Hargrove. I was just saying to Ginny . . ."

"And why should they have light? Why should they get anything from us at all?"

". . . soon put an end to the problem."

My father is already here; I see that he is talking to Patrick Riley, the man who took over as the head of *Deliria*-Free America after Thomas Fineman was assasinated last month. Riley must have come up from New York, where the group is headquartered.

I think of what Cassandra told me—that the DFA worked with the Invalids, that Fred has too, that both attacks were

310

planned—and feel as if I'm going crazy. I no longer know what to believe. Maybe they'll lock me in the Crypts with Cassandra and take away my shoelaces.

I have to swallow back the sudden urge to laugh.

"Excuse me," I say as soon as Fred's grip on my elbow loosens and I see the opportunity to escape. "I'm going to get a drink."

Fred smiles at me, although his eyes are dark. The warning is plain: *Behave*. "Of course," he says lightly. As I make my way across the living room, the crowd presses tightly around him, blocking him from view.

A linen-draped table has been set up in front of the large bay windows, which look out onto the Hargroves' well-manicured lawn and impeccable flower beds, where blooms have been organized by height, type, and color. I ask for water and try and make myself as inconspicuous as possible, hoping to avoid conversation for at least a few minutes.

"There she is! Hana! Remember me?" From across the room, Celia Briggs—who is standing next to Steven Hilt, wearing a dress that makes it look as though she has stumbled accidentally into an enormous pile of blue chiffon—is frantically trying to get my attention. I look away, pretending not to have seen her. As she begins barging toward me, pulling Steven by the sleeve, I push into the hall and speed toward the back of the house.

I wonder whether Celia knows what happened last summer: how Steven and I breathed into each other's mouths, and let feelings pass between each other's tongues. Maybe Steven has told her. Maybe they laugh about it now, now that we are all safely on the other side of those roiling, frightening nights.

I head to the screened-in porch at the back of the house, but this, too, is packed with people. As I'm about to pass the kitchen, I hear the swell of Mrs. Hargrove's voice: "Grab that bucket of ice, will you? The bartender's almost out."

Hoping to avoid her, I duck into Fred's study, shutting the door quickly behind me. Mrs. Hargrove will only pilot me firmly back to the party, back to Celia Briggs, and the room full of all those teeth. I lean against the door, exhaling slowly.

My eyes land on the single painting in the room: the man, the hunter, and the butchered carcasses.

Only this time, I don't look away.

There's something wrong with the hunter—he's dressed too well, in an old-fashioned suit and polished boots. Unconsciously, I take two steps closer, horrified and unable to look away. The animals strung from meat hooks aren't animals at all.

They're women.

Corpses, human corpses, strung from the ceiling and piled on the marble floor.

Next to the artist's signature is a small, painted note: *The Myth of Bluebeard, or, The Dangers of Disobedience.*

I feel a need I can't exactly name—to speak, or scream, or run. Instead I sit down on the stiff-backed leather chair behind the desk, lean forward, and rest my head on my arms, and try to remember how to cry. But nothing comes except for a faint itch in my throat and a headache.

I don't know how long I have been sitting like that when I become aware of a siren drawing closer. Then the room is thrown, suddenly, into color: flashes of red and white burst intermittently through the windowpane. The sirens are still going, though—and then I realize that they are everywhere, both near and close, some wailing shrilly just down the street and some no louder than an echo.

Something is wrong.

I move out into the hall, just as several doors slam at once. The murmur of conversation and the music have stopped. Instead I hear people shouting over one another. Fred bursts into the hall and comes striding toward me, just after I've closed the door to his study.

He stops when he sees me. "Where were you?" he asks.

"The porch," I say quickly. My heart is beating hard. "I needed some air."

He opens his mouth; just then my mother comes into the hall, her face pale.

"Hana," she says. "There you are."

"What happened?" I ask. More and more people are flowing out of the living room: regulators in their pressed uniforms, Fred's bodyguards, two solemn-faced police officers, and Patrick Riley, wrestling on his blazer. Cell phones are ringing, and bursts of walkie-talkie static fill the hall.

"There's been a disturbance at the border wall," my mother

says, her eyes flitting nervously to Fred.

"Resisters." I can tell from my mother's expression that my guess is right.

"They've been killed, of course," Fred says loudly, so everyone can hear.

"How many were there?" I ask.

Fred turns to me as he's shoving his arms into his suit coat, which a gray-faced regulator has just passed him. "Does it matter? We've taken care of it."

My mother shoots me a look and gives me a minute shake of the head.

Behind him, a policeman murmurs into his walkie-talkie. "Ten-four, ten-four, we're on our way."

"You ready?" Patrick Riley asks Fred.

Fred nods. Instantly, his cell phone starts blaring. He removes it from his pocket and silences it quickly. "Shit. We better hurry. The office phones are probably going crazy."

My mom places an arm around my shoulders. I'm momentarily startled. It's very rare that we touch like this. She must be more worried than she seems.

"Come on," she says. "Your father's waiting for us."

"Where are we going?" I ask. She's already moving me toward the front of the house.

"Home," she says.

Outside, the guests are already amassing. We join the line of people waiting for their cars. We see seven and eight people piling into sedans, women in long gowns squeezing on top of one another in backseats. It's obvious that no one wants to walk the streets, which are filled with the distant sounds of wailing.

My father ends up riding in the front with Tony. My mom and I squeeze into the backseat with Mr. and Mrs. Brande, who both work in the Department of Sanitization. Normally, Mrs. Brande can't stop running her mouth—my mom has always speculated that the cure left her with no verbal self-control—but tonight we drive in silence. Tony goes faster than usual.

It begins to rain. The streetlamps pattern the windows with broken halos of light. Now, alert with fear and anxiety, I can't believe how stupid I've been. I make a sudden decision: no more going to Deering Highlands. It's too dangerous. Lena's family is not my problem. I have done all I can do.

The guilt is still there, pressing at my throat, but I swallow it down.

We pass under another streetlamp, and the rain on the windows becomes long fingers; then once again the car is swallowed in darkness. I imagine I see different figures moving through the dark, skating next to the car, faces merging in and out of the shadow. For a second, as we move beneath another streetlamp, I see a hooded figure emerging from the woods at the side of the road. Our eyes meet, and I let out a small cry.

Alex. It's Alex.

"What's the matter?" my mother asks tensely.

"Nothing, I—" By the time I turn around, he is gone, and

then I'm sure I only imagined him. I must have imagined him. Alex is dead; he was taken down at the border and never made it into the Wilds. I swallow hard. "I thought I saw something."

"Don't worry, Hana," my mother says. "We're perfectly safe in the car." But she leans forward and says, sharply, to Tony, "Can't you drive any faster?"

I think of the new wall, lit up by a spinning light, stained red with blood.

What if there are more of them? What if they're coming for us?

I have a vision of Lena moving out there, sneaking through the streets, ducking between shadows, holding a knife. For a moment my lungs stop moving.

But no. She doesn't know I was the one who gave her and Alex away. No one knows.

Besides, she is probably dead.

And even if she isn't—even if by some miracle, she survived the escape and has been squeezing out a living in the Wilds—she would never join forces with the resisters. She would never be violent or vengeful. Not Lena, who used to practically faint when she pricked a finger, who couldn't even lie to a teacher about being late. She wouldn't have the stomach for it.

Would she?

Lena

The planning goes late into the night. The sandy-haired man, whose name is Colin, remains sequestered in one of the trailers with Beast and Pippa, Raven and Tack, Max, Cap, my mother, and a few others he has handpicked from his group. He assigns a guard to watch the door; the meeting is invite-only. I know that something big is in the works—as big as, if not bigger than, the Incidents that blew part of a wall out of the Crypts and exploded a police station. From hints that Max has let slip, I've gathered that this new rebellion is not simply confined to Portland. As in the earlier Incidents, in cities all across the country, sympathizers and Invalids are gathering and channeling their anger and their energy into displays of resistance.

At one point Max and Raven emerge from the trailer to pee in the woods—their faces drawn and serious—but when I beg Raven to let me join the meeting, she cuts me down immediately.

"Go to bed, Lena," she says. "Everything's under control."

It must be almost midnight; Julian has been asleep for hours. I can't imagine lying down right now. I feel like my blood is full of thousands of ants—my arms and legs are crawling, itching to move, to *do* something. I walk in circles, trying to shake the feeling, and fuming—annoyed with Julian, furious with Raven, thinking of all the things I'd like to say to her.

I was the one who got Julian out of the underground. I was the one who risked my life to sneak into New York City and save him. I was the one who got into Waterbury; I was the one who found out Lu was a fraud. And now Raven tells me to go to bed, like I'm an unruly five-year-old.

I take aim at a tin cup that has been lying, half-buried in ash, at the edge of a burned-out campfire, and watch as it rockets twenty feet and pings off the side of a trailer. A man calls out, "Take it easy!" But I don't care if I've woken him up. I don't care if I wake the whole damn camp up.

"Can't sleep?"

I spin around, startled. Coral is sitting a little ways behind me, knees hugged to her chest, next to the dying remains of another fire. Every so often she prods it halfheartedly with a stick.

"Hey," I say cautiously. Since Alex left, she has gone almost

318

completely mute. "I didn't see you."

Her eyes go to mine. She smiles weakly. "I can't sleep either."

Even though I'm still antsy, it feels weird to be hovering above her, so I lower myself onto one of the smoke-blackened logs that ring the campfire. "Are you worried about tomorrow?"

"Not really." She gives the fire another prod, watches as it flares momentarily. "It doesn't matter for me, does it?"

"What do you mean?" I look at her closely for the first time in a week; I've been unconsciously avoiding her. There is something tragic and hollow about her now: Her cream-pale skin looks like a husk—empty, sucked dry.

She shrugs and keeps her eyes on the embers. "I mean that I have no one left."

I swallow. I've been meaning to speak to her about Alex, to apologize in some way, but the words never quite come. Even now they grow and stick in my throat. "Listen, Coral." I take a deep breath. *Say it. Just say it.* "I'm really sorry that Alex left. I know—I know it must have been hard for you."

There it is: the spoken admission that he was hers to lose. As soon as the words leave my mouth, I feel weirdly deflated, as though they've been swollen, balloonlike, in my chest this whole time.

For the first time since I sat down, she looks at me. I can't read the expression on her face. "That's okay," she says at last, returning her gaze to the fire. "He was still in love with you, anyway."

It's as though she's reached out and punched me in the

stomach. All of a sudden, I can't breathe. "What—what are you talking about?"

Her mouth crooks up into a smile. "He was. It was obvious. That's okay. He liked me and I liked him." She shakes her head. "I didn't mean Alex, anyway, when I said I had no one left. I meant Nan, and the rest of the group. My people." She throws down the stick and hugs her knees tighter to her chest. "Weird how it's just hitting me now, huh?"

Even though I'm still stunned by what she has just said, I manage to keep control of myself. I reach out and touch her elbow. "Hey," I say. "You have us. We're your people now."

"Thanks." Her eyes flick to mine again. She forces a smile. She tilts her head and stares at me critically for a minute. "I can see why he loved you."

"Coral, you're wrong—" I start to say.

But just then there's a footfall behind us, and my mother says, "I thought you went to sleep hours ago."

Coral stands up, dusting off the back of her jeans—a nervous gesture, since we are all covered in dirt, caked grime that has found its way from our eyelashes to our fingernails. "I was just going," she says. "Good night, Lena. And . . . thanks."

Before I can respond, she spins around and heads off toward the southern end of the clearing, where most of our group is clustered.

"She seems like a sweet girl," my mother says, easing herself down onto the log Coral has vacated. "Too sweet for the Wilds."

"She's been here almost her whole life." I can't keep the edge from my voice. "And she's a great fighter."

My mother stares at me. "Is something wrong?"

"What's *wrong* is that I don't like being kept in the dark. I want to know what the plan is tomorrow." My heart is going hard. I know I'm not being fair to my mother—it isn't her fault I wasn't allowed in to plan—but I feel like I could scream. Coral's words have shaken something loose inside me, and I can feel it rattling around in my chest, knifing against my lungs. *He was still in love with you.*

No. It's impossible; she got it all wrong. He never loved me. He told me so.

My mother's face turns serious. "Lena, you have to promise me that you'll stay here, at the camp, tomorrow. You have to promise me you won't fight."

Now it's my turn to stare. *"What?"*

She rakes a hand through her hair, making it look as though it has been styled with an electric current. "Nobody knows exactly what we can expect inside that wall. The security forces are estimates, and we're not sure how much support our friends in Portland have drummed up. I was urging a delay, but I was overruled." She shakes her head. "It's dangerous, Lena. I don't want you to be a part of it."

The rattling piece in my chest—the anger and sadness over losing Alex, and more than that, even, over this life that we string together from scraps and tatters and half-spoken words and promises that are not fulfilled—explodes suddenly.

"You still don't get it, do you?" I am practically shaking. "I'm not a child anymore. I grew up. I grew up without you.

And you can't tell me what to do."

I half expect her to snap back at me, but she just sighs and stares at the smoldering orange glow still embedded in the ash, like a buried sunset. Then she says abruptly, "Do you remember the Story of Solomon?"

Her words are so unexpected that for a moment, I can't speak. I can only nod.

"Tell me," she says. "Tell me what you remember."

Alex's note, still tucked into the pouch around my neck, seems to be smoldering too, burning against my chest. "Two mothers are fighting over a child," I say cautiously. "They decide to cut the baby in half. The king decrees it."

My mother shakes her head. "No. That's the revised version; that's the story in *The Book of Shhh*. In the real story, the mothers don't cut the baby in half."

I go very still, almost afraid to breathe. I feel as though I'm teetering on a precipice, on the verge of understanding, and I'm not yet sure if I want to go over.

My mother goes on, "In the real story, King Solomon decides that the baby should be cut in half. But it's only a test. One mother agrees; the other woman says that she'll give up claim to the baby altogether. She doesn't want the child injured." My mother turns her eyes to me. Even in the dark, I can see their sparkle, the clarity that has never gone away. "That's how the king identifies the real mother. She's willing to sacrifice her claim, sacrifice her happiness, to keep the baby safe."

I close my eyes and see embers burning behind my lids:

blood-red dawn, smoke and fire, Alex behind the ash. All of a sudden, I know. I understand the meaning of his note.

"I'm not trying to control you, Lena," my mother says, her voice low. "I just want you to be safe. That's what I've always wanted."

I open my eyes. The memory of Alex standing behind the fence as a black swarm enfolded him recedes. "It's too late." My voice sounds hollow, and not like my own. "I've seen things . . . I've lost things you can't understand."

It's the closest I've come to speaking about Alex. Thankfully, she doesn't pry. She just nods.

"I'm tired." I push myself to my feet. My body, too, feels unfamiliar, as though I'm a puppet that has begun to come apart at the seams. Alex sacrificed himself once so that I could live and be happy. Now he has done it again.

I've been so stupid. And he is gone; there is no way for me to reach him and tell him I know and understand.

There is no way for me to tell him that I am still in love with him.

"I'm going to get some sleep," I tell her, avoiding her eyes.

"I think that's a good idea," she says.

I've already started to move away from her when she calls out to me. I turn around. The fire has now burned out completely, and her face is swallowed in darkness.

"We make for the wall at dawn," she says.

Hana

I can't sleep.

Tomorrow I will no longer be myself. I will walk down the white carpet, and stand under the white canopy, and pronounce vows of loyalty and purpose. Afterward, white petals will rain down on me, scattered by the priests, by the guests, by my parents.

I will be reborn: blank, clean, featureless, like the world after a blizzard.

I stay up all night and watch dawn break slowly over the horizon, touching the world with white.

Lena

I'm in a crowd, watching two children fight over a baby. They are playing tug-of-war, pulling it violently back and forth, and the baby is blue, and I know they are shaking it to death. I'm trying to push through the crowd, but more and more people are surging around me, blocking my path, making it impossible to move. And then, just as I feared, the baby falls: It hits the pavement and shatters into a thousand pieces, like a china doll.

Then all the people are gone. I am alone on a road, and in front of me, a girl with long, tangled hair is bent over the shattered doll, piecing it back together painstakingly, humming to herself. The day is bright and perfectly still. Each of my footsteps rings out like a gunshot, but she doesn't look up until I am standing directly in front of her.

Then she does, and she is Grace.

"See?" she says, extending the doll toward me. "I fixed it."

And I see that the doll's face is my own, and webbed with thousands of tiny fissures and cracks.

Grace cradles the doll in her arms. "Wake up, wake up," she croons.

"Wake up."

I open my eyes: My mother is standing above me. I sit up, my body stiff, working feeling into my fingers and toes, flexing and unflexing. The air is hung with mist, and the sky is just beginning to lighten. The ground is covered with frost, which has seeped through my blanket while I was sleeping, and the wind has a bitter, morning edge. The camp is busy: Around me, people are stirring, standing, moving like shadows through the half darkness. Fires are sparking to life, and every so often, I hear a burst of conversation, a shouted command.

My mother reaches out a hand and helps me to my feet. Incredibly, she looks rested and alert. I stomp the stiffness out of my legs.

"Coffee will get your blood moving," she says.

It doesn't surprise me that Raven, Tack, Pippa, and Beast are already up. They are standing with Colin and a dozen others near one of the larger fire pits, their breath clouding the air as they speak in low tones. There is a stockpot of coffee on the fire: bitter and full of grains, but hot. I start to feel better and more awake after I've had only a few sips. But I can't bring myself to eat anything.

Raven raises her eyebrows when she sees me. My mother gestures to her, a motion of resignation, and Raven turns back to Colin.

"All right," he's saying. "Like we talked about last night, we move in three groups into the city. First group goes in an hour, does the scouting, and makes contact with our friends. The main force doesn't budge until the blast at twelve hundred hours. The third group will follow immediately afterward and head straight to the target. . . ."

"Hey." Julian comes up behind me. His eyes still have a puffy, just-awake look, and his hair is hopelessly tangled. "I missed you last night."

Last night, I couldn't bring myself to lie down next to Julian. Instead I found a free blanket and made my bed out in the open, next to a hundred other women. For a long time, I stared up at the stars, remembering the first time I came to the Wilds with Alex—how he led me into one of the trailers, and unrolled the tarp that served as its ceiling so we could see the sky.

So much between us went unsaid; that is the danger, and beauty, of life without the cure. There is always wilderness and tangle, and the path is never clear.

Julian begins to reach for me, and I take a step backward.

"I was having trouble sleeping," I say. "I didn't want to wake you."

Julian frowns. I can't bring myself to make eye contact with him. Over the past week, I've accepted that I will never love Julian as much as I loved Alex. But now that idea is overwhelming, like a wall between us. I will never love Julian like I love Alex.

"What's wrong with you?" Julian is watching me warily.

"Nothing," I say, and then repeat, "Nothing."

"Did something—" Julian starts to say when Raven whirls around and glares at him.

"Hey, Jewels," she barks out, which she has taken to calling Julian when she's annoyed. "This isn't gossip hour, okay? Shut it or clear out."

Julian falls quiet. I turn my eyes to Colin, and Julian doesn't try to touch me or move closer. The sky is now streaked with long filaments of orange and red, like the tendrils of a massive jellyfish, floating in a milk-white ocean. The mist rises; the earth begins to shake itself awake. Portland, too, will be stirring.

Colin tells us the plan.

Hana

On my last morning as Hana Tate, I drink my coffee onto the front porch, alone.

I had planned to take a final bike ride, but there is no hope of that now, not after what happened last night. The streets will be crawling with police and regulators. I'll have to show my papers, and field questions I can't answer.

Instead I sit on the porch swing, taking comfort in its rhythmic squeaking. The air is morning-still, cool and gray and textured with salt. I can tell it will be a perfect day, cloudless and bright. Every so often, a seagull cries sharply. Other than that, it's silent. Here there are no alarms, no sirens, no hint of the disturbance last night.

But downtown, it will be different. There will be barricades and security checks, reinforced security at the new wall. I remember, suddenly, what Fred told me once about the wall—that it would be like the palm of God, cupping us forever in safety, keeping out the diseased, the damaged, the unfaithful and unworthy.

But maybe we can never be truly safe.

I wonder whether there will be new raids in the Highlands, whether the families there will be once again displaced, and quickly dismiss the concern. Lena's family is beyond my reach. I see that now. I should have seen that always. What happens to them—whether they starve or freeze—is none of my business.

We are all punished for the lives we have chosen, in one way or another. I will be paying my penance—to Lena, for failing her; to her family, for helping her—every day of my life.

I close my eyes and picture the Old Port: the textured streets, the boat slips, the sun breaking loose of the water, and the waves lapping against the wharves.

Good-bye, good-bye, good-bye.

I mentally trace a route from Eastern Prom to the top of Munjoy Hill; I see all of Portland spread vastly below me, glittering in new light.

"Hana?"

I open my eyes. My mother has stepped onto the porch. She holds her thin nightgown close to her body, squinting. Her skin, without makeup, looks almost gray.

"You should probably get into the shower," she says.

I stand up and follow her into the house.

Lena

W e've moved to the wall. There must be four hundred of us, massed in the trees. Last night, a small task force made the crossing, to prepare last-minute for the full-scale breach today. And earlier this morning, another small group—Colin's people, hand-selected—got over the fence on the west side of Portland, close to the Crypts, where the wall has not yet been built and security has been compromised by friends, allies, on the inside.

But that was hours ago, and now there is nothing to do but wait for the signal.

The main force will breach the wall at once. Most of

Portland's security will be busy at the labs; I've gathered that there is a large event there today. There should only be a limited number of officers to hold us off, although Colin is worried that last night's breach didn't go as smoothly as planned. It's possible that inside the wall, there are more regulators, more guns than we think.

We'll just have to see.

From where I am crouching in the underbrush, I can occasionally see Pippa, fifty yards off, when she shifts behind the juniper bush she has chosen to conceal her. I wonder if she's nervous. Pippa has one of the most important roles of all.

She is in charge of one of the bombs. The main force—the chaos at the wall—is meant mostly to enable the bombers, four in total, to slip unnoticed into Portland. Pippa's end goal is 88 Essex Street, an address I don't recognize, probably a government building, like the rest of the targets.

The sun inches up into the sky. Ten a.m. Ten thirty a.m. Noon.

Any minute now.

We wait.

Hana

"The car's here." My mother rests a hand on my shoulder. "Are you ready to go?"

I don't trust myself to speak, so I nod. The girl in the mirror—blond tendrils of hair pinned and pulled back, eyelashes dark with mascara, skin flawless, lips penciled in—nods as well.

"I'm very proud of you," my mother says in an undertone. People are bustling in and out of the room—photographers and makeup artists and Debbie, the hairdresser—and I imagine she is embarrassed. My mother has never in her whole life admitted to being proud of me.

"Here." My mother helps me slip into a soft cotton robe, so

my dress—sweeping, long, and fastened at the shoulder with a gold clip in the shape of an eagle, the animal to which Fred is most often compared—will remain spotless during the short drive down to the labs.

A group of journalists is clustered outside the gates, and as I emerge onto the porch, I am startled by the glare from so many lenses turned in my direction, the rapid-fire *click-click-click* of the shutters. The sun floats in the cloudless sky, a single white eye. It must be just before noon. I'm glad as soon as we make it to the car. The interior is dark, and cool, and I know that no one can see me behind the tinted windows.

"I really don't believe it." My mother plays with her bracelets. She's more excited than I've ever seen her. "I really thought this day would never come. Isn't that silly?"

"Silly," I echo. As we pull out of the subdivision, I see that the police presence has been redoubled. Half the streets leading downtown have been barricaded, patrolled by regulators, police, and even some men wearing the silver badges of the military guard. By the time I can see the sloped white roofs of the laboratory complex—where Fred and I will be married in one of the largest medical conference rooms, big enough to accommodate a thousand witnesses—the crowd in the streets is so dense, Tony can hardly inch the car along through it.

It seems as though all of Portland has turned out to watch me get married. People reach out and knuckle the hood of the car for good luck. Hands thump against the roof and the windows, making me jump. And police wade through the crowd, moving people aside, trying to clear a space for the car, intoning, "Let 'em through, let 'em through."

A series of police barricades has been erected just outside the laboratory gates. Several regulators move them aside so we can pass into the small paved parking lot just in front of the lab's main entrance. I recognize Fred's family's car. He must be here already.

My stomach gives a weird twist. I haven't been to the labs since my procedure was completed, since I entered a miserable, chewed-up girl, full of guilt and hurt and anger, and emerged something different, cleaner and less confused. That was the day they cut Lena away from me, and Steve Hilt, too, and all those sweaty, dark nights, when I wasn't sure of anything.

But that was really only the beginning of the cure. This—the pairing, the wedding, and Fred—is its conclusion.

The gates have been locked behind us again, and the barricades restored. Still, as I climb out of the car, I can feel the crowd pressing closer, closer—itching to come in, to watch, to see me pledge my life and future to the path that has been chosen for me. But the ceremony will not begin for another fifteen minutes, and the gates will remain closed until then.

Behind the revolving glass doors, I can see Fred waiting for me, unsmiling, arms folded. His face is distorted by the glare and the glass. From this distance, it looks as though his skin is full of holes.

"It's time," my mother says.

"I know," I say, and I pass in front of her, into the building.

Lena

It's time. The rifle shots explode simultaneously in the distance—a dozen of them at least—and just like that, we are moving as one. We are running out of the trees, hundreds of us, drumming up mud and dirt, the rhythm of our feet like a single, swollen heartbeat. Two rope ladders appear over the side of the wall, then another two, and then three more—so far, so good. The first of our group reaches a ladder, jumps, and swings upward.

In the distance, a band is playing a wedding march.

Hana

utside the laboratories, the guards—nearly two dozen of them, arrayed in spotless uniforms—fire off their rifle salute, signaling that the ceremony can proceed. The large windows of the conference room are open, and through them we can hear the band begin to play a wedding march. Most of the onlookers have not been able to squeeze into the labs and will be clustered outside, listening, straining to see through the windows. The priest is wearing a microphone so his voice will be amplified, so it will reach every member of the assembled crowd, touch them with his words of perfection and honor, of duty and safety.

A platform has been erected in the center of the room, just

in front of the podium where the priest will conduct the ceremony. Two participants, both dressed symbolically, in lab coats, help me onto it.

When Fred takes my hands in his and lays them on top of *The Book of Shhh*, a small sigh travels the room, an exhalation of relief.

This is what we are made for: promises, pledges, and sworn oaths of obedience.

Lena

I'm halfway up the ladder when the alarms begin to sound. A second later there is another explosion of gunfire. There is nothing coordinated about these shots; they explode in rapid staccato, deafeningly close, and just like that the air is a symphony of shouts and shots and screams. A woman straddling the wall topples backward and tumbles to the ground with a sickening thud, blood bubbling from her chest.

Only a tenth of our number has made it over the wall. The air is suddenly thick with gun smoke. People are yelling—*go, stop, move, stop where you are or I'll shoot!* For a second I freeze on the ladder, swinging, petrified—my hands slip a little, and I barely manage to right myself before falling. I can't remember how to move. At the top of the ladder, a regulator is hacking at the ropes with a knife.

"Go. Lena, go!" Julian is beneath me on the ladder. He reaches up and pushes, jolting me back into my body. I begin working my way upward again, ignoring the searing pain in my palms. Better to fight the regulators on the ground, where we have a chance—anything is better than swinging here, exposed, like a fish on a line.

The ladder shudders. The regulator is still working feverishly with his knife. He is young—he looks somehow familiar—and sweat is matting his blond hair to his forehead. Beast has just made it to the top of the wall. There's a crack, and a small yelp, as he drives his elbow into the regulator's nose.

The rest happens quickly: Beast gets his fist around the man's knife and thrusts; the regulator slumps forward, eyes unseeing, and Beast heaves him unceremoniously over the wall, as though he is a sack of garbage. He, too, thuds when he hits the ground: Only then do I recognize him as a boy from Joffrey's Academy, someone Hana once spoke to at the beach. My age—we were evaluated on the same day.

No time to think about that now.

Two more strong pulls get me to the top of the wall. I slide onto my stomach, pressing hard into the stone, trying to stay as small as possible. Compact. The inside of the wall is crisscrossed with scaffolding left over from construction. Only a few portions of the stone catwalk, meant for patrols, are complete: There are bodies tangled everywhere, people fighting, locked together, struggling for the advantage.

Pippa is working her way grimly up the ladder to my right. Tack has dropped into a crouch on the scaffolding; he is covering her, sweeping a gun from left to right, picking off the guards who are rushing us from the ground. Raven goes behind Pippa, the handle of a knife gripped in her mouth, a gun strapped to her hip. Her face is taut, and focused.

Everything registers in bursts, flashes:

Guards running at the wall, materializing from guard huts and warehouses.

Sirens wailing: police. They've been quick to respond to the alarms.

And beneath this, a squeeze in my gut—the landscape of roofs and roads; the grim-gray flow of pavement; Back Cove, shimmering in front of me; parks dotted in the distance; the sweep of the bay, beyond the distant white blot that is the laboratory complex: Portland. My home.

For a moment, I'm worried I'll faint. There are too many people—bodies swarming and swinging, faces contorted and grotesque—and too much sound. My throat burns with smoke. A piece of the scaffolding has caught fire. And still we haven't gotten more than a quarter of our number over the wall. I can't see my mother; I don't know what happened to her.

Then Julian has made it over, and he wraps an arm around my waist and forces me to my knees.

"Down! Down!" he's shouting, and we thud hard onto our knees as a series of bullets lodge into the wall behind us, spraying us with fine dust and stone-spit. The scaffolding groans and sways beneath us. Guards have massed on the ground, heaving its supports, trying to topple it.

Julian shouts something. His words are lost, but I know he is telling me that we need to move—we need to get to the ground. Next to me, Tack has reached back to help Pippa over the wall. She moves clumsily, weighted down by the backpack she carries. For a second, I imagine that the bomb will go off right here, right now—the blood and fire, the sweet-smelling smoke and the ricocheting stone shrapnel—but then Pippa is safely over the wall and climbing to her feet.

Just then a guard on the ground swings his rifle toward Pippa, locks her in his sights. I want to scream—I want to warn her—but I can't make a sound.

"Down, Pippa!" Raven launches herself over the wall, knocking Pippa out of the way just as the guard squeezes the trigger.

Pop. The littlest noise. A toy-firecracker sound.

Raven jerks and stiffens. For a second, I think she is only surprised: Her mouth goes round, her eyes wide.

Then she begins teetering backward, and I know that she is dead. Falling, falling, falling . . .

"No!" Tack lunges forward and grabs hold of her shirt before she can tumble back over the wall, pulling her down and onto his lap. People are swarming all around him, seething like rats over the scaffolding, but he just sits there, rocking a bit, cupping her face in his hands. He wipes her forehead, brushes the hair away from her face. She stares up at him sightlessly, her mouth open and wet, eyes shock-wide, black braid coiled against his thigh. His lips are moving—he's speaking to her.

And now there is a scream inside me, silent and huge, like a black hole tunneling deep through my center. I can't move, can't do anything but stare. This is not how Raven dies—not here, not in this way, not in one flimsy second, not without a fight.

Pop goes the weasel. The child's game comes back to me then, the way we used to chase one another around the park. *Pop. You're it.*

This is all a child's game. We are playing with shiny tin toys and loud noises. We are playing two-sides, like we used to when we were children.

Pop. White-hot pain blazes through me, past me. I bring my hand to my face instinctively and feel for injury; my fingers graze my ear and come away wet with blood. A bullet must have just clipped me.

The shock, even more than the pain, wakes me up, kicks my body into motion. There weren't enough guns to go around, but I have a knife—old and blunted, but still better than nothing. I wrestle it out of the leather pouch around my hips. Julian is making his way down the scaffolding, swinging along the crisscrossed iron bars like a monkey. A guard tries to grab hold of one of Julian's legs—Julian twists and brings his foot, hard, into the guard's face. The guard staggers back, releasing him, and Julian drops the remaining few feet to the ground, into the chaos of bodies: Invalids and officers, our side and their side, merging into one enormous, writhing, bloody animal.

I scoot to the edge of the catwalk and make the jump. The few seconds I am airborne—and a target—are the most terrifying. I am totally exposed, totally vulnerable. Two seconds—three seconds, tops, but it feels like an eternity.

I hit the ground, nearly on top of a regulator, and take him down with me as my ankle twists and I tumble onto the gravel. We are a wild tangle—momentarily entwined, struggling to gain the advantage. He tries to aim his gun at me, but I get his wrist in my hand and twist backward, hard. He yelps and drops the gun. Someone kicks it, and the gun spins away from my fingers, into the gray-dust chaos.

Then I see it barely a foot away. The regulator spots it at the same time, and we reach for it simultaneously. He's bigger than I am, but slower, too. I have it in my hand, close my fingers around the trigger a full second before him, and his fist connects with nothing but dirt. He roars, enraged, and lunges for me. I swing the gun up, catch him in the side of the head, hear a crack as the gun connects with his temple. He goes slack, and I launch myself to my feet before I can be trampled.

My mouth tastes like metal and dust, and my head has started to throb. I don't see Julian. I don't see my mother or Colin or Hunter.

Then: a rocking mortar-blast, an explosion of stone and white caulk-dust. The blow nearly takes me off my feet. At first I think one of the bombs must have been triggered accidentally and I look around for Pippa, trying to clear my head of the ringing, of the stinging, choking dust, just in time to see her slip, undetected, between two guard huts, heading for downtown.

Behind me, one of the scaffolds groans and begins to topple. There is a sharp swell in the screaming. Hands dig at my back as everyone presses forward, trying to break free from its path. Slowly, slowly, groaning, it teeters—and then accelerating, crashes to the ground, splintering, trapping the unlucky ones beneath its weight.

The wall is now sporting a gaping hole at its base; I realize this must have been the work of a pipe bomb, an explosion jerry-rigged by the resistance. Pippa's bomb would have ripped the wall in two.

Still, it's enough; our remaining forces are spilling through the opening, a current of people who have been pushed or forced out, dispossessed and diseased, flooding into Portland. The guards, a ragged line of blue-and-white uniforms, are swallowed up in the tide, pushed back, and forced to run.

I've lost Julian. No point in trying to find him now; I can only pray that he is safe, and that he'll make it out of this mess unharmed. I don't know what happened to Tack, either. Part of me hopes that he has retreated over the wall with Raven, and for a second I imagine that once he has gotten her back to the Wilds, she'll wake up. She'll open her eyes and find that the world has been rebuilt the way she wanted it.

Or maybe she won't wake up. Maybe she is already on a different pilgrimage, and has gone to find Blue again.

I push my way toward the place I saw Pippa vanish, struggling to breathe in the smoke-clotted air. One of the guard huts is burning. I flash back to the old license plate we found, half-buried in the mud, during our migration from Portland last winter.

Live free or die.

I stumble over a body. My stomach heaves into my mouth—for a split second, I'm overcome by blackness, coiled tight in my stomach like Raven's hair on Tack's leg, Raven's dead, *oh God*—but I swallow and breathe and keep going, keep fighting and pushing. We wanted the freedom to love. We wanted the freedom to choose. Now we have to fight for it.

At last I break free of the fighting. I duck past the guard huts, breaking into a run on the gravel path that divides them, heading for the sparse group of trees that encircles Back Cove. My ankle hurts every time I put my weight down on it, but I don't stop. I swipe my ear quickly with my sleeve and judge that the bleeding has already slowed.

The resistance may have a mission in Portland, but I have a mission of my own.

Hana

The alarms go off just before the priest can pronounce us husband and wife. One moment, everything is quiet and ordered. The music has died down, the crowd is silent, the priest's voice resonates through the room, rolls out over the audience. In the quiet, I can hear each individual camera shutter: opening and closing, opening and closing, like metal lungs.

The next moment everything is motion and sound, shrieking chaos, sirens. And I know, in that instant, that the Invalids are here. They've come for us.

Hands grab me roughly from all sides.

"Move, move, move." Bodyguards are piloting me toward

the exit. Someone steps on the end of my gown, and I hear it rip. My eyes are stinging; I'm choking on the smell of too much aftershave, too many bodies crowding and pulling.

"Come on, hurry it up. Hurry it up."

Walkie-talkies explode with static. Urgent voices shout in a coded language I don't understand. I try to turn around to look for my mother and am nearly carried off my feet by the pressure of the guards moving me forward. I catch a glimpse of Fred surrounded by his security team. He's white-faced, yelling into a cell phone. I will him to look at me—in that moment I forget about Cassie, I forget about everything. I need him to tell me we're okay; I need him to explain what's happening.

But he doesn't even glance in my direction.

Outside, the glare is blinding. I squeeze my eyes shut. Journalists jostle close to the doors, blocking the way to the car. The long metal barrels of their camera lenses look for a second like guns, all directed straight at me.

They're going to kill us all.

The bodyguards fight to clear space for me, shouldering apart the rushing stream of people. At last we reach the car. Once again, I look for Fred. Our eyes meet briefly across the crowd. He's heading for a squad car.

"Take her to my house." He yells this to Tony, then turns around and ducks into the back of a police car. That's it. No words at all for me.

Tony puts a hand on top of my head and directs me roughly into the backseat. Two of Fred's bodyguards slide in next to me, guns out. I want to ask them to put their weapons away, but my brain doesn't seem to be working correctly. I can't remember either of their names.

Tony jerks the car into gear, but the knots of people gathered in the parking lot mean that we're trapped. Tony leans on the horn. I cover my ears and remind myself to breathe; we're safe, we're in the car, it will be okay. The police will take care of everything.

Finally, we begin to move forward, plowing steadily through the dispersing crowd. It takes us nearly twenty minutes to make it out of the long drive leading down to the labs. We turn right onto Commercial Street, which is clotted with more foot traffic, then zip against traffic into a narrow one-way street. In the car, everyone is silent, watching the blur of people in the streets—people running, panicked, undirected. Even though I can see people openmouthed, shouting, only the sound of the alarms penetrates the thick windows. Strangely, this is more frightening than anything—all these people voiceless, screaming silently.

We barrel down an alley so narrow, I'm positive we'll get stuck between the brick walls on either side of us. Then we turn down another one-way street, this one relatively free of people. We blow straight past the stop signs, and jerk left into another alley. Finally, we're really moving.

It occurs to me to try and reach my mother on her cell phone, but when I dial her number, the phone system keeps returning an error. The system must be overloaded. I suddenly feel very small. The system is security; it is everything. In Portland, there is always someone watching.

But now it seems the system has been blinded.

"Turn on the radio," I tell Tony. He does. The National News Service patches in. The announcer's voice is reassuring, almost lazy—speaking terrifying words in a tone of total calm.

"... *breach at the wall* ... *everyone urged not to panic* ... *until the police can restore control* ... *lock doors and windows, stay inside* ... *regulators and every government official working hard in tandem*—"

The announcer's voice cuts off abruptly. For a moment there is nothing but static. Tony spins the dial, but the speakers continue buzzing and popping, letting out nothing but white noise. Then, suddenly, an unfamiliar voice comes in, overloud and urgent:

"*We are taking back the city. We are taking back our rights and our freedom. Join us. Take down the walls. Take down the*—"

Tony punches the radio off. The silence in the car rings out, deafening. I flash back to the morning of the first terrorist attacks, when at ten a.m., in the middle of a peaceful, every-day Tuesday, three blasts went off simultaneously in Portland. I was in a car then, I remember; when my mother and I heard the announcement on the radio, we didn't believe it at first. We didn't believe it until we saw the smoke clotting the sky, and saw the people begin to stream past us, running, pale, and the ash began to drift like snow.

Cassandra said that Fred let those attacks happen, to prove

350

that the Invalids were out there, to show that they were monstrous. But now the monsters are here, inside the walls, in our streets again. I can't believe that he would let this happen.

I have to believe that he will fix it, even if it means killing them all.

We've finally shaken off the chaos and the crowds. We're near Cumberland now, where Lena used to live, in the quietly run-down residential portion of the city. In the distance, the foghorn in the old watchtower on Munjoy Hill begins blowing, sending mournful notes beneath and beyond the alarms. I wish we were heading home instead of to Fred's house. I want to curl up in my bed and sleep; I want to wake up and find that today was all just a nightmare that has pushed through the cracks, past the cure.

But my home is no longer my home. Even if the priest did not get to finish his pronouncement, I am now officially married to Fred Hargrove. Nothing will ever be the same.

Left onto Sherman; then right into yet another alley, which will dump us onto Park. Just as we reach the end of the alley, someone runs out in front of the car, a gray blur.

Tony shouts and slams on the brakes, but it's too late. I have time to register the tattered clothing, the long, matted hair—*Invalid*—before the impact carries her off her feet. She spins across the hood—fans for a second against the windshield—and drops out of sight again.

Anger crests inside me, sudden and startling, a stabbing peak of it that breaks through the fear. I lean forward, shouting,

"It's one of them, it's one of them! *Don't* let her get away!"

Tony and the other guards don't need to be asked twice. In an instant, they're rocketing into the street, guns drawn, leaving the doors of the car hanging open. My hands are shaking. I squeeze them into fists and lean back, taking deep breaths, trying to calm down. With the doors open, I can hear the alarms more clearly, and distant sounds of shouting, too, like the echo-roar of the ocean.

This is Portland, my Portland. In that moment, nothing else matters—not the lies or the mistakes, and the promises we've failed to keep. This is my city, and my city is under attack. The anger tightens.

Tony is hauling the girl to her feet. She is fighting, although she is outnumbered and completely outmatched. Her hair is hanging in her face, and she's kicking and scratching like an animal.

Maybe I'll kill this one myself.

Lena

By the time I make it onto Forest Avenue, the sound of the fighting has faded, swallowed by the shrill cries of the alarms. Every so often I see a hand twitching at a curtain, a fishbowl-eye peering down at me and then vanishing just as quickly. Everyone is staying locked up and locked in.

I keep my head down, moving as quickly as I can despite the throbbing in my ankle where I landed on it wrong, listening for sounds of squads and patrols. There's no way I'll be mistaken for anything but an Invalid: I'm filthy, wearing old, mud-splattered clothes, and my ear is still streaked with blood. Amazingly, there's no one on the streets. Security forces must have been diverted elsewhere. This is, after all, the poorer part of town; no doubt the city doesn't feel these people need protection.

A path and a road for everyone . . . and for some, a path straight into the ground.

I make it to Cumberland without problems. As soon as I step onto my old block, I feel for a moment as though I'm caught in a still life from the past. It seems forever ago that I used to turn down this block on my way home from school; that I used to stretch here after my runs, placing one leg on top of the bus-stop bench; that I would watch Jenny and the other kids playing kick the can, and open up the fire hydrants for them when it got hot in the summer.

It *was* a lifetime ago. I'm a different Lena now.

The street, too, looks different—saggier, as though an invisible black hole is spiraling the whole block slowly down into itself. Even before I reach the gate in front of number 237, I know that the house will be empty. The certainty is lodged like a hard weight between my lungs. But I still stand stupidly in the middle of the sidewalk, staring up at the now-abandoned building—*my home, my old house, the little bedroom on the top floor, the smells of soap and laundry and cooked tomato*—taking in the peeling paint and the rotting porch steps, the boarded-up windows, the faded red *X* spray-painted on the door, marking the house as condemned.

I feel as if I've been punched in the stomach. Aunt Carol was always so proud of the house. She wouldn't let a single season go by without repainting, cleaning out the gutters, scrubbing the porch.

Then the grief is replaced by panic. Where did they go?

What happened to Grace?

In the distance, the foghorn bellows, sounding like a funeral song. I start, and recall suddenly where I am: in a foreign, hostile city. It is no longer my place; I am not welcome here. The foghorn blows a second, and then a third time. The signal means that all three bombs have been successfully dropped; that gives us an hour until they blow and all hell breaks loose.

That gives me only an hour to find her—and I have no idea where to begin.

A window bangs shut behind me. I turn just in time to see a white-moon worried face—looks like Mrs. Hendrickson—disappear from view. One thing is obvious: I need to move.

I duck my head and continue hurriedly down the road, turning as soon as I see a narrow alley between buildings. I'm moving blindly now, hoping that my feet will carry me in the right direction. *Grace, Grace, Grace.* I pray that she might somehow hear me.

Blindly: across Mellen, toward yet another alley, a black gaping mouth, a place of sideways shadows to conceal me. *Grace, where are you?* In my head, I'm screaming it—screaming so loudly it swallows up everything else and whites out the sound of the approaching car.

And then, out of nowhere, it's there: the engine ticking and panting, the window reflecting light in my eyes, blinding me, the squealing wheels as the driver tries to stop. Then pain, and a sensation of tumbling—I think I'm going to die; I see the sky revolving above me, I see Alex's face, smiling—and then I feel the hard bite of pavement underneath me. The air gets knocked out of me and I roll over onto my back, my lungs stuttering, fighting for air.

For a confused moment, watching the blue sky above me, strung taut and high between the roofs of the buildings, I forget where I am. I feel like I'm floating, drifting across a surface of blue water. All I know is I'm not dead. My body is still mine: I twitch my hands and flex my feet just to be sure. Miraculously, I managed to avoid hitting my head.

Doors slam. Voices are shouting. I remember that I need to move—I need to get to my feet. *Grace.* But before I can do anything, hands grab me roughly by the arms, haul me to my feet. Everything is coming to me in flashes. Dark black suits. Guns. Mean faces.

Very bad.

Instinct takes over, and I begin twisting and kicking. I bite down on the hand of the guard who is gripping me, but he doesn't release me, and another guard steps forward and slaps me in the face. The blow stings and sends a fiery explosion across my vision. I spit blindly at him. Another guard—there are three of them—aims his gun at my head. His eyes are as black and cold as cut stone, full of not hatred—*cureds don't hate, cureds don't hate and they don't care, either*—but disgust, as though I am a particularly disgusting brand of insect, and I know then that I will die.

I'm sorry, Alex. And Julian, too. I'm sorry.

I'm sorry, Grace.

I close my eyes.

"Wait!"

I open my eyes. A girl is emerging from the backseat.

She is dressed in the white muslin of a new bride. Her hair is elaborately knotted and curled around her head, and her procedural scar has been highlighted with makeup, so it looks like a little colored star just beneath her left ear. She is beautiful; she looks just like the paintings of angels we used to see in church.

Then her eyes land on me, and my stomach wrenches. The ground opens underneath me. I can hardly trust myself to stand.

"Lena," she says calmly. It is more of an announcement than a greeting.

I can't bring myself to speak. I can't say her name, even though it screams, echoing, through my head.

Hana.

"Where are we going?"

Hana turns toward me. These are the first words I have managed to say to her. For a second she registers surprise, and something else, too. Pleasure? It's hard to tell. Her expressions are different, and I can't read her face anymore.

"My house," she says after a brief pause.

I could laugh out loud. She's so ridiculously calm; she could be inviting me over to surf LAMM for music, or curl up on her couch and watch a movie.

"You're not going to turn me in?" My voice is sarcastic. I know she's going to turn me in; I knew it the moment I saw the scar, saw the flatness behind her eyes, like a pool that has lost all its depth.

Either she doesn't detect the challenge or she chooses to ignore it. "I will," she says simply. "But not yet." An expression flickers across her face—a momentary uncertainty—and she seems about to say something else. Instead she turns back to the window, chewing her lower lip.

That bothers me, the lip-chewing. It is a break in her surface of calm, a ripple I didn't expect. It's the old Hana peeking out of this shiny new version, and it makes my stomach cramp again. I'm overwhelmed by the momentary urge to throw my arms around her, to inhale her smell—*two dabs of vanilla at the elbows, and jasmine on her neck*—to tell her how much I've missed her.

Just in time, she catches me staring at her and presses her mouth firmly into a line. And I remind myself that the old Hana is gone. She probably doesn't even smell the same. She hasn't asked me a single question about what has happened to me, where I've been, how I came to be in Portland, streaked with blood and wearing dirt-encrusted clothing. She has barely looked at me at all, and when she does, it is with a vague, detached curiosity, as though I'm a strange animal species in a zoo.

I'm expecting us to turn toward West End, but instead we head off-peninsula. Hana must have moved. The houses here are even larger and statelier than in her old neighborhood.

I don't know why I'm surprised. That is one thing I have learned during my time with the resistance. The cure is about control. It's about structure. And the rich get richer and richer, while the poor get squeezed into narrow alleys and cramped apartments, and told they are being protected, and promised they will be rewarded in heaven for obedience. Servitude is called safety.

We turn onto a street lined with ancient-looking maple trees, whose branches embrace overhead to form a canopy. A street sign flashes by: Essex Street. My stomach gives another violent twist. 88 Essex Street is where Pippa has planted the bomb. How long has it been since the foghorn blew? Ten minutes? Fifteen?

Sweat is pooling under my arms. I scan the mailboxes as we pass. One of these homes—one of these glorious white houses, crowned like cakes with latticework and cupolas, ringed with wide white porches and set back from the street on vivid green lawns—is going to blow in less than an hour.

The car slows to a stop in front of ornate iron gates. The driver leans out his window to punch a code into a keypad, and the gates whir smoothly open. It reminds me of Julian's old house in New York City, and amazes me still: all this power, all this energy flowing and pumping to a handful of people.

Hana is still staring impassively out the window, and I have the sudden urge to reach out and drive my fist through her image as it is reflected there. She has no idea what the rest of the world is like. She has never seen hardship or been without food, without heat or comfort. I'm amazed that she could ever have been my best friend. We were always living in two separate worlds; I was just stupid enough to believe it didn't matter.

Towering hedges surround the car on both sides, flanking a short drive that leads to another monstrous house. It is larger than any we have seen thus far. An iron number is nailed above the front door.

88.

For an instant, my vision goes black. I blink. But the number is still there.

88 Essex Street. The bomb is here. Sweat tickles my lower back. It doesn't make any sense; the other bombs are planted downtown, in municipal buildings, like they were last year.

"You live here?" I say to Hana. She is getting out of the car, still with that same infuriating calm, as though we're on a social visit.

Once again, she hesitates. "It's Fred's house," she says. "I guess we share it now." When I stare at her, she amends, "Fred Hargrove. He's mayor."

I had completely forgotten that Hana was paired with Fred Hargrove. We'd heard rumors through the resistance that Hargrove senior had been killed during the Incidents. Fred must have taken his father's place. Now it begins to make sense that a bomb was planted in his home; nothing is more symbolic than striking the leader directly. But we've miscalculated—it isn't Fred who will be at home. It's Hana.

My mouth feels dry and itchy. One of her goons tries to grab me and force me out of the car, and I wrench away from him.

"I'm not going to run," I practically spit, and slide out of the car on my own. I know I wouldn't get more than three feet before they opened fire. I'll have to watch carefully, and think, and look for an opportunity to escape. No way am I going to be within three blocks of this place when it blows.

Hana has preceded us up the porch steps. She waits, her back to me, until one of the guards steps forward and opens the door. I feel a rush of hatred for this brittle, spoiled girl, with her spotless white linens and her vast rooms.

Inside, it's surprisingly dark, full of lots of polished, dark oak and leather. Most of the windows are half-obscured by elaborate drapery and velvet curtains. Hana starts to lead me into the living room, and then thinks better of it. She continues down the hall without bothering to switch on the light, turning back only once to look at me with an expression I can't decipher, and finally leads me through two swinging doors and into the kitchen.

This room, in contrast with the rest of the house, is very bright. Large windows face out over an enormous backyard. The wood here is shaved pine or ash, soft and nearly white, and the counters are spotless white marble.

The guards follow us into the room. Hana turns to them.

"Leave us," she says. Illuminated by the slanted sunlight, which makes it appear as if she is glowing slightly, she once again looks like an angel. I'm struck by her stillness, and by the quietness of the house, its cleanliness and beauty.

And somewhere in its underbelly, buried deep, a tumor is growing, ticking toward its eventual explosion.

361

The guard who was driving—the one who had me in a headlock earlier—makes noises of protest, but Hana silences him quickly.

"I said, leave us." For a second, the old Hana resurges; I see the defiance in her eyes, the imperial tilt of her chin. "And close the doors behind you."

The guards file out reluctantly. I can feel the weight of their stares, and I know that if Hana were not here, I would already be dead. But I refuse to feel grateful to her. I won't.

When they are gone, Hana stares at me for a minute in silence. Her expression is unreadable. Finally she says, "You're too skinny."

I could almost laugh. "Yeah, well. The restaurants in the Wilds are mostly closed. They're mostly bombed, actually." I don't bother keeping the edge out of my voice.

She doesn't react. She just keeps watching me. Another beat of silence passes. Then she gestures to the table. "Sit down."

"I'd rather stand, thanks."

Hana frowns. "You can treat that as an order."

I don't really think that she'll call the guards back if I refuse to sit, but there's no point in risking it. I slide into a chair, glaring at her the whole time. But I can't get comfortable. It has been twenty minutes at least since the foghorn blew. That means I have less than forty minutes to get out of here.

As soon as I sit, Hana whirls around and disappears into the back of the kitchen, where a dark gap beyond the refrigerator indicates a pantry. Before I can think of escape, she reemerges, carrying a loaf of bread wrapped in a tea towel. She stands at the counter and slices off thick hunks, slathering them in butter and piling them high onto a plate. Then she moves to the sink and wets the tea towel.

Watching her turn on the faucet, watching the steaming water that appears instantly, I am filled with envy. It has been forever since I've had a proper shower, or gotten to clean myself except in frigid rivers.

"Here." She passes me the hot towel. "You're a mess."

"I didn't have time to do my makeup," I reply sarcastically. But I take the towel anyway, and touch it gingerly to my ear. I've stopped bleeding, at least, although the towel comes back flecked with dried blood. I keep my eyes on her as I wipe off my face and hands. I wonder what she is thinking.

She slides the plate of bread in front of me when I've finished with the towel, and fills a glass with water, along with real ice cubes, five of them rattling joyfully together.

"Eat," she says. "Drink."

"I'm not hungry," I lie.

She rolls her eyes, and once again I see the old Hana float up into this new impostor. "Don't be stupid. Of course you're hungry. You're starving. You're probably dying of thirst, too."

"Why are you doing this?" I ask her.

Hana opens her mouth and then closes it again. "We were friends," she says.

"*Were*," I say firmly. "Now we're enemies."

"Are we?" Hana looks startled, as though the idea has never occurred to her. Once again, I feel a flicker of unease, a squirming feeling of guilt. Something isn't right. I force the feelings down.

"Of course," I say.

Hana watches me for a second more. Then, abruptly, she gets up from the table and moves over to the windows. Once her back is to me, I quickly take a piece of bread and stuff it in my mouth, eating as quickly as I can without choking. I wash it down with a long slug of water, so cold it brings a blazing, delicious pain to my head.

For a long time, Hana doesn't say anything. I eat another piece of bread. She can no doubt hear me chewing, but she doesn't comment on it or turn around. She allows me to keep up the pretense that I am not eating, and I experience a brief burst of gratitude.

"I'm sorry about Alex," she says at last, still without turning.

My stomach gives an uncomfortable twist. Too much; too quickly.

"He didn't die." My voice sounds overloud. I don't know why I feel the urge to tell her. But I need her to know that her side, her people, didn't win, at least not in this case. Even though of course, in some ways, they did.

She turns around. "What?"

"He didn't die," I repeat. "He was thrown into the Crypts."

Hana flinches, as though I've reached out and slapped her. She sucks her lower lip into her mouth again and starts chewing. "I—" She stops herself, frowning a little.

"What?" I know that face; I recognize it. She knows something. "What is it?"

"Nothing, I . . ." She shakes her head, as though to dislodge an idea there. "I thought I saw him."

My stomach surges into my throat. "Where?"

"Here." She looks at me with another one of her inscrutable expressions. The new Hana is much harder to read than the old one. "Last night. But if he's in the Crypts . . ."

"He's not. He escaped." Hana, the light, the kitchen—even the bomb ticking quietly underneath us, moving us slowly toward oblivion—suddenly seem far away. As soon as Hana suggests it, I see that it makes sense. Alex was all alone. He would have gone back to familiar territory.

Alex could be here—somewhere in Portland. Close. Maybe there's hope after all.

If I can only get out of here.

"So?" I push up from the chair. "Are you going to call the regulators, or what?"

Even as I'm talking, I'm planning. I could probably take her down, if it comes to it, but the idea of attacking her makes me uneasy. And she'll no doubt put up a fight. By the time I get the better of her, the guards will be on top of us.

But if I can get her out of the kitchen for even a few seconds— I'll put the chair through the window, cut through the garden, try to lose the guards in the trees. The garden probably backs up onto another street; if not, I'll have to loop around to Essex. It's a long shot, but it's a chance.

Hana watches me steadily. The clock above the stove seems

to be moving at record speed, and I imagine the timer on the bomb ticking forward as well.

"I want to apologize to you," she says calmly.

"Oh yeah? For what?" I don't have time for this. We don't have time for this. I push away thoughts of what will happen to Hana even if I manage to escape. She'll be here, in the house . . .

My stomach is clenching and unclenching. I'm worried the bread will come straight back up. I have to stay focused. What happens to Hana isn't my concern, and it isn't my fault, either.

"For telling the regulators about 37 Brooks," she says. "For telling them about you and Alex."

Just like that, my brain powers down. *"What?"*

"I told them." She lets out a tiny exhalation, as though saying the words has given her relief. "I'm sorry. I was jealous."

I can't speak. I'm swimming through a fog. *"Jealous?"* I manage to spit out.

"I—I wanted what you had with Alex. I was confused. I didn't understand what I was doing." She shakes her head again.

I have a swinging, seasick feeling. It doesn't make any sense. Hana—golden girl Hana, my best friend, fearless and reckless. I trusted her. I loved her. "You were my best friend."

"I know." Again she looks troubled, as though trying to recall the meaning of the words.

"You had *everything*." I can't stop my voice from rising. The anger is vibrating, ripping through me like a live current. "Perfect life. Perfect grades. Everything." I gesture to the spotless kitchen, to the sunshine pouring over the marble counters like drizzled butter. "I had nothing. He was my one thing. My only—" The sickness surges up and I take a step forward, clenching my fists, blind with rage. "Why couldn't you let me have it? Why did you have to take it? Why did you always take everything?"

"I told you I was sorry," Hana says again mechanically. I could shriek with laughter. I could cry, or tear her eyes out.

Instead I reach out and slap her. The current flows down into my hand, into my arm, before I know what I am doing. The noise is unexpectedly loud, and for a moment I'm sure the guards will burst through the door. But no one comes.

Instantly, Hana's face begins to redden. But she doesn't cry out. She doesn't make a sound.

In the silence, I can hear my own breathing—ragged and desperate. I feel tears pushing at the back of my eyes. I'm ashamed and angry and sick all at once.

Hana turns slowly back to face me. She almost looks sad. "I deserved that," she says.

Suddenly I am overcome with exhaustion. I am tired of fighting, of hitting and being hit. This is the strange way of the world, that people who simply want to love are instead forced to become warriors. It's the upside-down nature of life. It's all I can do not to collapse into a chair again.

"I felt terrible afterward," Hana says in a voice hardly above a whisper. "You should know that. That's why I helped you escape. I felt"—Hana searches for the right word—"*remorse*."

"What about now?" I ask her.

Hana lifts a shoulder. "Now I'm cured," she says. "It's different."

"Different how?" For a split second, I wish—more than anything, more than breathing—that I had stayed here, with her, that I had let the knife fall.

"I feel freer," she says. Whatever I was expecting her to say, it isn't this. She must sense that I'm surprised, because she goes on. "Everything's kind of . . . muffled. Like hearing sounds underwater. I don't have to feel things for other people so much." One side of her mouth quirks into a smile. "Maybe, like you said, I never did."

My head has started to ache. Over. It's all over. I just want to curl up in a ball and go to sleep. "I didn't mean that. You did. Feel things, I mean, for other people. You used to."

I'm not sure she hears me. She says, almost as an afterthought, "I don't have to listen to anybody anymore." Something in her tone is off—triumphant, almost. When I look at her, she smiles. I wonder whether she's thinking of anyone in particular.

There is the sound of a door opening and closing and the bark of a man's voice. Hana's whole face changes. She gets serious again in an instant. "Fred," she says. She crosses quickly to the swinging doors behind me and pokes her head into the hall tentatively. Then she whirls around to face me, suddenly breathless.

"Come on," she says. "Quick, while he's in the study."

"Come on where?" I say.

Hana looks momentarily irritated. "The back door leads

onto the porch. From there you can cut through the garden and onto Dennett. That will take you back to Brighton. Quickly," she adds. "If he sees you, he'll kill you."

I'm so shocked that for a moment I just stand there, gaping at her. "Why?" I say. "Why are you helping me?"

Hana smiles again, but her eyes stay cloudy and unreadable. "You said it yourself. I was your best friend."

All at once, my energy returns. She's going to let me go. Before she can change her mind, I move toward her. She presses her back against one of the swinging doors, keeping it open for me, poking her head into the hall every few seconds to make sure the coast is clear. Just as I'm about to scoot past her, I stop.

Jasmine and vanilla. She still wears it after all. She *does* smell the same.

"Hana," I say. I'm standing so close to her, I can see the gold threaded through the blue of her eyes. I lick my lips. "There's a bomb."

She jerks back a fraction of an inch. "What?"

I don't have time to regret what I'm saying. "Here. Somewhere in the house. Get out of here, okay? Get yourself out." She'll take Fred, too, and the explosion will be a failure, but I don't care. I loved Hana once, and she is helping me now. I owe this to her.

Once again, her expression is unreadable. "How much time?" she asks abruptly.

I shake my head. "Ten, fifteen minutes tops."

She nods to show that she has understood. I move past

369

her, into the darkness of the hallway. She stays where she is, pressed against the swinging doors, rigid as a statue. She lifts her chin toward the back door.

Just as I'm placing a hand on a door handle, she calls to me in a whisper.

"I almost forgot." She moves toward me, her dress rustling, and for a moment I am struck by the impression that she is a ghost. "Grace is in the Highlands. 31 Wynnewood Road. They're living there now."

I stare at her. Somewhere, deep inside this stranger, my best friend is buried. "Hana—" I start to say.

She cuts me off. "Don't thank me," she says in a low voice. "Just go."

Impulsively, without thinking about what I am doing, I reach out and seize her hand. Two long pulses, two short ones. Our old signal.

Hana looks startled; then, slowly, her face relaxes. For just one second, she shines as though lit up by a torch from within. "I remember . . ." she whispers.

A door slams somewhere. Hana wrenches away, looking suddenly afraid. She pivots me around and pushes me toward the door.

"Go," she says, and I do. I don't look back.

Hana

I have counted thirty-three seconds on the clock when Fred bursts into the kitchen, red-faced.

"Where is she?" His armpits are wet with sweat, and his hair—so carefully combed and gelled at the ceremony—is a mess.

I'm tempted to ask him who he means, but I know it will only infuriate him. "Escaped," I say.

"What do you mean? Marcus told me—"

"She hit me," I say. I hope that Lena left a mark when she slapped me. "I—I cracked my head on the wall. She ran."

"Shit." Fred rakes a hand through his hair, steps out into the hall, and bellows for the guards. Then he turns back to me.

"Why the hell didn't you let Marcus take care of it? Why were you alone with her in the first place?"

"I wanted information," I say. "I thought she was more likely to give it to me alone."

"Shit," Fred says again. The more worked up he gets, strangely, the calmer I feel.

"What's going on, Fred?"

He kicks a chair suddenly, sending it skittering across the kitchen. "Goddamn *chaos*, that's what's going on." He can't stop moving; he clenches his fist, and for a moment, I think he might go for me, just to have something to punch. "There must be a thousand people rioting. Some of them Invalids. Some of them just kids. Stupid, stupid. . . . If they knew—"

He breaks off as his guards come jogging down the hall.

"*She* let the girl get away," Fred says, without giving them a chance to ask what's wrong. The scorn in his voice is obvious.

"She hit me," I repeat again.

I can feel Marcus staring at me. I deliberately avoid his eyes. He can't possibly know that I let Lena escape. I gave no indication that I knew her; I was careful not to look at her in the car.

When Marcus's eyes pass back to Fred, I allow myself to exhale.

"What do you want us to do?" Marcus asks.

"I don't know." Fred rubs his forehead. "I need to think. Goddamn. I need to *think*."

"The girl bragged about reinforcements on Essex," I say.

372

"She said there was an Invalid posted at every house on the street."

"Shit." Fred stands still for a moment, staring out at the backyard. Then he rolls his shoulders back. "All right. I'll call down to 1-1-1 for reinforcements. In the meantime, get out there and start combing the streets. Look for movement in the trees. Let's rout as many of these little shits as we can. I'll be right behind you."

"Got it." Marcus and Bill disappear into the hall.

Fred picks up the phone. I put a hand on his arm. He turns to me, annoyed, and hangs up.

"What do you want?" he practically spits.

"Don't go out there, Fred," I say. "Please. The girl said— the girl said the others were armed. She said they'd open fire if you so much as put your head out the door—"

"I'll be fine." He jerks away from me.

"Please," I repeat. I close my eyes and think a brief prayer to God. *I'm sorry.* "It's not worth it, Fred. We need you. Stay inside. Let the police do their jobs. Promise me you won't leave the house."

A muscle flexes in his jaw. A long moment passes. At every second, I keep expecting the blast: a tornado of wooden shrapnel, a roaring tunnel of fire. I wonder if it will hurt.

God forgive me, for I have sinned.

"All right," Fred says at last. "I promise." He lifts up the receiver again. "Just stay out of the way. I don't want you screwing anything up."

"I'll be upstairs," I tell him. He has already turned his back to me.

I pass into the hall, letting the swinging doors close behind me. I can hear the muffled sound of his voice through the wood. Any minute now, the inferno.

I think about going upstairs, into what would have been my room. I could lie down and close my eyes; I'm almost tired enough to sleep.

But instead I ease the back door open, cross the porch, and go down into the garden, being careful to stay out of sight of the large kitchen windows. The air smells like spring, like wet earth and new growth. Birds call in the trees. Wet grass clings to my ankles, and dirties the hem of my wedding dress.

The trees enfold me, and then I can no longer see the house.

I will not stay to watch it burn.

Lena

The Highlands are burning.

I smell the fire well before I get there, and when I'm still a quarter-mile away, I can see the smudge of smoke above the trees, and flames licking up from the old, weather-beaten roofs.

On Harmon Road, I spotted an open garage and a rusted bike mounted on the wall like a hunter's trophy. Even though the bike is a piece of crap, and the gears groan and protest whenever I try to adjust them, it's better than nothing. I actually don't mind the noise—the rattling of the chains or the hard ringing of the wind in my ears. It keeps me from thinking of Hana, and from trying to understand what happened.

It drowns out her voice in my head, saying, *Go*.

It doesn't drown out the blast, though, or the sirens that follow afterward. I can hear them even when I have made it almost all the way to the Highlands, cresting like screams.

I hope she got out. I say a prayer that she did, although I no longer know who I'm praying to.

And then I'm in the Highlands, and I can think only of Grace.

The first thing I see is the fire, which is leaping from house to house, from tree to roof to wall. Whoever set the fire did it deliberately, systematically. The first group of Invalids breached the fence not far from here; this must be the work of regulators.

The second thing I notice is the people: people running through the trees, bodies indistinct in the smoke. This startles me. When I lived in Portland, Deering Highlands was deserted, cleared out after accusations of the disease made it a wasteland. I haven't had time to think about what it means that Grace and my aunt are living here now, or consider that others might have made their home here as well.

I try to pick out familiar faces as they blur past me, darting through the trees, shouting. I can't see anything but form and color, people holding bundles of their belongings in their arms. Children are wailing, and my heart stops: Any one of them could be Grace. Little Grace, who barely made a sound—she could be shrieking in the half dark somewhere.

A hot, electric feeling is pulsing through me, as though

the flames have made their way into my blood. I'm trying to remember the layout of the Highlands, but my mind is full of static: An image of 37 Brooks, of the blanket in the garden and the trees lit gold by the dipping sun, keeps playing there. I hit Edgewood and know I've gone too far.

I turn around, coughing, and retrace my path. The air is full of cracking, thunderbolt crashes: Whole houses are engulfed, standing like shivering ghosts, burning white-hot, doors gaping, skin melting from flesh. *Please, please, please.* The word drills through my head. *Please.*

Then I spot the sign for Wynnewood Road: a short three-block street, fortunately. Here the fire has not spread so far and remains caught up in the tangled canopy of trees, and skating over the roofs, an ever-growing crown of white and orange. By now, the people in the trees have thinned, but I keep thinking I hear children crying—ghostly, wailing echoes.

I'm sweating, and my eyes are burning. When I ditch the bike, I struggle to catch my breath. I bring my shirt to my face and try to breathe through it as I jog down the street. Half the houses don't have any visible numbers. I know that in all probability, Grace has fled. I hope she was one of the people I saw moving through the trees, but I can't shake the fear that she might be trapped somewhere, that Aunt Carol and Uncle William and Jenny might have left her behind. She was always curling up in corners and hiding in hidden, recessed spaces, trying to make herself as invisible as possible.

A faded mailbox indicates number 31, a sad, sagging house,

smoke churning out of its upper windows, flames licking across its weather-beaten roof. Then I see her—or at least I think I do. Just for a second, I swear I see her face, pale as a flame, in one of the windows. But before I can call out, she vanishes.

I take a deep breath and dart across the lawn and up the half-rotted steps. I stop just inside the front door, momentarily dizzy. I recognize the furniture—the faded striped couch, the rug with its singed tassels, and the stain on the old red throw pillows where Jenny spilled her grape juice, still barely visible—from my old house, Aunt Carol's place on Cumberland. I feel as though I've stumbled directly into the past, but a warped past: a past that smells like smoke and wet wallpaper, with rooms that have been distorted.

I go from room to room, calling out to Grace, checking behind furniture and in the closets of several rooms that are totally vacant. This house is much larger than our old one, and there is not nearly enough stuff to fill it. She is gone. Maybe she was never here—maybe I only imagined her face.

Upstairs is black with smoke. I can only make it halfway to the landing when I am forced back downstairs, heaving and coughing. Now the front rooms, too, are on fire. Cheap shower curtains are tacked to the windows. They go up in one lick, letting off the stink of plastic.

I back into the kitchen, feeling like a giant has its fist around my chest, needing to get out, needing to breathe. I heave my shoulder into the back door—swollen with heat, it resists—and finally go stumbling into the backyard, coughing, eyes watering. I'm not thinking anymore; my feet are moving me automatically away from the fire, toward clean air, *away*, when I feel a shooting pain in my foot and I am falling. I hit the ground and look back to see what has tripped me: a door handle, a cellar, half-obscured by the long grass on either side of it.

I don't know what makes me reach back and wrench open the door—instinct, maybe, or superstition. A set of steep wood stairs runs down to a small underground cellar, roughly hacked out of the earth. The tiny room is fitted with shelves, and stocked with cans of food. Several glass bottles—soda, maybe—are lined up on the ground.

She's squeezed so far into a corner, I almost miss her. Luckily, before I can close the door again, she shifts, and one of her sneakers comes into view, illuminated in the smoky red light pouring in from above. The shoes are new, but I recognize the purple laces, which she colored in herself.

"Grace." My voice is hoarse. I ease down onto the top step. As my eyes adjust to the dimness, Grace floats into focus—taller than she was eight months ago, thinner and dirtier, too—crouched in the corner, staring at me with wild, terrified eyes. "Grace, it's me."

I reach out to her, but she doesn't move. I ease myself down a step farther, reluctant to go into the cellar and try to grab her. She was always fast; I'm afraid she'll duck and run. My heart is throbbing painfully in my throat, and my mouth tastes like smoke. There's a sharp, pungent smell in the cellar

I can't identify. I focus on Grace, on getting her to move.

"It's me, Grace," I try again. I can only imagine what I must look like to her, how changed I must appear. "It's Lena. Your cousin Lena."

She stiffens, as though I've reached out and shocked her. "Lena?" she whispers, her voice awed. But still she doesn't move. Above us, there is a thunderous crash. A tree branch, or a piece of the roof. I have a sudden terror that we will be buried in here if we don't move now. The house will collapse, we'll be trapped.

"Come on, Gracie," I say, invoking an old nickname. The back of my neck is sweaty. "We've got to go, okay?"

At last Grace moves. She strikes out clumsily with a foot, and I hear the tinkle of glass breaking. The smell intensifies, burning the inside of my nostrils, and suddenly I place it.

Gas.

"I didn't mean to," Grace says, her voice high-pitched, shrill with panic. She is crouching now, and I watch a dark stain of liquid spread on the packed dirt floor around her.

The terror is huge now: It presses me from all sides. "Grace, come on, sweetie." I try to keep the panic from my voice. "Come take my hand."

"I didn't mean to!" She starts to cry.

I scuttle down the last few steps and grab her, heaving her up onto my waist. She is awkward, too big for me to carry comfortably, but surprisingly light. She wraps her legs around my waist. I can feel her ribs and the sharp points of her hip bones. Her hair smells like grease and oil and—faintly, just faintly—like dish soap.

Up the stairs and into the world of flame and fire, air turned watery, shimmering with heat, as though the world is breaking apart into a mirage. It would be faster to set Grace down and let her run next to me, but now that I have her—now that she is here, clinging to me, her heart beating frantically in her chest, pounding its rhythm into mine—I won't let her go.

The bike is where I left it, thank God. Grace maneuvers clumsily onto the seat, and I squeeze on behind her. I shove off down the street, my legs heavy as stone, until momentum begins to carry us; and then I ride, as fast as I can, away from the fingers of smoke and flame, leaving the Highlands to burn.

Hana

I walk without paying attention to where I am or where I am going. One foot in front of the other, my white shoes slapping quietly against the pavement. In the distance, I can hear the roar of shouting voices. The sun is bright, and feels nice on my shoulders. A breeze lifts the trees silently, and they bow and wave, bow and wave, as I pass.

One foot, and then another foot. It's so simple. The sun is so bright.

What will happen to me?

I don't know. Maybe I will come across someone who recognizes me. Maybe I will be brought back to my parents. Maybe, if the world doesn't end, if Fred is now dead,

I will be paired with someone else.

Or maybe I will keep walking until I reach the end of the world.

Maybe. But for now there is only the high white sun, and the sky, and tendrils of gray smoke, and voices that sound like ocean waves in the distance.

There is the slapping of my shoes, and the trees that seem to nod and tell me, *You're okay. Everything will be okay.*

Maybe, after all, they are right.

Lena

As we get close to Back Cove, the trickle of people swells to a roaring, rushing stream, and I can barely maneuver my bike between them. They are running, shouting, waving hammers and knives and pieces of metal piping, surging toward some unknown location, and I'm surprised to see that it isn't just Invalids rioting anymore: It is kids, too, some as young as twelve and thirteen, uncured and angry. I even spot a few cureds watching from their windows above the street, occasionally waving, a show of solidarity.

I break loose of the crowd and bump the bike onto the churned-mud shores of the cove, where Alex and I made our stand a lifetime ago—where for the first time, he traded his happiness for mine. Grass grows high between the rubble of the old road, and people—injured or dead—are lying in the grass, letting out moans or staring sightlessly at the cloudless sky. I see several bodies facedown in the shallows of the cove, tendrils of red sweeping across the surface of the water.

Past the cove, at the wall, the crowd is still thick, but it looks like mostly our people. The regulators and police must have been driven back, farther toward Old Port. Now thousands of rioters are flowing in that direction, their voices unified, a single note of fury.

I ditch the bike in the shade of a large juniper and, at last, take Grace by the shoulders, examine her all over for cuts or bruises. She is shaking, wide-eyed, staring at me as though she believes I'll disappear any second.

"What happened to the others?" I ask. Her fingernails are coated with dirt, and she is skinny. But otherwise, she looks okay. More than okay—she looks beautiful. I feel a sob building in my throat, and I swallow it back. We aren't safe, not yet.

Grace shakes her head. "I don't know. There was a fire and . . . and I hid."

So they did leave her. Or they didn't care enough to look when she disappeared. I feel a wave of nausea.

"You look different," Grace says quietly.

"You got taller," I say. Suddenly I could shout for joy. I could scream with happiness while the whole world burns.

"Where did you go?" Grace asks me. "What happened to you?"

"I'll tell you all about it later." I take her chin with one hand. "Listen, Grace. I want to tell you how sorry I am. I'm sorry for leaving you behind. I'll never leave you again, okay?"

Her eyes travel my face. She nods.

"I'm going to keep you safe now." I push the words out past the thickness in my throat. "Do you believe me?"

She nods again. I pull her to me, squeezing. She feels so thin, so fragile. But I know that she is strong. She always has been. She will be ready for whatever comes next.

"Take my hand," I tell her. I'm not certain where to go, and my mind flashes to Raven. Then I remember that she is gone—murdered at the wall—and the sickness threatens to overwhelm me again. But I have to stay calm for Grace's sake.

I need to find a safe place to go with Grace until the fighting is done. My mother will help me; she'll know what to do.

Grace's grip is surprisingly strong. We pick our way along the shoreline, threading between the people—Invalids and regulators alike—injured, dying, and dead. At the top of the slope, Colin, limping, leans heavily on another boy and makes his way to an empty spot on the grass. The other boy looks up and my heart stops.

Alex.

He sees me almost immediately after I've spotted him. I want to call out to him, but my voice is caught in my throat. For a second, he hesitates. Then he eases Colin down into the grass and bends to say something to him. Colin nods, gripping his knee, wincing.

Then Alex is jogging toward me.

"Alex." It's as though saying his name makes him real. He stops a few inches away from me, and his eyes go to Grace, and then back to me. "This is Grace," I say, tugging her hand. She hangs back, angling her body behind mine.

"I remember," he says. There is no more hardness in his eyes, no more hatred. He clears his throat. "I thought I'd never see you again."

"Here I am." The sun feels overly bright, and all of a sudden I can think of nothing to say, no words to describe everything I've thought and wished and wondered. "I—I got your note."

He nods. His mouth tightens just a little. "Is Julian . . . ?"

"I don't know where Julian is," I say, and then instantly feel guilty. I think of his blue eyes, and his warmth curling around me when I slept. I hope he has not been hurt. I bend down so I can look Grace in the eyes. "Sit here for a minute, okay, Gracie?"

She folds herself to the ground obediently. I can't bring myself to step more than two paces away from her. Alex follows.

I lower my voice so Grace won't hear us. "Is it true?" I ask him.

"Is what true?" His eyes are the color of honey. These are the eyes I remember from my dreams.

"That you still love me," I say, breathless. "I need to know."

Alex nods. He reaches out and touches my face—barely skimming my cheekbone and brushing away a bit of my hair. "It's true."

"But . . . I've changed," I say. "And you've changed."

"That's true too," he says quietly. I look at the scar on his face, stretching from his left eye to his jawline, and something hitches in my chest.

"So what now?" I ask him. The light is too bright; the day feels as though it's merging into dream.

"Do you love me?" Alex asks. And I could cry; I could press my face into his chest and breathe in, and pretend that nothing has changed, that everything will be perfect and whole and healed again.

But I can't. I know I can't.

"I never stopped." I look away from him. I look at Grace, and the high grass littered with the wounded and the dead. I think of Julian, and his clear blue eyes, his patience and goodness. I think of all the fighting we've done, and all the fighting we have yet to do. I take a deep breath. "But it's more complicated than that."

Alex reaches out and places his hands on my shoulders. "I'm not going to run away again," he says.

"I don't want you to," I tell him.

His fingers find my cheek, and I rest for a second against his palm, letting the pain of the past few months flow out of me, letting him turn my head toward his. Then he bends down and kisses me: light and perfect, his lips just barely meeting mine, a kiss that promises renewal.

"Lena!"

I step away from Alex when Grace shouts. She has climbed to her feet and is pointing toward the border wall, bouncing excitedly on her toes, full of energy. I turn to look. For a second, tears break apart my vision, turn the world to a kaleidoscope of colors—color crawling up the wall, making a mosaic of the concrete.

No. Not color: people. People are surging toward the wall.

More than that: They are tearing it down.

Yelling, wild and triumphant, brandishing hammers and bits of the ruined scaffolding, or picking with their bare hands, they are dismantling the wall piece by piece, breaking the boundaries of the world as we know it. Joy surges inside me. Grace begins to run; she, too, is pulled toward the wall.

"Grace, wait!" I start to follow her, and Alex grabs my hand.

"I'll find you," he says, watching me with the eyes I remember. "I won't let you go again."

I don't trust myself to speak. Instead I nod, hoping that he understands me. He squeezes my hand.

"Go," he says.

So I do. Grace has paused to wait for me, and I take her thin little hand in mine, and soon I find that we are running: through the sun and the lingering smoke, through the grass on the shores that have become a graveyard, while the sun continues its indifferent rotation and the water reflects nothing but sky.

As we approach the wall, I spot Hunter and Bram, standing side by side, sweating and brown, swinging at the concrete with large pieces of metal piping. I see Pippa, standing on a portion of the wall that remains, waving a vivid green shirt like a flag. I see Coral; fierce and beautiful, she passes in and out of view as the crowd surges and shifts around her. Several feet away, my mother works with a hammer, swinging easily and gracefully, making it look like a dance: this hard and muscled woman I hardly know, a woman I have loved my whole life. She is alive. We are alive. She will get to meet Grace.

I see Julian, too. He is shirtless, sweating, balancing on a heap of rubble, working the butt of a rifle against the wall, so that it splinters and sends a fine spray of white dust onto the people beneath him. The sun makes his hair blaze like a ring of pale fire, touches his shoulders with white wings.

For a second, I feel a sense of overwhelming grief: for how things change, for the fact that we can never go back. I'm not certain of anything anymore. I don't know what will happen—to me, to Alex and to Julian, to any of us.

"Come on, Lena." Grace is tugging at my hand.

But it's not about knowing. It is simply about going forward. The cureds want to know; we have chosen faith instead. I asked Grace to trust me. We will have to trust too—that the world won't end, that tomorrow will come, and that truth will come too.

An old line, a forbidden line from a text Raven once showed me, comes back to me now. *He who jumps may fall, but he may also fly.*

It's time to jump.

"Let's go," I say to Grace, and let her lead me into the surge of people, keeping a tight hold on her hand the whole time.

We push into the shouting, joyful throng, and fight our way toward the wall. Grace scrabbles up a pile of broken-down wood and shards of shattered concrete, and I follow clumsily until I am balancing next to her. She is shouting—louder than I have ever heard her, a babble-language of joy and freedom—and I find that I join in with her as together we begin to tear at chunks of concrete with our fingernails, watching the border dissolve, watching a new world emerge beyond it.

Take down the walls.

That is, after all, the whole point. You do not know what will happen if you take down the walls; you cannot see through to the other side, don't know whether it will bring freedom or ruin, resolution or chaos. It might be paradise, or destruction.

Take down the walls.

Otherwise you must live closely, in fear, building barricades against the unknown, saying prayers against the darkness, speaking verse of terror and tightness.

Otherwise you may never know hell, but you will not find heaven, either. You will not know fresh air and flying.

All of you, wherever you are: in your spiny cities or your one-bump towns. Find it, the hard stuff, the links of metal and chink, the fragments of stone filling your stomach. And pull, and pull, and pull.

I will make a pact with you: I will do it if you will do it, always and forever.

Take down the walls.

Turn the page to discover
LAUREN OLIVER'S gripping novel
of friendship, courage,
survival, and hope

heather

THE WATER WAS SO COLD IT TOOK HEATHER'S BREATH away as she fought past the kids crowding the beach and standing in the shallows, waving towels and homemade signs, cheering and calling up to the remaining jumpers.

She took a deep breath and went under. The sound of voices, of shouting and laughter, was immediately muted.

Only one voice stayed with her.

I didn't mean for it to happen.

Those eyes; the long lashes, the mole under his right eyebrow.

There's just something about her.

Something about her. Which meant: Nothing about you.

She'd been planning to tell him she loved him tonight.

The cold was thunderous, a buzzing rush through her body. Her denim shorts felt as though they'd been weighted

3

with stones. Fortunately, years of braving the creek and racing the quarry with Bishop had made Heather Nill a strong swimmer.

The water was threaded with bodies, twisting and kicking, splashing, treading water—the jumpers, and the people who had joined their celebratory swim, sloshing into the quarry still clothed, carrying beer cans and joints. She could hear a distant rhythm, a faint drumming, and she let it move her through the water—without thought, without fear.

That's what Panic was all about: no fear.

She broke the surface for air and saw that she'd already crossed the short stretch of water and reached the opposite shore: an ugly pile of misshapen rocks, slick with black and green moss, piled together like an ancient collection of Legos. Pitted with fissures and crevices, they shouldered up toward the sky, ballooning out over the water.

Thirty-one people had already jumped—all of them Heather's friends and former classmates. Only a small knot of people remained at the top of the ridge—the jagged, rocky lip of shoreline jutting forty feet into the air on the north side of the quarry, like a massive tooth biting its way out of the ground.

It was too dark to see them. The flashlights and the bonfire only illuminated the shoreline and a few feet of the inky dark water, and the faces of the people who had jumped, still bobbing in the water, triumphant, too happy to feel the cold, taunting the other competitors. The top of the ridge was a shaggy mass of black, where the trees were encroaching on the rock, or the rock was getting slowly pulled into the woods, one or the other.

But Heather knew who they were. All the competitors had to announce themselves once they reached the top of the ridge, and then Diggin Rodgers, this year's sportscaster, parroted back the names into the megaphone, which he had borrowed from his older brother, a cop.

Three people had yet to jump: Merl Tracey, Derek Klieg, and Natalie Velez. Nat.

Heather's best friend.

Heather wedged her fingers in a fissure in the rocks and pulled. Earlier, and in years past, she had watched all the other gamers scrabbling up the ridge like giant, waterlogged insects. Every year, people raced to be the first to jump, even though it didn't earn any extra points. It was a pride thing.

She banged her knee, hard, against a sharp elbow of rock. When she looked down, she could see a bit of dark blood streaking her kneecap. Weirdly, she didn't feel any pain. And though everyone was still cheering and shouting, it all sounded distant.

Matt's words drowned out all the voices.

Look, it's just not working.

There's something about her.

We can still be friends.

The air was cool. The wind had picked up, singing through the old trees, sending deep groans up from the woods—but

5

she wasn't cold anymore. Her heart was beating hard in her throat. She found another handhold in the rock, braced her legs on the slick moss, lifted and levered, as she had watched the gamers do, every summer since eighth grade.

Dimly, she was aware of Diggin's voice, distorted by the megaphone.

"Late in the game . . . a new competitor . . ."

But half his words got whipped away by the wind.

Up, up, up, ignoring the ache in her fingers and legs, trying to stick to the left side of the ridge, where the rocks, driven hard at angles into one another, formed a wide and jutting lip of stone, easy to navigate.

Suddenly a dark shape, a person, rocketed past her. She almost slipped. At the last second, she worked her feet more firmly onto the narrow ledge, dug hard with her fingers to steady herself. A huge cheer went up, and Heather's first thought was: *Natalie.*

But then Diggin boomed out, "And he's *in*, ladies and gentlemen! Merl Tracey, our thirty-second gamer, is *in*!"

Almost at the top now. She risked a glance behind her and saw a steep slope of jagged rock, the dark water breaking at the base of the ridge. It suddenly seemed a million miles away.

Her stomach turned, and for a second the fog cleared from her head, the anger and the hurt were blown away, and she wanted to crawl back down the rock, back to the safety of the beach, where Bishop was waiting. They could go to Dot's for late-night waffles, extra butter, extra whipped cream. They could drive around with all the windows open, listening to the rising hum of the crickets, or sit together on the hood of his car and talk about nothing.

But it was too late. Matt's voice came whispering back, and she kept climbing.

No one knows who invented Panic, or when it first began.

There are different theories. Some blame the shuttering of the paper factory, which overnight placed 40 percent of the adult population of Carp, New York, on unemployment. Mike Dickinson, who infamously got arrested for dealing on the very same night he was named prom king, and now changes brake pads at the Jiffy Lube on Route 22, likes to take credit; that's why he still goes to Opening Jump, four years after graduating.

None of these stories is correct, however. Panic began as so many things do in Carp, a poor town of twelve thousand people in the middle of nowhere: because it was summer, and there was nothing else to do.

The rules are simple. The day after graduation is Opening Jump, and the game goes all through summer. After the final challenge, the winner takes the pot.

Everyone at Carp High pays into the pot, no exceptions. Fees are a dollar a day, for every day that school is in session, from September through June. People who refuse to pony up the cash receive reminders that go from gentle to persuasive:

vandalized locker, shattered windows, shattered face.

It's only fair. Anyone who wants to play has a chance to win. That's another rule: all seniors, but *only* seniors, are eligible, and must announce their intention to compete by participating in the Jump, the first of the challenges. Sometimes as many as forty kids enter.

There is only ever one winner.

Two judges plan the game, name the challenges, deliver instructions, award and deduct points. They are selected by the judges of the previous year, in strict secrecy. No one, in the whole history of Panic, has ever confessed to being one.

There have been suspicions, of course—rumors and speculation. Carp is a small town, and judges get paid. How did Myra Campbell, who always stole extra lunch from the school cafeteria because there was no food at home, suddenly afford her used Honda? She said an uncle had died. But no one had ever heard of Myra's uncle—no one, really, had ever *thought* about Myra, until she came rolling in with the windows down, smoking a cigarette, with the sun so bright on the windshield, it almost completely obscured the smile on her face.

Two judges, picked in secret, sworn to secrecy, working together. It must be this way. Otherwise they'd be subject to bribes, and possibly to threats. That's why there are two—to make sure that things stay balanced, to reduce the possibility that one will cheat, and give out information, leak hints.

If the players know what to expect, then they can prepare.

And that isn't fair at all.

It's partly the unexpectedness, the never-knowing, that starts to get to them, and weeds them out, one by one.

The pot usually amounts to just over $50,000, after fees are deducted and the judges—whoever they are—take their cut. Four years ago, Tommy O'Hare took his winnings, bought two items out of hock, one of them a lemon-yellow Ford, drove straight to Vegas, and bet it all on black.

The next year, Lauren Davis bought herself new teeth and a new pair of tits and moved to New York City. She returned to Carp two Christmases later, stayed just long enough to show off a new purse and an even newer nose, and then blew back to the city. Rumors floated back: she was dating the ex-producer of some reality TV weight-loss show; she was becoming a Victoria's Secret model, though no one has ever seen her in a catalog. (And many of the boys have looked.)

Conrad Spurlock went into the manufacture of methamphetamines—his father's line of business—and poured the money into a new shed on Mallory Road, after their last place burned straight to the ground. But Sean McManus used the money to go to college; he's thinking of becoming a doctor.

In seven years of playing, there have been three deaths—four including Tommy O'Hare, who shot himself with the second thing he'd bought at the pawn shop, after his number came up red.

You see? Even the winner of Panic is afraid of *something*.

So: back to the day after graduation, the opening day of Panic, the day of the Jump.

Rewind back to the beach, but pause a few hours before Heather stood on the ridge, suddenly petrified, afraid to jump.

Turn the camera slightly. We're not quite there. Almost, though.

dodge

NO ONE ON THE BEACH WAS CHEERING FOR DODGE Mason—no one *would* cheer for him either, no matter how far he got.

It didn't matter. All that mattered was the win.

And Dodge had a secret—he knew something about Panic, knew more about it, probably, than any of the other people on the beach.

Actually, he had *two* secrets.

Dodge liked secrets. They fueled him, gave him a sense of power. When he was little, he'd even fantasized that he had his own secret world, a private place of shadows, where he could curl up and hide. Even now—on Dayna's bad days, when the pain came roaring back and she started to cry, when his mom hosed the place down with Febreze and invited over her newest Piece of Shit date, and late at

11

night Dodge could hear the bed frame hitting the wall, like a punch in the stomach every time—he thought about sinking into that dark space, cool and private.

Everyone at school thought Dodge was a pussy. He knew that. He *looked* like a pussy. He'd always been tall and skinny—angles and corners, his mom said, just like his father. As far as he knew, the angles—and the dark skin—were the *only* things he had in common with his dad, a Dominican roofer his mom had been with for one hot second back in Miami. Dodge could never even remember his name. Roberto. Or Rodrigo. Some shit like that.

Back when they'd first gotten stuck in Carp (that's how he always thought about it—getting *stuck*—he, Dayna, and his mom were just like empty plastic bags skipping across the country on fitful bits of wind, occasionally getting snagged around a telephone pole or under the tires of some semi, pinned in place for a bit), he'd been beat up three times: once by Greg O'Hare, then by Zev Keller, and then by Greg O'Hare *again*, just to make sure that Dodge knew the rules. And Dodge hadn't swung back, not once.

He'd had worse before.

And that was Dodge's second secret, and the source of his power.

He wasn't afraid. He just didn't care.

And that was very, very different.

The sky was streaked with red and purple and orange. It reminded Dodge of an enormous bruise, or a picture taken of the inside of a body. It was still an hour or so before sunset and before the pot, and then the Jump, would be announced.

Dodge cracked a beer. His first and only. He didn't want to be buzzed, and didn't need to be either. But it had been a hot day, and he'd come straight from Home Depot, and he was thirsty.

The crowd had only just started to assemble. Periodically, Dodge heard the muffled slamming of a car door, a shout of greeting from the woods, the distant blare of music. Whippoorwill Road was a quarter mile away; kids were just starting to emerge from the path, fighting their way through the thick underbrush, swatting away hanging moss and creeper vines, carting coolers and blankets and bottles and iPod speakers, staking out patches of sand.

School was done—for good, forever. He took a deep breath. Of all the places he had lived—Chicago, DC, Dallas, Richmond, Ohio, Rhode Island, Oklahoma, New Orleans—New York smelled the best. Like growth and change, things turning over and becoming other things.

Ray Hanrahan and his friends had arrived first. That was unsurprising. Even though competitors weren't officially announced until the moment of the Jump, Ray had been bragging for months that he was going to take home the pot, just like his brother had two years earlier.

Luke had won, just barely, in the last round of Panic. Luke had walked away with fifty grand. The other driver hadn't

13

walked away at all. If the doctors were right, she'd never walk again.

Dodge flipped a coin in his palm, made it disappear, then reappear easily between his fingers. In fourth grade, his mom's boyfriend—he couldn't remember which one—had bought him a book about magic tricks. They'd been living in Oklahoma that year, a shithole in a flat bowl in the middle of the country, where the sun singed the ground to dirt and the grass to gray, and he'd spent a whole summer teaching himself how to pull coins from someone's ear and slip a card into his pocket so quickly, it was unnoticeable.

It had started as a way to pass the time but had become a kind of obsession. There was something elegant about it: how people saw without seeing, how the mind filled in what it expected, how the eyes betrayed you.

Panic, he knew, was one big magic trick. The judges were the magicians; the rest of them were just a dumb, gaping audience.

Mike Dickinson came next, along with two friends, all of them visibly drunk. The Dick's hair had started to thin, and patches of his scalp were visible when he bent down to deposit his cooler on the beach. His friends were carrying a half-rotted lifeguard chair between them: the throne, where Diggin, the announcer, would sit during the event.

Dodge heard a high whine. He smacked unthinkingly, catching the mosquito just as it started to feed, smearing a bit of black on his bare calf. He hated mosquitoes. Spiders,

14

too, although he liked other insects, found them fascinating. Like humans, in a way—stupid and sometimes vicious, blinded by need.

The sky was deepening; the light was fading and so were the colors, swirling away behind the line of trees beyond the ridge, as though someone had pulled the plug.

Heather Nill was next on the beach, followed by Nat Velez, and lastly, Bishop Marks, trotting happily after them like an overgrown sheepdog. Even from a distance, Dodge could tell both girls were on edge. Heather had done something with her hair. He wasn't sure what, but it wasn't wrestled into its usual ponytail, and it even looked like she might have straightened it. And he wasn't sure, but he thought she might be wearing makeup.

He debated getting up and going over to say hi. Heather was cool. He liked how tall she was, how tough, too, in her own way. He liked her broad shoulders and the way she walked, straight-backed, even though he was sure she would have liked to be a few inches shorter—could tell from the way she wore only flats and sneakers with worn-down soles.

But if he got up, he'd have to talk to Natalie—and even looking at Nat from across the beach made his stomach seize up, like he'd been kicked. Nat wasn't exactly *mean* to him— not like some of the other kids at school—but she wasn't exactly nice, either, and that bothered him more than anything else. She usually smiled vaguely when she caught him talking to Heather, and as her eyes skated past him, through

15

him, he knew that she would never, ever, actually look at him. Once, at the homecoming bonfire last year, she'd even called him Dave.

He'd gone just because he was hoping to see her. And then, in the crowd, he had spotted her; had moved toward her, buzzed from the noise and the heat and the shot of whiskey he'd taken in the parking lot, intending to talk to her, *really* talk to her, for the first time. Just as he was reaching out to touch her elbow, she had taken a step backward, onto his foot.

"Oops! Sorry, Dave," she'd said, giggling. Her breath smelled like vanilla and vodka. And his stomach had opened up, and his guts went straight onto his shoes.

There were only 107 people in their graduating class, out of the 150 who'd started at Carp High freshman year. And she didn't even know his name.

So he stayed where he was, working his toes into the ground, waiting for the dark, waiting for the whistle to blow and for the games to begin.

He was going to win Panic.

He was going to do it for Dayna.

He was going to do it for revenge.

Don't miss Lauren Oliver's
compelling first novel,
the *New York Times* bestseller

before
i
fall

They say that just before you die your whole life flashes before your eyes, but that's not how it happened for me.

To be honest, I'd always thought the whole final-moment, mental life-scan thing sounded pretty awful. Some things are better left buried and forgotten, as my mom would say. I'd be happy to forget all of fifth grade, for example (the glasses-and-pink-braces period), and does anybody want to relive the first day of middle school? Add in all of the boring family vacations, pointless algebra classes, period cramps, and bad kisses I barely lived through the first time around . . .

The truth is, though, I wouldn't have minded reliving my greatest hits: when Rob Cokran and I first hooked up in the middle of the dance floor at homecoming, so everyone saw and knew we were together; when Lindsay, Elody, Ally, and I got drunk and tried to make snow angels in May, leaving person-sized imprints in Ally's lawn; my sweet-sixteen party, when we set out a hundred tea lights and danced on the table in the backyard; the time Lindsay and I pranked Clara Seuse on Halloween, got chased by the cops, and laughed so hard we almost threw up—the things I wanted to remember; the things

3

I wanted to be remembered for.

But before I died I didn't think of Rob, or any other guy. I didn't think of all the outrageous things I'd done with my friends. I didn't even think of my family, or the way the morning light turns the walls in my bedroom the color of cream, or the way the azaleas outside my window smell in July, a mixture of honey and cinnamon.

Instead, I thought of Vicky Hallinan.

Specifically, I thought of the time in fourth grade when Lindsay announced in front of the whole gym class that she wouldn't have Vicky on her dodgeball team. "She's too fat," Lindsay blurted out. "You could hit her with your eyes closed." I wasn't friends with Lindsay yet, but even then she had this way of saying things that made them hilarious, and I laughed along with everyone else while Vicky's face turned as purple as the underside of a storm cloud.

That's what I remembered in that before-death instant, when I was supposed to be having some big revelation about my past: the smell of varnish and the squeak of our sneakers on the polished floor; the tightness of my polyester shorts; the laughter echoing around the big, empty space like there were way more than twenty-five people in the gym.

And Vicky's face.

The weird thing is that I hadn't thought about that in forever. It was one of those memories I didn't even know I remembered, if you know what I mean. It's not like Vicky was traumatized or anything. That's just the kind of thing *that kids do to each other. It's no big deal. There's always going to be a person laughing and somebody getting laughed at. It happens every day, in every school, in every town in America—probably in the world, for all I know. The whole point of growing up is learning to stay on the laughing side.*

Vicky wasn't very fat to begin with—she just had some baby weight on her face and stomach—and before high school she'd lost that and grown three inches. She even became friends with Lindsay. They played field hockey together and said hi in the halls. One time, our freshman year, Vicky brought it up at a party—we were all pretty tipsy—and we laughed and laughed, Vicky most of all, until her face turned almost as purple as it had all those years ago in the gym.

That was weird thing number one.

Even weirder than that was the fact that we'd all just been talking about it—how it would be just before you died, I mean. I don't remember exactly how it came up, except that Elody was complaining that I always got shotgun and refusing to wear her seat belt. She kept leaning forward into the front seat to scroll through Lindsay's iPod, even though I was supposed to have deejay privileges. I was trying to explain my "greatest hits" theory of death, and we were all picking out what those would be. Lindsay picked finding out that she got into Duke, obviously, and Ally—who was bitching about the cold, as usual, and threatening to drop dead right there of pneumonia—participated long enough to say she wished she could relive her first hookup with Matt Wilde forever, which surprised no one. Lindsay and Elody were smoking, and freezing rain was coming in through the cracked-open windows. The road was narrow and winding, and on either side of us the dark, stripped branches of trees lashed back and forth, like the wind had set them dancing.

Elody put on "Splinter" by Fallacy to piss Ally off, maybe because she was sick of her whining. It was Ally's song with Matt, who had dumped her in September. Ally called her a bitch and unbuckled her seat belt, leaning forward and trying to grab the iPod. Lindsay complained that someone was elbowing her in the neck. The cigarette dropped from her mouth and landed between her thighs. She started cursing and trying to brush the embers off the seat cushion and Elody and Ally were still fighting and I was trying to talk over them, reminding them all of the time we'd made snow angels in May. The tires skidded a little on the wet road, and the car was full of cigarette smoke, little wisps rising like phantoms in the air.

Then all of a sudden there was a flash of white in front of the car. Lindsay yelled something—words I couldn't make out, something like sit or shit or sight—and suddenly the car was flipping off the road and into the black mouth of the woods. I heard a horrible, screeching sound—metal on metal, glass shattering, a car folding in two—and smelled fire. I had time to wonder whether Lindsay had put her cigarette out.

Then Vicky Hallinan's face came rising out of the past. I heard laughter echoing and rolling all around me, swelling into a scream.

Then nothing.

The thing is, you don't get to know. It's not like you wake up with a bad feeling in your stomach. You don't see shadows where there shouldn't be any. You don't remember to tell your parents that you love them or—in my case—remember to say good-bye to them at all.

If you're like me, you wake up seven minutes and forty-seven seconds before your best friend is supposed to be picking you up. You're too busy worrying about how many roses you're going to get on Cupid Day to do anything more than throw on your clothes, brush your teeth, and pray to God you left your makeup in the bottom of your messenger bag so you can do it in the car.

If you're like me, your last day starts like this:

ONE

"Beep, beep," Lindsay calls out. A few weeks ago my mom yelled at her for blasting her horn at six fifty-five every morning, and this is Lindsay's solution.

"I'm coming!" I shout back, even though she can see me pushing out the front door, trying to put on my coat and wrestle my binder into my bag at the same time.

At the last second, my eight-year-old sister, Izzy, tugs at me.

"What?" I whirl around. She has little-sister radar for when I'm busy, late, or on the phone with my boyfriend. Those are always the times she chooses to bother me.

"You forgot your gloves," she says, except it comes out: "You *forgot* your *gloveths*." She refuses to go to speech therapy for her lisp, even though all the kids in her grade make fun of her. She says she likes the way she talks.

I take them from her. They're cashmere and she's probably gotten peanut butter on them. She's always scooping around in jars of the stuff.

"What did I tell you, Izzy?" I say, poking her in the middle of the forehead. "Don't touch my stuff." She giggles like an idiot and I have to hustle her inside while I shut the door. If it were up to her, she would follow me around all day like a dog.

By the time I make it out of the house, Lindsay's leaning out the window of the Tank. That's what we call her car, an enormous silver Range Rover. (Every time we drive around in it at least one person says, "That thing's not a car, it's a *truck*," and Lindsay claims she could go head-to-head with an eighteen-wheeler and come out without a scratch.) She and Ally are the only two of us with cars that actually belong to them. Ally's car is a tiny black Jetta that we named the Minime. I get to borrow my mom's Accord sometimes; poor Elody has to make do with her father's ancient tan Ford Taurus, which hardly runs anymore.

The air is still and freezing cold. The sky is a perfect, pale blue. The sun has just risen, weak and watery-looking, like it has just spilled itself over the horizon and is too lazy to clean itself up. It's supposed to storm later, but you'd never know.

I get into the passenger seat. Lindsay's already smoking and she gestures with the end of her cigarette to the Dunkin' Donuts coffee she got for me.

"Bagels?" I say.

"In the back."

"Sesame?"

"Obviously." She looks me over once as she pulls out of my driveway. "Nice skirt."

"You too."

Lindsay tips her head, acknowledging the compliment. We're actually wearing the same skirt. There are only two days of the year when Lindsay, Ally, Elody, and I deliberately dress the same: Pajama Day during Spirit Week, because we all bought cute matching sets at Victoria's Secret last Christmas, and Cupid Day. We spent three hours at the mall arguing about whether to go for pink or red outfits—Lindsay hates pink; Ally lives in it—and we finally settled on black miniskirts and some red fur-trimmed tank tops we found in the clearance bin at Nordstrom.

Like I said, those are the only times we *deliberately* look alike. But the truth is that at my high school, Thomas Jefferson, everyone kind of looks the same. There's no official uniform— it's a public school—but you'll see the same outfit of Seven jeans, gray New Balance sneakers, a white T-shirt, and a colored North Face fleece jacket on nine out of ten students. Even the guys and the girls dress the same, except our jeans are tighter and we have to blow out our hair every day. It's Connecticut: being like the people around you is the whole point.

That's not to say that our high school doesn't have its freaks— it does—but even the freaks are freaky in the same way. The Eco-Geeks ride their bikes to school and wear clothing made of hemp and never wash their hair, like having dreadlocks will somehow help curb the emission of greenhouse gases. The Drama Queens carry big bottles of lemon tea and wear scarves even in summer and don't talk in class because they're "conserving their voices." The Math League members always have ten times more books than anyone else and actually still

11

use their lockers and walk around with permanently nervous expressions, like they're just waiting for somebody to yell, "Boo!"

I don't mind it, actually. Sometimes Lindsay and I make plans to run away after graduation and crash in a loft in New York City with this tattoo artist her stepbrother knows, but secretly I like living in Ridgeview. It's reassuring, if you know what I mean.

I lean forward, trying to apply mascara without gouging my eye out. Lindsay's never been the most careful driver and has a tendency to jerk the wheel around, come to sudden stops, and then gun the engine.

"Patrick better send me a rose," Lindsay says as she shoots through one stop sign and nearly breaks my neck slamming on the brakes at the next one. Patrick is Lindsay's on-again, off-again boyfriend. They've broken up a record thirteen times since the start of the school year.

"I had to sit next to Rob while he filled out the request form," I say, rolling my eyes. "It was like forced labor."

Rob Cokran and I have been going out since October, but I've been in love with him since sixth grade, when he was too cool to talk to me. Rob was my first crush, or at least my first *real* crush. I did once kiss Kent McFuller in third grade, but that obviously doesn't count since we'd just exchanged dandelion rings and were pretending to be husband and wife.

"Last year I got twenty-two roses." Lindsay flicks her cigarette butt out of the window and leans over for a slurp of coffee.

"I'm going for twenty-five this year."

Each year before Cupid Day the student council sets up a booth outside the gym. For two dollars each, you can buy your friends Valograms—roses with little notes attached to them—and then they get delivered by Cupids (usually freshman or sophomore girls trying to get in good with the upperclassmen) throughout the day.

"I'd be happy with fifteen," I say. It's a big deal how many roses you get. You can tell who's popular and who isn't by the number of roses they're holding. It's bad if you get under ten and humiliating if you don't get more than five—it basically means that you're either ugly or unknown. Probably both. Sometimes people scavenge for dropped roses to add to their bouquets, but you can always tell.

Acknowledgments

There are many, many people who helped and supported me as I was writing the Delirium trilogy: The list is too long to enumerate, and I'm sure to forget someone. Thank you to my friends, my family, my brilliant editor and agent, and all the people at HarperCollins; I am so grateful for your continued belief in my books.

I'd like to thank, most importantly, the fans who have made my career possible, who inspire and galvanize me to write more and better. Thank you for passionately identifying with Lena; thank you for your messages on Facebook, Goodreads, Twitter, etc.; thank you for loving Alex (or Julian!), for counting down the days between book releases, for badgering me to release even sooner, for blogging and posting and liking and making the online space such a dynamic place for book lovers. Thank you to every blogger who has championed my books, and even the ones who haven't. Thanks to every teacher, librarian, educator, or parent who has recommended one of my books to a teen; thanks to every teen who has passed along one of my books to a bestie.

With love and gratitude,

Lauren